# Advance Praise for Shade

"From its stunning first scene to its heartwarming last, *Shade* is a striking tale of mystery and danger that kept me hooked. This is Olson's finest work yet, and reading it, one gets the feeling he's just getting warmed up."

**Robin Parrish**
Author of *Relentless* and *Merciless*

"Unseen enemies. Questioned sanity. The weighing of reality. All the things I like in a book! The shadows are not silent. I lost sleep over this book. I got goose bumps from this book. The kind of scary that you crave and cringe at, *Shade* offers up a monster made more frightening by its originality. Thanks a lot, John Olson—because of you, I will not walk alone at night for a long time to come."

**Tosca Lee**
Author of *Demon: A Memoir* and *Havah: The Story of Eve*

"John B. Olson is a seasoned storyteller, and Shade is quite a story! As the heat turns up, and as menacing tones and brooding characters abound, the theme of God's grace boils to the surface. A few years back, Olson gave us a new twist on Jekyll & Hyde; now he puts his own fast-paced spin on the Dracula story. I can only hope there's a sequel in the works!"

**Eric Wilson**
Author of *Field of Blood* and *A Shred of Truth*

"*Shade* is a smart, gripping thriller. John B. Olson whips you along in a breakneck odyssey through a hellish paradise lost—and keeps you up all night doing it."

**Melanie Wells**
Author of *My Soul to Keep* and *When the Day of Evil Comes*

"Things that go bump in the night are not all figments of overwrought imaginations or evidence of mental illness. As our heroine discovers, evil personified preys on the ignorance of its victims. Lock your doors and windows, leave the lights on, and hunker down for a splendid, spine-chilling read."

**Donita K. Paul**
Author of the *DragonKeeper Chronicles*

"I am more than a little intrigued with where the author will take this series, but I am strapped in for what is going to be a ride of supernatural proportions!"

**RelzReviews**

"A rare combination of page-turning thriller and characters so well drawn that you will think about them long after the story is finished."

**Kathryn Cushman**
Author of *A Promise to Remember* and *Waiting for Daybreak*

"John Olson draws us into a swirling, surreal world, made more terrifying because it inhabits the ordinary places of a young woman's life. Best of all, while the story conveys horror in vivid strokes, it also paints the beauty of humble, noble, sacrificial love through a character that will live me for a long time."

**Sharon Hinck**
Author of the Sword of Lyric series

"An intelligent, fast-paced novel that keeps the reader guessing until the very last page. *Shade* portrays deep spiritual truths while continuing to stretch the envelope."

**Hannah Alexander**
Author of the Hideaway series

"A classic good-versus-evil tale that resonates long after the end. If you haven't discovered John B. Olson by now, there is no better place to jump in!"

**Bookshelf Review**

# JOHN B. OLSON

## SHADE

A NOVEL

**B&H**
PUBLISHING GROUP

Nashville, Tennessee

978-0-8054-4734-7


Published by B&H Publishing Group
Nashville, Tennessee


Dewey Decimal Classification: F
Subject Heading: MYSTERY FICTION \ FANTASY
FICTION \ PARANOID SCHIZOPHRENICS—FICTION


Scripture quotations are from the Holy Bible, New
International Version, copyright © 1973, 1978, 1984 by
International Bible Society.

1 2 3 4 5 6 7 8 • 11 10 09 08

To Peter Sleeper
*"A man of many companions may come to ruin,
but there is a friend who sticks closer than a brother."*
Proverbs 18:24 (NIV)

# I

*When I consider how my light is spent,*
*Ere half my days, in this dark world and wide,*
*And that one talent which is death to hide*
*Lodged with me useless, though my soul more bent*

*To serve therewith my Maker, and present*
*My true account, lest he returning chide,*
*"Doth God exact day-labor, light denied?"*
*I fondly ask. But Patience, to prevent*

*That murmur, soon replies: "God doth not need*
*Either man's work or his own gifts; who best*
*Bear his mild yoke, they serve him best. His state*

*Is kingly: thousands at his bidding speed,*
*And post o'er land and ocean without rest;*
*They also serve who only stand and wait."*

John Milton

# Prologue

A moonlit night. Silver-frosted shadows frozen in the stillness of an early Minnesota fall. A weathered farmhouse looms over a fog-cloaked bog, leaking soft candlelight from a second-story window. Flickering silhouettes beat against the windowpanes. Clacks and sharp cries, injecting the silence with echoes of ringing pain.

Rising out of the mist, a dark shadow rolls through the clearing. Blotting out the farmhouse. Obscuring the moon.

———

"RECITE THE GATEWAY PROPHECY. Now!" A hooded man swung a staff in a sweeping arc toward a young boy's face.

"'The ancient enemy'"—the boy ducked and hopped backward on feet bound together with new hemp rope—"'in the last dark days of hunt shall rise up to destroy the Standing.'" The boy twisted his staff upward, deflecting the next blow in a fluid motion that circled his staff beneath his master's defense. "'Only the long-awaited shall stand.'"

The man sprang back, spun around, and swept at the boy's feet. But the boy leaped into the air even as he brought his staff down on the man's shoulder, pulling back on the blow an instant before impact.

"Good!" The old man smiled against the strain of another swing.

"'By becoming the enemy, he shall shield the world from the enemy's dark—'" The boy flinched, just managing to parry the next blow. He shuddered as a cold shiver crawled up his spine. Something . . . something dark . . . touched his mind like a foul stench.

"What is wrong, child? You've dropped your guard."

The boy frowned up at his beloved master. "Do you not feel it?"

"Feel what? Are you ill?"

"I don't know. It's awful—wicked!"

"Don't use slang with me, boy. If it's wickedness you feel, you need look no further than yoursel—" A rasping gurgle choked off the old man's voice. His eyes rolled back, then clamped shut until the creases surrounding them showed white against blood-red skin. Veins bulged at his neck as his lips drew back from his teeth in a piercing scream.

"*Evil!*" The man's howl echoed around them as he smashed his staff into the boy's shoulder, knocking him to the floor.

The boy tried to roll to his feet, but the force of the blow left him stunned. The air around him swirled with rage. A deep, dark unquenchable hunger.

"Pay attention, foundling!" The old man glared down at him, his face twisted into a mask of loathing and disgust. "Think you get a second chance with *It*?" The master swung his weapon down upon the boy's now upheld staff. "Never underestimate its capacity for evil." The staff struck again, sending pain radiating through the boy's arms. "No atrocity is ever too small. Too twisted. Too profane!"

Again and again he rained blows down upon the boy's staff until it splintered in his aching hands. The boy rolled to the side, dimly aware of a sharp smack inches away from his ear. Springing to his feet, he hopped to the window and dove at it headfirst.

But the window mullions were too heavy.

With a sickening crunch he bounced off the window and sank to the floor.

A crash sounded above his head. The spray of glass and splintered wood. Shielding his eyes with his hands, he pushed onto his feet. "Master, please. I don't under—"

Pain exploded in his arm as a powerful blow knocked him back through the jagged window. Icy darkness. The shriek of howling wind. He hit the ground with a soul-jarring thud.

*Pain.*

*Glorious, wonderful, delicious pain!*

Every heartbeat, every movement that convulsed his body with searing fire was answered with surges of perverse pleasure. Lying in the weeds, curled around his throbbing arm, a dark presence pressed down on him, rose up within him.

The sound of a slamming door broke him free from the nightmare's grip. He struggled to his feet but tripped on the rope and toppled back to the ground. A dark shadow, invisible to the eyes but chilling to the soul, passed over him as he lay on his side fighting with his good hand to work the rope over his bare feet.

A low growl rumbled in the night. Feet free at last, the boy rose to a crouch and searched the swirling darkness. The sound . . . it was all around him. Everywhere, nowhere, filling his mind, his soul, the spaces in between.

The angry voice of his master lashed out at him from the front of the house. The boy sprang to his feet and fled for the barn.

Leaping against the bolted door, he attempted to run up its reinforced surface but slipped and crashed back to the ground.

Risking a backward glance at his approaching master, he took a deep breath and then, his right arm dangling, picked his way up the exterior braces of the door. He jumped out into space, twisting in the air to catch with one hand the rope that dangled from the loft beam overhead. He clung desperately to the rope, wrapping his legs and feet around it as he squirmed his way toward the overhanging beam.

A dark, rumbling growl filled the night, freezing him where he clung. A sharp cry of agony followed by a rasping wheeze. Wave upon wave of unholy exultation battered him as he clung, trembling, to the rope. He looked down at the twisted shadow on the ground, but even without seeing he knew.

His master was gone.

The steady, familiar presence had disappeared. For the first time in his life, he was alone.

A blurred, man-shaped shadow moved toward him. The hazy figure flickered like a moth beating erratically against the light. Hunger. A dark, terrible longing. Invisible eyes locked onto him. An irresistible tug on his soul. He was hungry. So very hungry. There was no escape. Weariness sang through him. Despair. Surrender. He had to give up. Climb down. He moved to lower himself down the rope . . .

Searing pain exploded in his right arm. The boy cried out, blinking into the night as if waking from a nightmare. His fingers tightened, and he clung to the rope for his life. The dark presence reached toward him from below, but he didn't look down.

*Relax. Release the rope. All will be well.*

"No!" Scrambling blindly against the tears and pain, heedless of the crashing of the barn door and the roar that echoed in his mind, he pulled himself onto the overhanging beam.

He couldn't escape. Mustn't.

Gritting his teeth, he stepped out onto the practice cable that stretched between the barn and the old farmhouse.

He couldn't do it. It was too dark. He was weak, cowardly, full of loathsome sin.

Fixing his eyes on the light from the second-story window, he took a faltering step, feeling for the thin cable with his bare feet.

He was going to fall. He had never practiced in the dark.

A jolt passed through the cable and rattled in his mind like a thunderclap.

And then he ran.

Across the cable, over the rooftop, down the trellis. Through field after field after screaming, shrieking field, he ran. Through the night and long into the morning until exhaustion left him panting in his sleep, cradling his arm in the fork of a tree in front of a small Minnesota farmhouse.

## ∾ 1 ∾

A tear ran down Melchi's cheek, losing itself in the curl of his wild beard. He had found his dear friend Telémakhos, but not the way he had hoped. Crouching at the edge of the graveled trail, he pulled the well-worn copy of *The Odyssey* out of the mud.

He knew he should be grateful to recover his book at all, but the cover was so muddy and torn . . . it was difficult to conjure up the appropriate feelings of gratitude. He dabbed at the mud with the dusty sleeve of his tattered overcoat and slid the book into the duct-taped pocket of his innermost jacket.

Now if he could just find his other treasures . . .

He searched the area in an ever-expanding circle. Twenty yards ahead a patch of white caught his eye. His *Reader's Digest* family! He ran up the trail and retrieved the ragged magazine clipping from a tangle of dusty ivy. Smoothing the picture across his thigh, he drank in the image of two laughing parents pushing their daughter on a swing. At least *it* had escaped the mud. He leaped to his feet and continued searching until he found a white corner protruding from a puddle. Just beyond that a half-dozen newspaper clippings clung to a thicket of tall weeds.

He reached down with a sigh and pulled the old Polaroid free of the water. Miss Lila had given him the photograph after he helped load her things onto the moving truck. He wiped the picture on the cleanest part of his sleeve and inspected the likeness of the kindly old lady. Not too bad, considering. If he could just find his backpack, he'd be okay. It would take forever to find a replacement. People hardly ever threw out backpacks.

Melchi gathered the newspaper clippings and arranged them by date. A few of them were missing, but that didn't matter. He still had the last three: "Three Homeless Found Mutilated," "Sunset Teen Still Missing," "New Evidence in Golden Gate Murders."

Turning to make sure he was still alone, he rolled up the wad of clippings and stuffed them into the lining of his inner jacket. Then he sprang to his feet and took off down the trail, searching from side to side as he ran. At every intersection he dropped onto all fours and searched for fresh disturbances in the sand. The thief was almost certainly following the path to Stanyan Park, but Melchi couldn't afford to take any chances.

Halfway to Stanyan, Melchi finally found what he was looking for. A complete set of footprints. His thief was definitely another homeless. A man, from the size of the prints. He wore two different types of boots: the left sole was worn and smooth, like a cowboy boot, while the right sole had a shallow wavy tread. Most likely a hiking boot. And yes, his homeless was headed toward Stanyan Park. Either he was one of the crazies, or he was a long-timer. Either way, for him to risk stealing from another homeless, he was probably in pretty bad shape.

Melchi sprinted down the trail with long, ground-eating strides. When the long-timer's section of Stanyan Park came into view, he slowed to a less conspicuous pace and made for a cluster of homeless men lolling in the shade of a large pine tree. He had seen most of them before, but that didn't mean anything. The homeless kept pretty much to themselves; he didn't really *know* any of them.

One of the men, a snake-faced Caucasian with long greasy black hair, backed away at Melchi's approach. Melchi raised himself to his full height and stepped closer, intentionally invading the man's space. The man's eyes went wide, and he fell back onto the ground, revealing a pair of matching athletic shoes. Melchi turned back to the others and stared down at their feet. They all shifted and a few mumbled, but that was only natural. He towered head and shoulders above even the tallest of them. Unfortunately, none of them displayed the furtive, down-turned eyes of a guilty conscience. And none of them were wearing mismatched boots.

Melchi walked past the men and turned toward the fashionable section of the park across from the McDonald's. He didn't expect to find his homeless playing Hacky Sack, but there were still a lot of commuters out. The thief could be working the sidewalks to pay for his next meal.

Melchi was halfway across the park when he noticed a covered shopping cart sitting by a clump of windswept trees. Among the trees, wrapped in an old blanket, lay an old man. Melchi recognized his own wool blanket even before he spotted the mismatched boots on the man's feet. This was his homeless—the man who threw his dear Telémakhos into the mud. The man who stole the best pack he ever owned.

Melchi marched up to the man and spoke in a deep grating voice. "I have come for my pack."

The man didn't move.

"I have come for my pack." Melchi reached out and shook the sleeping man.

The old-timer sputtered and opened his eyes.

"I have come for my pack."

The man's eyes went suddenly wide. With fluttering, trembling limbs, he staggered to his feet and stumbled toward his cart. "Didn't know. Didn't know it was you." He reached a shaking hand behind him and rummaged under the tarp. "Thought it belonged to nobody. Didn't know . . ." The man pulled out the battered nylon backpack and thrust it forward, cringing behind it as if it were a shield. "Thought it was nobody's. Nobody at all . . ."

Melchi took the bag and pulled back on the zipper. It was still there! He took out a bundle and shucked off one plastic bag after another until he came to a small hardcover book. Relief surged through him.

He had his Milton back, and it was perfect.

Then Melchi frowned. "Where is the spray bottle? It is very important."

"Didn't know. Nobody . . . Didn't know it was you . . ." The old man turned and started pulling things from the shopping cart. Crumpled trash bags, twisted knots of clothing, clumps of soggy fast-food wrappers . . .

"About as big as my hand, a white spray bottle, full of clear liquid."

Finally the man pulled out a spray bottle and turned to show Melchi.

"Did you use any of it? Did you get any of the liquid on your skin?"

The man shrank back against the cart. "I didn't know. I didn't. Didn't know . . ."

Melchi took the bottle and held it up to the light. It was still full. Maybe all would be well after all. He reached down and retrieved his blanket from the ground. Then, wrapping his Milton back in the plastic bags, he folded his blanket around it and slipped the whole bundle back into his pack.

"Taking the backpack was wrong. Do you understand? Beware the curse: 'For every one that stealeth shall be cut off as on this side.'" Melchi watched as the man went back to digging in his cart. Apparently the import of his words were lost on the man. He stood already too close to the veil.

"I am sorry." Melchi bowed his head and turned to walk back to Golden Gate Park. The man was still murmuring to himself as Melchi crossed the street and broke into a jog.

Half a day! He had wasted half a day tracking down his backpack. Half a day he could have been inspecting graveyards, searching for underground vaults or mausoleums, hidden gateways to the great inter-dimensional beyond. There would be no time tonight. He hadn't visited the roof of the mental hospital for days. Tonight was supposed to be his night for a stakeout.

He pulled his Telémakhos out of his pocket and thumbed through its well-worn pages. The text was still readable, but the cover was a mess. He'd need a clean cloth to remove the mud. And if he didn't repair the tears soon, the whole front cover might fall off.

Besides, he hadn't seen the Booklady in two days. She might need some help with boxes. And he was so . . . he might as well admit it. He was hungry, and she would probably offer him something to eat.

A visit to the Booklady would be selfish and totally irresponsible, but he was so tired. He hadn't slept since yesterday morning, and then only for a few hours. Would it hurt so much to take a break? Just a few minutes, and then he would sprint the distance to the mental hospital. It would take hardly any time at all.

Melchi looked up at the setting sun. If today were Tuesday, he would have to get there fast. He broke into an all-out run and sped across a hard-packed trail. Without breaking stride, he hurdled a four-foot oleander and weaved through a stand of evergreens until he reached a towering cedar. Leaping into the air, he grabbed a high branch and pulled himself up and over in a single, fluid motion. Then, racing like a squirrel through the branches of the tree, he came to a heavy rope stretched between the cedar and an enormous eucalyptus twenty feet away. He scanned the forest floor below and then stepped out onto the rope and walked quickly across it to a rope-mesh platform woven between two large branches.

No time for a ceremony. He grabbed the knotted string of a blackened silver medallion and slipped it over his head. Then, digging inside a canvas duffel bag, he brought out a handful of sharpened stakes and tucked them into his overcoat pocket as he felt his way back across the tightrope. He plummeted down the tree in a barely controlled free fall and hit the ground with a smack.

Tuesday nights the Booklady went home early. He hoped it wasn't Tuesday.

One eye on the dying sun, he swerved and dodged and ducked his way through the park to burst out onto the city streets at a full run.

He slowed to a walk before reaching the Booklady's store and smoothed back the tangles of his wild hair, using his fingers as a crude comb. A yellow light shone from the part of the window that wasn't covered by shelves. Warmth and comfort and light. Delicious. His mouth was already watering. Maybe if she still hadn't eaten . . .

*No!* Melchi swallowed and turned away from the shop. The Booklady had given him food two nights ago. He had no right to expect more. He was being selfish, carnally self-indulgent.

He started to step away from the building, but the staccato clack of high heels brought him up short. Somewhere, farther up the hill, a woman was walking through the semi-darkness. For all he knew, she could be a Standing, walking alone and unprotected into the clutches of the eternal enemy. No, she wasn't alone. He could just make out the soft scrape of another pair of feet. A man, judging by his weight—probably wearing athletic shoes. The woman would be fine.

Brushing his hair away from his eyes, Melchi glanced back at the bookstore. How could he even think of delaying? He still hadn't checked the morgue, and then there were the rooftops, and the disappearance of the sixteen-year-old boy . . .

But he was tired and Telémakhos was torn. He listened as the taps of the lady's shoes faded into the distance. No, he had to try. How would he feel if someone else were killed while he indulged his flesh? He would check out the rooftops first and spend the rest of the night at the mental hospital.

"Well?" The Booklady's gravelly voice sounded from within the store. "Are you going to come in, or am I going to have to bring your supper out to you?"

He froze where he stood. "I am sorry to disturb you. It is me, Melchi." Was he not obligated to enter now? Out of respect for his elder? Perhaps, if he only stayed a little while . . . What could thirty minutes possibly hurt?

A bell clanged as he tugged on the weathered door. Just like a real home. He ducked beneath the doorway and turned sideways to squeeze between the overloaded shelves on either side of the entrance. The air was heavy with stale cigarette smoke and the musty smell of old books. So inviting. Deliciously warm. He stood with bowed head before the Booklady's cluttered counter, shuffling his feet as he waited for her to look up from the books spread open before her.

The Booklady slid her reading glasses up onto her head and pushed a straggle of gray hair behind her ears. "In the mood for some fried chicken? I've got mashed potatoes too. Made 'em myself. Hungry?"

"I am fine, thank you. It is good of you to offer, but you must not feel like you have to give me food every time I visit. You do too much as it is."

"Hmmph. I'm hungry. I've been waiting for you all day. Thought you were going to come yesterday."

"I am sorry. I—"

"I didn't eat until 7:30, but that's all right. I'm sure you've got better things to do with your time than visit with a grouchy old lady."

"No, that is not it at all. I love being here. You are the best friend I have."

"Hmmph." The Booklady smiled severely and lit a cigarette. "Too bad you're not hungry. There's too much for just me. I guess I'll just have to throw most of it away."

"Well, I guess I could eat a little. If you really have enough."

"If I really have enough? Hmmph." The Booklady reached under the counter and pulled out a large box of chicken. "Think I can eat all this myself?" Her features softened as Melchi stepped closer and examined the contents of the box. "Come on, boy, help yourself. I'll get us forks for the potatoes."

Melchi took a small chicken leg and moved behind the counter to his spot on the floor. He knelt, holding the chicken upright before him like a candle, and whispered a short prayer. "Holy One, for your overgenerous providence, for your abundant kindness and mercy, we give Thee thanks. Amen." When he opened his eyes, the Booklady stood over him with a Tupperware bowl full of mashed potatoes.

"How long has it been since you've eaten, Melchi?"

He looked down at the floor, his ears beginning to burn.

"I thought so. I was only asking because"—she plopped a dollop of potatoes on a paper plate and put it on the floor in front of him—"because, I don't know. I just wish you would come by more often. I don't get much company, you know."

"I am sorry. I don't wish to presume upon your generosity. You do too much as it is. I have nothing to offer in return."

"Fiddlesticks! You clean the shop. You unload the truck and arrange the books. I should be paying you, you know. If the IRS ever found out about you, they'd slap my butt in jail for violating labor laws."

Melchi twisted to sit cross-legged next to her chair and looked up at the shopkeeper with a grin.

"So eat now! The chicken's already cold, if that's what you're waiting on." The Booklady put three more pieces of chicken on his plate and nibbled at her own piece.

Melchi gobbled down the chicken, trying his best to be appropriately thankful. It was very good. Perfect. He tried to think of something to say, but words failed him. The warmth of the bookstore; the rich, salty chicken; the creamy, peppery potatoes. It was too much. He could only look up at the Booklady and hope she would understand how much more he wanted his piteously inadequate thank-you to convey. She picked at her food and gazed down on him with that pinched little smile.

For all of Melchi's size, he could never eat very much at one time. When the meal was over, the Booklady gave him a damp paper towel for his hands and then took up her book and started reading. Melchi pulled his overcoat and backpack off and then took his copy of *The Two Towers* from one of the shelves. He opened it to his place and sat back down in his spot by the Booklady's chair.

He drank in the heady words, savoring them as he had the chicken. Delicious.

A gentle touch brushed across his hair. Melchi went rigid, not sure what to do. Another touch sent an electric jolt prickling down his neck. She was combing his hair. He should do something. It had to be wrong. He would be *marime*. Unclean.

He knew he should leave, but he couldn't. He sat, transfixed, drinking in the strange sensations. It was so . . . wonderful. If only it could last forever. He turned his head away to hide the tears that streamed down his cheeks.

This was what it meant to have a mother.

# 2

*Chocolate.* Hailey opened her eyes slowly, squinting against the glaring light of Tiffany's shabby-chic lamp. The rich smell of chocolate tickled at the back of her brain. Hadn't she been eating ice cream?

Jerking suddenly awake, she grabbed at the sticky container of Häagen-Dazs on her lap. *Great . . . just great!* It had tipped over while she slept, leaving a chocolaty smile on her sweatshirt. She sucked tentatively at the stain and climbed to her feet to inspect the damage. A large brown blob stood out against the off-white fabric. The sofa looked like one of her old neighbor's Holsteins. Tiffany was going to have a Rocky-Road meltdown.

The soft scrape of footsteps sounded at the door. Hailey whirled around. The sound of a muffled voice. A *male* voice . . .

*God, please . . . not again!* Glancing around the living room, she flipped over the sofa cushion and stuffed the ice-cream container under the coffee table. Then, gathering up a stack of photocopied journal articles, she ran toward the stairs.

The dead bolt slid back with a snap.

"Oh good, you're awake."

Her roommate's slurred voice shamed Hailey into stopping. "Barely. I'm on my way to bed right now. G'night, Tiff." Hailey started up the stairs without turning around.

"Come on, silly. It's Friday night. You gotta stop working sometime. Besides, I got someone I want you to meet."

Hailey brushed back her hair and wiped a sleeve across her mouth before turning around. Not just one, but two guys stood in the doorway. Hailey couldn't believe it. Her roommate had the morals of an alley cat, but this . . .

Then she noticed how tall the redhead was. So that's what her roommate was up to.

Tiffany tugged on the redhead's arm, but the shorter guy stepped in front of them. He looked part Asian, with that silky black hair and those soft, handsome features.

"Hi, I'm Louie. Glad to meet you. Tiff's told me all about you."

Hailey shook his hand, careful not to fall into her habitual slouch. "Hi Louie. Good to meet you too. A minute later and we'd have met in . . . I mean, well, if you'd have gotten here a minute later, I'd have been in . . . ." Hailey cast a longing look up the stairs. So much for being smooth. "Look, I have to get up really early in the morning."

"Sorry about that. Tiff said you were a night owl, and, well . . . here we are."

"That's okay." She grimaced as the words escaped her lips. Why couldn't she just tell them to go away? Tiff never worried about being rude.

Her roommate pulled the lanky redhead forward and took Louie possessively by the arm. "Hailey, I want you to meet Mark. Mark, this is Hailey."

Mark reached out to take Hailey's hand.

"Mark's a scientist-kinda doctor, and you're a doctor-kinda scientist, right? You're both brains and must have tons and tons in common."

*Like we're both skyscrapers.* Hailey forced a smile and turned to look him in the eye. "Hi Mark. Nice to meet you."

"Hi."

"Well, my job is done. I'd stay and talk, but I'm sure the conversation would be way above my head." Tiff let out a dull laugh that clanked like a cowbell flung down a concrete stair. "Louie and I'll just leave you two scientists to get acquainted." She ducked under Louie's arm and pulled him toward the stairs.

"Wait a second." Hailey moved to block their way. "You haven't told me . . . anything about Mark."

"Yeah, I did. He's a med student. What more do you need? He's smart, rich, obviously good-looking."

Hailey forced a smile as the ungainly student shuffled his feet. It wasn't his fault he'd been dragged into this. He seemed almost nice.

Tiff stepped behind her, making for the stairs. Hailey made one last attempt to halt the invasion. "So what about you, Louie? What do you do?"

"He's a med student too. But he's already taken." Tiff grabbed Louie by the arm, and the two tromped up the stairs.

"But . . ." Hailey sighed as the couple disappeared from view. She turned and studied her roommate's idea of a perfect match for her. Mark had a long face and unruly hair. He was easily six foot five. At least she'd be able to wear heels.

"Sorry if that was embarrassing. I shouldn't have let them talk me into coming. Were you going to bed?"

"Not anymore."

"Oh." Mark fidgeted with his hands and turned to look around the room. "So . . . Louie says you're a scientist. What field?"

"Biochemistry. I'm a third-year grad student in Werner's lab." Hailey cast one last look up the stairs and trudged over to the sofa. The whole room reeked of chocolate.

"What kind of research are you doing? I'm really interested in biochemistry."

"Mark, there's something you should know." She dumped the articles on the coffee table and plopped down on the sofa. "I'm nothing at all like my roommate."

"Okay."

"Birds of a feather may flock together, but I'm not a bird and I'm not into flocking. We're just sharing a room until they finish remodeling my apartment. My real roommate is staying with a friend, and I . . . I'm babbling like an idiot, aren't I?"

"No problem." Mark moved to the sofa and sat down beside her. "I really am interested in biochemistry."

"Wait until you've done it awhile. The interest dims a little when you're playing personal handmaiden to a billion demanding bacteria."

"Right . . ." Mark went back to studying his hands. "So what do you think about the epidemic?" He shifted in his seat, stretching out his arm to rest it on the back of the sofa.

She scooted away from him and pulled her legs up, hugging her knees to her chest.

"Hailey?"

"I'm sorry. I—" She glanced at his arm. "I just realized. I have to go back to the lab. I started a culture this afternoon, and the bugs have been growing a lot faster since I changed their media. It was really good meeting you." She leaned forward. *Come on. Take the hint. Please.*

"Right now? I could go with you if you want. You shouldn't be walking alone—not with all the stuff that's been happening lately."

"That's okay. I do it all the time. One of the hazards of the trade. And I really shouldn't let you in the lab."

"Top-secret research, huh?"

"Something like that." Hailey slid onto the edge of the couch. "I really should get going."

Mark didn't move.

"Okay . . ." Hailey pushed up onto her feet and started across the room.

"I'm going back up the hill anyway, so I might as well come along." Mark followed her to the door, hovering over her as she fumbled with the dead bolt. "Louie's probably not going to be leaving anytime soon." He nodded in the direction of the stairs.

Hailey's face was beginning to glow. She opened the door and pushed out into the cold San Francisco night. A fog-drenched breeze blew icy needles through her sweatshirt. She really should have gone back for a jacket, but all her clothes were in Tiffany's room.

And she was *not* going in there.

Pulling her hands inside her sleeves, she hurried up the street. A damp fog hung in the air, muffling the streetlights in a shroud of glowing orange. Mark's footsteps slapped the sidewalk a few steps behind her. She could hear him huffing and puffing up the steep hill.

"So what do you think about the epidemic? Think it could be caused by prions?" Mark pulled even with her, blowing on his hands.

"What epidemic? What are you talking about?"

"Sudden onset dementia." He drew out the words like a waiter at a froofy restaurant. "Three cases in the last two weeks—all of them from the Sunset district."

"Three cases don't exactly make an epidemic."

"Maybe, but we think they may have had contact with one another. And Frates called in Prusiner for a consultation. All the interns have been talking about it."

"A new form of mad cow disease?"

"Maybe."

"And maybe not." Hailey didn't put much stock in the UCSF rumor mill. All the same, she wished she'd sent back the burger she'd gotten at Deli Nine. It had been awfully rare.

A tremor of nausea shuddered through her body. She stopped and searched the darkness. Her back and arms tingled with the chill of cold sweat. Sensations of overwhelming dread crawled up her spine. What was going on? She was shaking from head to foot.

"Are you okay?" All of a sudden Mark was in front of her, staring into her face. "Hailey?"

"Huh? Yeah, okay. Fine." As suddenly as they had appeared, the strange sensations passed, leaving her weak and trembling. "Just thinking about a hamburger I probably shouldn't have eaten." Hailey took a deep breath and started walking. Speaking of hamburgers, she was starting to get hungry. *Very* hungry. She wanted so much to—what?

She shuddered and quickened her pace. Turning into the entrance of the UCSF parking garage, she passed through a dimly lit corridor between two sets of bike cages. She stared at the convex safety mirror mounted at the end of the passage. Funny, she had never noticed the mirror before. She couldn't see anybody near the elevator, which should have comforted her. Instead, it only made her more uneasy. When she got to the elevators, she pressed the up button and waited. Was Mark planning to follow her up?

The elevator opened with a ding, and Mark stepped in front of her. He reached around her to hold the door, brushing her back with his arm. Hailey stumbled inside and hit the button for the top floor. Slumping against the back wall, she watched the display above the doors light their upward progress.

"You know, I bet this is the only place in the world where you can get in at the ground floor, go up ten floors and walk out of the building on ground level." Mark licked his lips and smiled.

"Go up nine floors, you mean." Hailey kept her eyes on the level indicator, willing the elevator to go faster.

"No, you're forgetting the stairs. The elevators go to level I; then we have to take the stairs up a level to get to the Parnassus Street entrance."

The elevator doors opened, and Hailey stepped out with Mark right behind.

"Right, there are ten floors total, but we only go up nine." Hailey turned back to see a frown on Mark's face and then jogged up the stairs two at a time. Before he could catch up with her, she pushed through the doors and turned to wave. "Bye, Mark. Thanks for the walk!"

She ran across the street and up the steps of the science building, digging in her pocket for her keys. Unlocking the heavy glass door, she turned just enough as she pulled it open to assure herself Mark wasn't still following.

The door closed behind her with a sigh. Hailey shivered. A chill brushed across her mind, leaving behind the disturbing aftertaste of decay and wet rat. She hurried toward the elevators, fighting the urge to break into a run. Hollow footsteps echoed loud and lonely in the empty marble hallway. Stepping into a waiting elevator, she punched the ninth-floor button and leaned back against the wall. The door shut with a clank, sealing her in.

"Stupid! How could I have been so stupid!" she blurted out at the elevator ceiling. "I can't believe I did it again. He wasn't so bad. I can't—"

The elevator opened onto the ninth floor, and Hailey fell suddenly silent. The floor was quiet as a tomb. What was she doing there anyway? What was *wrong* with her?

Hailey lunged forward to escape the closing doors. Walking through the halls, the swish of her jeans, the tap of her shoes, the wheeze of her breathing—everything seemed to shout her arrival.

She held her keys with both hands to keep them from jingling as she eased the key into the lock and opened the door of the lab. The room was dark. Where was everybody? She turned the lights on and checked her watch. It was only 12:30.

She circled the room, glancing behind each lab bench before returning to her desk. Digging in the bottom drawer, she came up with a granola bar and wolfed it down. She reached for another one, but it wasn't what she wanted. She was hungry but not for granola. Sliding the desk drawer silently back into place, she cast a wary glance at the door.

"This is stupid!" she hissed. "Check the stupid bugs and get your stupid self home to bed where you belong." She stopped the shaker bath and pulled out a flask. The medium was already milky. She should check their optical density, but . . .

A burning sensation rumbled up her spine and into her brain, erupting in a fiery plume of rage.

Forget it! She could start another stupid culture tomorrow. She hated having her life ruled by bacteria. She hated spectrophotometers. She hated the whole stupid lab, the whole stupid school!

She screamed and flung the flask at the floor. It burst into a blossom of jagged-edged liquid. Kicking a glass shard into the wall, she pushed her way out of the room.

Hunger welled in her chest, churning, raging, beating at the walls of her sanity. She started to run, but the floor teetered beneath her feet, throwing her sideways against the wall. Anger exploded in her mind, filling her, surrounding her, flowing through her.

A soft tapping sound stabbed through her senses like a honed knife. Something was behind her. She could feel it watching her, feel its hunger. Hailey tried to turn, but her muscles wouldn't respond. A will, stronger than her own, bound her. Steel bands, cutting into her muscles, pressing in on her chest until she couldn't breathe.

Shaking with the effort, she pushed herself away from the wall. The hallway before her dimmed and then separated as another image invaded her vision.

The image of herself as seen from behind.

A ragged scream erupted from her lips. She tottered forward— just enough to keep herself from falling—then, propelled by an explosion of fury, she broke into an all-out run. Down the hallway, past the elevators, through the stairwell door. Leaping down the stairs a quarter flight at a time, her screams punctuated only by sobbing breaths, Hailey spiraled downward. Half jumping, half falling, she plummeted toward the first floor.

*There's no escape. There can never be escape!*

She burst through a set of steel doors at the bottom of the stairs and stumbled out into the moonlit darkness. A construction sign stood by a roped-off sidewalk. Ripping the temporary sign out of the ground, she jammed its metal post through the two door handles and yanked down on the end to bend it into place.

A low rumble sounded on the other side of the door. She backed away, screaming. It was coming for her. She could feel it seeping through the doors! She turned and ran for the campus security office. Mr. Hemphill was on duty. He'd be able to help. He *had* to be on duty.

A wave of nausea bent her double, sending her crashing into a parked car. She rolled over and over across the cold cement, clawing at the foul presence that enveloped her. Putrid. Slimy. She felt it slithering into her mind. She was worthless trash. Rotten. Unspeakably dirty.

*Yes, go to campus security.* Honey-sweet words oozed through her brain. *Go to campus security. Go and wait.*

"No!" Hailey sprang to her feet and charged down the street. Shrieking, screaming, clawing and scratching at the voices swirling in her head, she bounded down the hill. Darkness. She needed someplace to hide. Her shouts turned to whimpering sobs as she willed herself to calm. She had to *focus*, think through her options. Tiffany's apartment? A stranger's?

Making for the lit doorway of the closest townhouse, she scrambled up the concrete steps and jabbed at a glowing doorbell. *Come on. Answer the door!* The rage was starting to come back. With one last shake of the door handle, she turned and fled back down the sidewalk.

A wall of darkness rose up before her at the end of the road. Golden Gate Park. She ran out into the street bordering the park and waved her arms. Where were all the cars? The road was always busy. *Always.* Did they know something she didn't? White-hot fury erupted inside of her. They hated her. The whole stupid world wanted to see her dead.

*No!* Hailey shook herself, tried to clear her mind. She stumbled across the street and leaped over the ditch. The presence knew where she was. Vaulting a low fence, she plunged into the cloying darkness. Tree branches slashed at her face and tore at her arms, but she kept running, zigzagging back and forth to lose herself in the tangle of vines, limbs, and leaves. If she didn't know where she was, maybe it wouldn't either. This was her only chance.

Running until she couldn't run anymore, Hailey limped to her right and collapsed into a dark thicket.

*Calm down. Calm down.* She lay in the semi-darkness, hugging her knees to her chest. Throat open. Mouth open. No vocal chords. A remote part of her brain fought for control. She couldn't stop the sobs that wracked her body, but she had to be quiet. She buried her eyes in her hands, let the rush of her breathing fill her world.

The snap of a twig tugged her back into awareness. Something was moving—a shadow through the trees. She gulped back a swallow of air and fought against burning lungs to quiet her breathing, but still it advanced. Headed straight for her.

Hailey jumped to her feet and started to run, but her foot caught in a tangle, and her ankle turned beneath her. She hit the ground hard and rolled onto her back to face her pursuer.

It was a man. And in his hand he brandished a knife.

## ~ 3 ~

How could he have been so weak? Melchi carried box after box of books from the supply room and arranged them on the overflowing bookstore shelves. The few minutes he had allowed the Booklady to touch his hair could well cost him his life. Worse. The life of another. He was marime—unclean. His investigations would have to be postponed until after the duration of his penance. If he survived that long.

But first he had to demonstrate his gratitude. The Booklady had given him food. She left the bookstore late, letting him read much longer than usual. He didn't have much time.

Taking up his bucket and mop, he scrubbed the floor of the bathroom and then dusted the bookshelves with a feather duster while he waited for the floor to dry.

As he stepped back into the bathroom to clean his mop, a burning sensation tickled at the back of his mind. He leaped across the room and swatted at the light switch, plunging the room in darkness. Clenching his eyes shut, he backed against the bathroom wall as the crushing weight of darkness pressed in on him from all sides.

A silent scream quivered up his spine. He held his hands over his ears, but he couldn't shut it out. Rage washed through him like water through a saturated sponge. *Not tonight. Please, not tonight. Holy One, help me. Please don't let it hunt tonight.*

A tremor snapped his head back, bashing it into the hard edge of the cast-iron sink. Another silent scream. Pain and terror—the cries of a woman . . .

A child of the Standing.

*Please, no.* Melchi crawled out from under the sink. What could he do? He was marime. Besides, he'd never be able to find it in time. If only he hadn't been so lazy. Ortus always told him it would be his undoing.

Feeling for the bucket of dirty water, Melchi emptied it into the toilet. There was nothing he could do. Nothing. Not only had he spent the night in self-indulgence, but the Booklady had touched his hair. If it found him, it would kill him. And if it found him in the Booklady's store . . .

Clamping his eyes shut, he crawled across the floor. *Holy One, we thank Thee. Holy One, hide us in Thy almighty hands.* He repeated the words over and over, letting them fill his mind, willing them to blot out all awareness of his surroundings. Climbing to his feet at the front door, he pushed it open, and the bell clanged before he thought to grab it.

The cold night air bore down on him with searching eyes. *Holy One, hide us. Holy One, hide us.* He opened his eyes and fumbled with the lock, imagining he was closing the massive door of a great castle. The dragon was coming; he had to lock the gate. The dragon was coming. He turned and fled into the night, letting the city buildings spin by him in a dark and dreamy blur.

Up a hill, down a street, up another hill, over, across, around, he closed his eyes and flung himself between two parked cars. With burning lungs he pressed himself against the asphalt, letting the cold seep into his bones. A sudden hush fell over the city. Soft, gentle silence. The bookstore was safe. It had to be. Maybe the woman had managed to escape too. He hadn't felt the exultation of a death cry.

Melchi climbed to his feet and jogged back down the hill toward the park. He didn't have a choice. He had to reach the safety of his nest. There was nothing else he could do. The Booklady had touched his hair. He was unclean. If it caught him, he was dead.

Safe within the cover of the forest, Melchi started to relax and fell into the rhythm of a slow trot. It was unusually cold out, even for San Francisco. He tried to blank his thoughts and forget himself like Ortus had taught him, but a vague worry gnawed at the corner of his mind.

*The scream.* The Mulo had found another Standing. If it hurt her, it would be his fault. He was worse than a murderer. The Holy One could never use such a damaged tool. He was so selfish, wretched, vile . . .

The image of the trembling old-timer leaped into his mind. What if he didn't have another blanket? Melchi cast the thought aside. Of course he had a blanket. He was a homeless. Blankets were essential.

But what if he had been forced to steal? What if his blanket had been stolen by someone else? Melchi wrestled with the thought, but it wouldn't go away.

Leaping high into the air, he caught the limb of his cedar and swung himself up to the safety of his nest. He pulled the blanket out of his pack and spread it out on the rope mesh. He didn't deserve such comfort. How could he even think of sleep after everything he had done?

But he couldn't go out into the night. He was unclean. If the Mulo found him, it would kill him. Melchi searched for a new argument, but he was already climbing down the tree. The night was too cold.

He couldn't have another death on his conscience.

He slunk along a dark path, hugging the blanket to his chest. The man was so old. The pathos in his eyes hit him like a slap to the face. How could he have been so heartless? So selfish? Why couldn't he do anything right?

A vision filled his mind. The old man lying unprotected on the ground, too spent to shiver against the cold night air. He started to run.

Faster. He had to go faster.

———————

HAILEY SCOOTED AWAY FROM the skeletal man standing over her. She looked up, numb, disbelieving, as he sauntered toward her, knife advanced, mumbling and nodding to himself. Working up his nerve.

This couldn't be happening. It couldn't. A whining, simpering moan sounded in her ears. With a start she realized it was coming from her. Some detached part of her being rose above her panic and observed the advancing man with shocking emotional flatness. She was supposed to scream, but she couldn't for the life of her remember how. She could only stare like a silent spectator in a dream.

The man reached toward her with the long blade of his knife and slid it slowly under the bottom edge of her sweatshirt. Cold metal touched her skin, shattering her calm like a dropped flask. Her whole being retched as she lost herself in a single, prolonged, soul-tearing scream.

———————

A LOUD SCREAM ROCKED the night. Melchi skidded to a halt, spinning about in an effort to locate its source. It was a woman's scream, and it came from nearby.

He plunged through the undergrowth, crossing his arms before his face as he crashed through the tearing branches. It was too dark. There was no way he could find her.

A flash of silver. Ahead and to his left. The vague shadow of a man. Without slowing, Melchi adjusted his course and plowed through the intervening saplings.

The man turned to meet him just before impact. Only then did Melchi see the knife.

———— ·+· ————

A LOUD CRASH SOUNDED through the trees. Hailey snapped back into herself. Her attacker turned to face the noise. He swung the knife around just as a dark figure launched itself at him.

The knife flashed as the rescuer whirled up and over her attacker, pulling him down with a sickening snap. An agonizing scream tore through the night.

Hailey sat rigid as a dark shadow rose from the ground. The knife in its hand glinted in the moonlight. Raising it in the air, the shadow launched it spinning into the trees.

The moonlight caught the man's heavily bearded face. Hailey gasped, suddenly overwhelmed by a deep abiding sorrow. Tears streamed down her cheeks as she looked up at the huge man standing before her.

He stood wide-eyed and stoop shouldered, staring back at her. He was enormous, and his eyes . . . She saw herself as in a mirror. She was so beautiful. Painfully, agonizingly beautiful. If only she could—he could?

"No!" Hailey screamed. It was still in her head. *He* was in her head.

The giant jumped back and searched the clearing with wide, darting eyes. Mouth open wide, chest heaving, he stood at a half crouch, balanced on the thin edge of indecision. To pounce on her? To dart away? Hailey was afraid to move. She didn't want to trigger either reaction.

Fear rippled across her spine. The sensation was all too familiar yet so completely different. Was it her fear or his she felt? Did she feel anything at all?

She stared back at the wild man, not daring to blink. Fingers outspread, head thrust forward, he circled her with intense, probing eyes. Sparkling pools of moonlight. Two shining stars, fixed and certain above her spinning, careening world. The stars grew brighter, larger, filling the night with their light.

A gasp tore her eyes from the giant's. The wiry man had risen from the ground and was charging. Her giant just stood there, mute and staring. Then, in a flash of motion, the charging man went sailing over his head. Across the clearing, crashing into a shadowy hedge.

The giant turned toward the flailing man. "That was bad. Go now and trouble us no more! Stray from the straight and narrow one more time, and I shall surely find you."

The skinny man cursed and climbed out of the tangle of bushes, hugging his right arm to his body. The giant turned toward Hailey, head bowed and eyes turned downward. Her attacker stood watching him, considering. Then with an oath he turned away and fled through the surrounding trees.

"I am sorry," the big man said at last in a broken, uneven voice. "I did not intend to break his arm. It happened too fast . . . I didn't get a chance to . . . but that's not an excuse. I should have thought of something else. I am very sorry."

Hailey stared at the man in front of her, blinking against the distortion of her tears.

"Are you unwell?" He spoke slowly, as if speaking to a child.

Hailey nodded her head and tried to stand, but her ankle collapsed beneath her.

The man jumped back, his face distorted with pain.

"No, it's okay!" Hailey felt herself tossed in a sea of raging emotions. What was happening to her?

"You're hurt." The man took a step forward and then stopped. He rocked back and forth, hands clenching and unclenching, staring at the ground, listening, longing . . .

Hailey forced her eyes away. She had to get a grip. He was just a normal guy. A street person. Something else was going on. Food poisoning maybe? Sudden-onset dementia?

Climbing onto her knees, she pushed herself up onto her right foot and tried to stand, but a dark wave crashed over her, tipping her off balance. She took a step, and her ankle flashed out in pain. The man reached toward her and then pulled away to let her fall backward in a crumpled heap.

"Please help me." She fought through a storm of swirling emotions. "Please. I'm sick. I need to get to a doctor."

"Wait here. I will return soon."

"No!" She didn't mean to shriek. "Please, don't leave me. Not here!"

"What can I do?"

"Help me up. I know I can walk. Please . . . don't leave me."

The man turned away. "I—can't."

Hailey crawled after him, reached out for his leg. He wanted to help. She knew he wanted to help, but he was afraid. Of her?

The man stepped out of reach, and she collapsed back onto the ground. Something was wrong. She had to get to a doctor. She had to get out of there.

He stooped down next to her, reached out a halting hand. Was he trembling or was it her? His touch would kill her. Kill him?

He gasped as one of his hands slid behind her back. An arm hooked under her knees, and he lifted her gently from the ground.

*So close.* She wrinkled her nose and turned her face away. She wanted so much to hold him. She was so close.

A dark canopy of interlacing silhouettes moved across the orange-tinted sky. He carried her through the park, holding her away from his body. She could feel his tension, hard as steel, stabbing into her bones.

"Put me down. I'm too heavy."

"But you're hurt."

"I'm too . . . tall. You can't carry me." Panic rose up inside Hailey. She was so awkward, so huge. He shouldn't, couldn't—

"You're not heavy at all; you're—" His voice choked off.

Hailey sucked in her breath. *Beautiful.* He was going to say beautiful. Warmth suffused her body. She sank into its soft embrace, relaxed as it soothed the tension from her shoulders. An alarm rang out inside her head. He was a stranger. A filthy, smelly homeless man. But somehow it didn't seem to matter.

Leaning against his chest, she reached her arms around his neck. A gasp sounded next to her ear. She was so close . . . She clung tighter to the giant as a storm of raging emotions beat down on her. She was so beautiful. Too beautiful. Too achingly, wondrously beautiful!

"Holy One, please help me . . ." What was she saying? How long had they been standing like this? Why weren't they moving? She had to see a doctor—a *real* doctor. Did she even want to be a doctor? She wasn't even sure anymore. *Holy One, help me. Please . . . hold me.*

A fiery rage cut through her turmoil like a knife. She could feel it beating against her, insinuating itself into her mind like a foul stench. The monster was back. It was getting closer. She could run, but she would never be able to escape.

Hailey clasped the giant tighter, burying her face in his chest. Sinewy bands stood out like bulging cords beneath his coat. Knotted and twisted. So horribly deformed. Pushing herself away, she looked up into his eyes. Who was he? *What* was he? None of it made any sense at all.

———

MELCHI BROKE INTO AN all-out run, straining to hold on to the girl as she struggled and twisted in his arms.

"Try to quiet your mind," he hissed in her ear. "The Mulo searches for us. It knows we're here."

"Put me down!" The girl beat against his chest and face with a hail of flailing fists. "Something's wrong. I need to see a doctor!"

"But the Mulo! It will kill you." Melchi stopped at the edge of the park, searching the surrounding city. The park was the safest place for them. They could lose themselves in the trees. But the girl. She said she needed a doctor . . .

"Please." The girl went limp in his arms. He could feel her shuddering as sobs convulsed her body. "Please don't hurt me."

"I'd never—it's the Mulo. I—" Melchi cast one last look back at the park and leaped out into the street. She was sick. Possibly dying. He could feel the razor edge of pain cutting beneath her fear.

Charging up the hill, he dodged in and out between the trees and parked cars. If the Mulo found him, it would kill him. Especially now. How could he have been so weak? To be touched by the Booklady was bad enough, but to touch such a beautiful girl, willfully and of his own volition . . .

If he could just get her to the hospital before the Mulo found them.

He was halfway up the hill when it hit him. A wave of twisted exultation, lashing at his back like a bullwhip. The Mulo was at the edge of the park.

It knew where they were.

"It has found us. I cannot hold it off long." Melchi stopped and tried to lower the girl to the ground, but she clung tighter to his neck. "You must go from here. Run as fast as you can. Find a place to hide."

"No, please . . . don't leave me. I can't walk. Don't make me go. Please . . ."

Melchi stood rigid, fighting a million temptations at once. His heart pounded against his ribs. The Mulo was coming. He had to do something. He couldn't let it get to her.

Swinging her legs back over his arm, he started running. Up the hill, out onto the road. It didn't matter if it saw them now.

"Yell for the police as soon as you're inside." Melchi called out as he turned at the top of the hill. "I will do what I can to slow it down."

The girl's head lolled against his chest. Her eyes were open, but she didn't seem to understand.

"Did you hear me? Call the police. They cannot stand long against it. You must find someplace to hide."

Melchi was gasping for breath as the semicircular drive of the hospital building jolted into view. The Mulo was right behind them. They wouldn't make it. He was too weak, tired, filled with loathsome sin.

The glass doors slid open as he pounded into the emergency room lobby. "Police!" Melchi shouted between heaving breaths as he set the girl on the floor. "Remember, you must hide!" He called back over his shoulder as he turned and fled back through the open door. "Try to stay calm. It can hear your emotions!"

The doors shut behind him with an ominous clank. He stepped away from the building and reached out with his mind. Faces pressed in on him from all sides. Terror, confusion, unbridled hysteria. The girl's emotions swirled around him like a raging sea. A bright and shining beacon the Mulo would be able to see for miles.

Jogging out into the street, Melchi turned in a tight circle to search the gloaming shadows. "I know you are here! It is me you want. Come out and get me!"

The night air pressed down on him, holding him like a vice. White hot needles prickled at his skin. He could feel the malice closing in. Putrid, dirty, unspeakably evil. He stumbled forward and almost tripped over a bulge in the pavement. He had to get away from the hospital, but he was too tired. So weak . . . He took a few more staggering steps and lurched to the side. How could he walk? How could he even move? He was starving to death. He'd been hungry for so long. So hungry. Hungry for . . . the girl?

A vision flashed before his mind's eye. Soft luminous eyes, a delicate oval face, shining black hair flowing like silk across slender shoulders. Melchi squeezed his eyes shut, jammed his palms into his eye sockets. He had to resist. Stand firm against the evil. Stand firm against . . . himself.

He *was* the evil. He always had been.

A low rumbling growl rattled through his frame. Right behind him. Too late to run.

The Mulo was already here.

"LET GO OF ME!" Hailey swung her fists and kicked out with her right foot. "It's here. Don't you feel it?" She wrenched free of the doctors' grasp and flung herself at the floor.

A half-dozen hands caught her and forced her backward, pinning her to the bed. Faded green togs. The smell of ethanol. A heavy strap pressed down on her chest. "No, please! It's killing him!" She kicked out, crying out in pain as her ankle was snared and lashed against the bed.

An antiseptic face filled her vision. Cool hands cupped her face. "I need you to calm down, okay? Calm down and tell us what's wrong. We can't help you if you don't tell us what's wrong."

"They're fighting. It's trying to kill him—the giant who rescued me."

"Shhh . . . It's okay." The doctor's head bobbed up and down. "We'll take care of it. I promise you, but first I need you to tell me your name. Do you remember your name?"

"Hailey Maniates."

"Good." The man smiled and nodded. "Now Hailey. Tell me who's fighting. Do you know where they are?"

"Don't you feel it? In the air. All around. He's hurt. The giant that rescued me."

The doctor glanced at one of the others. "And this giant. Who's he fighting?"

"Not a *giant* giant. A huge homeless man. He rescued me from a skinny guy with a knife—back in Golden Gate Park."

"And they're still in the park. You think they're still fighting?"

"No, they're here. Somewhere near the hospital. I can feel them. The homeless man and . . . some kind of a monster. I know what this sounds like, but I'm not crazy! I'm a grad student—here at UCSF. Something attacked me in my lab. It was in my head.

I saw myself through its eyes. The giant carried me and now he's—"

A wall of rage hit her in the chest. Twisted pleasure. Intense pain. Hailey screamed and tried to squirm free of her bonds. It was coming for her. The air was thick with it. She could feel it getting closer.

She kicked out and shrieked as pain stabbed up from her ankle. The storm clouds swirling in her mind parted to reveal the doctor's intense face. He was shouting at her. Calling her name.

"—any medication? What drugs have you been taking? It's okay. You aren't in any trouble. We need to know in order to help you."

Her arm was forced back. The prick of a needle in her vein.

"No! Let me go!" Hailey jerked her hand back and swung at the doctor's face. "It's coming. It'll kill me! You can't hold me against my will. Let me go!"

"Where's that Geodon?!" The doctor grabbed her flailing head with both hands. "And get that other hand secured. Now!"

"No . . . you can't!" Hailey arched her back, pushing back against her bonds. "It's coming. Please . . ."

"Hailey, I need you to listen to me, okay?" The doctor's fingers tightened around her face. "You're perfectly safe. What you're experiencing isn't real. It's just a hallucination. I'm going to give you a sedative to help you calm down, okay? The sedative will make everything better."

"Hallucination?" Hailey's voice broke. Hot tears streamed down her face, tickling her ears. "No . . . it can't be. The knife. He cut my sweatshirt. I could see myself through his eyes!"

A needle-sharp pain jabbed into her shoulder, pumping her arm full of biting coolness.

"No. Please . . ."

A tingling chill spread out through her body, easing into her mind like a long drawn-out sigh.

A cruel laugh rumbled up her spine and echoed in her brain. The monster was coming for her. And this time it knew she couldn't escape.

———————

MELCHI SPUN IN A powerful roundhouse kick, but his leg swished through empty mist. Crouching low to the ground, he braced himself for the charge as dark phantoms danced at the periphery of his vision. Lurid shadows. The stench of decaying flesh.

"Show yourself, Mulo!" He held up his pendant and turned in a tight circle.

The snap of fluttering fabric. Behind him, to his left.

He turned toward the sound, searching the blackness of a recessed doorway. The flicker of shadow against darkness off to his right. An echoing laugh to his left. It was all around him. Suffocating, pressing down on him like a crashing wave.

Melchi backed away from the hospital as the streetlights around him sputtered and dimmed. Hatred beat down on him from every direction. Putrid, malicious . . . it invaded his thoughts with degrading passions and blackest guilt.

The girl. He had touched her; he had raised his eyes to the beauty of her visage. He was already fallen. Even standing, he could not hope to stand.

Staggering backward, he turned and broke into a run as an explosion of rage swept over him. Tongues of scorching flame licked at the recesses of his mind, consuming all but thoughts of escape. He darted toward a tall building and vaulted off a low window sill. Hurtling through the air, his fingers closed around the bars of a second-story window as he slammed chest first into the concrete wall.

Running was useless. He was already dead.

Melchi kicked with his feet, tried to scrabble up the wall. The Mulo was right beneath him, reaching up for him. Lashing out at him with the force of its presence.

*Cease striving. Know that I am your god.* Smooth words insinuated themselves into his mind. *Relax. Be still. You have already fallen. You cannot be raised again.*

A soothing numbness seeped through Melchi's body. The bars were slipping. He could feel himself floating softly to the ground, buoyed up by the whisper-soft brushes of angels' wings. Rest. Total relaxation. He had worked so hard for so long. Didn't he deserve a break? Hadn't he earned it?

"No!" Melchi slammed his forehead into the concrete, clinging to the pain like a lifeline in a raging storm. Pulling with all his remaining strength, he climbed up onto the windowsill and hugged the bars to his chest. One more level. Just a little higher.

He jammed his fingertips into a seam in the concrete and pulled himself up the wall. Wedging his feet between the bars on the window, he regripped with his fingertips and pulled himself even higher. One more pull. Just a few more inches . . . His fingers closed over the edge of the third-story sill. Kicking with his feet, he pulled himself up onto the ledge.

Good. Just one more level. All he needed was—

The foul presence receded like a spent wave on the shore. Melchi gasped and sputtered in the cold clean air. He clung trembling to the wall, waiting for it to return. The last stroke of death after the illusion of calm.

Nothing. Leaning out from the building, he searched the empty streets below. The Mulo . . . had it broken off the attack? It didn't make sense. He had been as good as dead.

"The girl!" Melchi pushed away from the wall and pivoted as his coat whipped and crackled in the rushing wind. Windmilling his arms against the shrieking air, he smacked into the ground, buckling and rolling to absorb the impact.

His left foot screamed out in pain. Another stupid mistake. Tonight he couldn't do anything right.

"Here I am!" he shouted out into the darkness. "Come and get me!" He limped back to the hospital, ignoring the pain in his foot. If the Mulo got to the girl . . . how could he ever live with himself?

The glass panels of the hospital doors swooshed aside as he reached the entrance. Skidding to a stop inside the lobby, he reached out with his mind. She was here. Her panicked thoughts clung to him like a terrified child. She was frightened, weak, reeling from terrible pain.

A shout called after him as he plunged through a doorway and raced down a brightly lit corridor. Something was wrong. The girl's presence was getting weaker. Fading like a tiny ember removed from its fire. Her soul—it was as if it were being slowly siphoned away.

He stumbled to a stop and collapsed onto the floor as the last tremulous wisp of her presence faltered and finally winked out.

He had failed. Again.

## 4

The city lights smoldered, sodden orange sparks blown into a wash of mist, moon, and void. Nearsighted cars felt their way along narrow city streets, probing the murky darkness with soft reluctant lights. A smudge of texture, intermittent against the sheen of a fog-drenched street, moved toward the entrance of the hospital. Melchi leaned out over the edge of the roof and watched as it disappeared into the building.

Just a normal *gadzé*—one of the fallen. Probably another patient. Drawing back from the edge, he locked his cramped legs into a squatting position. His lower back burned, but he didn't relax a muscle. He deserved the pain. It was his fault she was dead. He could have prevented it. *Should* have prevented it.

But no. At the first show of force, he'd turned tail and scampered away like the sniveling coward he was. He didn't deserve to wear the mark of the Standing. He was a depraved, murderous, lecherous coward. He didn't deserve to be alive at all. This vigil was only the beginning of his suffering. Real penance would commence in the morning.

Melchi brushed the thought aside and reached out with his mind. Still no sign of the Mulo. Not even the faintest tremor. It had made its kill and escaped—probably through one of the back doors. The hospital buildings were all interconnected. The Mulo had its choice of a hundred different escape routes.

But why leave at all? He had been at its mercy. It could have taken him at any time. Why had it gone for the girl instead? Even if she were one of the Standing, had Melchi fallen so low he was no longer a threat? Was he so far gone as to be beyond all hope of redemption?

*Holy One. Please forgive me. Please . . .*

The girl's face flashed unbidden before his mind. Tear-stained eyes. Quivering lips. She had been so . . . beautiful. Hot coals ignited in his gut. He had killed her. He'd reached out and wantonly touched her leg. Breathed the warm perfume of her hair, felt its soft caress against his neck. And then he had killed her. Abandoned her to a fate far worse than death.

*Holy One, please . . . I have fallen so low. I cannot even ask for forgiveness without committing the transgression I ask to be forgiven for. I am hopelessly infected. Even repentance is beyond me.*

Rising onto stiff, tingling legs, he stepped toward the edge of the roof. A dark void opened out beneath him. One single step. It would be so easy to end his struggles. All it would take was one more step and he would never have to fail again. He would never have to hurt anyone else.

Far below him a dark figure moved down the street, dragging with it a blast of wind and fog. He leaned out over the edge, watching it drift toward the hospital entrance. The city beneath him tilted and whirled. He was suddenly tired. How many days had it been since he'd slept? His eyes wandered to a dark blot on the horizon. Golden Gate Park stood below him, a great abyss that swallowed up the light of the city. A cold, yearning, hungry abyss. He was cold and sleepy. His nest would be so warm . . .

Melchi started as if from a dream. Jerking away from the edge of the roof, he dropped down into a low crouch, listening, sifting through the shadows. What had he missed? He stepped back toward the ledge and searched the city streets one more time. The Mulo was out there somewhere. The murderer of his people. It had killed the girl, his parents, Ortus—everyone he had truly loved. He must not rest until he tracked it down—even if he *was* unclean. If it killed him, it killed him.

One way or another the long struggle would finally be at an end.

---

"HAILEY MANIATES." A DISEMBODIED voice floated through the darkness. "Hailey, time to wake up."

*Mom?* Hailey tried to wrap her mind around the concept. Something was wrong. She was missing something. Why couldn't she remember?

"It's almost lunchtime. You don't want to miss lunch." The singsong voice echoed through her mind, a jumble of words hovering just beyond her reach. "Come on. Wake up!" She felt herself being shaken. Ice-cold hands against her bare skin.

"Mmmm . . ." Hailey tried to form the word, but she couldn't say it. Then she remembered the fire. Her mother . . . it was impossible. She couldn't be here. Shouldn't be here.

Straining with all her might, she forced her eyes open and squinted up into the blearing brightness. A hazy figure moved toward her, a blur of blue and pastel green.

"Good, you're awake. How are you feeling?" The woman reached down, touched Hailey's face, then sat back on some kind of padded stool.

Hailey watched her for what seemed like hours. What was she waiting for?

"Why don't we start with your name. Do you remember your name?" The woman was writing something. She could hear a faint scritching against a white clipboard. Gradually the sound faded. The woman was watching her, shaking her head with a tight-lipped frown.

"Are you having trouble talking? Nod your head if you can understand me."

Hailey managed a wooden nod. No . . . that wasn't right. "Of course I can talk." Her voice sounded slurred and distorted in her ears—like her tongue had fallen asleep during the night. "Why wouldn't I be able to talk?"

"Good!" The woman smiled and scritched on her clipboard. "Do you remember your name?"

"Hailey Maniates." Hailey rolled onto her side and looked around the Spartan room. The table, dresser, bed—everything was bolted down. "Where are we? Who are you?"

"I'm Dr. Victoria Goldberg. I'm here to assist in your treatment."

"Treatment?" Hailey looked down at her feet. When had they changed her into pajamas? "But I don't need treatment." She managed to lift her foot. Her ankle was wrapped in an elastic bandage. "It's just a sprained ankle. Why would I need treatment for a sprained ankle?"

"The emergency-room doctors said you were trying to escape from some kind of . . . monster. A monster and a giant, do you remember? They said you heard voices in your head."

*The monster* . . . the hallway outside her lab. Running through the darkness. Golden Gate Park.

"Hailey? What is it? What do you remember?"

"What?" Hailey turned to face the doctor, tried to focus on her face. "I already told them. He wasn't a giant—just a big homeless man. He rescued me from a guy who was . . . attacking me."

Thin, lipstick-smeared lips tightened into a crinkled line. Just above them a furrowed field of bleached peach fuzz grew in the shade of a sharp aquiline nose. It wasn't human. It didn't even seem real.

"Do you remember hearing voices? Seeing yourself from someone else's eyes?"

The voice made Hailey jump. She shook her head and forced her eyes to meet those of the woman.

"So you didn't hear voices?" The woman's eyes narrowed. She already knew. Somehow she already knew.

"Not exactly voices . . ." Hailey closed her eyes and tried to concentrate. She shouldn't be talking about this, but what could she do? She couldn't lie. "It was more like emotions. I could feel what the homeless man was thinking. It was almost like being inside his head."

"And the monster? He was in your head too?"

"Look, I know what it sounds like, but I didn't imagine it. I'm not crazy." Hailey tried to sit up, but the room tilted around her, tipping her off balance.

The woman caught her by the arms and eased her back onto the pillow. "Nobody thinks you're crazy. I'm just trying to help. And I can't help you if you don't tell me what happened."

"But I don't know what happened. It's all a blur. I was probably in shock. Did you ever consider that? Shock from my ankle. Shock from being attacked by a man with a knife."

"It's possible." The woman scribbled something on the clipboard. "And where were you when you were attacked? What were you doing?"

"I . . ." Hailey closed her eyes and shook her head. "You can't hold me here. My ankle is fine. I want to go home."

"I'm sorry." The woman shook her head, sadly it seemed. Hailey could almost believe she really cared. "Just one more question, okay?"

Hailey took a deep breath and tried to focus on the woman's face.

"Did the voices ever tell you to do something you knew was wrong? To hurt somebody, for example. Maybe even yourself?"

"I didn't hear voices!"

The woman stared hard at Hailey and jotted a note on the clipboard.

"I'm serious. It just felt . . . different. Like someone was standing right behind me. I could feel how much he wanted to hurt me. It was like he was giving off thought waves. I don't know. Vibrations or something. It was almost like a taste or a smell. I'm sure there's a perfectly rational explanation for what happened. I just don't know what it is yet."

"And you consider yourself a rational person, that is correct?"

"I already told them. I'm a scientist . . ."

"Do you believe in the supernatural?"

"I know what you're getting at, but no, I don't believe in monsters. It was just a figure of speech. I was terrified. I didn't know what was happening to me."

"But what about ghosts? Spirit guides, angels . . . God?"

"Look . . . just because I believe in God, doesn't mean I'm crazy. It takes just as much faith to believe the materialistic premise of science as it does to believe in God. More than 80 percent of the population believes in God. What are you going to do, have them all committed?"

"We don't want to have anyone committed. I'm just gathering information, that's all."

"But why? Why does it matter whether I believe in God or not?"

The woman pursed her lips and looked down at the clipboard. When she finally looked up, she seemed to have made up her mind about something. Hailey waited for her to speak.

"While you were tranquilized, the doctors ran several tests on you. They had to rule out the possibility of a tumor or physical trauma."

Hailey's heart froze in her chest. "What did they find?"

"Nothing to be concerned about. No tumors or indications of stroke or the like. But your brain scans were highly unusual. The right posterior superior parietal lobe of your brain was lit up like a Christmas tree. We've never seen that area so active."

Hailey searched the woman's face for a cue. "And this is bad?"

"Not necessarily. It's just unusual, that's all. This brain center is responsible for your sense of self. Where does Hailey end and the rest of the world begin? It's called the god center because it's active during prayer and meditation. Some neurologists think its activity may even give some segments of the population the illusion of God's existence, that sense of otherness that might easily be mistaken for the presence of the supernatural—in your case, monsters. Or the illusion that other people's emotions have gotten into your head."

"So you think that's what happened to me? It was . . . that center of my brain?"

The woman frowned and shook her head. "Maybe. But there's a lot we don't understand. Is this the first time you've experienced an episode like this?"

Hailey nodded and the doctor scribbled another note on the clipboard.

"Yet you believe in God. Why is that?"

"Because I'm a scientist. God is the only thing that makes sense."

"But don't most scientists think . . ."

"What? That just because they have a materialistic explanation for speciation, they've somehow disproved God's existence?

Like that makes sense. Even if we had a mechanism for abiogenesis, how life came into being in the first place, even if we could explain what happened before the Big Bang, that still wouldn't disprove God."

Goldberg frowned and shifted on the stool. "I'm not arguing. I'm merely trying to ascertain whether you might have had an episode in the past and assumed it was God. Has God ever talked to you? Have you ever felt . . . *His* presence?"

Hailey turned and looked up at the ceiling. No matter what she said, Goldberg was going to take it the wrong way. She couldn't win.

"Hailey?"

"I already told you. I've never heard voices. I didn't hear voices last night."

"But that sense of otherness. The feeling of God's presence?"

"It's not the same thing. Last night didn't make me feel loved and accepted. It didn't help me stop lying or control my temper or get over my fears." Hailey pushed herself up until she was sitting upright on the bed and looked Goldberg in the eye. "Last night was one hundred and eighty degrees, totally and completely different from anything I've ever experienced. Nothing else even comes close."

The doctor looked down at her clipboard and scribbled a long note before finally looking up. "You're twenty-four, right?" There was something about her voice. She knew more than she was telling.

Hailey nodded. "What do you think it is?"

"It's way too early for a diagnosis. We don't even—"

"But you have a theory. What's your initial hypothesis?"

The doctor searched her eyes for several seconds. Finally she shook her head. "It's too early to say for sure, but you seem to have all the classic symptoms of paranoid schizophrenia. Your description matches it perfectly, and you're exactly the right age for its onset. The brain scan is unusual but not inconsistent. We know so very little about the physiological causes of the disease. It could well be related."

"But you weren't even there. How do you know things didn't happen just like I said? How do you know I didn't really feel their emotions?"

"Hailey, think about what you're saying." The woman leaned forward and took her by the hand. "You're a scientist. What's the scientific basis for what you're describing? I know it's hard to accept, but if you're ever going to be able to cope with this condition, you're going to have to accept it. There's no such thing as monsters or demons or ESP or people talking in your head. It's important that you keep thinking like a scientist. You have to go with the facts. Don't let yourself be swayed by what you think you might have experienced. Sometimes our brains can play tricks on us. You have to go with what you know to be true."

"If I can't trust my brain, how do I know what I think is true is actually true? How do I even know I'm having this conversation?"

A stern look. More scribbling on the clipboard.

"I was joking, okay?" Hailey leaned forward and tried to read the upside-down notes. "I'll ignore everything that falls outside the realm of common experience. If I ever hear voices, I promise not to listen to them. Can I go home now?" She swung her legs over the side of the bed and started to step down, but the woman held out a hand.

"I know this is going to be hard to accept, but I can't let you go. Not yet."

Hailey searched the woman's face.

"You've been admitted to this facility under what's called a section 5150—a mandatory seventy-two-hour hold for treatment and observation. You have a right to a hearing, but if you go that route, I'll be forced to testify against you. It would be much better for everyone concerned if you'd focus your energy on getting well. If you cooperate with the treatment and don't give us any reason to believe you could be a danger to yourself or others, then we'll be able to talk about releasing you at the end of the hold."

Hailey tried to take it all in. "And if I don't cooperate?"

The doctor didn't flinch. "We'll be forced to recommend a longer stay."

---

ATHENA LEANED AGAINST THE blistered balcony railing and looked out over the sleeping city. A fine mist hung in the air, soaking into her skin with a tingling chill.

She brushed a strand of limp green hair from her face and glanced back through the peeling French doors. Cerridwen, Brigantia, and Maeve were yipping like dogs at Benedict's feet. Brigantia with her expensive leather, Cerridwen with her blacker than black hair, Maeve with her new fangs. It was so pathetic. They thought they were so sexy, so unconventional. But they were all a bunch of sheep. Mindlessly following one another, falling all over themselves in their eagerness to fit in.

Athena turned away. She was tired of their little fantasy trips. Tired of the whole charade. Even the real world would be better than this. Shallow commercial reality with its tabloid neighborhoods and smiling billboard citizens.

She leaned far out over the railing, stretching out her hands toward the black ribbon streets below. Her feet gritted across the concrete, sending a shiver up her spine. If she slipped, if she flipped over the rail and tumbled into the icy blackness below, how many of her so-called friends would even care? For all their Gothic love of darkness and despair, for all their teenage obsession with death and dying, were any of them capable of real mourning? In a world of self-serving dreams, could there ever be true loss?

A braying laugh sounded behind her. Maeve, no doubt, trying to snake Benedict away from her. The snotty little prep-schoolie didn't care that it would put Athena back out on the streets again, that she'd have to start all over on her *letter of no record* application. Just to prove she didn't have a birth certificate so the government could reject her application to get a social security number. But what did Maeve care? She had a cushy job at the Metreon and a mom with an expensive car. To someone like her, Benedict was just the flavor of the week.

Athena grabbed the railing and pulled herself back onto the balcony. Turning to strike a languid pose, she watched Benedict and his little black-clad harem through half-closed eyes. They hadn't even noticed her. They were too busy laughing at Smythe who was strutting back and forth, waving his arms like an arthritic bat. Idiot.

At least Benedict had a job. And she had to admit, he was tolerably good-looking. With his pale skin and bleached-white hair, he stood out like a beacon against his pack of let's-all-use-the-same-shade-of-hair-dye friends. But he wouldn't hold out long. He had about as much backbone as a jellyfish. If she jumped off the balcony right now, she wondered how long it would take for one of the schoolies to take her place. A week maybe? A day? As long as it wasn't Maeve, she didn't really care.

She turned back to the night, but a flash of silver caught her eye. Something in Smythe's hand. She watched as Smythe led Benedict toward the bedroom. And then she saw it. An old-fashioned straight razor.

Athena pushed her way through the doors and started after Benedict, but Maeve moved to block her way. Brigantia circled around behind her, smiling so that the tips of her canines rested on the thin dark line of her lower lip.

"Benedict, if you—"

A chill stabbed up Athena's spine, filling her brain with a deep, terrible longing. Hunger. Ravenous desire. For a sickening moment, the world tilted and swayed. Raw anger boiled in the air, roaring in her ears like a wounded beast.

Panting, she turned to face the girls. Maeve's lips were moving, but the roar overpowered her voice. A hand was reaching for her. Cerridwen's face, close and hideously distorted.

"Are—you—okay?" Black lips, smeared and hideous. Cheap plastic fangs.

Athena dove onto the floor and rolled through a forest of shuffling feet. Something was out there. Somewhere outside. She had to get away. Had to—

Her terror subsided like a crashing wave drawn back into the sea. She turned and stared up at the girls standing around her in an astonished half circle.

"Are you okay?"

"What's wrong? You look like you're going to throw up."

Athena staggered onto her feet and brushed invisible dirt from her loosely fitting gown. "Didn't you feel it?"

"Feel whath?" Maeve pushed up on her ridiculous teeth.

"You're joking, right?" Athena studied each girl in turn. "You felt it. You had to."

Vacant looks. Brigantia turned to Cerridwen and started laughing.

"The . . . I guess it was an earthquake. We don't have them in London, you know." She swung around as a gasp escaped the next room. Benedict was either laughing or crying. She couldn't tell which.

## ⤳ 5 ⤳

*God, why?* Hailey pounded her forehead into the damp chill of her institutional pillow. *Why are You letting this happen? Why aren't You doing anything? Is it the medication? Is that what I'm supposed to think? That Your presence has all been a delusion?*

She flipped onto her back and yanked the pillow out from under her head to hug it to her chest. The ceiling tiles overhead pressed down on her, thick and impenetrable as steel blast shields. She had been on the drugs for two days. Two days of absolute silence. Of her prayers bouncing like rubber bullets off the drab institutional walls.

If she really had paranoid schizophrenia, why did everything feel so wrong? Why were the memories still so vivid? It had all seemed so real . . .

But wasn't that the way the disease worked? Wasn't that the problem? It felt real, but it couldn't have been. Monsters? Reading strangers' minds? Feeling their emotions? None of it made any sense—not practically, not scientifically, not experientially. Disease was the only logical explanation. If she hadn't freaked out in the lab, she wouldn't have run out into the park and she never would have been attacked by the skinny guy. That part, at least, had been real. The gash in her sweatshirt proved there had been a knife.

Goldberg was right. Hallucinations were dangerous. She had to get them under control. She could have been killed. If it weren't for the giant, she would have been killed. Assuming, of course, he even existed.

But how could he have been an illusion? He'd carried her to the hospital. She couldn't have walked by herself. Could she? She could remember it so well. The tension in his arms, the feeling of his shoulders, twisted and hard and knotted.

But even then, hadn't she known something was wrong? He had picked her up like a Barbie doll, carried her an arm's length away from his body. That sort of thing only happened in dreams. She knew better than that. She was a behemoth. Way too big to be carried, no matter how big the guy was. The physics were all wrong.

But if she were going to dream up an imaginary rescuer, why not imagine someone polished and clean who looked like Tom Cruise? She could still remember the way her hero smelled. People didn't hallucinate smells. Did they?

Footsteps sounded outside the door. The soft clank of the heavy doorknob. Hailey threw off the pillow and pushed herself into a sitting position as the door swung open.

"Hailey Maniates?" A man in a rumpled tweed sports coat poked his head into the room and frowned. "I'm sorry . . ." He paused and combed his fingers through a mop of disheveled sandy hair. "The woman at the desk said it was the fifth door on the right, but I wasn't sure if . . ." His voice trailed off as he looked her up and down. "You're not Hailey Maniates, are you?"

"Why wouldn't I be?" Hailey tugged down on her pajama top and leaned back on her hands to keep her stomach from bunching.

The man grinned and stepped into the room. "Let's just say you don't exactly look the type to spend a Friday night alone in a research lab."

"Oh? And what exactly does that type look like?"

"I, ah . . ." The man ran his fingers through his hair again. "I'm Detective Smiley." He smiled to match his face to his name. "I'm here to ask you a few questions. They tell me you had quite a scare Friday night."

*"Detective Smiley?" As in . . . police detective?* Hailey sat up straighter. Maybe they didn't think she was crazy after all.

She studied the man as he patted down the pockets of his jacket. There was something odd about his stance. His shoulders were uneven, and his left arm hung still at his side. "Okay!" He pulled a notebook from his pants pocket and held it under his dangling arm as he fished a pen out of his jacket. "The hospital report says you were attacked by a man in Golden Gate Park? Friday night just—" he glanced at his watch—"two days ago?"

Hailey nodded. "I didn't think they believed me."

"Actually, they didn't have a choice." The detective shrugged. "There was a weapon involved so they had to report it, and I understand there was some physical evidence as well?"

"A sprained ankle and a long slice through my sweatshirt." Hailey studied the detective as he struggled to write in his notebook. "If you get me out of here, I could show you where it happened. There's bound to be footprints. Signs of a scuffle. We might even be able to find the knife. The guy that rescued me threw it out into the trees. If it's still there, I'm sure I could find it."

"That won't be necessary, actually."

"I know what you're thinking, but I wasn't imagining it. I've got a sliced sweatshirt to prove it! Where else could I have gotten—"

"It's okay. I believe you." The detective raised his good hand. "I wouldn't be here if I didn't."

"So get me out of here. Tell them I'm telling the truth."

"It's not that simple, but I'll do what I can, okay?" The man fixed her with an uneven smile. "But first I was hoping to get a description of the man who attacked you."

"Well, it was dark, so I didn't get a very good look at him. He seemed fairly young, probably in his teens or early twenties. And skinny. With a sunken face and dark hair. He was probably only five foot ten or eleven."

"Anything unusual about his chin? Did you see his chin?"

Hailey shrugged. "It was dark. The guy that rescued me got there almost right away."

"The guy that rescued you? What can you tell me about him?"

"Why? He didn't do anything wrong." Hailey shifted on the bed, watching him out of the corner of her eye.

"Just trying to be thorough." The detective smiled and moved to lean against the other bed.

"Well, he was tall and stocky, and he had a beard and long curly hair."

"Stocky? As in athletic?"

"Not really. He was—"

"What color was his hair?" The detective leaned forward and licked his lips. There was something about his eyes . . .

She felt like an injured deer in the middle of a wolf pack.

"I'm sorry, what did you say?"

"His hair. What color was his hair?"

"Brown, but—"

"Not black?" Suddenly he was standing over her, fixing her with a baleful stare.

"No." Hailey looked down at the floor. "Why?"

"I was just wondering. How you could tell if it was, as you said, so very dark."

"The only people with naturally black hair are of Asian descent, and he definitely wasn't Asian."

"I see. Was he carrying any weapons? Was he wearing any distinguishing jewelry, a pendant perhaps?"

"Carrying any weapons? What are you getting at?" Hailey stared back, resisting the almost overwhelming urge to look away. "He risked his own life to save me. He's no criminal, I can tell you that for sure. He had every opportunity to—"

"I'm sorry. You misunderstand my intentions." The detective's face relaxed into a smile. "I'm merely trying to get a description of the only witness in this case. Homeless people are never difficult to locate if you know where to look."

"Oo . . . kay." Hailey looked back down at the floor. Had she told the detective her rescuer was homeless? She couldn't remember.

"Was he carrying any weapons?"

"Oh, yeah—I mean no. He didn't have any weapons."

"Yet you told the doctors he took the knife away from the perpetrator and might even have broken the man's arm. Without a weapon?" The man stepped closer. Hailey could feel his eyes boring through the top of her head.

"He was strong, okay? He carried me as if I were a baby." Hailey risked another glance up. He was still staring. Had he blinked while she wasn't looking?

"You say he carried you? You were that close? Surely you must remember something about him. Something unusual, maybe. Something to help us identify him."

"No, nothing." Hailey shook her head. Why wouldn't he leave her alone? Couldn't he tell she was tired?

"Nothing at all? Are you absolutely sure? Of course not. You remember something. Something about his eyes, his clothes. He was wearing gloves perhaps. Carrying a spray bottle?"

Hailey shook her head. "I think I need to lie down now."

"Of course."

Hailey heard the bed creak as the man stood up and walked over to the door.

"Let me know if you remember anything else, no matter how insignificant. I assure you I'll give this case my closest attention."

"Thanks, I will." Hailey flashed him what she hoped was a winning smile. "And please, tell the doctors you believe me. They think I imagined the whole thing."

"I promise. I'll do everything I can." The detective backed through the door. Another uneven grin and the door closed behind him.

Hailey stared at the wall, turning the new information over and over in her mind. Not only did the detective believe her, but he seemed to know way more than he was telling. That proved she wasn't crazy, didn't it? Something else was going on. Maybe something big.

A loud knock made her jump. The door opened, and Dr. Goldberg stepped into the room. "Everything still okay? No more dizziness? No abnormal vision or disorientation?"

Hailey shook her head. "And I still know my name and the date, and I still don't hear voices."

"Okay. Just checking. Remember, we'll be getting together this afternoon at 2:30." She turned to walk through the door.

"Dr. Goldberg, wait."

"What?" The doctor's smile evaporated. In its place was a tight-lipped frown.

"The detective just now. He said he believed me about the attack. I think he knows what happened to me."

"What detective? What are you talking about?" Goldberg moved across the room to stand over Hailey's bed.

"The detective. He was following up on my attack." Hailey waited for comprehension to dawn. "You know. The emergency room doctors file a police report. . . . They send a detective to investigate?"

"And this detective," Goldberg's voice was suddenly all fresh air and sunshine, "he's here in the room right now?"

"No!" Hailey turned away and sighed. "He came and left a few minutes ago. I'm not imagining things. Check with the front desk. They gave him directions to the room!"

"Hailey," Goldberg spoke her name gently, "police aren't allowed in here to see patients—not without my approval."

"Don't tell me. Tell him. His name is Smiley, Detective Smiley. Call the police station. They'll tell you he was here."

"No need to get excited. Of course he was here." The singsong was back in her voice. "So what did he have to say? Start from the beginning. I want to hear everything."

---

ANOTHER MISSING BOY. THAT made three in less than a week! Melchi tucked the newspaper clipping into his coat pocket and jogged up a narrow residential street. Three teenagers—all living within a couple of miles of one another. It had to be the Mulo. But what was it doing? They couldn't *all* be the Standing. Ortus had said there weren't that many left. Forty or fifty, thinly scattered across the globe. And the Standing didn't live in houses; they had to be gadzé. But what would the Mulo want with normal teenagers?

He slowed to a stop at a faded Art Deco tucked between two Victorians. The street number matched the address from the phone book, but there were two other Smythes living in the area. It could be the wrong house. He ambled up the street, searching the windows for signs of life. An ominous silence radiated from the houses. It was as if the whole neighborhood was holding its breath, waiting for the next blow to fall, a last bit of bad news to confirm the unspoken fears of a whole community.

This was the place. It had to be. Snapping his fingers, Melchi wheeled around and jogged back in the direction he had come. He knew he looked suspicious, but it couldn't be helped. The whole neighborhood was on edge. He wouldn't have much time.

Darting across the sidewalk and a patch of brown weeds, he vaulted the gate between the house and its neighbor and ran between the buildings to a small, refuse-strewn yard. Weathered wooden stairs climbed the back of the building to a door on the second floor. It was almost too easy. Bounding up the steps a half flight at a time, he crept out onto the second-floor landing and turned to survey the silent neighborhood. So far so good. Climbing onto the railing, he jumped up and caught the edge of the roof. Then, kicking out with his feet, he swung himself up and over the edge of the roof and rolled across its gravel-and-tar-covered surface.

Flattening himself against the roof, he reached out with his senses, sifting through the sounds, feelings, and smells of the neighborhood. A small dog yipped across the street, three or four houses away. Distant laughter. The drone of passing cars . . .

He rolled onto his hands and knees and searched the rooftop for signs of a struggle. The police would have already checked inside the house, but they wouldn't think to check the roof. The gadzé, as a rule, were hopelessly limited to two-dimensional thinking. They couldn't track a Mulo if it was right on top of their heads. He crept across the gravel surface, sweeping his eyes back and forth across his path. There it was! Right by the edge of the roof: a faint depression in the tar. The outline was sharp and brittle. It was definitely fresh—less than twenty-four hours old. He leaned out over the edge and checked the wall below. A dark peeling window stood right beneath him, propped open by the heavy end of a broken pool cue.

Flipping over the edge of the roof, Melchi swung himself onto the windowsill and ducked inside. The room was dark and claustrophobic. Piles of clothes littered the floor, linen capes, fishnet shirts, studded leather bands, all of them the blackest shades of black. The room was just like the others, right down to the posters covering the walls. Oppressive, sinister images peered down at him from every direction. Darkness, malice, violence—the air was heavy with it.

Melchi tiptoed across the room and checked the CD covers piled on top of a small stereo. Same style of music, same manic obsession with disorder. Everything seemed to fit. He dropped to his hands and knees and started digging through the piles of junk under the bed. There it was, just like the others. He pulled a carved wooden box out from under the bed and eased its lid open. An old-fashioned straight razor gleamed silver against the black velvet lining. Cotton balls, rubbing alcohol, a small mirror. A black-and-white photograph of a dark-haired girl in leather and black lace. Behind the picture was a single strand of bright green hair.

An almost undetectable tremor passed through Melchi's frame. A noise? A change in the wind? No, it couldn't be. The neighborhood was perfectly quiet. Too quiet.

Something was wrong.

Shoving the box under the bed, Melchi pushed the pile of clothes back on top of it and bounded across the room to the open window. Two cars were parked out front. They hadn't been there before. The faint hum of another car sounded from the street behind the house. It wasn't moving.

Melchi backed away from the window. They couldn't have left the cars. He would have heard them. What if he—

The doors of both cars flew open and four men stepped out onto the street. Climbing onto the windowsill, Melchi leaped out and grabbed the overhanging roof, swinging himself up and over its edge.

"Police! Stay right where you are!" The commanding voice rang out as Melchi rolled across the skittering gravel surface. Climbing to his feet, he listened as an answering shout sounded from the backyard. Barked orders. Bursts of walkie-talkie static erupted from every side of the house.

He was trapped.

———+·+———

HAILEY HOBBLED PAST A cluster of empty tables. The walking boot they'd given her for her ankle clacked against the slick tile floor, making her feel like Long John Silver. Somewhere behind her a blaring television filled the recreation room with the buzz of hollow voices. The scrape of chairs to her left, the babble of incoherent voices to her right. It was too much. How was she supposed to think with all this Clockwork Orange going on around her? The drugs, the isolation, the incessant noise—it was enough to make anybody crazy.

She eased herself onto a vinyl sofa and checked the clock for the thousandth time that morning. Almost ten a.m. When had they brought her in? Dr. Goldberg said they could only hold her for seventy-two hours. She had to be past the time limit now. Had they forgotten about her? Had Goldberg decided to have her committed after all?

It wasn't fair. She had tried to cooperate. She'd done everything they asked her, answered all their stupid questions, taken their stupid medicine. She had even admitted that the whole voices-in-the-head thing had been a hallucination. So why were they still holding her? It couldn't be the detective's visit. The police department had confirmed everything. Goldberg had told her herself.

"There you are! I've been looking for you."

Hailey jumped as Dr. Goldberg clacked across the floor to stand in front of her. Jim, her heavyset, green-togged contact person, stood right behind Goldberg, muscular arms folded across his chest. Finally. This was it. The confrontation she'd been waiting for.

"So, how are you feeling?"

Hailey swallowed and forced her eyes back to Goldberg. "I haven't heard any voices if that's what you mean. I'm always sleepy, and this medicine makes me feel like I'm swimming through a pool of molasses. But other than that, I'm great. Perfectly normal in every way."

"Good. I'm very pleased." Goldberg smiled and looked down at the ever-present clipboard. "Any dizziness, nausea, disorientation?"

Hailey shook her head, bracing herself against the arm of the sofa. "I'm fine." She enunciated the words carefully. She wasn't giving Goldberg any more ammunition. If they wanted to have her committed, they were going to have to base it solely on the doctors' testimony.

". . . are the times and dates for your therapy sessions. The address and directions are at the bottom of the page." Goldberg held out a folded slip of paper.

Hailey reached out and took it, searching Goldberg's eyes. What had she missed? Were they extending her therapy? She nodded and tried an ambiguous smile.

"I need to stress, it's absolutely imperative that you show up for your appointments. We've stabilized your condition, but the real healing happens in therapy. Understand?"

Show up for her appointments? They were giving her a choice? Hailey nodded and glanced over at her contact person. He didn't seem to be paying attention.

"If you have a conflict, call us and we'll reschedule, but make sure you come. You don't want to end up back here, do you?"

Hailey started to nod, caught herself, and then shook her head.

"Good. And remember, you have to take your medicine. Every day without fail. I don't care how it makes you feel; you have to take it. To stop taking it is to invite the direst of consequences. You could be institutionalized, injured, or even worse. I can't tell you how many people have ended up critically injured or dead, all because a patient thought she was getting better and stopped taking her medicine. This is serious. I won't release you if you don't agree to keep taking it."

Hailey nodded. "But when can I stop taking the medicine?"

Goldberg's face clouded.

"I mean, after going through all the therapy . . . and taking the drugs and cooperating with my treatment in every way. Is it possible I could get to the point where I don't have to be on medication at all?"

"I think this may be a subject for a future session, okay?"

"I'm not asking for a binding promise; I just need to know the odds. How many patients get to the point where they don't need the medicine?"

Goldberg pursed her lips and looked down at her clipboard. "Your roommate will be here to pick you up in fifteen minutes. You'll need to gather up your things." She stood aside to let Jim reach down and help Hailey to her feet.

Hailey followed them through the rec room and down the hallway leading to her room. Tiffany, of all people, was coming to get her. She never would have thought she'd be so happy to see her roommate.

She stopped at the door and stood back to let Jim open it for her. "How many cases of paranoid schizophrenia have been cured?" She used her most professional, detached voice. "Does Geodon have any curative effects or does it simply mask the symptoms?"

"Hailey, I'll be honest with you." Goldberg stepped into the room and sat down on the edge of the other bed. "Paranoid schizophrenia is a permanent condition. The drugs can reduce the symptoms of psychosis, but they aren't a cure. There's a lot of ongoing research, but so far no real cure has presented itself."

*Permanent?* Hailey felt the room closing in on her. "There has to be some hope. I mean, I can't keep taking the drugs forever. They make me too sleepy. I can't think—"

"I didn't say forever. And remember. We're not even certain of the diagnosis yet."

"But what's the likelihood? Based on what you know right now, what do you think is the probability I have paranoid schizophrenia?"

Dr. Goldberg looked down at her clipboard. Hailey could almost feel her considering and rejecting different diagnoses. "This is still way too early, but if I had to say now, I'd have to give it a probability of more than 90 percent."

"So how do you decide for sure? Do I stop taking the drugs and wait to see what happens?"

The doctor shook her head. "Hailey. This is important. The medication isn't optional. You have to accept the fact that you'll be taking it for a long time—probably for the rest of your life."

# ᙭᙭ 6 ᙭᙭

Melchi crouched on the roof, listening to the shouts and footsteps surrounding the building. The roof shook as a crash sounded somewhere beneath him. The pounding of heavy footsteps. They were coming up the stairs. He ran to the center of the roof and slid to a halt. The house next door was an easy jump—eight feet away and two feet up. But the next jump was impossible to judge, and that was the critical one.

Shouted instructions sounded beneath him. The thud of footsteps running across the floor. He backed to the edge of the building and took a running start. Leaping across the gap, he landed lightly on the shingled roof and skidded onto his back to keep from sliding down the gentle slope. No time for second-guessing. He pushed onto his feet and sprinted across the roof. The next house was much farther away. The closer he got, the more impossible the jump looked. He needed more height, more speed!

Planting his foot on the very last shingle, he launched himself across the fifteen-foot gap. Adrenaline surged through his body. He was coming in too low. He wasn't going to—

*Oomph!* He slammed stomach first into the edge of the roof. The impact folded his body around the jutting eave. For a breathless second he hung, clinging to the roof, then his weight dragged him slowly back over the edge. Reaching out with a flailing hand, he managed to grab the corner of a flimsy rain gutter and hold on tight as the gutter peeled away from the house, swinging him in a wide, jerking arc along the side of the house. The gutter tore away with a ringing *snap,* and he crashed into an overgrown hedge.

Fighting to catch his breath, Melchi struggled free of the flattened bushes.

"I got him!" Two heads topped the plank wall surrounding the backyard behind him. Two police officers with guns.

Melchi staggered across the lawn and vaulted over the opposite fence. The wail of sirens bore down on him from all directions. They were getting closer.

He ran across the yard and ducked behind a small redwood growing at the corner of a dirty gray house. Leaping into the air, he caught a low branch and swung himself up and over. One more branch. Another . . .

"This way! Around the other side!" The two officers clambered over the fence and ran across the yard as Melchi hugged the trunk to his chest. The foliage was too thin. If they looked back, they would be able to see him.

He eased himself around the tree as the men climbed over the fence and disappeared into the next yard. Shouting followed. It wouldn't take them long to figure out what he'd done. They would be back.

Melchi snaked his way through the smaller, denser branches at the top of the tree and, giving the area a quick scan, climbed out onto the roof. Two police cars blocked the street ahead, and a string of flashing lights wrapped around the other two sides of the block.

Crouching low, he crept across the roof and leaped the gap onto the house he had fallen from. Then climbing almost to the ridgeline, he ran back along the roof and hurled himself across the fifteen-foot void. He hit the roof with inches to spare and pressed himself flat against the shingles.

No shouting voices. No bursts of static. It was as safe as it was going to get. He ran across the roof and leaped back onto the flat roof of the missing boy's house.

He lay on his back, listening as the sounds of pursuit drifted farther down the street. So many police officers. What did they think, that he had taken the boy and was coming back to admire his handiwork? It didn't make sense. None of it made sense. The boy lived in a real house; he wasn't the Standing. The posters on his walls were filled with the icons and imagery of the Mulo's followers. Why would the Mulo take one of his own?

The squad cars pulled away from the house, and there was a lull in the activity. No footsteps, no radios, nothing. Melchi crawled over to the edge of the roof and surveyed the area. This was as good as it was going to get. Leaping from roof to roof, he made his way across the block until a tall sweet gum provided a sheltered way to the ground.

Then zigzagging through the residential parts of the Sunset District, he worked his way toward the park, jumping at every noise, diving for cover at the sound of every passing car. With the Mulo on the hunt, the city had never been safe, but now even the brightly painted townhouses seemed to glare down at him with frosty malevolence. He was a criminal now. A sociopathic vandal. He had torn up an expensive rain gutter. Crushed a beautiful flowering bush. It would take him years to pay for all the damage.

A police cruiser turned down the road, forcing Melchi to take refuge in the gutter behind a parked car. The car kept moving and disappeared at an intersection two blocks away. He crawled onto his feet, but another patrol car was coming at him from the opposite direction. He dropped back onto the ground. It seemed they were searching the whole city for him. How was he going to make it back to the park?

When the car finally passed, Melchi darted across the road and ran down a narrow street. The Booklady's store was only a few blocks away. He skidded to a stop at an intersection and searched up and down the cross street before racing on. One more block, a few hundred feet, twenty yards . . .

He hit the door, swung it open with a jingle, and slammed it shut behind him. Then leaning against an overflowing bookshelf, he panted and tried to catch his breath.

"Well?" The Booklady appeared at the head of the crowded entryway. "Are you going to tell me what's wrong, or am I going to have to beat it out of you?"

Melchi's heart dropped into his stomach. He shouldn't have come here. If he told her what happened, would that make her a criminal too?

A police siren sounded behind him. He turned and listened at the door. It was coming from the direction of the boy's house. Had someone spotted him running down the street?

"I'm waiting." The Booklady's voice grated against the sound of the retreating siren.

Melchi turned slowly and looked down into her frowning face. "I didn't mean to do anything wrong. It was an accident."

"Didn't mean to do what?" Her eyes squinted. Was she angry at him? Disgusted by what he had done? Could she read the guilt on his face?

Melchi looked down at the floor. "I am sorry. I don't know what else to say. Please forgive me for betraying your trust."

"You can start by telling me what happened." She looked him up and down, burning through his skin with the heat of his shame. "Come on. A religious boy like you? It couldn't have been too bad."

Melchi just stared at the floor.

"Are you going to tell me now, or do I have to call the police and ask 'em myself?"

————

A KNOCK SOUNDED AT Hailey's door, and Dr. Goldberg walked inside. "Hailey, time to go. Your roommate's here."

Hailey stood and steadied herself against the foot of her bed. A strange woman stepped into the room. Bright yellow glasses, orange fly-away hair, a pink and green floral T-shirt . . .

"Hi, I'm Susan Boggs. Melissa's been staying with me until your apartment is ready."

*Boggs?* Hailey's voice caught in her throat. Why did it have to be Boggs? She was famous at the university, the darling of the department. She had published three papers in *Science* in less than three years.

"Hi, I'm Hailey. I . . ." She clunked forward and shook the fourth-year grad student's hand. "It's good to meet you."

Dr. Goldberg stood back, frowning at the whole awkward exchange. "I thought you were roommates."

"Actually, Boggs is my roommate's roommate. Just for the month. It's really—"

"Melissa, Hailey's normal roommate, is staying with me until their apartment is finished." Boggs stepped forward and cast a mysterious look in Hailey's direction. "Melissa's out of town, but I'd be happy to have Hailey stay with me until she's back."

The doctor took Boggs aside. "And you'll be around to keep an eye on her? She has to take her medicine every day."

"Absolutely. No problem." Boggs turned another look on Hailey. Was it guilt? An apology for selling her out to the shrinks?

Hailey just stood there, looking from Boggs to Goldberg. Between the two of them there was enough pent-up drama to fuel an entire high-school musical. "I'm not an invalid, you know. I can take care of myself. When I say I'll take the medicine, I'll take the medicine. I don't need any babysitters spying on me."

"Of course not." Goldberg stepped forward and took Hailey by the hand. "But we prefer to release our patients into someone's care. Standard procedure. Patients living alone have a much higher recidivism rate than patients supported by friends and family."

Hailey shrugged her words aside. Boggs was looking around the room like it was a festering prison cell.

"We should probably get going."

Hailey grabbed her backpack and followed Boggs's eyes to the table by her bed. No flowers, no cards or letters or care packages. Just a backpack with a toothbrush and a few clothes. She wasn't even wearing makeup. How pathetic could she get? She was a charity case. At the mercy of her roommate's temporary roommate—someone she didn't even know.

Dr. Goldberg ran through an endless list of instructions while Boggs looked on, a first-row seat, surround-sound, eyewitness to the train wreck of the century. All Hailey could do was dig her fingernails into the palm of her hand and pray the show would be over soon. Finally, mercifully, a health tech walked into the room with a wheelchair and then, just like that, Goldberg headed for the door. No handshakes, no good-bye, just a "see you at our Wednesday appointment," and she was gone. On to the next sheet on her clipboard.

Hailey stared at the floor as the health tech wheeled her down the hallway. The light tap of Boggs's feet sounded small and hesitant behind her back. Hailey glanced up at the closed doors lining the walls. She could almost feel Boggs's revulsion, sense her thoughts: *What kind of crazies are hiding inside here? What kind of a crazy did I volunteer to drive home?*

The tech stopped at the front desk and handed Hailey a stack of papers to make it all official. She was a documentable, certifiable, card-carrying crazy now. She'd have to wait two years before she could carry a gun. So much for that AK-47 assault rifle she'd been eyeing at the university bookstore.

Four signatures later Hailey and her keeper were out the door. Hailey hobbled like an invalid toward Boggs's waiting car. She could almost hear the institution's collective sigh of relief. One more potential lawsuit gone. She was officially on her own.

"Here. Let me help you." Boggs took Hailey by the arm and helped her into the old-fashioned VW Bug. "I would have scooted the seat back if I'd known . . ."

"I was a one-legged behemoth?" Hailey tried to fold herself into the tiny compartment. Even at her best she wasn't very coordinated, but with one foot in a walking cast and her brain shrunken by the drugs to the size of a pea, she felt like an overgrown marionette with only one string.

"Sorry about the car. I should have borrowed another one. These were designed for Oompa Loompas, not fashion models."

*That's right. Butter up the crazy person before she snaps and goes Ninja Turtle all over your car.* Finally, after hoisting herself back onto the parking brake, Hailey managed to get her booted foot inside the car.

Boggs closed the door and hurried around the car to slide like a ballerina behind the steering wheel. "Where to? Want to get some coffee or something?" She bit her lip and turned a wide-eyed look on Hailey before starting up the car.

"Look. I appreciate your picking me up, but I know you need to get back to your research. I don't want to take up any more of your time."

"No problem. I know this cute little coffee shop on Seventeenth Street. They've got the best ham-and-ginger croissants. I know it sounds weird, but you've got to try one. They're really good."

"You don't have to do this."

"Do what? Talk you into getting coffee?"

"Babysit the girl from the loony bin. I don't know what Dr. Goldberg told you, but I'm not crazy. I'm not going to do anything stupid, and I don't need anybody looking over my shoulder. The only thing wrong with me is they're making me take drugs for a condition I probably don't even have."

"I wasn't trying to . . ." Boggs's eyes clouded. "Look, I'm sorry if it looked like I was taking sides. But Melissa's out of town, and they made it sound like they weren't going to let you go if you didn't have anybody to look after you. Their words, not mine. I was just trying to help. They said your parents were . . ." Boggs bit her lip and turned back to her driving.

*Go ahead. Feel sorry for the poor little orphan girl.* The poor orphan Amazon who was so crazy they couldn't trust her with dental floss and sharp pencils. Hailey turned away and stared out at the blurred row of parked cars whizzing by. What was she going to do? Go back to work like nothing had happened? Goldberg already called her advisor. Soon everybody in the whole department would know. They already thought she was mental because she was a Christian. Now they'd treat her like a sleep-deprived land mine. A female land mine, no less. During the wrong time of the month.

It was too much. First she couldn't trust her senses, and now she wasn't supposed to trust God? What did that leave? Them? The keepers of the asylum? She couldn't live life that way.

She might as well be dead.

*Why, God? First my parents and now this? What good could possibly come of me being crazy?*

The car turned and pulled over to the side of the road. "Hailey." A warm hand touched her shoulder. "I'm really sorry. Please, if there's anything I can do to help . . ."

A shudder passed through Hailey's frame. Her face was suddenly hot. Tears burned in her eyes, but she couldn't make them stop. She turned away as a strangled sob convulsed her body.

"It's okay, Sweetie. It's okay." An arm wrapped around her shoulders and pulled her into a gentle embrace. "I'm right here." Boggs's soft voice soothed through her tears. The steady stroke of a hand moving across her hair.

Hailey leaned against Boggs's shoulder for what seemed an eternity. Boggs. The übergenius. The bright and shining star of the department.

Finally, Hailey pulled away and wiped a sleeve across her face. She was a soggy mess. She didn't want to think what she had done to Boggs's T-shirt.

"I've always wanted to meet you." Boggs voice was whisper soft. "Melissa talks about you all the time. She says you're a very special person."

"A special slobby mess." Hailey wiped her face with her other sleeve and tried to conjure up a smile.

"I'm serious. She says you're the kindest, most thoroughly consistent spiritual person she's ever known."

"Whatever that means." Hailey glanced at Boggs. Was she making fun of her?

"It means your faith is making a difference. It means she's noticing. Asking questions."

"My faith?" Hailey studied Boggs's face. It didn't sound like an accusation. "What are you trying to say? This isn't exactly . . . I'm really not in the mood for an argument right now."

"I'm not trying to argue. I'm just . . ." Boggs's lips tightened into a thin line. "I know I don't talk about it that much, not like you, but I'm a Christian too."

Boggs, a Christian? Hailey didn't know what to say.

"So when the hospital called and said you needed a ride, I guess I just want you to know . . . if you need to talk, I'm right here."

"Thanks." What was she supposed to say now? "There's really not that much to tell. Friday night while I was working in the lab, someone . . . tried to attack me. I ran down the stairs and barred the doors with a signpost. Then, like an idiot, I ran down the hill and tried to hide in the park." Hailey paused to let Boggs give voice to the unspoken question in her eyes. She noticed the small jeweled cross at Boggs's throat. Had she always worn a cross? Why hadn't she noticed it before?

"So . . ." Boggs drew out the word. "Is that when you sprained your ankle?"

Hailey nodded. "This skinny guy found me hiding and came at me with a knife. As scary as it was, it was almost a relief to see him. Like he wasn't as bad in person as he was in my imagination. Anyway, that's when I fell and twisted my ankle. He held the knife to my stomach, and I just screamed." Hailey closed her eyes. She could still hear the crash of the big man running through the woods. The splintering of half-grown saplings.

"It's okay. You don't have to talk about it if you don't want to."

"I'm fine." Hailey opened her eyes. "This is the good part. This huge guy shows up and takes the knife away from the little guy like he was a baby. You aren't going to believe this, but he was absolutely gorgeous."

"What did he look like?"

Hailey turned to look out the window. She could still see him, the long matted hair, the thick curly beard, his misshapen hunched back. Whatever possessed her to describe him as gorgeous?

"He was huge—at least six foot seven. I . . . guess I tend to notice things like that." Hailey made a face and looked down at her hands. "And solid as a redwood. Picked me up like I didn't weigh five pounds."

"Picked you up?"

Hailey nodded. "Because of my ankle. He carried me all the way to the emergency room."

Boggs frowned and bit her lip.

"I'm not kidding. He really carried me."

"I believe you. It's just that . . . why did they send you to the . . . you know? Why did they think you were hallucinating?"

Hailey lowered her eyes. Boggs's cross shimmered and sparkled in the morning sunlight. She was going to have to tell someone eventually. They would all want to know. "It wasn't so much what happened as what I felt while it was happening." She glanced at the windows and then back at the star grad student. "When I was in the lab, I . . . didn't actually see the man that tried to attack me. It was more like I could feel him in my head. Like I'd just stepped inside this huge cloud of evil. At one point I even thought I saw myself from behind. It was like I was looking at myself through his eyes."

Boggs's mouth dropped open into a silent O. "I'm not doubting you. It just sounds so creepy. I would have passed out in a puddle of pee."

"I know what it sounds like, but it wasn't my imagination. This was way too vivid. My imagination isn't that good."

"And that's why they sent you to the psych ward?"

"That and what happened with the guy that rescued me. I could feel his thoughts too. And when they started fighting . . . I guess I sort of freaked out."

Boggs shook her head. "I can't imagine going through all that. The fact that you managed to get away in the first place. It's all so incredible. You were under so much stress! I would have flown apart at the seams. It's no wonder your mind, you know . . ."

"My mind?" Hailey's eyes started to burn. "Look, I know what I felt. I was there and, frankly, you weren't."

"Hailey, I'm just saying that sometimes, when something traumatic happens to us, our minds play tricks on us. It's a natural part of our survival mechanism."

Hailey turned in her seat as the world started going hazy. "I think I should go home now."

"Hailey . . . it's not that I don't believe you. I'm just trying to consider all the options."

"I get what you're saying." Hailey stared out the window, focusing on the vague outline of a parking meter. So this was her life now. Everyone thinking she was crazy, no matter what she said. Wonderful. "I promise to keep taking the medicine, but I really have to go home now."

---

MELCHI SAT ON THE floor behind the Booklady's counter. A chocolate chip cookie lay untouched on the napkin in front of him. The Booklady perched on her stool and looked down at him like a bird of prey. Her eyes were harsh and penetrating, but the corners of her mouth turned up with the traces of a suppressed smile.

Melchi stared at the floor. "I am sorry. I don't know what to say."

"How about the truth?"

The words weren't harsh, but they struck Melchi like a blow to the face. Tears pooled in his eyes. He felt like he was going to be sick.

The Booklady's features softened. "I'm sorry Melchi, but I think of us as friends. I want to help you, but I can't if you're just going to sit there sulking like a bump on a log."

"That is why I should not be here. I don't want you to get hurt."

"How on earth could I get hurt? This old lady might surprise you. I'm a lot tougher than I look."

"You are safer not knowing."

"Don't I at least have the right to know what this great danger to me is? I think you're being very inconsiderate in not telling me."

Melchi looked down at his cookie. If he *was* putting her in danger, didn't she deserve to know? It had always been his secret, but would it not be permissible to tell one other person—for her own protection?

He cleared his throat and looked up. She had given him so much food, let him read so many books. But he wasn't supposed to tell. That was the law . . .

"Melchi, if that's your real name—"

Melchi winced. "I am sorry. I always meant to tell you. My real name is Melchizadek. My master gave it to me when I was a little baby. He didn't know the name my parents gave me."

"Your *master*? What do you mean, master?" The Booklady frowned down at him.

"My master raised me after my parents died." Melchi looked back at the floor. "They were murdered."

He could hear the Booklady's slow release of breath. "Go on."

"It killed my master too when I was still a boy. And now it wants to kill me."

"It? What *it*? Who wants to kill you?"

Melchi shook his head. He had said too much. It wasn't safe to talk about it. Especially not now.

"And why were you hiding from the police? What's with you and the sirens?"

Melchi took a deep breath and let it out slowly. "A teenager is missing from the Sunset district. I was at his house looking for clues, but someone must have seen me and called the police."

"Lands! Looking for clues? Whatever for?"

"I think it might have taken him."

"You mean the person who killed your parents? Why didn't you just explain?"

"To the police?" Melchi couldn't believe he'd heard her right. "They would take me away. Lock me in an institution. I would be dead in less than a week."

"Why? What have you done? Why are you so afraid of the police?"

"Because of my parents. My master always said—"

"Melchi, did you have anything to do with your parents' death?"

"No, I was just a baby, but—"

"Then why would the police lock you away?"

"Because I am an orphan. I don't have any of the papers . . . My master said that if they found me, and I didn't have the right papers, they would take me—"

"Hogwash. Your so-called master was the one who needed to worry about the police. If you haven't done anything wrong, you don't have anything to fear from the police. I think we should call them right now and straighten everything out." The Booklady reached for the phone.

"No!" Melchi jumped up and put a hand on the phone. "Please, don't. There's more . . ."

"I'm waiting."

"I don't live in a house. I sleep in a nest in Golden Gate Park. I know it is illegal, but I don't know where else to go."

The Booklady raised her eyebrows, waiting.

"And today, while I was running away from the police, I fell off a house and broke a big piece of metal off the roof."

"I'm sure all that can be explained." The Booklady reached for his hand, forcing him to let go of the phone.

"Please don't. It would kill me. I am the only one who can stop it."

"What *it*?" the Booklady demanded. "What are you talking about? You haven't said one thing yet that makes sense."

*So angry.* Melchi raised an arm to protect his face. He must have really done something wrong.

"Can't you see I want to help you? What are you so all-fired afraid of?" The Booklady punched a single digit on the phone and waited.

Melchi sank to the floor and buried his face in his knees. What could he tell her? What was he permitted to say? When he looked up, her finger was still poised over the phone. Then the words came in a hoarse whisper, dim echoes of the catechism his master had drilled into him since his infancy.

"The ancient enemy, in the last dark days of hunt, shall rise up to destroy the Standing. Only the long-awaited shall stand. By becoming the enemy, he shall shield the world from the enemy's dark threat." Melchi hesitated. He did not wish to frighten her, but he could not turn back now. "The ancient enemy is here, searching the city for the lost dimensional gateway. To get past the gateway's guardian, the enemy needs a Standing. If it ever finds one, the long-awaited may not be able to stand."

He took a deep breath and looked the Booklady in the eye.

"I am the long-awaited Child of Standing."

# 7

"Welcome to McDonald's. May I take your order?"

Hailey stared up at the backlit menu. The writing blurred and shimmered under the distorted haze of a half-dozen meal deals. This was crazy. How could she still be so sleepy? She had overslept her alarm by five hours.

"Can I help you?"

She wiped a sleeve across her eyes and tried to concentrate on the pimple-faced youth. The longer she stayed on the medicine, the worse the fog seemed to get. How was she supposed to get her work done? She felt like a zombie with a hangover.

"Hello? Ma'am?"

"Okay . . ." Hailey dug a hand in her pocket, pulled out a wad of bills and handed a twenty to the guy at the counter. "I'd like . . . ten hamburgers, please."

"Is that for here or to go?"

Hailey just stared at him. If she didn't get off the drugs soon, this would be her future. Hailey, the super-sized burger flipper. She'd slept through both of her classes *and* the meeting with her advisor. If she wanted to stay in grad school, she didn't have a choice. She had to find her homeless man and prove she wasn't hallucinating.

The cashier mumbled something and pushed a white bag across the counter. It was warm and surprisingly heavy. What was she going to do with ten hamburgers? Maybe she *was* crazy.

She clomped out the door of the McDonald's, swiveling on the heel of her walking boot like a cowboy after a long ride. Crossing the busy street, she walked out into the crowded park, staying as far as possible from the clusters of ragged people littering the trampled lawn.

Two scraggly men watched her from the shade of an evergreen, following her with hollow eyes. She veered toward the more crowded section of the park, hugging the McDonald's bag to her chest to hide it behind the oversized sleeves of her UCSF sweatshirt. There had to be somebody she could ask. Why weren't there any women?

Just ahead of her a group of leather-clad punks stood in a tight circle kicking a Hacky Sack. Metal spikes, piercings, angry tattoos. They looked rough, but at least they were alert enough for intelligent communication.

"Excuse me, but have you guys seen a big man with long curly brown hair and a beard? He's about six foot seven and wears a long black coat." Hailey waited as they continued to kick the bag. "He's enormous, built like a linebacker. You couldn't miss him."

The sack hit the ground, and one of the guys stepped toward her. His ears were pincushioned with spikes and loops. Three silver rings pierced his left nostril. "We arrive to here only yesterday. We do not know many friends yet." His thick accent sounded like a cross between British and German. He smiled, looking her up and down. "You would like to join us?"

"Sorry, I would, but I . . ." Hailey looked down at her foot.

"He is your boyfriend you are looking for?"

Hailey took a step backwards. "No, but I really need to find him soon. Thanks."

She turned and almost ran into a haggard old man wearing a stained army jacket and no shirt. "Excuse me, sir, but have you seen a—"

"Spare a dollar? I gotta get medicine." The man shoved a dirty piece of paper in Hailey's face. "I got this 'scription says I gotta get medicine. It cost a hundert dollars."

Hailey stepped back and looked around the park. Digging in her pocket, she pushed a wrinkled five-dollar bill toward the man and turned away.

"God bless you, ma'am. God bless you. I ain't beggin'. I got this doctor bill . . ."

*God bless you?* She took a deep breath and turned back to the old man. "Please. Have you seen a really big man who lives here in the park? He's about six foot seven and has long curly brown hair and—"

"Bless you, ma'am. You're a angel of mercy, that's all what you are. A angel of mercy."

Hailey dug in the McDonald's bag, handed the man one of her hamburgers, and mumbled a feeble apology. Another man stepped in front of her. Two others followed her with their eyes. If she didn't hurry she'd be trapped. She spun and hobbled past the German teens. The guy with pincushion ears was still staring at her. She could feel the darkness of his thoughts oozing into her brain.

Limping toward the sidewalk, she pushed her way past another leering man. These people couldn't help her. The whole idea was stupid. She took off toward the medical school. If the drugs kept her from doing biochemistry, what made her think she'd be able to track down a homeless man? She wasn't a detective. She should have talked to Smiley. He could have helped her. It was his job to help her.

A strange feeling cut through the haze of her thoughts. Turning, she scanned the park behind her. A low hill separated her from the rest of the park. There, between a row of windswept evergreens, an old white-haired man sat huddled under a wool blanket.

Hailey hefted the McDonald's bag. He was an old man. What could it hurt? She limped over to him and cleared her throat. He just sat there, rocking back and forth with his eyes partly closed.

"Excuse me. Sir?"

The man's eyes opened slowly, and he stared up at her like he was in a trance.

"Have you seen a man, about six foot seven with curly brown hair and a beard?"

The man pulled the blanket tighter about his shoulders and stared.

"Long curly hair and a bushy beard—a really big man?" Hailey held up her arms to signal the man's height and breadth.

The man's eyes narrowed. "Didn't know it was his. He gave it to me. It's mine now." He pulled the blanket off his shoulders and hugged it in a ball to his chest. "Didn't know. He gave it to me."

"Who? Who gave it to you?"

"He *gave* it to me."

"Who gave it to you? Was it a big man?"

The old man looked up at her with wide eyes. He was rocking back and forth again—was that a nod?

"It's all right. I'm not going to take your blanket. I brought you some hamburgers." Hailey held out the McDonald's bag, but the man gripped his blanket even tighter. "It's okay." She set the bag on the ground and backed away.

The man looked down at the hamburgers and nodded. His forehead wrinkled into a cascade of leathery folds. He seemed to be thinking.

"It's okay. I'm his friend. Did he give you the blanket?"

"I didn't know. Thought it belonged to nobody. He *gave* it to me."

"Who?" Hailey leaned forward, cooing in her gentlest voice. "Who gave you the blanket? I'm his friend. I want to give him hamburgers too."

The man leaned forward close enough for Hailey to smell the stench of his breath. He spoke in a hushed whisper. "The one."

"Where is he? Do you know where I can find him?"

The man lunged for the McDonald's bag and let out a hoarse scream.

Hailey jumped back and tripped over the uneven ground. "It's okay. You can have them!" Flailing about, she rolled onto her hands and knees and climbed onto her feet. The man was still shrieking. People were staring. A pack of haggard men were coming her way.

She made for the edge of the park, hobbling as fast as the walking boot would allow. A man's voice cried out behind her. Running footsteps. A shaft of sunlight dazzled her eyes as the ground dropped out from under her feet, tipping her forward onto hot black asphalt. A car horn blared. The squeal of skidding tires. Trembling from head to foot, she pulled up on the bumper of the rocking car and stumbled across the street.

A circle of babbling voices closed in on her. Leather and chains. A multicolored Mohawk. Hailey turned and started to run, but her boot caught on the curb and sent her tumbling into the sidewalk. She crawled toward a sheltering doorway and froze. A man's dark shadow fell across her path. She turned her head and squinted against the sun. A Mohawk-crowned punk was standing over her. He crouched down next to her and leaned in close, reaching out for her with a sickly white hand.

ATHENA HELD HER DRESSES up to the light and frowned. The fabric was getting so thin she could see all the way through them. Maybe if she redyed them. Benedict had some black dye. If she soaked them extra long . . . or better yet, if she dyed her skin underneath the dresses . . .

No. What she really needed was a new dress. If she didn't get a social security number soon, she was going to have to start wearing Benedict's clothes. And then she'd really look like a priss.

She held the oldest dress up to her and inspected herself in the mirror. If the party was warm enough, maybe thin wouldn't be so bad. Benedict certainly wouldn't mind. The dress was wide and billowing, so it would totally engulf her. Make her look pale and emaciated. Very sexy. She smiled at her reflection and leaned closer to check her lipstick. The sheen of the black fabric really brought out the green in her lips. Okay. The old dress it was.

She wadded up the other dress and stuffed it into her backpack. Tonight would be great. She hadn't been to a party in ages. And Benedict said it was going to be upscale—*très* lav. Free drinks. There was even supposed to be food. She couldn't wait.

"Notice anything different?"

Athena gasped and whirled around. "Benedict. I hate when you do that! And what did you do to your hair?"

"Like it?" Benedict struck a pose to let her see the back of his head. His hair was Goth black and slicked back like a used car salesman.

Athena put on her most charming smile. "When did you get home? I didn't hear the door."

"Who says I used the door?" He smiled, revealing a set of long pointed canines.

"Would you take those stupid things out of your mouth!"

"Yes, ma'am, Miss Athena-Belle," he replied in an exaggerated southern accent and pulled the plastic caps off his teeth.

Athena looked down and took a deep breath. Her British accent was practiced to perfection—except when she got mad. Only then did her southern Gypsy roots begin to show through.

"Notice anything else?" Benedict stepped closer.

"Besides the fact that you totally ruined your hair?"

"Black is closer to my natural color, you know—much more befitting my true nature."

"Is that what this is all about? Your little vampy trip?"

"Hey, like that's real sensitive."

"You could have at least told me. I could have done a much better job."

"I will next time, okay? I guess I'm just nervous about tonight." Benedict's voice dropped to a whisper. "Foster says there's this guy at the party that could really turn me."

"Turn you? Please tell me this isn't one of those role-playing parties."

"No, this is for real. He says there's a real immortal. He's already turned Smythe."

"Smythe's traded his brain for a set of dice. If you think I'm going to spend the night babysitting a bunch of preadolescent fanty-boys . . ."

"It's not like that. It's a real party, and I want to be with you. Foster just said . . . well, never mind what he said." Benedict stepped closer to Athena and leaned close to stare into her eyes. "Notice anything else?"

"What did you do to your eyes?" Benedict's eyes were solid black, dilated so much that his irises didn't show at all.

"Look deep and know that I am hungry for you."

Athena swallowed back the retort forming on her lips. It wasn't worth it. The last thing she wanted was to spoil the party.

She turned to let him kiss her cheek. There would be time for a good fight after the night was over.

---

HAILEY STARED UP AT the Mohawked punk. Thin, pale, almost bloodless white, his mouth gaped open as he looked into her eyes. Gleaming white teeth against black lifeless lips.

"You must be careful. A man from the hotel has been following you."

"What hotel? What—"

A car horn blared. A man's voice, calling out her name.

The punk spun around in a blaze of sunlight and disappeared.

"Hailey. Hailey Maniates. Are you okay?"

Raising herself off the sidewalk, she searched up and down the street, shielding her eyes with a scraped and bleeding hand. Where had he gone? How could he have moved so fast?

"Hailey!"

She looked up into a long face framed with unruly orange hair.

"Mark? What are you doing here?"

The med student crouched beside her and eased her back onto the sidewalk. "What happened? Did you hit your head?" He pulled back on her eyelids, moving a finger back and forth in front of her eyes.

Hailey shook him off and tried to sit up. "I'm fine. Did you see him? A skinny guy with a Mohawk? Where did he go?"

"What guy?"

"He was right here, leaning over me. You had to see him. A big, rainbow-colored Mohawk."

"I saw you fall down in front of a car. Did it hit you? What happened?"

"I'm fine. It didn't hit me, but I need to talk to the Mohawk guy. It's important. Which way did he go?"

"What guy?" Mark was staring at her like she was crazy. "There was a ton of people crowding around you, but I didn't see any Mohawks. I parked the car as soon as I saw you fall. I got here as fast as I could."

Hailey reached up and let Mark help her onto her feet.

"What happened? I saw you trying to run in that . . . boot. And what happened to your foot?"

"It's sort of a long story." She brushed at a scrape on her palm and dusted herself off, feeling for cuts and bruises. "I sprained my ankle Friday night. Right after you dropped me off at the lab I was . . . attacked."

"Attacked? Are you serious?

Hailey shrugged. "I guess I was in the wrong place at the wrong time. A homeless guy with a knife jumped me."

"Oh my gosh. So you came out here to try to find him? Let me give you a ride home." Mark reached toward her arm and hesitated. "Or should I take you to the emergency room?"

"No, I'm fine, but a ride would be nice—if you don't mind. My ankle's about to explode."

"Sure." Mark helped Hailey to his car, fussing over her like a mama hen.

"It's all right. I've got it. It's just a sprain—doesn't mean I'm an invalid, you know."

"Sorry." Mark shut the door and ran around the car. He got in and struggled with unsteady hands to get his seat belt on.

"Nice Mustang."

"Thanks. I got it because it had more headroom than a Porsche." He fumbled with his keys in the ignition and the car lurched forward with a cough. He turned an uneasy smile on her. "Works better with the clutch." His ears almost matched his hair.

"Mark, just a second. Before we go I've been wanting to ask you about sudden onset dementia."

"S.O.D.?" Mark turned in the driver's seat, casually draping an arm over the steering wheel. "What do you want to know?"

"I need to know all the diagnostics, epidemiology, mechanisms—whatever you can tell me."

"Why? Because of that hamburger you ate? I don't think that's how it's transmitted."

"I just need to know. What are its symptoms?"

"There's no way you could have it. From what I hear its majorly debilitating—really serious stuff."

"I just need to know the symptoms."

Mark started the car and pulled out into the street in a wide U-turn. As he passed though the intersection, Hailey looked back at the spot where she'd talked to the old homeless man. The man was gone. The shopping cart that had been right beside him was gone too.

"To be honest, Hailey, I don't know any of the details, but I gather that one minute a person is fine and the next minute he's a raving lunatic."

"How long do the episodes last?"

"What do you mean? From what I hear it's permanent. They don't have a cure yet. They're still trying to figure out what's causing it."

Hailey didn't know whether to be relieved or more worried. She wasn't exactly a raving lunatic, but still . . . "Do you know if the patients respond to antipsychotics? Have they tried Geodon?"

Mark shrugged. "I can't imagine them not trying it."

Hailey nodded. If they responded to antipsychotics, they wouldn't be calling it a new disease.

"Hailey? I, um . . . was wondering how you're feeling."

"Why? What makes you ask?" She glanced at him out of the corner of her eye, trying to read his expression.

"I know you probably feel terrible right now, but do you think you might feel better by this weekend?"

"My ankle won't be better, if that's what you mean. I'll have to cancel the marathon I was planning to run."

"Good. So you'll have an opening in your schedule."

Hailey searched Mark's face.

"I was just wondering if you could . . . if you were feeling okay, would you like to go out to dinner with me? Maybe Friday night?"

Hailey shook her head. Hadn't he been listening? "Mark, I'm really—" She stopped mid-sentence. Was she doing it again? No, it was foolish to even consider it. There was way too much going on in her life. Being a certified nutcase was the best excuse in the world. "Mark, I'm sorry, but I'm a mess right now. I've been sick, and the medicine I've been taking is turning me into Dawn of the Dead. You saw what it did to me back there. I belly flopped right in front of a car."

"But you've still got to eat, drugs or no drugs. And sitting down at a nice restaurant is a lot easier than cooking."

Hailey did a mental inventory of the cupboards and freezer. No. She couldn't. "I'm sorry Mark, but my life is a mess—"

"That's okay. We don't have to go anywhere fancy. Sukhothai or maybe Little Bangkok?" He turned to her with large, Clifford the Big Red Dog eyes.

"Mark . . ."

Mark sighed and his expression took on a serious look. "Louie's making Tiff dinner Friday night and wants me out of the way."

"Sorry." What was she apologizing for?

"I could get you home early. Say by nine? That'd give you plenty of time to train for your next marathon."

"Mark . . . it's not that I don't like you . . ."

"Great! I'll pick you up at 7:30—unless you want to eat earlier. Or later. We could—"

"Okay. 7:30 is fine. I'll be sure to wear my Birkah so you don't lose your appetite." She held up her scraped and bruised arms. "Honestly. Look at me. I look like I just walked through an explosion."

"You look fine. More than fine. In fact, I don't suppose you'd want to go get something to eat now?"

Hailey shook her head to clear the cobwebs from her brain. Had she really agreed to go out with this guy? What had she been thinking? "Thanks for the offer, but I've kind of got some stuff going on that I probably need to start sorting out." She stared out the car window.

Probably? No probably to it. She needed to sort out her life. Now.

## 8

Melchi melted into the gloom of a dark alleyway, pressing himself flat against a graffiti-stained wall. A pair of headlights swept down the street. The fifth police cruiser that night. He stepped out onto the sidewalk as soon as the car was past. The Booklady said he didn't have anything to fear from the police, but she knew only part of the story. As long as the Mulo lived, every official in the city had to be considered dangerous. The Mulo's influence couldn't be overestimated. The higher the official, the greater the threat.

Slinking from shadow to shadow, he crept up the street toward the entrance of an underground BART station. A blank-faced commuter walked toward the station, studiously ignoring the ragged man huddled at the top of the steps. The ragged man held up a plastic cup and muttered a few incoherent words as the commuter hurried past him and disappeared down the stairs.

Pulling a paper-towel-wrapped sandwich from his pocket, Melchi stepped out into the light and crouched down in front of the ragged man. "Wake the eyes of the city. I must find a girl with long green hair. Dressed like the others—black with leather or rubber or lace."

The man stared back at Melchi with penetrating blue eyes. "Still searching for parties?" His voice grated like gravel sliding across steel.

"They have another list for me?" Melchi glanced up and down the street and slipped the sandwich to the man.

"They say Haight Street. Big expensive hotel."

"Thank you." Melchi took the man's hand in his. "Remember. Find the teenager with long green hair. The enemy of the gateway never sleeps."

The man didn't respond. His attention had already drifted to the sandwich.

"I'll see you tomorrow." Melchi patted the man on the back, letting his hand rest an extra few seconds on his shoulder. "The Holy One will keep you safe." Glancing once more around the intersection, he cut across the street and ran up the hill toward the Haight-Ashbury district.

*A big expensive hotel.* He should have known. Melchi zigzagged through the city, keeping to the narrower, darker side streets. The Mulo had targeted a hotel in New Orleans. Parties every weekend, hundreds of noisy, alcohol-addled guests—the perfect hunting ground. Melchi should have checked the hotels weeks ago.

Turning down another side street, he backpedaled to a halt. There, less than fifty feet ahead of him, a group of dark figures was walking up the sidewalk. He ducked into the shadow of a row of ancient townhouses and followed them up the hill. There were eight of them, all dressed in black. Some of them were drinking alcohol, so they couldn't be teenagers, but they could have passed for even younger. He crept closer, reaching out with his mind. No presence. And none of them seemed to have green hair. Still, they definitely fit the pattern.

Melchi followed them to a busy intersection. Sure enough, it was Haight Street. A shudder tingled up his spine as they turned left and headed up the hill toward a tall building. This was it. The night he had been training for! Hunger burned in his chest as he stalked up the busy street. The hotel was definitely expensive looking. Another group was just going in. Black leather, filmy dresses. A man and woman crossed the street. The woman's dress was so thin . . . Melchi looked down at the ground, but the image had already burned into his brain. White-hot flames rose up in his chest. A swarm of fiery voices buzzed in his ears—

*The Mulo!*

Melchi backed away from the hotel, searching up and down the crowded street. There were too many people. Too many voices. A foul presence slithered through his awareness. Alien, sinister, full of hatred and envy. Something was wrong. So many voices . . .

He turned and started running back through the shadows, dodging in and out between the skulking partygoers. How could there be more than one? It was impossible, but . . . the hotel was swarming with Mulo.

*Holy One, we thank Thee. Holy One, hide us in Thy almighty hands.*

Vaulting a metal fence, he plunged down a dark alley and ducked behind a pile of loose trash.

*Holy One, hide us.*

He pressed his hands to his eyes and tried to block out the voices that buzzed like a swarm of angry hornets in his brain. He had to stand firm, to quiet his heart. He took a deep breath, focusing on the smell of stale urine and wet cardboard.

If he could feel them, then they most certainly could feel him.

———+·+———

THE BALLROOM THROBBED TO the driving rhythm of the five-guitar band. Blasting and pounding, surging, surrounding, the music battered its way through the wildly gyrating crowd. Athena swayed back and forth at the edge of the gathering, a slender reed finding its own rhythm in the staccato blasts of the musical storm.

Clenching her eyes tight, she willed the chest-kicking bass to purge her of the fury rising up like a thunderhead inside her. She wanted to dance, to hurl herself against the blast, to let it hold her, lift her off her feet, carry her high above the storm. But Benedict, Mr. I-promise-we'll-dance-himself, was preening in front of the other fanty-boys.

Then the lead singer started to croon, and Athena opened her eyes. His voice was melodic, every word sung with perfect-pitch precision. Pathetic. Where was the energy? The passion? She might as well face it—the band sucked. They weren't going to do anything but industrial garbage. She might as well go home.

She pushed her way through the crowd. What was she doing there anyway? The whole place was wrong. Polished brass, cut-glass mirrors, crystal chandeliers, Tweety-bird band boys. Somebody somewhere must have gotten their wires crossed. Any second they would realize the crowd wasn't doing formal wear under all that leather. Then the police would arrive and throw everyone out. She tried to imagine a cluster of gray-heads in tuxedos and sequin gowns partying in an abandoned warehouse, drinking spiked beer and rocking to real music.

Athena threaded her way through the crowd to one of the drink tables. A man in a black vest and bow tie poured her a glass of champagne and called her "ma'am." Whoever set this party up had a whacked sense of humor.

She waded back into the mob, searching for familiar faces. She recognized one or two people, but most were college age or even older. A man covered in tattoos stood in a corner wearing nothing but a G-string and his ink. Another man with a riding whip and a red and black cape led a leggy woman in a black corset by a heavy chain attached to a metal collar around her neck. A heavily powdered woman in a black hoop skirt. A good-looking man wearing black rubber. Some wore fangs, but most seemed normal enough.

A hand grabbed her from behind and spun her around.

Athena glared at Benedict. "Too late!" she shouted over the music. "Go back and play with your dice-rolling playmates. I'm blowing." She managed to control her anger just enough to keep the drawl out of her voice.

"I'm done with them. The rest of the night is all you. I'm ready to dance." He moved closer to her, swaying with the music. "Didn't I tell you this was going to be cool? What do you think?" Benedict nodded toward the bow-tied waiters at the drink table.

"This place is dead. I'm going to a *real* party."

"It's still early. It'll pick up. Come on, I want to dance."

"Too little, too late, roller-brain." Athena turned to the ballroom entrance and started to push her way through the crowd.

Benedict grabbed her arm and spun her back. "Come on. I said I would dance."

"And I said *no!*" Athena yanked her arm free.

His eyes widened and his mouth dropped open.

"And take off those stupid fangs! I'm *sick* of your fantasy games!" She didn't care who stared. She'd had it with this lame party, and she'd had it with him.

Benedict took the fangs out of his mouth and put them in a pocket. "I said I'm sorry."

Athena's muscles tensed. An icy chill crept up her spine. She wanted body and soul to tear Benedict to pieces. She took a deep breath and exhaled slowly, willing herself to relax. *Calm down. It's not worth it.* She turned to walk away, but a tall, skinny guy with a beautiful rainbow-colored Mohawk caught her eye.

*So retro . . .*

Athena stopped and stared. His skin was pasty white, his features sensitive and delicate but not effeminate. And he was so thin, delightfully emaciated.

"Benedict! Wait a second. I need to talk to you." The Mohawk punk was shouting over the noise.

"What do you want, Blaise?" Benedict's tone wasn't hostile, but Athena could tell they weren't friends. Which made the punk even more appealing.

"Foster said you're here to be turned. Is that true?" The punk stepped in front of Benedict as he tried to go around him.

Benedict tugged on Athena's arm, but she shook herself free.

The punk turned on her with a smile. "Hi, I'm Blaise . . ."

"I'm Athena." She swayed before him, trying to come up with a compliment for his retro look that wouldn't sound totally goofed.

Benedict reached for her arm, but she warned him off with a look.

"Just hear me out, okay?" Blaise stepped back in front of Benedict. "Smythe is missing. He might even be dead. These guys are dangerous. You shouldn't be here."

"So why are *you* here, Blaise? Jealous that Smythe got turned and you didn't? Worried they'll choose me over you?"

"I'm just here to warn everybody, and then I'm out. These guys are dangerous. I was a fool before. If I'd known . . ."

An invisible wave swept through the ballroom like a gust of wind. Anger. It hit Athena square in the chest, leaving her dizzy and out of breath. She looked around the room and noticed several others looking around as well. Blaise stood frozen in mid-sentence, but Benedict didn't seem to have noticed.

Athena stepped closer to Blaise. "Did you feel that?"

Benedict pushed between Blaise and Athena. "Feel what? What's going on?"

Blaise grabbed Athena and Benedict by the arms and tried to pull them toward the exit. "We've got to get out of here. Now!"

The room rumbled with another wave that traveled through Athena, shaking her to the core, waking a slumbering hunger, a thirst . . . for what? What was happening?

The room flashed with light and sound. A guy in a black robe. A girl in lace. They jostled and bumped against her. She fell to the ground and was hauled immediately to her feet and pushed forward again. Benedict yelled in her ear. Why wouldn't he quit yelling? Why wouldn't—

An arm wrapped around her, yanking her out of Blaise's grip. She twisted and kicked her feet, but Benedict held on.

"Come on, Benedict!" Blaise stood panting before them, his eyes wide and frightened. "We've got to get out of here before it's too late."

"And I said leave us alone!" Benedict shouted over the din.

Athena wrenched herself free and pulled her twisted dress down around her waist.

"Look! You wanna be turned? You want to be immortal?" Blaise spat out the words. "Then come with me. Immortality lies with me—not these guys. They'll turn you, all right. Turn you stone-cold dead."

The crowd around them stood back, tittering nervously. A silver-haired man in a charcoal suit pushed his way forward to stand between Benedict and Blaise. The man studied the two combatants.

"Well, what do we have here?"

"This jerk is trying to drag my date from the party."

"Was he?" The man stared Blaise up and down and frowned. "We shall see about this. Who are you? Reveal yourself."

Blaise stared back in defiance. His face tightened. Veins stood out at his temples and neck.

"A most curious weave . . . most curious. What are you hiding? Answer me!"

Blaise's features softened into a smile. "My friends and I were just leaving. We didn't mean to cause any trouble."

"So that's what you want? The girl?" He stared hard at Athena and laughed. "Get out of here, hedge-weaver. You have no idea who you're dealing with. If the master were here, he'd burn you to the ground, hedge and all."

Athena's stomach twisted and churned as she fought to catch her breath. The air around her crackled with tingling electricity. She took a step back into the crowd of onlookers as the man fixed her with an intense stare. She raised her chin and stared back at him. He looked to be about forty or fifty, graying hair, neatly trimmed mustache, piercing dark eyes. For an instant she felt it: burning, overpowering desire. The sensation subsided almost immediately, leaving her weak and trembling. She had to get out of there. She couldn't breathe. She took another step toward the door, but the man reached out a hand.

"I beg your pardon, Miss—"

Athena ignored him and took another step.

The man let out a hissing breath. "I do not wish to detain you, but would you accept this small token as an apology for this regrettable scene? I am sorry for my own display of detestable manners."

Athena brushed past him, but a sparkle of red in his outstretched hand made her pause. He held a piece of jewelry, a cluster of sparkling diamonds surrounding a large red stone. The setting was ornate and old-fashioned. It almost looked real.

"If you will please forgive my embarrassing display, I'm sure the owner of the hotel will wish to apologize further—Saturday at a private dinner he is holding here at the hotel?"

Athena couldn't take her eyes off the red stone. "You want to give this to me because . . . ?" She was afraid to continue. She didn't want to break the spell.

"As an invitation to dinner, Saturday at seven. Will you come?"

The hushed whisper of jealous female voices. Athena felt like the heroine of a Cinderella fairy tale. She took the brooch from the man's hand and hefted it. It was majorly heavy. It couldn't be real. Could it?

"Oh yes. My employer is very fond of rubies. He buys only the finest."

Heart pounding, Athena pressed the brooch to her chest. Her head was light, and her legs felt weak. "Thank you. I don't know what to say." Who was she kidding? She lifted her eyes to the man's and smiled. "I mean, yes. Of course. Dinner Saturday. It'll rock my world."

---

HOLY ONE, WE THANK *Thee. Holy One, hide us in Thy almighty hands . . .*

Melchi clambered up a metal drainpipe, feeling his way through the cloying darkness. He was a fiery dragon, scaling the walls of a doomed castle. Death and destruction were his to dispense. He was powerful, his rage absolute.

Hot flares burned at the back of his mind. A foul caress prickled at his skin. *Holy One help me. They're too close. Too strong!* He reached the end of the pipe and stretched out to grasp the edge of the roof. A tremor shuddered through his body as he swung out over the void. He was too weak. Too dirty. He couldn't make it.

*Holy One, hide us. Holy One, be our shield.* Kicking and flailing, he pulled himself over the edge of the roof and climbed onto his feet, a weary knight breaching the dragon's cave. Bright diamonds crunched under his feet as he pressed forward. An icy wind blasted through him, freezing him to the core. He pushed through the storm to the edge of a great precipice and looked out over the countryside. Green calming fields, a bright sunny sky . . .

Gradually the dark wave receded, leaving him trembling and gasping for breath. He opened his eyes and looked out over the neighborhood. The hotel was lit up like a beacon. He was almost a block away, but he could easily make out the features of the dark figures streaming in and out through the gleaming metal-and-glass doors. What were they doing? Didn't they realize the danger they were in? The air was thick with it. Couldn't they feel it?

He stepped toward the edge of the roof. No, he couldn't risk an attack. Not now. It would be suicide. Any closer and they'd swarm down on him like an army of locusts. He stepped back and watched the grim spectacle. So many people. He had to think of something. He couldn't just let them walk like sheep to the slaughter.

The roar of an engine interrupted his thoughts. A large dump truck was rumbling up the street. Melchi watched as it turned in front of the hotel and circled around to the back of the building. A weight sank into the pit of his stomach. No, it wasn't possible.

This was the United States. One of the busiest, most visible cities in the country.

He paced back and forth across the roof. He had to do something. Even if they killed him, didn't he have to at least try? A silent scream blasted through his senses. The presence was unmistakably feminine. The girl from the park? He ran to the edge of the roof and searched up and down the street. It was getting closer, stronger. She was definitely one of the Standing. The sweetness was almost obscene against the backdrop of such corruption and filth.

Then he saw her. From the back. A tall brunette dressed in a black silky gown. She had escaped the Mulo. Somehow she had tracked it to its lair and come out alive. He ran to the back of the roof and scrambled over the edge, feeling for the pipe with his feet. Releasing his hold on the roof, he clung to the pipe and tried to slide down its rusty, bracketed surface. Too slow. He wasn't going to make it. The girl's presence was starting to fade.

Pushing away from the wall, he plummeted through the darkness. Something soft crushed beneath his feet, spinning him sideways to crash into the ground. Pain exploded through his head, flashing in red and white clouds before his eyes. His right arm, his ribs, his knee. He'd been foolish to jump. The girl . . .

He was losing her.

Melchi staggered to his feet and pushed past the crumpled trash can. Limping around to the front of the building, he searched the crowded street. There she was, a block away. Heedless of the tumult buzzing through his brain, he ran after her. She was wearing a clingy dress and long black gloves. He slowed to a walk as he came up behind her. Her presence . . . why couldn't he feel it anymore? He was just about to call out to her when she turned with a startled gasp.

Even in the dark he could tell it wasn't her. He stopped and watched as the stranger quickened her pace and hurried off into the night. He had been a fool. If he'd felt anything, it had to be someone else. He turned and looked up at the brightly lit hotel. What was he supposed to do? Fight all of them?

A straining engine rumbled through the neighborhood. The dump truck was leaving the hotel. He ran down the sidewalk and leaped onto a dark telephone pole as the heavy truck roared past him. He'd only managed to shimmy partway up the pole, but it had been enough to see over the side of the bed. The truck had been empty when it pulled up to the hotel.

But it was leaving full.

## 9

Athena pulled the smudged glass door open and pushed her way into the gloom of the rundown pawn shop. She hefted the brooch in her hand. If she could just get enough money for her own apartment . . . It was possible. Even costume jewelry was valuable if the quality was good enough.

She looked around the cluttered shop. The early morning sun lit the barred window, casting the shop in striped shadows. No one was here.

She was just about to leave when a graying man stepped from a back room and turned sideways to squeeze behind the counter. He leaned back against a filthy wall and stared at her, waiting.

Athena held out the brooch. "How much could I get for this?"

The man took the jewel from her hand and examined it, holding it up to a dusty streak of light. "Twenty-five dollars."

"That's all?" Athena tried not to let her disappointment show. Against all reason she had allowed herself to get her hopes up. She'd barely slept all night. "How do you know it isn't real?"

"Don't matter. What matters is what folks'll pay for it."

Athena decided to gamble. "If it's a real ruby you could get a hundred times that much for it at a jewelry store. How about two hundred dollars?"

"Then why don't you take it to a jewelry store yourself? I don't buy nothin' hot. The offer stands at twenty-five."

"I didn't steal it. Someone gave it to me. A very rich man."

"Good for you."

"I'd like it back, please."

The man palmed the brooch and leaned over the creaking countertop, watching Athena with a self-satisfied smile.

Athena took a step back. "I work in the costume shop across the street. Had to show the brooch to my boss to get him to let me come here." She took a deep breath.

The man just stood there.

"I want the jewel back now. I've got to get back to work."

He held out the jewel and then jerked it away as Athena reached for it. "Okay, I'll give you a hundred dollars—way more'n it's worth."

"No thanks. I've got to get back to work."

"Suit yourself. Nobody'll beat that offer, but if they do, you come back here first before selling. That clear?"

Athena nodded and snatched the brooch out of his hand. She let the door slam behind her as she walked out into the biting wind. What an idiot! If she had a job, why would she be hawking jewelry at a pawn shop? The man didn't know what he was talking about. She'd have to risk taking it to a jeweler. If it was stolen, they would take it from her, but she wouldn't get into much trouble. And if she did, well that would take care of her room and board, wouldn't it? Better jail than going back home. But the man at the hotel wouldn't have risked giving a stranger stolen jewelry. It had to be costume.

She took a bus to the Market district and searched up and down the street for a jewelry store. There were a few shops of the gold-75-percent-off variety, but she needed an upscale shop. One that sold *real* diamonds.

Turning down a side street, she stopped in front of a respectable-looking storefront. *Johnson Family Jewelers. Free Cleaning.*

Taking a deep breath, she marched into the shop and looked around. Tiled floors, gleaming jewelry cases. Perfect. She headed straight for the engagement ring case. Even poor girls got married. Now the shopkeeper would have to pay attention to her.

A young natural blonde appeared and stood at a respectful distance while Athena pretended to examine the rings. Finally, after considering each ring twice, she looked up at the woman and smiled.

"Did you find something you like?" The woman stepped behind the counter and inserted a ring of keys into the back panel.

"Oh me, no. I'm just picking out a style—I'm not the one who will be buying it."

"Of course not." The woman's eyes sparkled in the lights as she leaned in closer. She wasn't wearing a diamond. Perfect.

"But I'm not worried. He has good taste in jewelry. Want to see what he just gave me?"

The woman leaned over the counter. "I'd love to." Her voice was low, almost conspiratorial.

Athena pulled the brooch from her pocket, wishing she'd thought to put it on before entering the shop.

"Wow," the woman breathed. "That's gorgeous. Can I hold it?"

Athena handed it over.

"It's beautiful. Is it a family heirloom? Did he say how long it was in his family?"

"That's just the thing. He gave it to me and didn't tell me a thing about it." Athena dropped her voice. "I know I'm being totally wicked, but what do you make of it?"

The woman walked to the back, motioning for Athena to follow. She held the brooch under a strong magnifying glass and touched it with a metal probe. "I'm not hurting it—just checking the settings. Sometimes on older pieces like this the settings need to be resoldered."

"So it's real? How much do you think it's worth?" Athena tired to make the question as casual as she could.

"Oh yes, it's real all right. And it's old. You can tell by the cut of the diamonds. This is just a rough estimate, and I'm not at all qualified to do appraisals, but I'd say the ruby alone is worth close to fifty thousand dollars. But this piece is an antique. It could be priceless."

Athena's head started spinning. Fifty thousand dollars. What had she gotten herself into? Now she *had* to show up at that party. People didn't give away fifty thousand dollars for nothing. There were always strings attached—and trying to cut those strings could be dangerous.

If not fatal.

---

ONE, TWO, THREE, GO . . .

Hailey tried to roll over but just didn't have the strength. She forced her eyes open and blinked against the filmy haze fogging her vision.

A dull knock sounded in her ears. Was it coming from downstairs? The knock sounded again, this time louder. Who would be coming over so early? She rolled over with a groan and felt for her alarm clock. Every muscle in her body ached. She felt like she'd just gone twenty rounds with . . .

2:15.

She pulled the alarm clock off the table and held it up to her eyes. 2:15 . . . in the afternoon? Her seminar!

She pushed herself out of bed and crumpled to the floor as her ankle gave way. The doorbell grated in her ears like fingernails on a blackboard. "I'm awake already! Hold on!" She hobbled across the bedroom and hopped down the stairs, leaning on the rail to maintain her balance.

The doorbell rang again.

"I said I'm coming!" Eight more hops and she was at the door. She shoved back the bolt and swung it open. *"What?"*

"I'm sorry. I—" Boggs backed away from the doorway. "I didn't mean to wake you. I was just . . ." Her eyes went suddenly wide. "Your arms and face . . . What happened?"

"No big deal. I tripped. The stupid drug they've got me on makes me so woozy . . . I might as well have the hallucinations."

"The drugs? I didn't realize they were so bad."

"Now you know. Anything else?" Hailey started to close the door.

"I was talking to Dr. Jennings, and I guess I just wanted to make sure you're okay."

"Did Dr. Goldberg send you? I took my medicine, if that's what she wants to know."

"Nobody sent me. I'm just worried. Dr. Jennings said you missed the seminar today."

"Because of the drugs." Hailey sighed and motioned Boggs inside. "I'm sleepy all the time. And even when I manage to stay awake, I can't think straight. I don't know how I'm going to do my work. I can barely cross the street, let alone design new protein purification procedures."

Boggs bit her lip and looked up at Hailey. "I also came by to apologize."

"Apologize?" Hailey limped across the room and plopped down on the sofa. "Apologize for what?"

"For not believing you. You're right. I wasn't there. I shouldn't have jumped to conclusions."

"What are you saying? Now you think I'm . . . not crazy? You think I actually saw myself through someone else's eyes?"

Boggs nodded.

"That's crazy. You need the antipsychotics more than I do."

"But I thought you said—"

"I know what I said, but think about it. How could I see through someone else's eyes? How does mind reading work? What's the mechanism?"

Boggs sat down on the sofa next to Hailey and swung around to face her. "Just because we don't understand something doesn't mean it didn't happen. To jump to a conclusion based entirely on the supposition that we know everything there is to know about the universe—now *that's* crazy."

"So the guy that attacked me, you actually think I could feel his thoughts?"

"Maybe."

"Please," Hailey pushed up from the sofa, "don't feel like you have to humor me. Being in denial never helped anyone."

"Or maybe you were feeling someone else's thoughts. Didn't you say you couldn't see the attacker at first? Didn't you say the guy with the knife didn't seem that bad compared to what had been chasing you?"

Hailey turned away and hopped over to the stairs.

"Hailey, I'm trying to say I believe you. What's so bad about that?" Boggs's voice followed her up the stairs. "I thought you'd at least listen."

"And I thought you were trying to help." Hailey stopped at the top of the stairs and slumped against the wall. "Listen, I appreciate what you're trying to do, but it isn't helping. I know it couldn't have been real. I'm ready to accept that now. I'm a paranoid-schizophrenic-nutso head-case. It's the only thing that makes sense."

"No, it's not." A hand touched Hailey's shoulder, a gentle pressure, turning her away from the wall. "Hailey, there's a big universe out there. There are so many things we don't know anything about. We'll never get anywhere if we assume everyone who comes across something we don't understand is crazy."

"So what do you think it was? Aliens? The Loch Ness monster?"

"I don't know, but I'm almost positive it wasn't a hallucination."

"How can you say that? You don't know. You weren't even there."

"Could a hallucination rip a steel door off its hinges?"

"What are you talking about?" Hailey turned and looked Boggs in the eye. "The doors at the bottom of the stairs? I went by the department yesterday. They were fine."

"But did you check with the physical plant?"

"What?"

"The guys at the physical plant said they'd had to rehang the doors over the weekend. They'd been ripped completely off their hinges."

Hailey leaned back against the wall. She wasn't hearing this. This was a hallucination too.

"Hailey, the sign you said you used to bolt the doors? I found it last night. The pole had been sheered completely in half."

*Impossible.* A hundred different thoughts buzzed in Hailey's head.

"Don't take this wrong, but I don't think your imagination is that good." Boggs's gaze was so intense it almost hurt.

"So what was it? What do you think happened?"

"I don't know." Boggs shook her head slowly. "But I don't think those drugs are helping."

"You think I should stop taking them? What if I have another hallucination?"

"Then you better hope it's not carrying a knife."

# II

Oh, if such an one was to come from God, and not the
Devil, what a force for good might he not be in this
old world of ours. But we are pledged to set the world
free. Our toil must be in silence, and our efforts all in
secret; for in this enlightened age, when men believe not
even what they see, the doubting of wise men would be
his greatest strength. It would be at once his sheath and
his armour, and his weapons to destroy us, his enemies,
who are willing to peril even our own souls for the safety
of one we love—for the good of mankind, and for the
honour and glory of God.

Bram Stoker, *Dracula*

# ∽ 10 ∾

Hailey stepped out of the shower and wrapped herself in a towel. The bathroom fan grated and whined in a futile attempt to ventilate the steam-filled room. She sighed. It was good to be able to think again. She almost felt like a real person. A real person with a real date. How long had it been? She took a hand towel and was wiping a spot on the mirror when a rattling buzz sounded through the roar of the fan. The doorbell.

She grabbed her watch and checked the time. 6:55? She'd told Mark 7:30! Another buzz. Hailey flipped a towel back over her head and ripped her bathrobe from its hook. Why did he have to be so annoying?

She hobbled down the stairs and yanked the door open to the limit of its safety chain. "I thought we agreed on 7:30. I'm not ready yet." She stood behind the door, keeping far back from the narrow opening.

"Hailey?"

"Boggs?" Hailey shut the door, slid back the chain, and pulled it open again. "I'm sorry. I thought you were someone else. Come in."

Boggs studied Hailey as she stepped into the room. "I didn't mean to disturb you. I could come back later if you want."

"No, I'm glad you're here. Come in. Have a seat." Hailey limped across the room and leaned against the back of the sofa.

"So how are you feeling? You seem a lot better than yesterday."

"I'm still a little sleepy, but other than that, fine. I'm beginning to remember what it felt like to be me."

"So no voices or hallucinations? Things too strange to be true?"

"Like the star of the department coming over to check up on me?"

"I'm sorry. I wasn't trying to pry."

"No! It's fine. It's great, actually . . . having someone who cares enough to come all the way out here? How could that be a bad thing?"

A shy smile lit Boggs's features. "I'm glad you're okay. Last night I was so worried I couldn't sleep. I kept thinking, *What if she starts having hallucinations again? What if she runs out into the street and gets hit by a car?*"

"Well, then we'd know, wouldn't we?" Hailey stood and hobbled to the stairs. "Mind coming upstairs? I've got to get ready for a date."

Boggs's eyes went wide. "A date?"

"You don't have to look so surprised."

"I'm not . . . I mean . . . Considering all you've just been through, don't you think it's a little soon? You just went off the drugs."

"To be honest I probably wouldn't have agreed to go if I hadn't been spaced out by the drugs in the first place. But what can I do now? He'll be here in half an hour."

"Call him and tell him this is a bad time." Boggs followed her up the stairs. "He'll understand. Does he know about last week?"

"Not really. I think he knows something is up." Hailey stepped into the bathroom and started blow-drying her hair. "He was there when the whole thing started," she called out to be heard over the whine of the dryer, "and I'm pretty sure I asked him about S.O.D. the other day when he asked me out."

"Wait a second. This guy was there? You never told me that." Boggs's frowning face stared back at Hailey from the mirror. With her round glasses she looked like a crazed barn owl.

"Don't worry. He's harmless enough. He's a med student at the university."

"And you call *that* harmless? How long have you known him?"

"Since Friday night, but he—"

"Hailey! What if this guy had something to do with your attack? Call him right now and tell him you can't go. He could be dangerous!"

"Trust me. This guy is anything but dangerous." She switched off the dryer and watched Boggs through the mirror while she put on her makeup.

"But what if there's a connection? Maybe you're allergic to his cologne. Maybe he's been working with dangerous substances."

"Or maybe you've been watching too many late-night movies." Hailey stepped around Boggs and headed for the bedroom. "Just a second. I need to get changed." She shut the door behind her and rummaged through her closet. Some casual slacks and a nice shirt. Something that said dressy without looking too desperate.

"Hailey, I really don't think this is a good idea." Boggs's voice came through the door. "You didn't see the sign. It was snapped like a toothpick."

"Trust me. Mark couldn't break a *real* toothpick. There's no way it could have been him."

"But what if he had help?"

"So now it's a conspiracy?" Hailey shook her head and finished buttoning her shirt. "This is ridiculous. Nobody's going to break down two metal doors to get at a geeky grad student. It doesn't make sense."

"Either that or you were hallucinating. Take your pick. Either way, I still don't think you should go."

Hailey checked her watch. 7:22. Maybe Boggs was right. She really shouldn't be walking around on her ankle. Mark would understand. She strapped on her walking boot and clunked over to the window. Maybe they could go to dinner next weekend. Raising the blinds, she looked out onto the street below.

Too late. Mark's red Mustang was parked out front.

"Mark's already here. I really have to go." She grabbed her jacket and opened the bedroom door.

Boggs was pacing back and forth in the hallway, looking like the little red hen.

"It's okay. I'll be fine. Here, you can check him out." Hailey led Boggs over to the window. "I could use a second opinion."

They looked out the window, waiting for Hailey's date to appear.

"What's he doing?" Boggs's voice sounded in Hailey's ear. "He's not still inside the car?"

Hailey shrugged.

"He could be waiting at the door. You know, working up his courage to knock."

"Right. Because I'm so scary."

"Maybe I should go." Boggs turned for the door. "He probably sees my car and is waiting for me to leave."

"Why? Do you know him?"

"No." Boggs stopped and turned slowly. "It's just . . . I'm not exactly a guy magnet. I think I make them uncomfortable."

Hailey studied Boggs's expression. Was she serious? "Every time I see you at school you're surrounded by guys."

"Talking science. People always talk to me about science. Never about, you know, life—the stuff that really matters."

"Probably because they're intimidated. I know I was. But that was before I knew you." Hailey stepped toward her friend. She didn't seem to be angry. "Now I just . . . think you're great. I can't imagine a better friend." She put her arm around Boggs and coaxed her back to the window.

A mischievous grin spread across Boggs's face. "I hope you know what you're getting yourself into."

"And I hope *you* don't. If you did, you'd probably run and hide."

The two looked through the window in silence for what felt like several minutes. Still no sign of Mark.

"Not exactly eager to see me, is he?" Hailey left Boggs at the window and gathered her wallet and keys.

"It's not 7:30 yet, maybe he's—wait, there he is. He's getting out of the car." Boggs pulled back from the window. "He's kind of tall, but he looks harmless enough."

"I guess." All of a sudden Hailey wasn't so sure. The doorbell rang at exactly 7:30. Why did that bug her so much? She took a step toward the stairs, but Boggs cut in front of her.

"Listen." Boggs's face was suddenly serious. "I don't care what he says: Stay in a public place. Don't go anywhere alone with him."

Hailey nodded and took another step.

"And if you start feeling even the tiniest bit strange, call me. You have my number, right?" The doorbell rang again.

"I really shouldn't keep him waiting." She started down the stairs.

"And if you start having hallucinations, don't run out into the street," Boggs called after her. "If it doesn't seem dangerous, just ignore it."

Hailey hurried across the living room and opened the door. "Hi Mark. This is Boggs—a friend of mine from the department."

"Oh hi, um, Boggs. You're not . . . is she . . . ?"

"I've got to run." Boggs stepped in front of Hailey. "Nice meeting you, Mark. Take good care of Hailey. And don't stay out too late. She hasn't been feeling very well and needs her rest."

Mark nodded and shot a questioning look at Hailey.

"See you, Boggs. Thanks for everything."

Mark walked Hailey out to the street and held the door open for her as she climbed into the car. She watched as he walked stiffly around the car and slid behind the wheel. Could Boggs be right? Could Mark be connected to the attacks? He had been there at the university, and at Stanyan Park too. And she had definitely felt funny at Stanyan—right before the guy with the Mohawk showed up.

"So are you hungry?" Mark started up the car and pulled out onto the street. "I was thinking we'd try Sukhothai, if that's okay with you. Or we could try someplace else. I'm up for anything. Whatever you want."

"Thai is fine." She smiled and looked out the window. Sukhothai was close by and on a busy little street. Boggs would approve. Maybe it was a little close to Stanyan Park, but so was her apartment. She couldn't avoid every homeless person in the city; she'd never be able to step outside the house.

They drove in nerve-wracking silence for several blocks. "Here we are." Mark pulled the car over right before the Ninth Avenue intersection. "I could let you out here so you don't have to walk. It might take me a while to find parking."

"Thanks." Hailey flashed him a smile. "Sukhothai, right?"

"If that's okay. I know a nicer place downtown . . ."

"No, Sukhothai is fine. I'll get us seats." Hailey climbed out of the car and waved as Mark gunned the engine and pulled away from the curb with a squeal. "Don't rush on my account," she murmured under her breath and watched as his car disappeared around the next intersection.

Maybe he saw a spot and would be right there. She waited a few minutes just to be sure and then started down the block to the restaurant. Why had she agreed to do this? Boggs was right. She needed to rest. Tiff wouldn't be bringing anyone home tonight, and she would have had the apartment to herself.

Hailey forced a smile as a passing couple stared at her. Her ankle was starting to throb again. She really shouldn't be walking on it. She would have to get back early to put some ice on it. Mark would understand.

A burly man in a denim jacket brushed by her, knocking her off balance. She stumbled to the side. *Of all the rude—*

Footsteps behind her. She was blocking their way.

"I'm sorry, I . . ." Her words blurred together in an unrecognizable stream. Wide-eyed faces filled her vision. They were staring at her, hiding their laughter behind contorted expanding and contracting faces. She backed against a wall. Cold roughness seeped into her bones.

Others were staring. A group of teenagers. Two guys and two girls. They were looking at her. One of the guys smiled. Did he think she was pretty? She opened her mouth, but the word froze on her lips. What would he do if she kissed him? She stepped away from the building, and the sidewalk shifted beneath her feet. She felt herself falling. The world spun around her in lazy, freeze-frame motion. She squeezed her eyes shut and braced herself for impact, but she never hit the ground. Finally, she opened her eyes. She was still standing. The guy stood so near, watching her, looking into her eyes. The girls crowded around her, pressing her back against the wall. Were they jealous? The guy was talking. His lips were so close. She could reach out and touch them.

She reached out her hand and a distant motion distracted her. Her hand, far, far beneath her. Reaching toward a crowd of circling people, just the tops of their heads. She was a butterfly, fluttering through the sky.

*No!* She jerked back her hand and bit the soft flesh at the base of her thumb. Voices swelled around her. She could see them clearly now. Pushing herself away from the wall, she turned and looked up. On the roof, two stories above her, the silhouette of a man disappeared behind the edge.

Anger erupted all around her, melting the bystanders like wax in a fiery furnace. She stamped her foot and clung to the pain, a hand-hold in the sweeping torrent. Her only shelter against the storm.

Pushing through the distorted faces, she ran across the street. *No. I shouldn't be reacting.* She slowed to a stop as squealing brakes sounded all around her. Angry voices. The blast of urgent horns.

"Calm down. None of this is happening. It isn't real." Hailey hobbled forward and pushed her way into a dimly lit bar. The air was heavy with the smell of wood polish and beer. She shouldered past a group of staring people. *It's not real. It can't be real.* Following a sign to the ladies' room, she stumbled inside and bolted the door behind her.

Then, leaning with her back against the door, she sank onto the floor and buried her face in her hands.

———

MELCHI LAY BACK ON the rooftop and pressed his palms to his eyes. A deep ache flowed from his legs through his lower back and up into his neck and shoulders. It felt so good to rest. He felt like he was floating. Above the rooftops, up into the deepening sky, he was an evaporating puddle of rainwater on a hot day, rising up to become one with the clouds.

A distant shout wrenched him back to reality. He groaned as he sat up and looked back over the edge of the roof. Nothing. Only a slow trickle of cars and pedestrians. No more trucks. No more seething presences. Just a fancy ornate building lighting up the night sky. The Mulo had already moved on. He was wasting valuable time.

Reaching into his pocket, Melchi pulled out the Booklady's watch. 8:05. There was a chance she would still be at the store. Maybe if he hurried he could catch her before she left. He wouldn't be gone that long. Yesterday the trucks hadn't started until 9:00. He'd have plenty of time. Besides, he hadn't eaten in a day and a half. And what if she needed her watch back? What if she had a new shipment of books that needed to be shelved?

But what if the Mulo came back? He pulled a piece of cardboard out of his pocket and checked his notes. Yesterday three dump trucks had come and gone from the hotel. The first arrived at 8:56 p.m.; the last had left at 2:15 a.m. It would be stupid for him to give up now. He needed to know what they were carrying. One thing was for sure: It wasn't all drywall.

Last night he'd gotten a good look inside the last truck as it pulled into the hotel. The bottom of the bed had been covered with a layer of busted-up drywall. And when the truck left, those same chunks of drywall had been on top of the load. Whatever they were carrying, they were going to a lot of trouble to disguise it. But what could it be?

Melchi tried to shake off the nauseating feeling settling over him. It couldn't be. It was too much. There had been four truckloads.

*So audaciously evil no one had wanted to believe it could be true.* Ortus's words rang like cymbals in his mind. *Never underestimate its capacity for evil. No atrocity is ever too small. Too twisted. Too profane.*

A distant rumble snapped Melchi back to attention. Another dump truck was pulling away from the hotel. When had it gotten there? Had he fallen asleep? He thrust a hand into his pocket and grabbed the Booklady's watch, but a strange sensation brushed his senses. Weak, tremulous, only the tiniest spark of life . . .

Melchi jumped to his feet and reached out with his mind. It was coming from the back of the truck. Something under all that rubble was alive!

Running to the back of the building, he looped his rope around an old exhaust vent and swung out over the edge of the building. His climb down the wall was agonizingly slow. By the time he reached the ground he could just hear the faintest hum of the truck as it faded into the distance. Cutting across the block, he vaulted a fence and ran across a gloomy school yard. The truck was moving way too fast. Even if it took the same route as the others, he would never be able to intercept it.

He turned left at the next street and was moving fast when he saw it. The truck was stopped at an intersection over two blocks away. He put his head down and ran harder. The sensation was still there. Whatever it was, it was still alive. He looked up and almost fell on his face. Two shadowy figures were climbing out of the back of the truck.

The light changed and the truck started forward as the figures jumped and tumbled to the ground. Slowly they stood up and looked around. They seemed dazed, confused—and so tiny. Children?

A pang stabbed through Melchi's heart. He was about to call out to them when one of them turned and looked his way. Then they were running, scampering away in the opposite direction.

"Wait! I'm a friend. I'm here to help!" As he ran after them, a set of headlights swung out onto the street—aimed right at the children. "Look out! Get out of the road!" Melchi ran faster, waving his arms wildly to attract the driver's attention.

The children veered to the side and darted between two town-houses. Melchi jogged after them. There they were, two shadows at the base of a tall wooden fence.

"It's okay. I won't hurt you." He slowed to an unthreatening walk. "I'm here to help."

Before he could even react, a tiny shadow leaped into the air. It hovered like a bird against the orange-tinted gloom. And then, in a streak of fluttering shadow, it flew into the night.

He looked down and gasped. The children were gone.

———————

HAILEY TOOK A DEEP breath and released it in a long wavering stream. The pounding on the bathroom door was becoming more insistent. She climbed unsteadily to her feet and checked herself in the mirror. Not too bad, considering. She unlocked the door and pulled it open a tiny crack to peek outside.

The door pushed in on her before her eyes had a chance to adjust to the light.

"It's about time. What were you doing? Taking a shower?" A hard-faced woman in a black sleeveless T-shirt walked into the bathroom and turned on Hailey with a scowl.

"Sorry. I wasn't feeling well." Hailey backed out into the hall and the door slammed shut in her face. She squinted at the line of women standing against the wall. "Sorry," she murmured again and limped back into the bar. An empty table stood in a dark corner of the room. She dropped into one of the chairs and pulled the cell phone out of her pocket.

What would she tell Boggs? Had it been another hallucination, or had it really happened? She stared at the phone, trying to sort through the tangle of images. No bruises, no cuts. No physical evidence of any kind. Just a man on the roof looking down on a crowd of crazy people. The whole thing was crazy. Like a nitrous-oxide-induced dream.

"What can I get for you tonight?" A spiky-haired redhead with a short apron pulled tight around her waist was watching Hailey over a pen and notepad.

"What? Um . . . could I have a glass of water? I'll order something, but could, um, could I have a menu?"

The waitress pointed to a blackboard over the bar. Pink, orange, and green chalk proclaimed the specials of the day. Hailey looked back to the waitress, but she was already talking to the man at the next table.

What should she do? Mark would be worried sick. Or mad. She didn't know him well enough to know which. She looked at her watch. Almost 8:40. Surely he wouldn't still be waiting in the restaurant. Besides, she had promised she'd call Boggs just as soon as anything happened.

She flipped her phone open and punched in Boggs's number.

Boggs answered on the first ring. "Hello, Hailey? Are you okay?"

"Boggs, I . . . I think I may have had another attack."

"Are you okay? What happened?"

"I'm fine, but I think someone may have been watching me. Either that or the whole thing was a hallucination. I really can't tell."

"Who was it? Did you recognize him?"

"No, it was too dark. It could have been anybody—or like I said, I could have imagined the whole thing."

"Where are you now? Are you sure you're okay?"

"I'm in a bar on Ninth Avenue—across from Sukhothai. I'm fine, but would you mind giving me another ride? I got separated from Mark, and I don't think I should . . . I mean, if there really *is* someone watching . . ."

"Are you sure you're safe there? Maybe I should call the police."

"No, I'm fine. Really. There's a ton of people here. If you could just give me—"

"I'll be right there, okay? Stay right where you are. Whatever you do, don't go anywhere by yourself."

"Okay." Hailey looked out the window front. "It's right across from Sukhothai, about three buildings down."

"I'm on my way."

The line clicked dead. Hailey closed her phone and looked up at the menu as the waitress bustled over and plunked a glass of water on the table. She ordered a burger with avocado, grilled onions, and garlic sauce. When the waitress left, she turned in her seat to watch the door. Boggs wouldn't mind waiting. Would she? She was so incredibly hungry. She hadn't eaten anything substantial all day.

An older couple stepped into the bar and stood looking around the room. Most of the tables were full, but there were still seats at the bar. Maybe she should move and let them have her table. Boggs would be here in just a few minutes.

She was about to get up when a man seated at the center of the room caught her eye. He smiled at her and got up from his table, tall and straight as a ramrod, in an expensive suit that seemed entirely out of place in the shabby little bar. Hailey looked down at her water and took a tiny sip. The guy was gorgeous. Straight off the movie screen.

Suddenly the man was standing over her. She started to look up, but her stomach clenched in a sudden spasm. She covered her mouth with her hand and swallowed back the bile rising into her throat. What was *wrong* with her? She had to get a grip. Pushing her hair out of her face, she looked up and returned the man's dazzling smile.

"The restaurant seems to be full. May I share your table?" The man's eyes locked onto hers, freezing her in a moment of heart-stopping agony.

A shudder passed through her frame. Animalistic revulsion, alien and twisted. Like the time she had helped Dr. Antipova remove a live dog brain for imaging in an NMR. She pushed the image from her mind. It wasn't real. None of it was real. "Actually I have to leave in a few minutes."

"I am sorry to hear that." Without taking his eyes off her, the man lowered himself into a chair. "I'm sure your company would have proven most scintillating."

"What?" Hailey turned toward the door. "What makes you say that?"

"Are you a professor or a student?"

He nodded at the UCSF logo on her wallet. His eyes sparkled. Large, luminous, dark as deepest night. A woman could lose herself in those eyes. Any sane woman would kill for the chance. Which left her out.

"I'm sorry." She shook her head to clear her mind. "I'm a student—at UCSF."

"A medical student?"

Hailey's eyes were drawn back to his face. Fine smile lines crinkled the corners of his eyes. What was he doing at her table? Why was he even talking to her?

"A graduate student perhaps? In what field?" He spoke with the tiniest hint of an accent. She couldn't quite place it. Yugoslavian maybe? Hungarian?

She forced her eyes to the table. She was gawking like an idiot tourist. "Oh yeah, my field . . . biochemistry. I'm in biochemistry."

"Ah, better still. Tell me, what do you think of these newest prions? Is our Dr. Prusiner right?"

"Prions?" Hailey snapped back to attention. "Why are you interested in prions?"

"No particular reason. I've been following the new research. Extremely intriguing."

"You're a scientist too?"

The man laughed. "No, I'm afraid not. I just became fascinated with biochemistry a few years back when your Dr. Prusiner won the Nobel Prize. He is a remarkable man—quite interesting."

Hailey nodded.

"But I am a man with too many interests—one interest gives way to another, and so on in an infinite chain. I fear I am far too easily distracted." His eyes seemed to drift. Was he checking her out? No. He was still looking her in the eye.

"So what do you, um . . . do?" Hailey glanced over at the door. What was taking Boggs so long?

"I am in—" his slow, ponderous smile seemed to hold a multitude of meanings—"finance. Not as stimulating as biochemistry, but it does gives me leisure to pursue my studies."

"Studies? Are you a student too?"

"Not formally. I am a student of life. The library is my university, and people such as yourself are my professors."

Hailey felt herself nodding. He was so dramatic. It was like having dinner with a Shakespeare play.

"My name is Sabazios."

The foreign name rolled around in her mind. *Sa-bay-shus.* What nationality was a name like that? "Hi, Sabazios. I'm Hailey."

"A pleasure to meet you, Hailey." He inclined his head and reached out his hand palm up.

Hailey reached out and shook the offered hand. His skin was cold and smooth as porcelain. She thrilled at the faint caress of his touch as his hand slid from hers.

"So what are you studying now, Sabazios?"

"For the moment I am fascinated with literature. The good, honest literature of the twentieth century—not the narrow-minded, bigoted twaddle your university system seems to be so enamored of at the moment."

"And what literature is that—that you like, I mean?" Hailey fought to keep a straight face. Was this guy for real?

"E. M. Forster, Donald Barthelme, Virginia Woolf—all so much more refined, so much more realistic than man's first faltering attempts at putting pen to page. Yet Shakespeare and Milton are still hawked from the pulpits of America's university systems. Why? Because they are enjoyable? Because they capture the truth of the human condition? Because of their fine craft? No, it's all propaganda. Intellectual snobbery."

"It sounds like somebody had a bad experience in Literature 101."

"You jest, but can you honestly say you enjoyed reading Shakespeare or Milton or Donne or any of the others so touted by the literary intellectuals?"

"I read *Romeo and Juliet* in high school, and I remember really liking it."

"But what of Milton? Was *Paradise Lost* not the most boring and ridiculous piece of fiction ever to pass itself off as literature? Who can get through three pages?"

"I don't know. Never read it. I guess I spent too much time in the lab."

"Believe me, Hailey, you were spared a monumentally painful ordeal."

Hailey allowed herself to smile. It had been a long time since she had been with someone so passionate. She felt swept away by the force of his feelings. It was a nice change from dry, unfeeling science.

"Woolf, on the other hand, she holds me like a spell."

Hailey listened as Sabazios extolled the virtues of Woolf and Forster, letting herself be lulled by the gently rocking waves of his impassioned voice. The room was deliciously warm, and he was intoxicatingly close. She sighed and let his perfect features fill her vision, blotting out all the ugliness of the world. Wide, black, sparkling eyes. She was falling into their depths, swimming in their liquid brightness.

A voice sounded at the back of her mind, distant and remote. Ringing with half-forgotten urgency. She tried to shut it out, but Sabazios had stopped talking. He had turned away.

"Hailey? Are you okay?"

"What?" Hailey forced herself to be alert. "Boggs?"

"Sorry I took so long. I couldn't find a parking place anywhere." Boggs rattled her keys in her pocket. "Are you ready to go?"

Hailey shook her head. "Can we wait a few more minutes? I just ordered a hamburger."

"Another one?" Boggs's eyes went wide as she looked down at the table.

"What?" Hailey looked down, and there, sitting in front of her, was a hamburger. "When did that get here?"

Sabazios cleared his throat.

"Oh, I'm sorry. Boggs, this is Sabazios."

He rose from his seat and inclined his head to Boggs. "I am very pleased to meet you, Boggs."

"Um, hi." Boggs glanced at Hailey.

"Please, allow me." Sabazios held a chair out for Boggs. "I had just invited Hailey to a party when you came in, Boggs. If she will do me the honor of attending, I would of course take her home."

He did? Hailey tried to think back to their conversation, but her head was too muzzy. Boggs was cocking an eyebrow at her. What was her problem? Why couldn't she just be happy for her that a man like this seemed to be interested in her? Still, as much as she'd like to go, she was finding it difficult to stay awake.

Hailey pressed a hand to her temples. "I'm sorry, Sabazios, but I'm tired. I should get home now."

"Until tomorrow then." Sabazios held her with beautiful dark eyes.

"Tomorrow?"

"The dinner party at my hotel. Surely you're not reconsidering?"

"No, tomorrow is fine." She shut her eyes, trying to replay their conversation in her mind. "What time again?"

"Seven o'clock." Sabazios flashed her another breathtaking smile. "I'll send my driver by your apartment at 6:45."

"My apartment?" Hailey asked. "You know where I live?"

"You just told me. Eleventh Avenue, right? The address is indelibly etched in my memory." He took Hailey's hand and pressed it to his lips. "Until tomorrow then." He gave a slight bow and wove his way through the crowded room.

Hailey shuddered as he pushed through the door. Was it just her or had the room suddenly gone ice cold?

# 11

Boggs rounded on Hailey as soon as they stepped out of the bar. *"What* were you thinking?"

"What? Sabazios? What was I supposed to do? Tell him to go away?"

"What were you even doing with him? I thought you had an attack. I thought you were on a date with Mark."

"I don't know." Hailey's voice choked off. She blinked hard and looked down at the ground. "I just couldn't . . . think."

"It's okay." An arm wrapped around her and guided her down the sidewalk. "I'm sorry. I've just been so worried. Tell me what happened."

"That's just it. I don't know. When Mark dropped me off, everything was fine. And then everything sort of went crazy. Like the whole world went out of focus. I did what you said and tried to ignore it, but—"

"Wait a second." Boggs stopped at her car and unlocked the door. "Mark dropped you off. So he wasn't with you?"

"No, he was off looking for a parking place." Hailey squirmed into the car and waited for Boggs to get in on the other side. "It was the same kind of thing as last Friday night. I felt like I could see myself from overhead, but this time I looked up and saw a man watching me from the roof."

"Did you get a good look at him? What did he look like?"

"It was too dark. He was just this shadowy blob."

"But you're sure he was a man? It couldn't have been a woman?"

"I don't know. Maybe." Hailey shrugged and buckled her seat belt as Boggs pulled out into traffic.

"And where did Sabazios come in? Was he there too?"

"No." Hailey shut her eyes and tried to remember. "As soon as I saw the man, I did what you said. I ran into the bar and locked myself in the bathroom until I could think straight again. And then, while I was waiting for you to get there, I think I must have had a relapse. This good-looking guy, Sabazios, comes walking up and asks if he can sit down. I think he was just trying to help. It had to be obvious I was in trouble. I know I looked a wreck."

"Hardly. Maybe a little damsel-in-distress-like but hardly a wreck."

"I don't even remember what I said. Everything sort of went fuzzy again. Next thing I know, you were there and I sort of had a date."

Boggs looked over at her and made a face.

"I'm serious. I honestly don't remember the conversation. At least not much of it. I know we talked about literature, and I seemed to be having a good time."

"Well, even so. I don't think you should go out with him. At this point I don't think you should go out with anybody. I don't even think you should leave the house."

"You think I should start taking the drug again?"

Boggs was silent for a long time. She stopped at a light and drummed on the steering wheel with her fingers. "I don't know.

Don't you think it's weird that it's only happened twice—and both times you had just been with Mark?"

Hailey nodded. "And there might have been a third time. I was on the drugs at the time, but I kind of remember falling in front of a car and freaking out. This weird guy with a Mohawk came up to me and said something bonkers and then—*bam!*—he was gone, and Mark was there claiming he hadn't seen anybody. I remember feeling woozy. When Mark asked me out, I was too dazed to say no—just like Sabazios. Only when Sabazios asked me, I'm pretty sure I didn't want to say no."

Boggs shot her a dark look.

"What? Sabazios is gorgeous. You have to at least admit that."

"And how long have you known him?"

"You saw him. He was a perfect gentleman. You can't be suspicious of everyone."

"Come on, Hailey. You just met him. You don't know a thing about him."

"We talked. For that matter I haven't known *you* that long either. Are you saying I shouldn't trust you?"

"All I'm saying is that—"

Their headlights flashed across a man sneaking out of a corner store. Tall. Bearded. Long curly hair. Hailey gasped.

The homeless man!

"Quick, stop the car! I've got to get out."

"What's wrong? Are you sick?" Boggs turned a worried look on Hailey and pulled the car over to the side of the road.

"I just saw him! The homeless man! He was leaving that bookstore. I've got to get out!"

"What homeless man?" The car started picking up speed again. "What are you talking about?"

"He was . . . he was the one that . . . Remember the guy that rescued me from the crazy with the knife? I think I just saw him!" Hailey turned in her seat and searched the street behind them. "Please, pull over. I've got to talk to him."

Boggs was watching her like one of the shrinks.

"I saw him. I'm not making this up!" Hailey twisted back around and pushed the passenger door open.

"Hailey, no!" The car squealed to a stop as Hailey threw off her seat belt and climbed outside. She hobbled toward the intersection at a stiff-legged jog.

"Hailey, wait." Boggs ran up beside her. "What are we doing? Who are we looking for?"

"The guy that rescued me. I think he might have been homeless." She plodded to a stop at the intersection and looked up and down both streets. "I know I saw him. I wasn't making it up." She strode over to the corner building and checked the door. It was locked. She stepped back and stared at the sign. It was a bookstore. Why would he be coming out of a bookstore?

Boggs's heavy breathing came up behind her. A light touch on her shoulder. Hailey shut her eyes and waited.

"I know what you're thinking, but I'm not crazy. My seeing him proves it. I'm not going back on the drugs."

Boggs didn't say anything for a long time.

Finally, Hailey couldn't stand it anymore. "What?"

"Don't you think we should get you home now? It's getting late, and you still need to call Mark. He's probably worried."

---

HAILEY OPENED HER EYES to a stream of morning sunlight. She settled back on the sofa and stretched, luxuriating in the gentle quiet of the new day. Wasn't it Saturday? She sighed and stretched her arms out over her head. *Clunk!* Something small and heavy clattered to the floor. The telephone. She rolled onto her side, and a hundred dark memories came flooding back to her. Hiding in the bathroom, the pressing crowd, the shadow watching her from the roof . . .

She sat up and searched the room. No, she was all right. It hadn't been real. It couldn't have been. She'd had another episode. It was all a hallucination. But what about the homeless man? She had seen him sneaking out of a bookstore. Had he been a hallucination too? It didn't feel like it, but how far could she trust her feelings? How far could she trust anything?

She strapped her walking boot around her foot and crept up the stairs. She didn't want to go through another night like that, even if it meant living the rest of her life as a zombie. She eased the door open and peaked into Tiffany's room. Good. She and Louie were already gone. Hobbling over to her dresser, Hailey opened the bottom drawer and pulled out her bottle of pills.

If she went back on the drugs and the attacks went away, it might not be rigorous proof, but at least the nightmares would be over. And if the attacks didn't go away, then at least she'd know for sure. Unless she was too muzzy-headed to realize she was being attacked. Was that what had happened in the park? The guy with the Mohawk had been trying to tell her something. Was he warning her about an attack?

Hailey walked into the bathroom and poured herself a glass of water. The homeless man was the key. He could feel it too. He knew what was happening to her. If she could only find him, get him to explain everything to Boggs, it would prove she wasn't crazy. They couldn't both be suffering from the same delusion.

If she could just find him . . . that is, if he wasn't a hallucination himself.

Clunking back to her room, she tossed the pills back in her dresser and hastily changed her clothes. The homeless man had been leaving the bookstore. After hours. Maybe someone there would know something about him. Maybe he was there now.

She grabbed a jacket and started down the stairs but stopped at the bottom to run back up and wash her face and brush her teeth. Then, after doing her makeup and running a brush through her hair, she was down the stairs and out the door.

Golden light beat down on her, warming her against the crisp, cool breeze. She closed her eyes and looked up at the sky, letting the sun hit her full in the face. The previous evening's nightmares faded in the sun's burning brightness. The memories seemed thin and insubstantial. How could any hallucination stand up to the hard reality of such a beautiful morning?

*God, thank you. This was just what I needed.* She walked down the hill and turned onto the street with the bookstore. As long as she didn't react to them, the hallucinations couldn't hurt her. She would be fine. After all, she had managed to carry on an entire conversation in the middle of an episode.

The thought of Sabazios's chiseled features and dark eyes thrilled through her, adding to the sun's warmth. It was only a dinner party. Other guests would be there to pick up the conversation if it lagged. Attack or no attack, as long as she kept her wits about her, she'd be fine.

Hailey crossed the street and scanned the faces of the other pedestrians as she neared the corner shop. Good—it was open. A sign hung in the window. *Elsewhere Books: Mystery, Science Fiction, Fantasy.* She pushed the door open and walked past a narrow aisle. Books were stacked everywhere—on top of the shelves, on the window ledges, in the aisles. An elderly woman looked up from behind the counter and smiled.

"Can I help you find anything in particular?"

"Uh, maybe." Hailey browsed the shelves, searching for an opening to bring up the subject of her homeless man.

"If you don't know the author, maybe if you describe it to me. I might have an idea." The old woman was watching her with a curious expression.

Hailey grasped at the first title she could think of. "So do you have, um, *Paradise Lost?*"

"*Paradise Lost*?" The woman fixed Hailey with a funny stare and then came out from behind the counter. "Sorry to say, but we mainly carry science fiction and fantasy here. You should try Hardaway's down the street. They carry a lot of secondhand classics."

"Thanks." Hailey could feel the color rising in her cheeks. "How about this then?" She grabbed a book off the shelf. *Tarzan of the Apes*. At least she had heard of it. Avoiding the woman's eyes, she carried it to the counter and dug in her wallet for a five.

"I thought you said you didn't carry the classics." Hailey nodded at a stack of books topped with *Robinson Crusoe*.

"Oh, these." The woman's face crinkled into a smile. She slid the books back behind the counter and looked back up at Hailey with another strange expression. "These are for a friend."

Hailey nodded and looked around the store. "This is a great bookstore. Have you ever had any trouble with break-ins?"

"Not much in here worth stealing, really. Why do you ask?"

"Um, I . . ." Hailey decided to lay her cards on the table. "Last night I was driving past the store and saw a man leaving. Really tall, with a beard and long curly dark hair. He seemed to be sneaking out, like he didn't want to be seen."

"And what's your interest in this man?" The woman's eyes danced. She knew something Hailey didn't, and whatever it was, she seemed to think it was funny.

"So you know about him? He really was here?"

"Maybe." Again the mischievous smile. "Was the man you saw strong with a handsome face and kind, gentle eyes?"

Hailey stared back at the woman. What was she getting at?

"How long have you known Melchi?"

"Melchi? Is that his name? Do you know where he is? I really need to talk to him."

A shadow fell across the woman's face. She turned and carried a stack of papers behind the counter.

"Please, it's important. I have to talk to him."

The woman was silent for several seconds, then looked up. "You still haven't told me how you know him."

"I know this is going to sound crazy—" she chose her words carefully—"but I think he may have saved my life."

"*May* have saved your life?"

"A man with a knife attacked me in Golden Gate Park. Then this huge homele—um . . . Melchi, rescued me. Took away the man's knife and tossed him around like a chew toy." She looked the woman in the eyes. So far she seemed to believe her. "But there was something else too. Something chased us up the hill, and Melchi seemed to know what it was. I know it sounds crazy, but I was attacked again last night. If Melchi has any information . . ."

The woman put a sallow hand on Hailey's forearm. She frowned into Hailey's eyes for a long second and then shook her head sadly. "I can't tell you where to find Melchi; I don't think anyone can. He comes and goes as he pleases. Like a ray of sunshine on a cloudy day. But I can give him your message. If he wants to talk to you, I'm sure he'll be able to find you. A lot easier than you'd be able to find him."

Hailey closed her eyes and took a deep breath. "I can't tell you how much this means to me. Just knowing he actually exists.

I was beginning to think I was crazy." She looked up and smiled her thanks to the kindly old woman.

"Yep, Melchi has that effect on everybody. Makes us all wonder if we're a little crazy. Sometimes I think he's the only sane human being on the planet."

Hailey nodded and started toward the door but stopped. This was crazy, but she couldn't just leave it to chance. "Tell him my name is Hailey Maniates. He can find me at Eleventh Avenue near Judah. It's a dirty blue house with peeling paint."

There, she'd done it. Boggs would kill her if she found out, but for once she didn't care. She had to talk to this Melchi.

Soon.

———————

MELCHI CROUCHED ON THE roof of an old frame house. She was inside. He could feel her presence fluttering like butterfly wings against his mind. "Hailey Maniates." He whispered the name out loud. That's what the Booklady had called her.

*Hailey Maniates.* So beautiful—like a Wordsworth sonnet.

An impression leaped into his mind. Cold, dark eyes. A stranger's handsome face. *No!* Melchi shut his eyes and forced the image from his head. This was wrong! He rose to his feet and stretched the feeling back into his legs. He shouldn't be here. His presence could lead the Mulo right to her.

He took a step and hesitated. If the Booklady was right and the Mulo had already discovered her, if it had managed to follow her last night . . .

He couldn't just stand by and let it find her. Memories boiled up like a geyser inside his head. Tear-stained eyes, tousled curls, the soft glow of moonlight on perfect skin. A deep yearning coiled like a constrictor around his chest. Crushing, suffocating, weighing him down.

*Holy One, please . . . Forgive me.* He dug his fingernails into his forearm, pressed harder, focused on the pain. How could he pretend to offer protection? He was worse than the Mulo! He stepped to the edge of the roof and reached out for an overshadowing tree.

A *click* sounded directly beneath him. The front door swung open, and the girl stepped out onto the porch. Melchi gasped. Dressed in a long, rose-colored gown, she looked for all the world like a fairy-tale princess. *The young Dawn with fingertips of rose . . .*

She turned this way and that, sending her hair tumbling in soft, silky cascades. She seemed to be looking for something. Melchi drew back from the edge of the roof, but a second later and he was peeking back over it again.

"I know you're here." She spoke in a loud voice. "Please come out. I need to talk to you."

Melchi jerked back away from the edge.

"Don't be afraid. I just want to talk, ask a few questions."

No, he couldn't . . . but Melchi took a deep breath, and before he could talk himself out of it, he leaped into the tree. Catching the branches only long enough to control his fall, he crashed from limb to limb and landed in a crouch at the tree's base.

The girl emitted a startled cry and backed toward the door.

"I am sorry. I did not mean . . ." Melchi took an involuntary step and then stopped.

"You didn't. I just didn't expect you to . . . come out of a tree." She took a cautious step toward him, hands outstretched like she was approaching a wild animal.

"I won't hurt you." Melchi spoke in his softest voice. "I only want to help."

The girl was smiling now. "I know."

Melchi took a step back. The ache in his chest was starting to expand. He shouldn't be here.

"It's okay." Her gentle voice coaxed him forward. "Please, just a few questions."

He nodded and swallowed at the tightness building in his throat.

"I never got to thank you. You saved my life."

Melchi looked down at a broken board on the porch. This was all wrong. His feelings . . . he shouldn't be here.

"My purse is inside. I'd appreciate it if you'd let me give you a reward."

"No! It is forbidden. I did not do it for—" He looked up help-lessly. "If I had been out patrolling as was my duty, I might have stopped the Mulo before it ever got to you. I might have prevented the whole attack. I am sorry."

"That's ridiculous. Surely you don't think it was your fault." The girl crept toward him and reached for his hand.

Melchi jumped back. "I must go." He barely managed to choke out the words. Lowering his eyes, he turned and retreated down the sidewalk.

Emotions rang out behind him like a pealing bell. "Please! I didn't mean it. Just a few questions. Please!"

So much pain. Tears welled in his eyes. What was he so afraid of? Why couldn't he just talk to her?

Uneven steps trailed behind him. Stabs of echoing pain every other step. "Please, back when you carried me . . . and on the porch, just now. . . . What's happening to me? Why does it feel like I can read your thoughts?"

"My thoughts?" Melchi stopped and focused on the ground in front of him, fighting to clear his mind. "You can hear what I'm thinking?"

"Sort of. I know it sounds crazy, but . . . I mean, *is* it crazy? Do you have any idea what's happening to me?"

"Do you hear actual words or is it more vague? Emotions . . . images and impressions . . ."

"The last part. Images and impressions."

"And what am I thinking now?"

"How should I know? That I'm a raving lunatic maybe? That you can't wait to get away from me?"

Melchi shook his head and turned to face her. What could he tell her? How much was she allowed to know?

The girl gasped. "You think I'm . . . beautiful. Too beautiful." She looked at him with wide, wondering eyes. "What's happening to me? How do I know that?"

"Anyone beholding you would think the same."

"What about . . ." The girl's eyes drifted to the right. "*Holy One*! That night you carried me, I kept hearing the words, over and over in my head. What does it mean? Am I just going crazy?" He could hear the desperation in her voice. Worse, he could feel it.

"Shush! Try to calm down. You must learn to control your emotions." Melchi lowered his voice to a whisper. "You are not crazy. You are—" He glanced up and down the street. He had to tell her. She was one of them. It was his duty. "What I am about to reveal is extremely important. You must never tell a soul. Understood?"

"Okay . . ."

"You feel my thoughts because you are a child of the Standing. Your soul resonates with the other dimension."

"The other . . .? What are you talking about?"

"Please, calm yourself. It is worse when you become excited."

"What's worse?"

Her voice was starting to get shrill. He shouldn't have said anything. She would bring the Mulo right down on them.

"Listen to me. Take a deep breath. Like this." Melchi breathed in and out slowly. "The Holy One has given you a great gift, but it comes with terrible responsibility. You are sensitive to the events that transpire on other, extra-dimensional planes of existence. But because you can feel the presence of the wanderers who walk those dimensions, they can also feel you. Especially when you are agitated or upset. To learn to control your emotions is your first responsibility as a child of the Standing."

"So you're saying you think this is really happening. That I really am feeling something. Why haven't I felt it before?"

"If you haven't been trained, the sensations are usually so faint as to be missed. But there is one wanderer, the Mulo, who walks with a foot in both dimensions. Its power is enormous. When it hunts, a child of the Standing can feel it for miles. Other times, it's as subtle as the whisper of the wind."

"This Mulo—you believe such a thing actually exists?"

Melchi nodded. "That night when I first saw you, the Mulo was hunting us. It could feel your confusion and pain."

*"Hunting. Us.* Why?" The girl's eyes were wide and staring. She couldn't take much more of this. It was too much information at once.

"The Mulo has always sought to destroy the Standing. There are many different teachings. Some say it needs a Standing to get through the gateway. Others say it seeks only to thwart the Holy One's purpose. Nobody really understands the reason."

"So you're saying this Mulo thing is trying to kill me?"

"You and me, all those who stand."

The girl was staring past him, her eyes glazed and unfocused. Finally she shook her head. "And you believe this? You actually

believe in mind-reading and other dimensions and monsters with
nothing better to do than wander around trying to kill people?"

"You yourself have felt it. At the hospital. I thought it had
killed you. One minute you were there, and the next you were
fading slowly away. How did you do it? How were you able to
escape?"

"Escape what?" Her forehead crinkled into a frown. "I
never saw anything. I just knew that something, somewhere was
fighting."

"Then what did you do? Did you pray a special prayer?"

"I don't know. I might have been praying. Mostly I was wres-
tling with a bunch of crazed doctors. They thought I was a basket
case. Shot me full of Geodon."

"Geodon?"

"It's an antipsychotic. They put me on it because they thought
I was crazy. They locked me in a mental hospital for three days!"

"An antipsychotic?" Melchi tried to wrap his mind around it.
"Like a Haldol-Lorazepam-benztropine cocktail? When did they
give it to you? How long were you on it?"

"What's this have to do with your monster thing? You say
I was attacked, but I never *saw* anything. I'm not even sure I felt
anything. How do I know this Mulo isn't a figment of your imagination? How do I know we're not *both* crazy?"

"A figment of my imagination couldn't have murdered my
parents. It couldn't have killed the man who raised me. A hallucination didn't murder seventeen people in Chicago, twenty-six
in New Orleans . . . Its trail of blood has spanned three millen-
nia. Before the Mulo came to this country, it killed thousands of
people in Romania and Bulgaria, millions in Nazi Germany, tens
of thousands in—"

"Wait a second! You don't seriously expect me to believe this
Mulo was responsible for the Holocaust? That's insane!"

"Is it? Adolf Hitler was a brilliant strategist. What possible reason could he have had for diverting so many critical resources away from the war effort? Why spend so much energy hunting down Gypsies and mental patients and Jews?"

"What do you mean Gypsies and mental patients? The Nazis were after the Jews."

"See what it has done? History has all but forgotten Himmler's 1937 decree, 'The Struggle Against the Gypsy Plague.' Over five hundred thousand Gypsies were killed during the Holocaust. Thousands of mental patients as well. The children of the Standing have always been wanderers. According to tradition we are not permitted to stay long in one place, to plant fields or dwell in houses. We have long hidden among the Gypsies. The Mulo knows this. He was striking at *us*. As for the mental patients, well, after all you have experienced, surely you must understand this strategy now."

The girl just stood there, watching him. Did she believe him? He searched her eyes but couldn't be certain. *Holy One, please. Help me convince her of the truth.*

"You must believe me. The Mulo is *very* real and *very* dangerous. It is not safe for you to be here. My advice is to get as far away from San Francisco as soon as possible. To remain here is to invite death."

"But—" The girl shook her head. "This is crazy. There's no such thing as monsters, and there's no such thing as reading minds. There's got to be another explanation. Something that doesn't involve invocations of the supernatural."

"You yourself said you prayed. Does this not mean you believe in a supernatural and holy God?"

"That's different. I—"

"The Holy One created the four or five dimensions we call our own. He is outside of them. Beyond them. Why is it so difficult to believe there are other dimensions as well?"

"But if you can't see them, how do you know?"

"And you see the Holy One?"

"No, but—"

"The test of sight is no proof—not for things which by their nature cannot be seen. But the Standing have been given other senses. And then there is the record of history, the evidence of the prophecies, dubious when pronounced but proven trustworthy through the test of time. The prophecies speak of other dimensions, entire worlds separate from our own. The Mulo has ever sought entrance to those worlds, access to almost limitless power. But one day the long-awaited one, the first guardian of the dimensional gateway, shall put an end to the enemy's dark threat."

"I can't—" The girl shook her head. "This is just too much."

"It is the truth."

"Maybe, but it's all happening so fast. You have to slow down if you want me to—"

The girl turned as a long shiny black car pulled up to her house. "Oh no. I forgot all about my date." She hurried over to the car as the driver got out and circled around to greet her.

Melchi studied the well-dressed man as he held the door open for her. Her date, she said. So clean and imposing in his beautiful black suit and white gloves.

Melchi reached toward him with his mind, hoping to find something—the tiniest indication that he was not what he seemed. But no . . . he was clean, as polished as his beautiful new car. Melchi looked down at his own clothes and then back at Hailey as she stood talking to the handsome young man.

What had he been thinking?

He looked down at the ground to mask his burning face. For all he knew the two of them were engaged to marry. The man in the beautiful suit and the young Dawn with fingertips of rose.

He turned away in shame. They were Odysseus and Penelope. And he was one of the greedy suitors.

How could he be so selfish? He should be happy for her. For them. But no . . . Ortus was right. He was far too easily distracted, vile and wicked through and through. He was the long-awaited. His responsibilities lay elsewhere.

And with the Mulo waxing ever stronger, Melchi was unlikely to live long enough ever to become distracted again.

———

HAILEY BALANCED ON ONE foot in front of the white-gloved chauffeur. "Please, tell him I'm sorry, but I just don't think I can make it tonight. I don't know why, but my ankle's swelling up like a grapefruit. I need to ice it down."

"Sure, I'll let him know." The driver shook his head. "My guess is he'll be pretty disappointed."

"I'm really sorry. I would have called, but a . . . an old friend came by, and we started talking, and the time just got away from me."

The driver nodded. A hint of a smile touched his lips.

"Could you make sure he knows?" Hailey scrambled to come up with something to say. Something kind without being too encouraging. "Please, just tell him I hope it works out another time? After my ankle has time to heal?"

"No problem."

Hailey watched the driver as he walked around the car and slid inside. He was still smiling. She hoped he wouldn't give Sabazios the wrong idea. The engine started and the limo pulled away.

"Sorry about that." She turned and looked up and down the sidewalk.

Her homeless man was gone.

# ৩ 12 ৩

Athena hurried down the dimly lit sidewalk, shivering against the damp night air. The hotel was further down Haight Street than she remembered. If she didn't move faster, she was going to be late.

Her new boots tapped out the urgency of her mission, each step rubbing bigger blisters onto her heels. She had spent thirty dollars on new clothes. Thirty dollars she didn't have. It had better be worth it.

She fingered the lump pinned to the inside of her dress. It wasn't too late. She could still catch a bus out of town. Maybe if she sold the brooch, she could start over in a new city. And why not? The bird was in her hand. What was she doing back at the bush?

But where would she go? She'd rather die than go back to her clan. San Francisco was her city now. She didn't want to live life on the run. If the Gypsies had taught her anything, it was that you didn't cross power. Handing fifty thousand dollars to a stranger— no explanations, no thinly veiled threats—well, that was true power. Either that or true stupidity.

She clacked across a side street as a black limo pulled in front of the hotel. A tuxedo-clad driver got out and walked into the building. She looked down at her new dress, happy she had spent the money. It was satiny black—right from the store. And much tighter-fitting than the rest of her dresses. She probably wouldn't wear it after tonight, but tonight was all that counted. If she could just get through the evening without having to give up the stone. Fifty thousand dollars. She would be set for life!

A shadow across from the hotel caught her eye. It looked like the guy from the party, the one with the rainbow Mohawk. What was his name? Blaine? Blaise? He was leaning against a dark building, staring at the hotel entrance. He turned his head, and she could see his lips moving ever so slightly, as if he were talking on a cell phone. What was he doing there? Waiting for her?

She was about to look for a side entrance when he pushed off the wall and started walking in the other direction. Good. He hadn't seen her. The last thing she needed was another scene. She tiptoed to the entrance and darted inside.

The lobby seemed a lot larger when it was empty. Marble and glass and gleaming brass. She stood in the entryway and looked around to get her bearings. What was she supposed to do now?

A man in a white turtleneck stood in a corner of the lobby, talking to the limo driver. Their tones were hushed, but Athena could tell the driver was being royally chewed out. A man in a black suit stood behind the front desk, frowning at her with disapproval. She raised her chin and clacked across the lobby to talk to him.

"Good evening. I have a dinner appointment with the owner." She spoke in her most aristocratic British accent. "Could you tell me where I might find him?"

"I'm sorry, but do you have an invitation?" She could just hear the undercurrent of contempt beneath his polished tone.

"The invitation was personal."

"I see." The man's supercilious laugh made her fingers clench. "Well that poses a problem, doesn't it?"

"Not for me, it doesn't." Athena glanced at the gold name tag above the man's pocket. "If you can't help me, Mr. Blakeney, then I shall leave. Kindly tell your employer Athena Cromwell was here to see him and you turned her away."

Athena turned her back on the man and started for the door. People like that grated her garters. She had almost made it to the door when a chill tingled up her spine.

"Excuse me. Ma'am?" Tapping footsteps behind her. "Are you here to see Mr. Vladu?"

"The owner?" Athena kept her voice controlled but held on to her anger in case she might need it later.

"Yes ma'am." The man in the white turtleneck interposed himself between her and the door.

"I was supposed to meet him for dinner, but Mr. Black-Eye, there at the desk—"

"I am Tristan Ibanescu, Mr. Vladu's assistant." The man gave a curt bow. "Please, accept my apologies. Mr. Blakeney will be dealt with later." He shot a dark look toward the desk. "If you would, please, follow me. I'd be happy to show you to Mr. Vladu's private dining room."

Athena followed Mr. Ibanescu, turning as she passed the desk to give Blakeney a triumphant smile. Even if she had to give the brooch back, the expression on the hotelier's face was worth it.

The assistant led Athena through a richly carpeted hallway and inserted a card in a slot next to a mahogany-paneled elevator. The door opened, and Ibanescu pressed the top button on the panel. The elevator lurched upward, making Athena feel weak in the knees.

"Did Mr. Vladu not give you an invitation?"

"I haven't actually met him yet. One of his managers invited me."

"Ah, you must mean Ericson. He met you at the party Wednesday night?"

Athena nodded, waiting for him to mention the brooch. Just then the elevator door opened, and she followed the man out into a broad hallway. Ahead of them, a pair of wide glass doors opened into a large, empty ballroom even more lavishly furnished than the one from the party. Ibanescu led her to an ornately carved door and paused.

"I'm sorry, but I'm afraid I missed your name."

"Athalia." She decided to give him her real name. If they did a background check, they probably already knew it anyway. "Athalia Pooro, but I go by Athena."

He opened the door to admit her into a lavish, candlelit room. "Miss Athena Pooro," he announced in a formal voice that caught her off guard.

She stood in the doorway while her escort crossed the room and whispered in the ear of a tall, good-looking man seated by himself at a large dinner table. Dozens of well-dressed guests stood in small clusters around the table. A few turned and nodded, but most kept on talking. Almost all of them were guys her age or a few years older. She could see only three other women. Two wore party dresses, but the other wore slacks. Narrow tables heaped with food lined the walls. It was incredible.

Athena stepped toward the ring of food-laden tables, but a man in a tuxedo blocked her way. Her eyes blurred, and she felt suddenly dizzy. "Get that glass out of my face!" The words were out of her mouth before she could control herself. Her vision gradually cleared, and the room righted itself once more. The attendant stood back from her, mumbling an apology. The weight of every eye in the room bore down on her, pinning her to the floor.

"I'm sorry." She kept her eyes fixed on the attendant. "You startled me. My eyes hadn't time to adjust to the light. Is that champagne? I would love some."

The man handed her an amber-filled glass, and she took a tentative sip before risking a look around the room. Most of the conversations had started up again, but a few heads were still turned her way. Good. Let them look.

The tall man at the end of the table caught her eye and raised his glass. Refusing to be intimidated, she raised her chin in a silent "what's up?" and walked over to the food tables. He was getting up, walking her way. She exhaled slowly. How was she going to play this game? It was too late for timid and invisible. She might as well have some fun. Spearing a stuffed mushroom, she held it poised in front of her, waiting for the man to say something.

"Good evening. I'm Sabazios Vladu."

She took a bite of the mushroom and chewed as she studied his face. The dude's eyes could feed a squad of cheerleaders for months. She swallowed and counted silently to ten. "Hi, Sabazios. I'm Athena." She paused and looked around the room before turning back to the man standing beside her. "Eat here often?"

His brow furrowed, then he smiled. "I suppose I do."

"Then maybe you could suggest something that's actually edible." She dropped the rest of the mushroom in a linen-lined basket next to the table.

Sabazios stared down at her with those intense dark eyes.

Resisting the urge to look away, she held his gaze and smiled. "No, it's not natural. If you look closer, you'll see I have purple roots."

The man broke into a dazzling smile. "Athena, I think I'm going to like you. You and I are going to get along fine."

"As much as I appreciate the vote of confidence, you certainly aren't making a good first impression, keeping a starving lady waiting. I'm about to blow away."

"Yes, yes, forgive me. Let's see what we can find for you."

Athena took his proffered arm and walked with him past the hors d'oeuvre tables. "And no raw fish or anything that could hatch into raw fish."

"How about the *Telemea de Carei*?" Sabazios pointed to a bowl of what looked like black olives stuffed with cheese.

Athena took a small bite. It was delicious, but she wrinkled her nose. "The Telemea is too salty—you taste it." She held up her toothpick, and Sabazios took a bite.

"You're right." He raised an eyebrow. "It *is* a little on the salty side. How about these *krathong thong*?" He pointed to a tray of tiny stuffed pastry shells.

Athena tried a tiny bite. "Americans. They make everything too salty—except for French fries. You can never have too much salt on a French fry."

Athena nibbled on the pastry while Sabazios pointed out other delicacies.

"Tell me, Ericson said he gave you a bauble at the party the other night."

"Oh yes, I meant to thank you. He said it was a gift from you, but you weren't there, and well, how could you have known?"

"I beg your pardon?"

"Not that red is totally out. I may do the red thing again, but right now—" she twisted a tuft of her hair—"it makes me look like a stop light. Way overly primary, don't you think?" Athena braced herself. This was where the swords came out.

Sabazios raised a finger and a waiter rushed over. *Uh oh.* She was in deep caviar now. What was he doing?

He whispered something in the waiter's ear, and the waiter left the room.

"I hope you told him that I like my fries salty."

Sabazios ignored her comment and walked to the head of the table. "Excuse me, everyone," his penetrating voice drew everyone's eyes toward him, "if I could have your attention." The room fell instantly silent. "If everyone would please be seated, dinner will be served immediately."

Sabazios sat down, and the guests followed his example. Athena hung back, waiting for everyone else to be seated. She didn't want to appear too eager. Besides, the others had seen her with Sabazios. It would be better if she was *forced* to take one of the seats closest to him.

The last guest was seated, leaving Athena the seat to Sabazios's right. She took another bite of pastry and counted to ten before moving to the table. While she was seating herself, the man in the white turtleneck came in and crouched beside Sabazios's chair. The two held a hushed conversation, and the man passed Sabazios something under the table.

"I suppose you're all wondering why you were invited here." Sabazios smiled and looked out over his guests.

Athena glanced around the table. She had assumed the others were in on the secret.

"Well, let me first introduce myself. I am Sabazios Vladu. Last year I was much like you—a guest at this table. At that time a different man sat in this chair. He offered me and the rest of the guests membership in a society called The Hand of Fellowship. The privileges were numerous—free use of the hotel's rooms and dining facilities, lavish gifts, exposure to an echelon of society I never dreamed existed. The obligations, however, were profound. When he or one of the senior members of the society died,

I agreed that if I were chosen to be his heir, I would continue the traditions of the society and at my death pass on all of my inherited wealth to a society member of my own choosing.

"To make a long story short, the man sitting in this chair died of a heart attack three months later, and I inherited an estate worth billions."

A gasp went up around the table. A group of waiters came in, as if on cue, and started serving the meal. Athena knew perfectly well it was all a scam, but what did they want with her? She was broke—not exactly a prime mark. No, the mark was one of the older men seated around the table. She was there to lend credibility to the story. But why give her the brooch? That was the part that didn't make sense. Well, at least her biggest worry was put to rest; Sabey wasn't a pimp.

Athena stopped picking at her plate and decided to eat in earnest. If she wasn't the main event, she might as well enjoy the sideshow. A hushed conversation gradually resumed around the table. The tone was, by and large, skeptical. By the sound of things, Sabey and his crew weren't going to net a very big haul.

The man to Athena's left turned to Sabazios and cleared his throat. He was one of the few men seated around the table that wore a suit. "Excuse me, Mr. Vladu, but I'm curious. What if one of us were in debt? I don't see how they could make much of a contribution to the deal you're proposing."

"I know what you're thinking, Mr. Summers. I thought the same thing myself a year ago, but there is no 'deal.' This isn't a pyramid scheme. At least not anymore. I must confess that it's possible it started out that way. Apparently the society has been in existence for more than five hundred years."

"Then I don't get it. In my experience things that seem too good to be true are always just that. I want you to know up front that I'm not going to sign anything. If you want me to leave now, just say the word."

All eyes turned to Sabazios. He rose slightly, pulled a wallet from his pocket and started counting out bills. Athena was close enough to see they were hundreds.

"You're welcome to leave anytime you wish, but let me assure you all, none of you will be asked to sign anything. You will not be asked to do anything but enjoy our hospitality—except, I should mention, this *is* a secret society. I would appreciate it if you didn't say anything to the media."

"Mmm-hmmm." Mr. Summers started to push himself away from the table but stopped short when Sabazios handed a stack of bills to Athena.

"Athena, would you please give this to Mr. Summers? He's a firm believer in the 'no free lunch' adage and seems intent on cheating himself out of what I must say is an extraordinarily fine meal."

Athena handed Summers the stack of bills—several thousand dollars, judging from the thickness.

Summers thumbed through the money and set it on the table. "I don't know what you're up to, Vladu, but I'm not having any part of it." He pushed himself from the table and moved toward the door, leaving the stack of bills behind. An attendant opened the door for him as he stormed out into the hall.

Silence filled the room. Athena watched Sabazios for a reaction but couldn't help a glance at the pile of money lying on the table. So tantalizingly close . . .

*Easy girl. The money's nothing compared to the brooch. Play it cool.*

"That was unfortunate," Sabazios said at last, shaking his head. "Mr. Summers needed two thousand dollars to keep his car. I know this because I took the liberty of having all of you screened. I apologize for this invasion of your privacy, but I had to make sure you didn't have any assets I might be accused of trying to steal. The world we live in has reached such a deplorable level of cynicism that it is difficult to act benevolently without being accused of criminal intent."

"One of the trials of being rich, eh, Sabazios?" Athena laughed, trying to lighten the mood.

"Not normally, I wouldn't imagine." His dramatic sigh whispered through the room. "It is my particular curse. When I accepted the inheritance, I agreed to induct new society members and regularly disperse to them a small fraction of my yearly profits."

"Well count me in," a pale, dark-haired guy across the table from Athena called out. "I'm happy to take any money you want to throw my way."

"Thank you . . ."

"Jason."

"Thank you, Jason. I knew someone would recognize my plight and offer their assistance." Sabazios nodded at a waitress, and the woman picked up the stack of bills and handed it to the wide-eyed youth."

"That's it? Just like that? You're just giving it to me?"

"Just like that."

"Well, in that case," the woman in slacks leaned forward, "I want to give you some assistance too."

Athena looked around as the room filled with giddy laughter. No doubt about it. Sabazios had them.

————

HAILEY FLOPPED DOWN ON the sofa and pounded her fists into the cushion. She was a scientist. Why couldn't she accept it? The homeless man was a hallucination. It was the only thing that made sense. There were no such things as extra-dimensional boogeymen. The monsters behind the Holocaust were all human. And mind reading or ESP or resonance or whatever else you wanted to call it—it just didn't exist. If she could read minds, why couldn't she read anyone else's? He had to be a delusion. The only way he could be real was if they both had the same delusion, and what were the odds of that?

But if he were a delusion, how had she gotten to the hospital? She couldn't have crawled. Her jeans hadn't gotten dirty enough. And she couldn't have walked either. She pulled her cell phone out of her pocket and punched in Boggs's number.

"Hailey? Are you okay?"

"I'm fine. Listen. I need to ask a really big favor. Remember that bookstore I thought I saw the homeless man coming out of? Could you take me there in ten minutes?"

"That's the really big favor?"

"If you need more time, I totally understand. I was just hoping to get there before it closed."

"No, it's fine. But why? Why the sudden rush?"

"I saw the homeless man."

"The guy that rescued you?"

"Yeah. But this time I had a chance to talk to him. He said a lot of crazy things—things way too crazy to be true. And I just . . ." She took a deep breath and let it out slowly. "I need to know whether he's a delusion or not."

"What? If you just talked to him . . . and didn't the woman at the bookstore say she knew him. Surely you don't think—?"

"Boggs, please. I just need to be sure. I'm sitting here, and I don't know if he's real or the bookstore was real or . . . I can't even be sure you're really real. It's driving me crazy—assuming I'm not crazy already."

"Hailey, stop it! Calm down. Listen to me. You're not crazy."

"I've got a psychiatrist and a big bottle of pills that say you're wrong."

"So? You were misdiagnosed. Big deal. These things happen all the time. The important thing is the evidence. We have physical evidence that someone attacked you. We have witnesses who confirm your homeless man exists."

"I have witnesses, as in me, the crazy person. I need independent corroboration."

"Okay, I'll be right over. Just stay right there. And stop torturing yourself!"

"Okay." Far easier said than done. Hailey hung up the phone and walked out onto the porch. It was already getting dark. The bookstore was probably closed.

Finally, Boggs pulled up in front of her house and tapped the horn.

Hailey clambered into the car and smiled at her new friend. "Thanks. I really appreciate your doing this."

"No problem. What are imaginary friends for?"

"Would you stop it? I'm serious!"

Boggs drove in silence while Hailey searched the empty sidewalks. The bookstore was dark when they got there. The sign in the window said it was closed.

"Sorry, Hailey. Maybe we can try again Monday?"

"He was at the store pretty late last night." Hailey looked to Boggs with her most pitiful puppy-dog eyes.

"Well . . . it's an awfully good parking place. It'd be a shame to waste it." Boggs turned off the car, and the two of them got out. Hailey walked over and checked the window. A faint light seemed to be coming from the back.

"Hello?" Boggs knocked on the door. "Hello? Is anybody there? We need help!"

A scrape sounded inside the shop. Soft footsteps.

"Please. It will only take a few seconds of your time."

The door opened to the chime of a bell, and the old woman poked her head out.

Hailey stepped forward. "Hi, I don't know if you remember me, but—"

"*Tarzan of the Apes*. I remember." The smell of fried chicken and stale cigarette smoke wafted through the door.

"I was wondering, if you have time, could we ask you a few questions?"

"About Melchi?" A knowing smile lit her face. "It's all right, Cupcake. I can vouch for him. He's one of the sweetest boys you'll ever find." She motioned for the girls to follow and led them back through the crowded store.

"I'm Susan Boggs, a friend of Hailey's."

The shopkeeper nodded and walked behind the counter where a small reading lamp lit a stack of open books.

"Hailey has been the victim of several attacks lately, and we're hoping to discover the cause. This man, Melchi, might have information that could help us if—"

"Melchi told me about the park." The old lady glared at Boggs. "The only reason he was there was because he was trying to help this girl. He didn't have anything to do with any attacks. He wouldn't hurt a fly."

"We have reason to—"

"I know he wouldn't." Hailey stepped forward. "He saved my life, and I'm very grateful. I don't think he's responsible for the attacks, but he said something this afternoon that makes me think he might have information that could help me. Do you know where he is?"

"I haven't seen him since this morning."

"Well, have you ever heard him use the words Mulo or the Standing?"

The shopkeeper nodded. "Melchi is very religious. And you know how priests are, filling boys' heads with foolishness and nonsense. But to Melchi it's all very real. If he talks about Mulo or boogeymen, it's because he believes what he's saying. One thing I know for sure, Melchi's no liar."

Boggs leaned forward. "So you're saying he actually believes in the Boogeyman?"

"Let me tell you something about Melchi. He's sharp as a tack. Lives in a whole different world than you and me. You girls are from the university, right?"

Hailey and Boggs nodded.

"Well, Melchi's had a hard life. His parents were murdered when he was a little baby. I doubt he's ever set foot in a proper school, but he's got a better education than you or I will ever have." The old lady looked Hailey in the eye, challenging her to disagree. "He has me check out science and math books from the library. And know what he does with them? He works the problems. Straight through. And I'm not talking easy math either. Calculus and linear algebra, and differ, diff . . ."

"Differential equations?" Boggs's eyes were wide.

"Works them straight through." The old lady smiled. "Hanged if I know if they're right, but they look like the examples in the books. And why would he spend his time reading and working if he wasn't doing them right?"

"Why do you suppose he needs to know so much math?" Hailey asked.

"I don't know. Just likes learning, I guess. Don't ask me how or why, but he even knows Latin. Do either of you girls know Latin?"

Hailey shook her head. "Do you know where he lives?"

"In the park." The woman laughed. "He calls it his nest, like he's a baby bird. But don't judge him by where he lives or how he dresses. Know what he does all day? He goes around trying to help people. Sometimes stays up all night, trying to save them from the bad guys. The boogeymen. That's what his Mulo are: all the hateful people in this city whose business it is to hurt others. People like that, Melchi can't even begin to understand them. No wonder they seem like monsters to him. And sweet girls like you are his children of the Standing. The ones he thinks it's his duty to protect. He takes it very serious. Thinks he's serving his God." The old woman's eyes met hers.

"He calls himself the long-awaited child of prophecy."

# ∽ 13 ∾

Athena leaned back in her chair and looked around the candlelit table. Bleary faces, drooping eyelids, contented moans. The buzz of excitement over Sabazios's offer had finally died down, and now the reality of how much food they had eaten was beginning to sink in. It was worse than Thanksgiving. She felt like she was going to explode.

She looked down at her half-eaten soufflé and pushed the plate away from her. The room tilted and swayed around her, like a mother rocking her child to sleep. A warm blanket of silence settled over her shoulders. Soft, soothing . . .

*No.* She shook herself and turned to face Sabazios. She had to say something. Something clever and witty and lively enough to keep her awake.

She was distracted by the sound of muffled voices. Shuffling feet at the door. A line of black suits and evening gowns were filing into the room to stand in a half circle around the table. Sagging faces. Vacant eyes. What was going on? Athena turned to the other guests. The guys on the far side of the table were staring past her with rapt, dazzled eyes. She followed their gazes across the room to a woman in a ridiculously low-cut gown. *Oh please* . . .

Athena rolled her eyes. What was Sabazios up to now?

She turned back to her host and smiled. He was talking to her. Something about a hand. Her hand?

The room shimmered like a desert mirage. He was reaching toward her, taking her by the hand. Red-hot fire burned up her arm, igniting her thoughts into a caldron of roiling passion. Dark eyes charged the air with pulsing energy. Probing tendrils of flame, burning through her skin, pushing into the darkness of her soul.

Deep in the back of her mind, a warning sounded, but it didn't make sense. Everything was perfect. The meal, the brooch, the company, everything. She watched in fascination as his lips moved. The musical lilt of his voice, the silent poetry of his eyes. He was so incredibly good-looking. How could she still be so hungry?

She leaned toward him and reached out to touch his face. He released her hand, pressed something hard into her palm. His voice washed through her, its waves reverberating, liquid echoes within her soul. *The emerald, jewel of the Amazon, blazing star of heaven, true light of Eve's pure soul.*

Her body quivered. She stood before him naked on a sandy beach, swaying to the silent music welling up inside her soul. He held out a golden chain, a sparkling emerald. Her gemstone. It was meant for her since the beginning of time. She was meant for it. He opened the clasp and slid the chain around her neck, brushing her neck with flames of golden fire.

She reached for his arms and pulled them tight around her. She would be his soon. His eagerness was a burning ache in her soul. To shed this body, crippled and useless. The room tilted, and she was free. She was behind herself watching. She saw herself sitting on the edge of her chair, leaning toward Sabazios. His eyes caught fire and stared right through her, filling the room with smoldering rage. And then she was back inside her body. Sabazios stood over her, glaring across the room.

She turned and the world spun around her like a top. Behind her stood a hunched man. Drool ran from a sagging mouth. Lopsided black eyes burned through her like a knife.

She stumbled out of her chair, holding onto the table for balance. "Bathroom. I've got to get to the bathroom." She barely recognized the slurred voice as her own.

A tuxedo appeared. Sabazios's concerned face. Why couldn't they understand? She hadn't had too much to drink. She just needed some air.

The room pounded beneath her feet. Bright lights flashed in her eyes. She was holding on to a man's arm. Mirrors and statues. Fountains of crystal light.

A door opened, and she was alone in a tiled room. Marble counters, brass mirrors, clamshell sinks. Drugged. That's what it had to be. She had been drugged. But why? She stumbled forward, watching as her reflection flickered in the mirror. Drifting to the right, back to the left, drifting to the right again. She was just tired, that was all, a calm voice reasoned inside her head. She should get some rest, a short nap on the glistening marble floor.

*No!* She slammed her knuckles against the counter, and her reflection came into focus. The necklace hadn't been a dream. A jewel-encrusted pendant hung around her neck. At its center was the biggest emerald she had ever seen.

Voices sounded at the door. Athena stumbled backward and slammed into a row of gleaming stalls. She could feel them, crawling around in her head. They wanted to take her. They knew where she lived.

Shutting herself in a stall, she pulled her keychain from her purse and used a key to pop the pin out of the hinge. One more hinge and she was dragging the heavy stall door over to the wall, bracing it against the bathroom door.

A loud knock echoed in her ears. An angry voice. The knob turned, and the door rattled on its hinges.

A blast of rage hit Athena in the chest, knocking her to the floor. She rolled backward, hit her head, rolled some more. Heavy thuds shook the bathroom. Angry voices buzzing in her brain. Bracing herself against a cold marble wall, she pushed up onto her feet.

Red silk curtains. An ornate window. She pried at the heavy latch until the window pushed open and a cool breeze struck her in the face. Far beneath her, the city opened out like the arms of a lover. Soft lights against a blanket of darkness. Off to the right, almost swallowed up by the darkness, a fire escape wound up the corner of the building. It was too far away. Too far by far.

A crash sounded behind her. The crack of splintering wood. She climbed up onto the windowsill, leaned out into the darkness and wind.

A low growl rumbled through her body, paralyzing her muscles. The night twisted around her. She could see herself framed in the window. Rigid and shaking with fright. Easy prey in the eyes of the hunter.

And then she jumped.

---

HAILEY SQUINTED AGAINST THE headlights of the VW Bug and waved as Boggs pulled the puttering car away from the curb. The old wooden porch creaked and groaned as she clunked up the steps and walked to the door. She fumbled in the darkness for a key and inserted it into the lock. The city was unusually still. She could hear the soft whisper of leaf scraping against leaf.

"Hello?" she called out into the night. "If you're out there, I really need to talk to you. I have a question about this Mulo you were talking about. I need to understand what it means to be one of your Standing people."

Ominous silence swallowed up her words. She opened the door and stepped inside. "Hello, Tiff?"

She clomped up the stairs and sat down on her bed, propping her foot up on her pillow. What did she do now? Sit back and wait for herself to go crazy? She wasn't made for inaction. She was a scientist—a researcher. If the world refused to give up its secrets voluntarily, her job was to grab it by the throat and wrestle them away by force. Starting with Mulo.

She pulled out her laptop and waited for it to boot. Even if Melchi had made bad people into monsters, the word had to come from somewhere. The whole child-of-the-Standing struggle between good and evil thing sounded far too well thought out, even if he was crazy. She clicked on her browser and typed *Mulo* into Google. It came back with over a million hits—acronyms, crosses between mules and horses, vampires . . .

*Gypsy* vampires! Spirits of the dead.

Melchi had talked about Gypsies. He'd thought it significant Gypsies had been massacred in the Holocaust. Gypsies and mental patients. Was there some sort of connection? Why hadn't she asked more questions? She should never have turned her back on him. What had she been thinking? The guy was jumpy as a hyperactive squirrel.

A dim memory percolated up through her thoughts. The detective at the mental hospital had been interested in Melchi. What was his name? Detective Smiley? Did he know something she didn't?

She pictured her homeless man dropping though the tree, landing catlike on the walk in front of her. He had been waiting for her, perched above her like a mountain lion waiting for its prey. She shuddered and set the laptop aside.

A loud creaking noise sounded somewhere above her. She sucked in her breath and froze, listening for the faintest indication of movement.

Silence.

She pulled out her phone and punched in Boggs's number.

"Boggs here."

"Boggs. This is Hailey. I—" She paused. Was that another noise?

"Hailey. Are you all right?"

"I guess so. I don't really know anymore. So much has—" A loud thump, right above her. It was definitely coming from the roof.

"Hailey? What's happening? Hailey?"

"Boggs," Hailey whispered into the phone, "I've got to go. I think someone's on the roof."

"Oh my gosh, lock the doors and stay away from the windows. I'll call 911."

"No, please . . . don't call the police. It might be him—the homeless man. I've got to talk to . . . I mean, if he didn't try to hurt me today, he couldn't be dangerous. Right?"

"What if it's not him? Hailey, this is crazy!"

"Just promise me. Don't call the police. I'll call them myself if it's not him."

"But what if it's—"

"Just don't call the police. Please. I've got to go now. Bye."

Hailey hung up and tiptoed down the stairs. She had to hurry. Boggs might call the police at any time.

She drew back the dead bolt with a loud snap and leaned trembling against the doorway. If she was wrong . . . if it wasn't Melchi. Or even if it was. The guy lived in a nest. He couldn't be the most stable isotope in the periodic table.

Her stomach churned as she stepped out onto the porch. How stupid could she get? At least the red shirts in slasher films carried flashlights.

*Crash!* Hailey's cell phone flew out of her hand as an overhead explosion plunged the house into darkness. She dove for the open doorway as pieces of plastic skittered across the porch. Slamming the door behind her, she struggled with the dead bolt, tugging on it, banging on it with her fists. She threw her shoulder into the door, again and again, until the bolt turned with a grating *chink*. Then, running through the dark room, she tripped over the sofa and landed in a heap on the floor.

The cell phone was busted. She had to find Tiff's land line.

Crawling on her hands and knees, she felt her way across the kitchenette. Irregular patches of moonlight outlined a shadowy cross. Skirting around the light, she felt her way across the counter. The base was there, but the phone wasn't on it. *Dear God. Please help me. Please don't let him find me.* Why hadn't she let Boggs call 911?

A rattling noise shook the tree by the porch. She swept her arms across the counter, across the kitchen table. The back of her arm hit something that went clattering to the floor. She pounced on the floor and grabbed up the receiver. Fumbling with the buttons, she finally hit the *talk* switch and the phone lit up like a beacon. She stabbed at the numbers and waited. The phone was dead.

*God, help me. Please.*

A woman's scream, sudden and shrill, echoed from the front of the house. Hailey collapsed onto the floor as an icy numbness spread outward from her heart.

It sounded like Boggs.

ATHENA LAY CRUMPLED AND panting on the frigid fire escape decking. Her right hip and stomach burned with nauseating pain. Probing tendrils of rage snaked through her mind. She couldn't escape. She was going to die.

Gritting her teeth against the pain, she clawed her way forward until her legs were free of the entangling bars. The image of a dark hand filled her mind. Twisting snakes, grotesque figures, invading darkness.

She climbed onto her feet and leaned against the rail. Sharp pain radiated out from her hip like an exploding sun. Probing eyes stabbed at her from the darkened windows. Fiery rage hung in the air, pressing down on her like a crowded mosh pit. She couldn't breathe. Her muscles refused to respond.

She leaned forward and fell, crashing into the metal deck. Pain tore through her body, ripping through her paralysis. She struggled forward on her hands and knees, tumbled down the spiraling steps. More steps, more falls. She tumbled down flight after flight, blind and numb to all but the urgency of her panic.

So close. She was going to make it! New energy surged through her body. She burst through the surface of a dark nightmare. Triumph!

Athena slammed her fist into a rail and shook her head to clear her mind. *No.* She couldn't go down. They were waiting for her.

She stopped and searched the surrounding darkness. She could feel their eagerness. At the bottom of the fire escape, a whole mob of them, waiting in the parking lot two stories below. Backing up against the building, she climbed over the fire escape railing and crawled out onto a small ornamental ledge. Pressing her body against the rough wall, she felt her way along the gritty surface.

Halfway to the corner she noticed the sloped roofline of an adjoining building just ten feet below. A few more feet. If she didn't land on the side facing away from the fire escape, she was dead.

She jumped from the ledge and smacked into the building. Tumbling down the shingled slope, she toppled off the roof and hit the ground with an agonizing thud. She lay still, too stunned to move. *Oh God . . . make the pain stop. Please.*

The sound of running footsteps tapped at the periphery of her agony. She struggled to stand, but her body refused to move. *God, please. If you're there . . .*

In a final burst of desperation, she crawled out of the entangling shrubs and ran.

From shadow to shadow, she pushed her way into the heart of the night. Footsteps echoing in her ears, the gasping sob of ragged breaths, she ran until she couldn't run any more.

Heavy footsteps. They were still behind her. Tendrils of sickening decay licked at the back of her mind. She couldn't outrun them; they were already in her head.

She cut across the street to an old garage wedged between two boarded-up warehouses. Throwing herself to the ground, she wriggled beneath a rusty gate. They were coming for her. They knew where she was.

She scrambled across the trash-covered pavement and burrowed beneath a pile of moldering cardboard, clenching her teeth as wave upon wave of exultation crashed against her brain.

———

MELCHI POUNDED DOWN THE hill, searching the side streets and alleyways to the right and left. A silent scream quivered up his spine. Her presence was so strong. Why couldn't he tell which direction she had gone? He slowed to a jog and circled a wide intersection. To the right maybe? Straight ahead?

A rumbling growl rattled through his skull. Whatever it was, it was getting closer. Melchi glanced back over his shoulder and ran on to the next intersection, but she wasn't any closer. If anything she was even farther away.

A high-pitched shriek sliced through the air. Behind him—off to the left. He ran back down the street and cut across the intersection. Through a parking lot, over a wall, out into the street. He heard a whimpering cry. There. Behind an overgrown chain-link fence.

Melchi ran, planted a foot in the middle of the fence, and vaulted over it, landing in a crouch on the other side. Framed against the reflected light of a white garage door, a hulking shadow carried the struggling figure of a girl—a girl with green hair!

The figure turned slowly, transferring the girl to one arm. Raw power crackled in the air. Twisted, primal, unspeakably evil.

Melchi balanced lightly on the balls of his feet, waiting for the lunge that would almost certainly end his life. Another low rumble climbed up his spine. He felt its presence as it reached out toward him. Filthy, hungry, and vile. Echoes of surprise and confusion mingled with the girl's terror. Something was wrong.

The girl cried out as she was flung against the building, and then, faster than thought, the creature charged.

Melchi met the attack with a foot to its midsection. Then, rolling with the charge, he lunged out with both feet, sending the creature crashing into the fence. The night exploded with rage. Melchi rolled onto his feet and probed the shadows for the girl. Finding an ankle, he lifted her struggling form off the ground, then lowering his shoulder, he rammed into the door of the garage.

The door frame groaned, but the heavy metal held. Taking a step back, he hurled his weight into the door again and bounced back as it burst open with a crash. He stepped into the shielding darkness, but his foot was grabbed from behind. Holding up the girl to protect her from the fall, he slammed into the floor. The girl struggled to her feet and ran inside as Melchi was dragged back into the moonlight. He kicked hard with his free foot and was rewarded with a savage bite to his calf. Twisting onto his back, he let the creature drag him through the door. Then, pulling his knees to his chest, he feinted with his right hand as he kicked both feet upward into the creature's chest. It flew through the air and landed with the crack of its head against the cement.

Melchi rolled onto his feet and plunged into the garage. Stepping to the side, he waited for the scraping steps and then slammed the door shut with all his might. A satisfying *whack* rattled the door just before it hit the frame. The sound of a large body crumpling to the ground.

Gritting his teeth against the rage filling his mind, Melchi felt his way to a rectangle of light at the back of the garage. The girl had run back outside. Terrified people always took the path that put the most distance between themselves and their fears— the path that always made tracking them easiest. He ran through the back lot and down a long narrow street.

Reaching out with his mind, he fought through the rage of the wounded beast. Finally, after what seemed an eternity, he felt it. Not the uncontrolled terror he'd been searching for but a weak, pulsating fear. Controlled and cautious, modulated by the frequency of an active mind. Melchi ran back toward the garage. She had turned to the side after all. Most likely she was hiding not far from the building. He quickened his step. The creature would start searching soon. He didn't have much time.

Melchi jogged back across the road and looked up and down the street. He could feel her. She was somewhere nearby, but where? Off to the left at the corner of a dark warehouse, he noticed a pile of trash next to a small trash can. The container was just big enough to hold her. He tiptoed back to the can and crouched down beside it.

"Don't be afraid. It's me. The man who tried to rescue you." Melchi spoke the words aloud to the plastic can. "It's not safe here. The creature is searching for you. It can sense your emotions."

Melchi waited for a reply, but the can was silent. "I give you my solemn vow that I will not knowingly hurt you. I am sorry that I touched you. I was trying to save your life." He paused again. He could feel her presence, strong and near. Fear. Indecision.

"I'm going to open the lid now. Please don't scream."

Melchi pulled the lid off the trash can and looked inside. The trash can was empty.

The rush of fabric and wind was all the warning he got before a sickening *thunk* to the back of his head filled his mind with pain and hot light.

He was unconscious before he hit the ground.

# ∽ 14 ∾

Hailey pressed herself against the wall of the kitchen as a loud creak sounded from the front porch. Footsteps—just outside the door. And then banging. A loud cry. She pulled the kitchen chairs around her as the shout cut through her panic, resolving itself into a vaguely familiar voice.

"Boggs?" Relief washed through her. She lay on the floor, drinking in the comforting voice.

"Hailey! Are you okay? Hailey?" More pounding at the door. "Hailey!" Then silence.

Hailey snapped back to herself. "In here. I'm in here!" She pushed her way through the chairs. "I'm in here. Don't go!"

"Hailey!"

"I'm here!" Eyes brimming with tears, Hailey ran across the room and pounded on the door. "Don't leave! I'm in here!"

"Are you okay? Can you unlock the door?"

Hailey opened the door and pulled Boggs inside. Then she put her shoulder to the door and slammed it shut. Sobs wracked her body as she tried to work at the lock with frantic, fumbling fingers. Boggs reached around her and turned the lock.

"It's okay, Hailey. Everything is going to be just fine." Boggs flipped the light switch up and down. "What's wrong with the lights?"

"He . . . they . . ." Hailey's stomach clenched into a hard knot. She couldn't control herself. The tears wouldn't stop. She dropped onto the couch and collapsed into Boggs's shoulder.

"It's okay, Sweetie. It's okay."

Soft whispers. Fingertips brushing through her hair. A sob shook her body. She was a little girl again, crying in her mother's arms. Trixie had gotten hit by a car. She was never going to see her again.

"It's okay. You're safe now. Everything's going to be okay."

Hailey lifted her head and wiped a sleeve across her eyes and nose.

"I'm sorry. I don't know what's gotten into me. It's just . . . I've been afraid so long. I can't do anything about it. It's never going to stop."

"Shhh . . . It's okay. It'll all be over soon."

"No it won't. I can't tell what's real and what's not. The doctor said there isn't a cure."

"Hailey, look at me."

Hailey wiped her eyes and searched her friend's face in the semidarkness.

"I was here this time. Something really came down from the tree. The power is off here, but every other house in the neighborhood has lights."

"Something's outside? But you—"

"Something ran right past me. I don't think it's out there anymore, but—"

"We've got to get out of here. He knows where we are." Hailey started to get up, but Boggs pulled her back down.

"The police will be here any minute. I called them before I came. But who's *he*? Who are you so afraid of?"

A knock sounded at the front door, making Hailey jump.

Boggs sat rigid, looking at the door with wide eyes. "Who is it?"

"Jim Murray. SF Police Department. We got a call."

Hailey rushed to the door and put her eye to the security peephole. The man outside aimed a flashlight at his chest. He was wearing a badge.

She unlocked the door and opened it wide. "Please come in."

The officer stepped inside and swept the light around the room. "We got a call that there was a problem here?"

"Y–yes. I was upstairs talking on the phone to a friend, and I heard someone on the roof." Hailey paused, wondering if she should let Officer Murray ask the questions.

Silence.

"And when I went outside to investigate, I heard a crash and the power went out. The phone went out too. My friend called the police."

"Okay, I'll check it out. Is everything okay inside?"

Hailey nodded.

The officer closed the door behind him. Boggs crossed the room and put an arm around Hailey.

A few minutes later, Officer Murray came back in.

"I think I found the problem. Looks like a rotten branch fell on the power line. It missed the telephone line though. Can I see your phone?"

"Over here." Hailey led him to the kitchen and retrieved the phone from the floor.

"Portables don't work when the power is off. Even with a battery backup, you have to put them back on the base first."

Hailey crossed the room to the corded phone and lifted the handset. A dial tone blared in her ear. "Now I really feel like an idiot. This one works fine."

"Well, it looks like everything is okay here. You probably just got a visit from a raccoon. Power company will come right out and fix that line." Murray turned toward the door.

"Officer Murray. I have something else to report too."

Murray turned to Hailey and waited.

"This is going to sound strange, but I was attacked last week by a man with a knife, and last night I think someone was following me."

The officer raised an eyebrow. "And you reported these attacks?"

Hailey nodded. "Do you know Detective Smiley?"

"Sure do. Used to work with him before he made detective."

"Well, I think he's working on the first attack, but I haven't told him yet about the second. Could you let him know I want to talk to him?"

"Sure, but I can take the report. You know, while I'm already here."

Hailey shook her head. "I need to talk to him personally. Tell him I . . . I've seen the homeless man that rescued me. The one he was so interested in. He'll know what I mean."

Officer Murray took out a notebook and started writing. "Okay, I'll tell him. We're a little undermanned right now, but I'm sure he'll get to you when he can." He flipped his notebook shut and moved toward the door.

"One more thing." Hailey stepped forward. "You said you knew Detective Smiley. What's he like?"

Murray stopped and raised an eyebrow again. "Is this a personal question or strictly professional?"

"What do you mean?"

Murray grinned. "Smiley is a great guy. A real hero. Not married or dating anyone as far as I know."

"That's not why I'm asking." She looked down at the floor. "Was he, um, recently injured?"

"His arm, you mean?"

Hailey nodded.

"It happened about a year ago when he was still in uniform. Story is, he almost got killed saving a little boy's life. At first he had a hard time coping, but he's a fighter. Doctors say there's no nerve damage. It could get better with time."

Hailey smiled. "Thanks. I appreciate your coming out."

Officer Murray nodded. "Don't worry. He's a good man. I'm sure he'll get back to you soon on this." He grinned again and opened the door. "Be a fool not to." The door shut with a click.

Hailey looked around the dark room, listening as a car started and drove off.

"Hailey, could you do me a favor?" Boggs put a hand on Hailey's shoulder. "I'm way too spooked to stay alone tonight. Would you mind spending the night at my place?"

"Sure." Hailey gave her friend a hug. "What good are fruitcakes if you can't pass them around?"

———

ATHENA LOWERED THE BRICK to the sidewalk and examined the man lying crumpled at her feet. What if he had been telling the truth? What if he really was trying to rescue her? She hadn't meant to hit him so hard, but he was way too big to take any chances.

Bracing a foot against a parking meter, she rolled him onto his side, but a lump behind his shoulders prevented her from turning him all the way over. She pressed her fingers to his wrist but couldn't be sure if she was doing it right. Great. If anybody saw her . . .

Digging through the trash she had emptied out of the trash can, she grabbed a paper-bag-wrapped bottle and pressed it into the big man's hand. There. That would buy her a little time.

"Okay, big guy. What are you packing?" Athena searched his pockets, and a bulge inside his coat caught her eye. She reached into the pocket, and her hand closed around something hard and cylindrical. She drew it out of his pocket, shielding it from the street with her body. It was a wooden dowel, sharpened on one end to a flattened point.

Not exactly what she was hoping for. She put the sharpened stick back in his pocket. Why was he carrying around a stake? She shuddered, not liking where her thoughts were leading. What if Benedict and his fanty boys were right? What if the whole vampire thing was real?

She checked the rest of his pockets and found a plastic spray bottle filled with clear liquid and a few newspaper articles but no money and no guns.

"Okay, big guy. If you aren't one of them, then I'm sorry about your head. But if you are, then remember this: Compared to what I'm going to do to you next time, this was just a love pat."

Climbing to her feet, she backed away from the body. Running would only draw attention. And speaking of attention, she had to do something about her hair. She reached down and tore a wide strip from the bottom of her dress and wrapped it around her head, tucking in as many loose strands of hair as she could feel. Thiry dollars down the drain. Oh well. She patted the lump under her dress. As long as she held onto the jewels, she was rich. She could afford a hundred dresses.

All she had to do was get out of town alive.

She strolled down the street, letting her eyes wander from side to side. A cold breeze blasted her in the face. It was getting colder, and she didn't have a coat. Where could she go now? They had to know where she lived. And if they already knew about Benedict, they probably knew about most of her friends. But would Benedict really sell her out if they offered to turn him?

She headed down a side street and began to run. Benedict knew all of her friends, every place she might try to hide. They had been hanging for months. There was only one place she could go. She made her way to the closest police station. They'd never have to know about the gems. If they were hot, the hotel gang wouldn't be able to report them. And even if they weren't, Sabey's boys had way too much to hide. But she had to be careful. They also had money, and money could buy anything—including little men in crisp blue uniforms.

A bank of fog rolled silently through the city, blocking out the light of the moon. She drifted through the dark deserted streets, keeping as much as possible to the shadows hugging the feet of the graffiti-stained buildings.

Finally she saw the lights of the police station, shining through the fog. Covering the bulge under her dress with her hand, she crept toward the entrance of the station. A wave of relief washed over her, sending goose bumps coursing up and down her spine. A wave of exultation.

Two dark figures stepped slowly out of the light. One of them lurched forward, radiating grotesque shadows against the fog-drenched light. Athena swallowed back the lump rising in her throat.

Suddenly she was hungry. Very hungry.

---

"OKAY BUDDY, UP YOU go! Easy."

Melchi dragged a stiff hand across his eyes. His head throbbed as he straightened his neck to sit up. Where was he? What was happening?

A hand grabbed his shoulder and pulled him forward. Melchi swung his arm in a tight circle to break the grip. Then, rolling backward, he threw himself into a back handspring and landed in ready position.

"What in the . . . well, I guess we don't have to go through the drunk tests."

Melchi squeezed his eyes shut, trying to bring them into focus.

"Easy buddy. Nobody wants a fight."

Gradually, he was able to make out the vague outline of a man holding a flashlight.

"I need to ask you a couple of questions. Just routine."

Light from the flashlight spilled onto the black-and-white car next to the curb. Right behind the officer, silhouetted against the fog, a telephone pole stood with staggered climbing bars starting about ten feet above the ground.

"First, I need to see some identification? Do you have a driver's license?"

Melchi stepped toward the police officer, holding out his hand. Then, leaping for the lowest bar on the pole, he pulled himself, hand over hand, up the pole until he was high enough to scamper to the top. Without pausing, he leaped from the pole to the roof of the adjacent building.

A quick glance confirmed the officer wasn't following him. Good. He was just standing there, shining his flashlight up and down the pole. Melchi crept to the back of the roof and climbed up the next building where he collapsed against an old air-conditioning unit.

A burning pain coursed up the back of his right leg. It felt like poison. Rolling up his pant leg, he examined the bite wound by the light of the fog-covered moon. It was warm to the touch. Red and puffy, scabbed over with dried blood.

No. It wasn't possible!

A Mulo's bite couldn't turn. Ortus had said the old stories were exaggerated. Silly superstition. It was just a nasty wound, nothing more.

*By becoming the enemy, he shall shield the world from the enemy's dark stain . . .*

*No!* Melchi tried to stand, but his vision darkened and he almost passed out. Strange sensations throbbed though his brain. He felt nauseous, twisted from the inside out. The prophecy. The part that had always scared him most. How else could he become the enemy? Ortus had never been bitten. How could he possibly know the Mulo's bite wouldn't turn? If bites couldn't turn, where did all the others come from? The hotel was swarming with Mulo-creatures.

He pushed himself to his feet and limped to the back of the roof. Easing himself over the edge, he dropped onto an old utility building and climbed down a rusty milling machine. Now what? Back to the roof to watch the hotel? A shudder passed through his frame. He had been watching them for days, and what good had it done? He wasn't any closer to defeating them. He was just putting off the inevitable. After all these years he had finally tracked the Mulo to its lair. It was his job to destroy it. He might not have much time.

The burning in his leg had already reached past his knee.

He took a deep breath and limped back toward the hotel. The creature carrying the green-haired girl had almost killed him. He hadn't even sensed it sneaking up on him. What hope did he have of defeating a whole building full of them? He needed a plan. Something to at least give him a chance. But every minute he delayed was another minute the Mulo might discover the girl.

*Hailey. The young Dawn with fingertips of rose . . .*

The memory of their conversation flooded back to him. He hadn't told her about the Mulo's creatures. He hadn't warned her about the hotel.

*Holy One, please . . . Just a few more minutes. Just one last chance to say good-bye.* He turned and started jogging in the direction of Hailey's house. The more he ran, the more his right leg burned. A strange sensation rang in his ears. He felt light-headed, dizzy.

*Holy One, forgive me. I didn't mean to touch the girl. I didn't think . . .*

Tears burned in his eyes, disrupting his vision. A deep aching hunger gnawed at his bones. *Holy One, please. Let her be home. Let me see her one more time.* He slowed to a jog as he turned onto her street. The house was dark. He'd have to wake her up. It was too important to risk a delay.

Heart pounding in his throat, he stepped toward the porch and faltered. There, sitting in front of the door, was an enormous bouquet of flowers. He crept up the steps and raised a hand to the door, but the smell of the flowers overwhelmed him. Star-shaped pinks, clustered white spears with red stripes, tiny white lace. So many different flowers—varieties he had never even seen before—all arranged in a beautiful glass vase.

He remembered the man in the beautiful suit with his white gloves and shiny black car. A man who lived in a real house, who had money to buy exotic flowers. A card poked out from the greenery. *Hailey* was written on the envelope in a beautiful, flowing script. What did he have to offer her? To be woken in the middle of the night just so he could satisfy his own selfish desires? And what if she came out in her nightclothes? What would he do then? What if his visit tarnished her reputation?

Melchi sank to the ground and buried his face in his hands. The thought of hurting her was too much to bear. His wasn't a life; it was a nightmare. Better to fight the Mulo and get it over with.

But first . . . one small gift. He shrugged out of his coat and pulled off his knapsack. Unzipping the bag, he was about to thrust his hand inside when a faint chill brushed across his mind. A distant stirring in the direction of the hotel. This was it.

It was time.

Melchi pulled out a small bundle and shucked off its plastic coverings. Then, stroking the faded blue cover of his Milton, he set it on the porch next to the door.

He wouldn't be needing it anymore.

Not where he was going.

---

BLUE SKIES AND SUNSHINE. How could she have been so paranoid? Hailey rolled down the passenger window and let the cool afternoon air whip her hair into a frenzy. A raccoon and a fallen branch. How stupid could she get?

She looked up the street at Tiffany's shabby little house and noticed a splash of color on the porch. Flowers? The bouquet was huge. Who could they be from? Sabazios? Maybe Boggs wouldn't notice.

"Hailey, flowers!" Boggs cried out the second she pulled up to the house.

"Wait here. I'll be right out with my stuff."

"Not on your life!" Boggs got out of the car and circled around to help Hailey unfold herself and get her walking boot out of the door. "You're not going back in that house until I check it out myself. Besides, I've got to see who your secret admirer is."

"Thanks, Mom." Hailey allowed herself to be pulled onto the porch. They were probably for Tiffany anyway.

No, the card had her name on it.

"Open it. Who's it from?"

Hailey opened the card and read it to herself and then aloud.

"'Sorry you still haven't recovered. If there's anything I can do to help, please call me at one of these numbers. Sabazios.'"

"You're not going to call him."

"Don't you think I should at least thank him? It seems like—" Hailey noticed a worn book sitting next to the flowers. She reached over and picked it up. *Paradise Lost*? That was the last book she'd expect to get from Sabazios. It wasn't even a new copy.

Boggs lifted the vase. "Want to bring them to my place?"

"We'd better leave them here. They'll never fit in your car." Hailey grinned, wondering what Tiff would think when she got home and saw that Hailey had been sent flowers.

She slipped the card inside the book and tucked the envelope back into the clip to let her roommate know who they were for. It would drive her crazy.

Opening the door, they stepped cautiously inside. Everything seemed normal. Boggs set the flowers on the coffee table and crept up the stairs.

"Everything's good up here." She called from the bedroom while Hailey checked the bathroom.

Hailey packed a shopping bag with her things while Boggs packed her laptop in its case. Then, leaving a note for Tiffany to let her know why the power was out, they threw Hailey's stuff in the back of the car and drove back to Boggs's apartment.

Boggs's apartment could only be described as boggling. Garage-sale furniture, Crayola-colored walls, homemade bookshelves stacked high with books. Piles of electronic debris were scattered everywhere. Hailey cleared a spot on the sofa and sat down with Sabazios's book.

Boggs picked up the pair of iPods Hailey had set aside and clipped them both to her waist. "Diastereo. See? I crossed the wires." She held up a single set of headphones attached to two different MP3 players. "A different song for each ear. I got the idea from chemical diastereomers and thought it might keep me from singing along with the music. Kind of a dumb idea, huh?"

"But in a brilliant sort of way." Hailey smiled and started flipping through the pages of Sabazios's book. Every square inch of the margins was covered in a fine script. She took out the card and compared the handwriting.

"They're different, see? The handwriting on the card and inside the book." Hailey held up the card and the book for Boggs to inspect.

"The card could have been written by the florist," Boggs suggested. "Or if this Sabazios guy is as rich as he looked, he probably had his secretary write it." She put the headphones on and danced back toward her bedroom.

Hailey angled the book to read one of the comments printed in the margin.

> *Man hath his daily work of body or mind*
> *Appointed, which declares his Dignity,*
> *And the regard of Heav'n on all his ways.*
>
> *Oh may I not an animal be, unseen by Holy Eyes*
> *But serve with every waking hour*
> *The Master of Land and Skies*

She smiled to herself, noting that the first three lines had been lifted from the adjacent passage. It wasn't hard to imagine the tall, proud man she had met in the bar taking it upon himself to rewrite Milton.

She tried to read the text of the passage, but her eye kept wandering back to the notes in the margins. It was like reading a diary—so intimate. Revealing. What had she said to make him so serious about her? She tried to think back to their conversation, but it was all a blur.

Boggs walked back into the living room. She had changed back into jeans and her hair was in a ponytail. "I've got to run if I'm going to make it on time. Are you sure you don't want to come?" She unlocked the front door of the building and took a key off her key ring.

Hailey looked up from her book. "Yeah, I'll be fine."

"Okay, help yourself to anything in the fridge." Boggs handed Hailey the key. "I'll try to be back by nine."

Hailey waved her friend out the door and turned back to Sabazios's notes. His comments were startlingly passionate. Every rambling monologue, every wordy description, every historical allusion seemed to excite his keenest interest. It didn't make sense. Why had he blasted the book at the bar? He obviously loved it.

She flipped to the front of the book, and his tone changed— from peals of ringing praise to thunderclaps of angry criticism. Every description of Satan bought a storm of protest from Sabazios's pen. Apparently, Sabazios disagreed with Milton's treatment of Satan, thinking the archfiend much less noble than Milton portrayed him.

Hailey was taken aback by his passion. It was almost unsettling. She flipped forward until she came to the end of book four. An entire page was blue with the ink of his pen.

> *Shee as a veil down to the slender waist*
> *Her unadorned golden tresses wore*
> *Dishevell'd, but in wanton ringlets wav'd*
> *As the Vine curls her tendrils, which impli'd*
> *Subjection, but requir'd with gentle sway,*
> *And by her yielded, by him best receiv'd,*
> *Yielded with coy submission, modest pride,*
> *And sweet reluctant amorous delay.*

*Oh Holy One, upon Thy mighty throne*
*How much more than a rib I'd gladly give?*
*My strength to fight for Thee and Thee alone,*
*My tongue to sing Thy praises while I live,*
*Mine eyes I give, they'll never leave her face,*
*My heart to love and serve her as my own,*
*For softness shee and sweet attractive grace.*

*Man, the near-sighted beast*
*    who moves past hill green and rose soft*
*    in the forced march of soldier's pace,*
*Is not blind who sees woman*
*    with the wonder of the moment*
*    reflected in her face.*
*He sees the greater beauty*
*    with vision magnified by love*
*    and made precious by her grace.*

She finished the page and devoured the notes in the margins of the following chapters. The flowery prose harkened back to another age. An age of chivalry, honor, and valor. An age of knights and fair ladies. An age of intense and passionate love. But it wasn't the intensity of the love that surprised her; it was the object.

Sabazios was in love with Eve.

Hailey picked up the phone and dialed the number on Sabazios's card. It was answered at the first ring.

"Hello, Sabazios speaking."

"Hi, Sabazios. This is Hailey Maniates. We met at that bar on Ninth Avenue?"

"Ah, yes. Hailey. How are you feeling?"

"I'm fine. I just wanted to thank you for the book and the flowers."

"The book? Yes, of course. They were the least I could do considering what you must be going through."

"I barely know what to say. I've been reading it all night. It's very moving. Beautiful. But I don't feel right about keeping it. I mean it's too . . . it must be very special to you."

"Yes. Quite." His voice sounded tight. Was he embarrassed?

"I'm sorry. I didn't mean to sound unappreciative, it's just that—"

"Hailey?" Sabazios's voice broke through her thoughts.

"Yes?" Hailey bit her lip. She was blowing it big time.

"I would much prefer continuing this discussion in person. Have you eaten dinner yet?"

"No." Hailey looked at her half-eaten sandwich. "I mean I haven't eaten—not really. I'd love to go to dinner, but I'm not dressed and—" Hailey stopped herself. She was doing it again. Why couldn't she just go out and have fun? Boggs herself had said she shouldn't be alone. And after reading his book, she knew beyond a shadow of doubt Sabazios was trustworthy.

"I'd love to go out to dinner."

"Marvelous. Is an hour too little time for you to make preparations?"

Hailey considered. "Better make it an hour and a half. I have to go home to change."

"Good then. I'll pick you up at your place in an hour and a half."

She set the phone down and stroked the cover of the faded book. Any man who could write with such nobility, such guileless and forthright passion, surely he was a man to be trusted.

Maybe . . . even more.

# III

*But you must remember that I am not as you are. There is a poison in my blood, in my soul, which may destroy me; which must destroy me, unless some relief comes to us. Oh, my friends, you know as well as I do, that my soul is at stake; and though I know there is one way out for me, you must not and I must not take it!*

Bram Stoker, *Dracula*

# ∽ 15 ∽

Hailey checked herself in the mirror. She needed more time. A rogue wave bulged from her hair on the left, and the right side was limp as overcooked spaghetti. She hurried over to the window and searched the street below. Not a car in sight. She unstrapped her walking boot and took a few experimental steps. Her ankle looked like she'd borrowed it from a hippo, but at least she could walk. A night without her walking boot wasn't going to kill her. It was only dinner.

Headlights traced a slow arc across the ceiling. A car was pulling up to the apartment. A fancy black car like a Jaguar or a Bentley. At least it wasn't a limo. Hailey watched as Sabazios got out of the car and strolled up to the door.

She whirled toward the mirror and examined herself once more before snatching up a sweater and limping down the stairs. If only she had thought to get the rose dress cleaned. Cobalt blue was a good color, but the rose looked so much better on her.

The doorbell sounded, and Hailey paused at the bottom of the stairs. Should she take the book along with her? It would be fun to discuss it with him, but what if it made him uncomfortable? The notes were awfully personal. Maybe when she knew him better.

She opened the door and suppressed a gasp. The man standing before her was right out of a dream. Finely chiseled features, dazzling black eyes, tall, athletic, immaculately dressed. Sabazios was stunning. More so than she remembered.

"Hailey, you look absolutely enchanting." Sabazios smiled and held out his arm.

Hailey raised a hand to the bulge in her hair. "Thank you." She reached out for his offered arm, wondering at her own audacity. Who was she even to touch the sleeve of this man's jacket? He was way out of her league.

"How's your ankle?" He paused to help her down the steps. "I see you're not wearing the cast anymore."

"Oh, it's fine, thank you." Hailey forced her eyes open and shook herself. *Come on Hailey. Wake up. Say something.*

"I'm glad to hear it." Sabazios opened the door for her, and she sank into the comfort of a plush leather seat. The dash sparkled with chrome and polished wood. She reached out and ran a finger across a line of leather stitching. The car was glowing, radiating comfort and warmth. Luxurious languor.

The car dipped and Hailey looked up into Sabazios's downturned face. He hadn't seemed so tall the other night.

"Like the car?"

*Like the car . . .* Hailey repeated the words to herself, waiting for the meaning to sink in. She was melting into the seat, sliding down into a Hailey-shaped puddle on the floorboards. All of a sudden she was so sleepy. She tried to sit up, braced herself against the floor with both feet. A twinge of pain traveled up her ankle and stabbed into her mind.

"Yes, I do." Hailey shook her head. They were already moving. "How fast will it go? Can you go faster?"

The hum of the engine deepened to a throaty roar. Hailey rolled her window down and leaned out into the wind. Cold air lashed at her hair, blasting through the fog swirling in her brain.

She would look like the bride of Frankenstein, but it couldn't be helped. Better an engaging monster than a sleeping beauty.

"I'm sorry. All of a sudden I'm so sleepy. It's not you. I just haven't been sleeping well lately."

"No apologies necessary. I fear I didn't give you much notice."

*Much notice?* Hailey pressed her foot to the floor until her ankle twinged. "Um . . . where are we going?"

"Sutro's at the Cliff House, if you'll be good enough to indulge me. Their new chef is actually quite good, and if the fog holds off, the view should be spectacular. The moon tonight is almost full."

Hailey nodded. She should say something, something witty and intelligent, but her words were lost in a rush of shadowy trees and pounding, swirling wind. She shut her eyes and let the world rush through her. The chill breeze washed down her body, caressing with fingertips of ice. The roar in her ears crowded out the rushing city, lifting her above its confusion, beyond her cares. She wanted to lose herself in the roar, but something at the back of her mind tugged her back.

Something was wrong.

She pushed through a shimmering veil and found only silence. Stomping her foot hard, she started awake. Sabazios was leaning over her seat. A warm hand clasped her shoulder. The car had stopped.

"Sorry to wake you." His black eyes drank in the night, leaving her strangely breathless. "But we're at the restaurant."

"Sorry." She shrugged and managed a weak smile. "I told you I was sleepy."

"Then I must work harder to keep you entertained." Sabazios circled the car and open her door.

She leaned on his arm as he escorted her into an open foyer. Glass ceilings, sparkling lights, murmuring voices. A dozen guests stood crowded in front of the host desk.

"I'll get us a table." Sabazios bypassed the waiting guests and spoke to the maître d' in a low voice. The man left his station and returned immediately with a waiter.

A gray-haired lady frowned at Hailey as Sabazios led her past the other guests. Hailey blushed and looked at the ground, watching their waiter's feet as he led them down to a private dining room at the back of the restaurant.

The waiter seated them and handed them menus. He smiled and bowed and droned on and on about the food. Dungeness crab . . . Calvados broth . . . smoked tomato coulis . . . Hailey tried to take it in, but she was too conscious of Sabazios's unblinking scrutiny. Her heart pounded in her ears as her senses burned with self-awareness. Finally, after what seemed an eternity, the waiter left the room. She swallowed back the lump of panic rising in her throat and looked down at the menu to avoid Sabazios's penetrating stare. The room was stiflingly hot; she could barely breathe.

Hailey rose from her chair and walked over to one of the windows to gaze out over the moonlit ocean. "This is beautiful." A bank of thick fog stood off the coast. Glowing with the reflected light of the moon, the mist rose up to mingle with the stars, a ghostly wall separating the land of light from a world of ghosts and shadows.

Sabazios's chair scraped. The tap of soft footsteps right behind her. Hailey felt her muscles tighten. *God help me. Please help me to be myself. Help me not to be afraid.* The touch of his hand tingled at the small of her back. She turned to face him, backing away to let his hand fall back to his side.

"It's funny, but I don't even know your full name." The fog in Hailey's brain was finally beginning to lift.

"I'm sorry. I should have properly introduced myself. I am Sabazios Vladu." He nodded in a slight bow.

"Sabazios Vladu." Hailey repeated the name, trying to place it. "What nationality is that?"

Sabazios shrugged. "I wish I knew. It's not the name I was born with. I was born Adam Kensington in Liverpool, England."

Hailey waited for him to continue.

Sabazios sighed. "When I was twelve, I was befriended by a wealthy gentleman named Sabazios Vladu. My family was poor, and he was good to us. He took me on holidays, paid for me to be privately educated—treated me like a son. When he died, he left his estate to me but with several conditions, one of which was that I should take his name. I suppose I could take back my old name—he's dead after all—but I keep the name of Sabazios out of respect for him. He was a kind man; the only obligation he laid on me was that I continue his system of benevolence in distributing his wealth."

"Wow. That's an amazing story." Hailey studied his face. Was he serious? "It's almost a Cinderella story. I can't believe it actually happened."

"Ah, but Cinderella stories happen all the time. You just have to be in the right place at the right time. And with the right prince." Sabazios reached in his pocket and pulled out a shimmering chain that sparkled red and gold in the dim light. He spread the chain on his hand and held it out to reveal an old, ornate necklace set with five large rubies. "For you, Hailey. A gift."

Hailey gasped. "It's beautiful, but I can't. I shouldn't. It's too . . . I mean I hardly know you."

"Nonsense. It's just a trifle. I want you to wear it. It will look lovely on you." Sabazios held the necklace toward her, but she backed away.

"I'm sorry, but I really can't accept it. I would feel too much of an obligation."

"No obligations. It's a gift. Nothing more. It is I who am under obligation—laid upon me by the late Sabazios. I must distribute a certain fraction of my earnings each year. I get to choose the form of the gift and, of course, the recipient." Sabazios smiled and held up the necklace. "And I can't think of a more beautiful form—or recipient."

A young waiter swept into the room and stopped, looking to Sabazios with wide, uncertain eyes. "Are you ready to order, sir? I could come back. . . ."

Sabazios slipped the necklace into his pocket. "I fear we haven't had a chance to look at the menu, but the grilled Pacific swordfish sounded fine. How about you, Hailey? Would you like him to come back?"

"No, I'm fine. What you're having sounds perfect." Hailey cringed. Why didn't she just hand him her brain and be done with it. Her brain and her self-respect, all boxed up and gift-wrapped with a Barbie-pink bow.

"And to drink?"

"A bottle of the finest red in your cellar."

The waiter raised his eyebrows and opened his mouth to say something but seemed to think better of it and clamped his mouth shut again. "Yes, sir. Will there be anything else?"

Sabazios looked to her before dismissing him with a wave of his hand.

Hailey retreated back to the table and sat down. The necklace was still in his pocket. Hopefully it would stay there. "I want to thank you again for the book. You're a wonderful writer. I'm very flattered you shared it with me."

Sabazios seated himself across the table from her and gazed into her eyes. "I must confess I'm not sure what you mean, but I thank you for the compliment."

Hailey nodded and tried to look away, but bold black eyes pulled at her heart until she could feel it, large and fluttery, in her throat. So handsome.

"I love what you wrote about Eve. It was so . . ."

Sabazios reached out a hand and placed it on hers. A burning warmth tingled up her arm, bringing her thoughts to a roiling boil. She took a deep breath and let it out slowly.

"It was so romantic."

She saw his lips move, but his eyes swallowed up all meaning. A nagging uneasiness rose up within her, and she lowered her eyes to the table. No. Not again. This time she wouldn't pull away.

She looked back up to expectant, confident eyes and plunged mind and soul into their depths. Candlelight flickered bright and cold within twin black orbs. Delicate white fish in a creamy sauce. Ruby-red wine swirled, lit from within by starbursts of shivering light. A blanket of fog flowed over them, shutting out the eyes of the moon. The flame burned brighter, radiating shimmering heat. The kiss of red rubies, cold and bright on quivering skin. Hailey leaned forward, yearning for the kiss, but a roaring wind held her back. She leaned into the storm, trembling and cold. Hair lashing in her face, she let its swirling tendrils hold her close in a numbing embrace.

The roar stopped. Sabazios was looking down at her through a crystal screen. She leaned into his arms, holding him tight, pressing her face into his lightly scented jacket. A pin prick, dull but insistent, stabbed into her mind. Burning like fire, it melted through the ecstasy of his embrace. Her ankle throbbed, pulsing to the rhythm of her pounding heart. She pulled away and balanced on her good foot, looking into the eyes of perfection.

"Shall we go in?" Gripping, echoing inside her soul, his voice penetrated like a command.

Hailey looked around in a confused daze. They were standing at the front door of Tiffany's apartment.

"What time is it?"

"Half past eleven." Sabazios's voice sent a surge of longing rushing through her body.

She searched the contours of his face. So gorgeous . . . and Tiffany would be there. She couldn't wait to see Tiff's face when she got a look at him. Hailey raised a hand to her neck and fingered one of the rubies.

"Sure, just for a little while. I have to get up early tomorrow."

———

MELCHI WOKE WITH A gasp. A trickle of sweat ran down his face. His head throbbed with a dull ache. Where was he? He tried to sit up, but his body refused to respond. A burning pain was crawling up from the back of his leg. The creature. He'd been bitten by a Mulo!

*By becoming the enemy, he shall shield the world from the enemy's dark stain . . .*

Gasping out loud, he climbed to his knees and focused blurry eyes on the dark cityscape surrounding him. He was still on the roof. Had he fallen asleep or passed out? He crawled to the edge of the roof and looked across the street to the brightly lit hotel. Reaching out with his mind, he sifted through the buzzing presences in the hotel. The Mulo wasn't there. Where could it have gone? He had been waiting all day.

*Hailey . . .*

Melchi grabbed his backpack and climbed onto his feet. What if the Mulo found her while he was asleep? He took a step and paused. If the Mulo had found her, she'd already be dead. But if he went to her now, chances were good he would lead it right to her. And the two of them together would send out a signal the Mulo could follow for miles.

He turned and settled back down on the roof. Might as well make himself comfortable. The Mulo might not come back for a long, long time.

HAILEY STOOD TO THE side as Sabazios swung open the door
and switched on the lights. She took a half step and hesitated as
her stomach churned. She felt a strong, almost overpowering urge
to turn and run. The room reeked of . . .

No, she was being ridiculous. It was the flowers. The flowers
just reminded her of her parents' death.

"Tiff! Are you here?" Hailey took a deep breath and stepped
inside. The dead bolt snapped shut with an ominous clank. "That's
funny. She's usually here Sunday nights. She has an 8 a.m. class on
Mondays."

"Tiff is your roommate?" Sabazios leaned against the back of
the sofa, taking in the contents of the room.

"Temporarily. I'm moving back in with my regular roommate
as soon as the construction is finished on our apartment building." Hailey started toward the sofa. Then she noticed the keys.
On the table by the door. Tiffany's keys.

"Tiff, are you upstairs?" Hailey walked to the bottom of the
stairs. "Tiff?"

A hand grabbed her shoulder. She cried out and turned.
Sabazios was leaning over her, charging the air with the force of
his presence. She stepped backward and hit the wall.

"Perhaps she stepped out for a moment." His eyes beat down
on her, pounding through the last shreds of her resistance.

"But she left her keys. Why would she—"

"Perhaps she didn't need them." Sabazios reached out and
cupped her face in his hands.

"Didn't . . . need them?" Hailey could barely whisper the
words. His touch soothed away all fears. She stood weak and trembling, transfixed by his eyes. They called out to her, raising an eager
response deep within her soul. Dark moons within a bright sky. She

leaned out over the void of space and felt it surrounding her, lifting her off her feet, placing her ever so gently upon a billowing cloud.

She lifted her hand to touch his marble face, impossibly smooth and cold. His lips moved. Strange words, deep and resonant, rumbled out into space. They were answered by other words not her own.

She sank into his arms. Her lips touched his.

A surge of passion. Terrible longing.

*Please God. Help me . . .*

*No!*

She tried to push him away, but he held her in an iron grip, boring into her mind with eyes of black fire.

A crash shook the room. She could feel herself being ripped in half as Sabazios pulled away.

The room was awash with boiling anger. A tidal wave of rage hit her in the face, rolling her over, knocking her to the floor. A roar, low and guttural, filled the room, a bracing focal point for her befuddled senses.

Hailey twisted away from the sound. The coffee table tipped in a cascade of sweeping blossoms. She scrambled across the floor, hit a wall, fell to the floor. Sabazios was crouching by the sofa, snarling like an animal at the foot of the sofa.

Quick, while he wasn't looking. Hailey climbed to her feet and froze. There, standing framed in the shattered doorway, stood her homeless man.

*Melchi.*

A sob convulsed Hailey, constricting her throat in the agony of paralyzing fear. "Help me. Please help me." She could only mouth the words. The sound wouldn't come.

Melchi took a step toward her, but Sabazios sprang at him, driving him with his shoulder back into the wall. The two rolled, struggling on the floor, splintering an end table, shattering a porcelain lamp. Inhuman growls and screams of rage filled the room. Hatred battered her senses. Flames of twisted passion, evil, guilt, rage—

Stomping her foot on the floor, she beat her fists against the wall. She had to get hold of herself. Had to regain control.

Melchi sailed through the air and crashed into a cheap particleboard desk. Sabazios advanced on him, slow and deliberate, murder burning bright in his eyes.

"Go! Get out of here!" Melchi's eyes locked on hers, filling her with the desperation of his plea.

She tore her eyes from his face and crept toward the door. *Quick, while the Mulo isn't looking!*

She lunged for the door and ran out into the night. Blinded by the sudden darkness, she hit the edge of the porch with a twisting step into nothing and slammed into the ground. Rolling, fighting for her breath, she crawled to her feet and ran screaming up the hill. Waves of anger lashed out at her. Screams of silent pain. She stumbled to a stop. Her homeless man, he needed help.

No. There wasn't anything she could do. Melchi's only hope of rescue waited at the top of the hill. She started running. Faster. Fighting through the pain, she pounded up the street. UCSF. Campus security. The police. She needed to find the police.

Gasping and sputtering, bent almost double by cramping muscles, she burst into the student center, stumbled down the stairs, and ran for the elevator.

*God please! Let me be in time.*

She slid between elevator doors and stabbed repeatedly at the button.

*God, please . . .*

The doors opened and Hailey plunged down a concrete hallway. She burst into the Campus Security office and crumpled to her knees. "Help me! Help!"

A door slammed. Pounding footsteps. "Hello? Dear Father, what happened?" A campus police officer slid to a stop before her, his hand gripping his holster.

"I'm—okay. A man—he's trying to kill—my friend. At my apartment!" She shouted out Tiffany's address.

The officer disappeared behind a counter and bellowed into a radio. "10-16 in progress. At . . . what's that address again?"

Hailey called out the address, gasped for breath, and called it out again.

"It's okay. The police are on their way. It's okay." The officer was looking down at her. "I'm going to call an ambulance now. Are you hurt?"

"No!" Hailey rolled onto her side, panting for breath. "No ambulance. I'm fine. But my friend—"

"It's okay. SFPD had a patrol only three blocks away. They'll take care of it. Tell me what happened."

Hailey picked herself up off the floor and leaned against the counter, listening to the bursts of coded messages pouring from the radio. She had done all she could. It was up to the police now. If they got there in time, they—

"Wait!" Hailey turned back to the officer. "Tell them it's the man in the expensive suit. He's the one that attacked me!" Hailey reached out and grabbed the officer by the arms. "The clean-cut guy. Not the one with the beard! Tell them now!"

She sank onto the floor. If the police didn't get the word in time, if they arrived on the scene and saw ragged, tattered Melchi fighting a handsome man in an expensive suit . . .

*God, please protect him. Please let him get away.*

She closed her eyes and thought back to her conversation with Smiley. Even if the police got the word, they might still go after Melchi. They would probably arrest him or . . .

Or worse.

Far, far worse.

# ◡◯ 16 ◯◡

Officer Bill Jennings pulled the squad car up to the curb. "Yep. This is the place." He opened the door and leaned his head out to listen. "Sounds pretty quiet. Any updates?"

Thad Parker, his rookie partner, flipped on the spotlight and played it along the building.

"What do you think you're doing?" Bill shut the door. "Why not phone ahead and let 'em know we're coming?"

"Dude! Look at that! They've bugged for sure!" Thad opened the door and started for the building.

"Get back in here!" Bill grabbed the shotgun from its mount and hurried after his partner. "Ted, wait for backup!" Great. Now he was doing it too. The whole precinct had started calling them Bill and Ted. Thought it was some kind of big joke. The best man on the force and the fool kid trying to get his head blown off. He'd warned the sergeant a hundred times, but all Collins could do was joke about busting up Bill and Ted. Ha, ha. Real funny. Especially after the millionth time.

Thad stood at the doorway training his flashlight around a dark room. The door lay on the floor, split almost in half.

"They said two men did this?"

Thad stood back to let Bill get a look at the trashed room.

"I don't like this. Let's get back to the car. Backup's on its way." Bill switched on his own flashlight and held it clamped with his left hand against the stock of the shotgun.

Thad looked at the shotgun and rolled his eyes. "I don't think so. Those guys are long gone." He stepped inside and made his way toward the kitchen area in the back, sweeping his light back and forth along his path.

Bill waited at the door. Fool kid was too cocky to understand. Handguns might be more maneuverable in close quarters, but staring down the barrel of a shotgun put a good dose of psychology on a bad guy. He'd been on the force sixteen years and never had to use it once.

He reached inside and flipped several light switches, but the power was dead. He was liking this less and less. He motioned for Thad to follow him outside, but Thad shook his head and started up the stairs.

*Of all the stupid, boneheaded . . .* Bill kicked a piece of broken glass, sending it skittering into the wall.

"Hey Bill, you better come up here. I think I found something."

A chill ran up Bill's spine. *Oh great! Tell 'em where you are, bonehead!* Leading his way with the shotgun, Bill crept across the room, holding the flashlight as far as possible from his body. He started up the stairs. Thad was making enough noise to wake the dead.

"Will you cut out the racket!" Bill hissed, spinning Thad around by the arm. His stomach churned. Chest heaving, he gripped the stock of his gun tighter, fighting the urge to embed it in Thad's thick skull. He bit his lip and loosened his grip. *Bonehead!* Probably wouldn't even phase him.

"See?" Thad whispered, pointing his flashlight at a dark carpet stain that had crept out from under a closed door.

Bill knelt and touched it with an index finger. It was still warm.

"Come on. Don't touch anything!" Bill hissed as he raced down the stairs. A terrible scream rang out behind him, ending in ominous silence. Bill leaped down the rest of the stairs and ran screaming across the room. Churning blood blotted out his vision; he was drowning in it, couldn't breath.

The floor slid out from under his feet, and he went down. Crashing into a sofa, rolling on the floor, he clawed his way out the door and leaped off the porch. His squad car. He was going to—

A crash sounded overhead. Wave upon wave of expanding blackness hit him in the back, driving him face first into the dirt. Ted! White-hot anger drilled into his brain, spreading to fill his mind. The boneheaded idiot would pay for this. The whole world was going to pay!

———————

"NO, I HAVEN'T BEEN drinking!" Hailey yelled into the receiver and turned to the campus security officer who was listening in on the other phone. "Jerry, tell the detective I'm not drunk!"

"It's okay. I believe you. I just have to ask for the report." Detective Smiley's voice was soft and soothing, like he was about to fall asleep.

Didn't he get it? Now wasn't the time for calm. This was the time for action. Melchi could be dead or dying, and all Smiley wanted to do was ask her questions?

"So you say that this homeless man broke down the door and attacked the man you were with, this Sabazios Vladu?"

"No. It wasn't like that. Sabazios was attacking me. Mel, m . . . my . . . the homeless man broke down the door to save me."

"But you said Mr. Vladu was just about to kiss you. He hadn't threatened you with physical violence, and you hadn't screamed or told him you didn't want to be kissed?" Smiley sounded tired and frustrated. "So tell me why this homeless man would think you were being attacked?"

Hailey bit her lip and looked across the room to get a nod from the security officer. "I know how this is going to sound, but it was like he was controlling me, keeping me from thinking. I don't know, I think maybe I was drugged. I can't explain it, but I know what I felt." Hailey pulled the telephone cord over the counter and slid down the wall to sit on the floor. "Why are we wasting time with questions when a man's life could be in danger?"

"Ms. Maniates, we're doing all we can. I've got men on the scene right now, but my main concern is your safety. I'm going to send a squad car over to pick you up and bring you to the station. You can't go home, and frankly I'd feel a lot better if you were somewhere safe. This may be a lot bigger than you think."

"But the homeless man isn't . . ."

"Regardless of who is or isn't a danger, I'd still feel better if you were under protection. Please."

Hailey looked at the security officer, who nodded his head.

"Okay, but it's Sabazios who's after me—not the homeless man."

"I'll send a squad car right over. Officer Hemphill, are you still on?"

"I'm here."

"Don't let her out of your sight until the officers arrive. Okay? They should be there in fifteen minutes."

"All right. You don't need to worry about that."

Hailey hung up the phone and buried her head in her hands while the two men exchanged details for some kind of a report. Melchi was innocent. Why wouldn't anyone listen to her?

Forty-five minutes later there was a knock at the door, and two uniformed police officers shuffled into the office. Officer Hemphill slid off the counter and slipped a half-eaten granola bar into his pants pocket, but Hailey just sat there on the floor.

"Hi, I'm Thad Parker, and this is Officer Bill Jennings." The young, dark-haired officer reached out to shake Hemphill's hand.

"I'm Jerry Hemphill." Jerry turned to shake Jennings's hand, but the older man gave no sign he had even noticed. He stood swaying on his feet with watery eyes and wide-gaping mouth.

"I'm afraid Bill's zoning. Cold medicine's knocked him out. I'm taking him home right after we escort Ms. Maniates back to the station."

Hailey stood and Officer Parker did a double take. "I'm sorry, Ms. Maniates. I didn't see you there." He took a step toward Hailey, and she pulled away.

"Jerry, shouldn't you check his ID or something?"

"It's okay, Missy. They're okay." He turned to Officer Jennings. "I'm sorry, but she's been through an awful lot tonight."

"I understand. I'd be worried about this clod too." Thad smacked Jennings on the chest. "Bill, wake up," he said in a loud voice. "Ms. Maniates wants to see your ID."

Officer Jennings fumbled with his back pocket, but Thad pushed his hand aside and pulled out the wallet himself, handing it to Jerry.

Jerry held the ID to the light. "He's okay, Missy. You'll be safe as long as Officer Jennings here isn't doing the driving."

Officer Parker chuckled and guided Hailey and his partner out the door.

———— • ————

MELCHI FELT HIS WAY up an almost vertical slope. His head, his leg, his whole body throbbed with pain. The heavy rasp of his breathing raged in his ears. He needed to be quiet. Somehow he had to slow his breathing. He wouldn't last another minute if it found him now.

*Holy One, we thank Thee. Holy One, hide us in Thy almighty hands.* The mantra replayed itself furiously in his head.

*Focus on the words,* the voice of his old master sounded over the prayer. *Let everything else fade away.* Ortus had been right about one thing: Even with all his training, the Mulo was much stronger than he. Stronger and faster. If he hadn't escaped when he did, he would already be dead. Or worse.

His foot slipped, sending a handful of pebbles skittering down the precipice below him. Too late to block it. He focused on his foot. Tried to imagine the smell of dog poop, a dark and lonely street with trash cans lined up in a ragged row. *Excuse me, sir, could you tell me what time it is?* But the Mulo's presence was still getting stronger. He had fooled it once; he wouldn't fool it again.

A thrashing noise sounded far below him. As steady as a steam engine, it moved straight for him, churning through the darkness like a heat-seeking missile. Abandoning stealth, Melchi opened his eyes and scrambled up the slope. With pounding heart and burning lungs he fought his way higher and higher, but the Mulo was gaining on him. It would catch him before he reached the top of the slope.

Coming to a grove of small eucalyptus trees, Melchi leaped into a tall straight tree and shinnied up its smooth surface. A jolt passed through the tree and into his body. A blast of anger washing through him from below. The tree shook and swayed back and forth until Melchi worried it would be uprooted. He climbed higher and higher until the tree bent, sagging under his weight. He swung the tree back and forth until it was leaning far out over the hill. Then, climbing hand over hand toward the top of the tree, he swung out over the void and—

The tree snapped with a loud *crack*. Melchi spun his arms around to keep himself upright as he plummeted through the air. He hit the slope and started sliding, barely slowing as he bounced and scraped his way down the gravelly hillside. Legs spread wide for balance, he let his overcoat and backpack take most of the abuse and prayed he wouldn't hit a tree.

He hit the bottom of the hill with a bone-rattling jolt and slumped forward under a rain of dirt and pebbles. Rolling onto his feet, he took off to the right. *To the park. To the park.* He chanted to the rhythm of his gasping breath. He didn't expect the trick to work again, but he had to try. His master's voice echoed in his mind.

*You are the long-awaited child of prophecy. To quit trying is the same as suicide. Same consequences, same punishment.*

Melchi urged himself to greater speed. If only he had brought his staff. He should have known. He should have been prepared. All his arguments about checking on the girl, all his rationale about protecting her—it had all been lies. He hadn't been prepared to confront the Mulo; he only thought to indulge his flesh. He had given in to the darkness. Again.

A stairway cut into the hill ahead of him. He veered toward it but tripped on an unseen snag and plunged forward onto his face. He lay in a patch of ivy, stunned and panting with short, rasping breaths. His ears rang. Great blooms of prickly red light danced before his eyes.

*The Mulo!*

Fighting his way to alertness, he struggled to his feet and crouched to await the attack. He spun in a slow circle, waiting, listening . . .

Silence.

His quadriceps began to tremble, but still he maintained the ready position. Where was it? It should have attacked by now.

Unless it had broken off the chase. And the only reason to break off the chase was . . .

Hailey.

———·—·———

HAILEY WALKED NEXT TO Officer Parker while his partner staggered along behind her. Their footsteps echoed off the dingy concrete walls. Even with a police escort, she felt nervous. Queasy pinpricks crawled up her spine. Her vision blurred. *She would soon have—*

She shook her head and tried to clear her mind. She would soon have what? What was wrong? Was she having another attack?

She glanced over her shoulder, and Officer Jennings stared back at her with open mouth and vacuous eyes. She turned back around but could still feel his eyes boring into the base of her neck.

Parker stopped at the elevator and pushed the down arrow on the panel. Hailey noticed the radio he wore on his belt.

"Would it be possible to use that?" She pointed at the radio. "To radio the officers at my apartment? I've been waiting to hear for over an hour."

The elevator door opened with a ring, and the three stepped inside. Officer Parker pushed the *A* button for the Irving Street entrance.

"Sorry about that. I thought you talked to the detective."

"I did, but he hadn't heard back yet. Did you hear the report? Is the homeless man okay?"

"You better wait and talk to the detective. We'll be there soon." Parker stared straight ahead at the elevator doors.

*He knew.* An icy weight settled into the pit of her stomach. He knew but didn't want to be the one to tell her.

"Please, just tell me one thing. I've got to know. Was he dead when they got there? If they hurt him . . ." Tears clouded Hailey's eyes, and she looked at her feet, blinking.

"No males were found at the apartment. Dead or otherwise."

"But they were—" Hailey frowned at Officer Parker's feet. The pants of his uniform hung in loose rolls above his shoes. Surely he—

Strong arms wrapped around her, pinning her arms to her sides. Her scream was cut short as a wide piece of duct tape was slapped across her mouth.

Hailey lifted her feet off the ground and kicked hard against the elevator doors, pushing her captor back against the wall. The doors opened. Parker grabbed her around the shoulders and tore her from his partner's grasp. His grip crushed down on her like a vise, pinning her arms to her sides. He dragged her out of the elevator and swung her around.

Waves of exultation tumbled across Hailey's senses. The garage lights melted into rings of rainbowed light. The garage was turning, spinning. She let her body go limp and collapsed almost to the floor before he caught her and pulled her upright. He was enormously strong. Much more powerful than he looked.

*Mulo.*

As the word leaped to her mind, Parker's grip around her tightened. He knew! Somehow he knew. Was he reading her mind?

Hailey stayed limp, waiting for her opportunity. Then, as he twisted her forward, she aimed a kick to his groin.

The man didn't even flinch. He fixed her with a triumphant stare and dragged her through the parking garage.

Hailey felt like she'd been kicked in the chest. She struggled, hooking a leg around his right leg, pulling with all her might. Parker jerked her to the side. Now her legs were flailing ineffectually in the air. He set her down next to a black-and-white police car and waited as Jennings struggled to open the door. Parker's grip was iron. She couldn't escape. No one could help her. It was pointless even to struggle, but—

"No!" Hailey kicked out at Officer Jennings, knocking the squad keys from his hand. If she could just get Parker to loosen his grip . . .

Looking back over his shoulder, she tried to feign the elation of being rescued. Even if he couldn't read her mind, he might be able to read her expression.

She struggled to control the muscles of her face, but the feelings wouldn't come. Happy thoughts. Graduation, Sugar Plump when she was a kitten. Bringing home first place for the district science fair. Her father had been so happy. He didn't even know she—

Jennings unlocked the door and swung it open wide.

*God, please! Help me.*

Hailey's eyes filmed over with tears, bright and dazzling. Her father had crushed her in his arms. The smell of his aftershave, strong and spicy, surrounding her, wrapping her in its masculine embrace.

*You are My precious daughter. I love you always. Beyond the bounds of time and place, you are Mine.*

A great rush of wind, soft and warm, buoyed her up, lifting her high into clouds of shining brightness. Her heart swelled within her, exploding with the warmth of sweet longing. The sun blazed down on her, overwhelming her with its radiance, filling her with its light.

*Dear Lord. Dear, precious Lord . . .*

Chest heaving, tears streaming down her face, she lay with her face pressed against a cold concrete floor. Running feet, vague and remote, tapped at the edges of her mind.

"Hailey! *Hailey!*"

The footsteps were calling her name.

# ∽ 17 ∾

Athena slammed into an empty trash can, sending it tumbling out into the deserted street. Great. Just when she was about to lose them. She stumbled after the can and pushed it further into the street and doubled back in the direction she had come.

She turned down a dark side street and ran. Now was the tricky part. The slow one could be anywhere. He had fallen way behind at the police station, lurching after her like a zombie in a horror movie. The analogy made her skin crawl. Okay, maybe he wasn't a zombie, but she still didn't want to run into him in the dark. Even the hotel would be better than that.

She made for a jeep parked on the side of the road and crawled into the darkness beneath it. Lying shivering on the cold asphalt, she peered out from behind the back tire. There he was. Her silent pursuer shuffled past the intersection at an awkward run.

Good, he saw the trash can. She scooted back further under the jeep and waited, straining her ears for clues to his position. She'd let him go another couple of blocks, and then she'd take off in the opposite direction. Maybe she could even get back to the police station before—

The shadowy form lurched back into the intersection and turned to shuffle straight for her. How did he know? Athena rolled out from under the jeep and ran. She was faster than he, but she couldn't run forever. What if the big man was right? What if they really could feel her emotions? No matter where she hid, they would always be able to find her.

No. She couldn't give in to superstition. That's probably what the man had wanted. Still, how had he found her? It didn't make sense. She lowered her head and kept running, looking down at the pavement in front of her feet. Without looking up, she took a right and then an immediate left. "Right, right, right turn," she repeated to herself, trying to project her thoughts into the surrounding night.

Another turn to the right. She kept her eyes focused on the sidewalk, fighting the urge to look up. *Another right. Another right.* The sidewalks blurred beneath her feet, and the rhythm of her breath filled her mind. She was so tired. Sleepy. She let the drowsiness wash over her, an opiate against her pain and fatigue. Finally, she slowed to a walk and leaned against a telephone pole to catch her breath. *No feelings. No pain. Another right.* She pressed her forehead against the pole to screen her eyes from the streetlight overhead.

A bright new flyer caught her attention. The Haight-Ashbury Hotel? She stood back to examine the advertisement. There would be another party at the hotel—a costume party.

*No feelings. No pain. Another right.* She couldn't run forever. The jewels weren't worth it. Nothing was worth it. But what would they do if she gave them back? It wasn't like she knew anything about their organization. Not really. If she didn't go to the police, they would eventually lose interest in her. As long as she didn't have their jewelry . . .

And there was a costume party tomorrow night. They would never expect her back at the hotel. It would be the safest place in town.

———·—·———

"HAILEY, ARE YOU ALL right?" the voice sounded, loud and insistent, above her head.

Hailey squeezed her eyes shut, trying to hold on to the dream. She felt a tugging, burning sensation on her cheek. Duct tape?

"What happened? Are you okay?"

The last lingering sensations of pleasure slipped away from her, leaving behind a deep yearning. It had been so beautiful. Why did it have to stop?

"It's okay." The voice cut through the sound of someone crying. "It's okay."

Hailey opened tear-filled eyes. She looked up into the face of her homeless man. Melchi.

"It was . . . so real. So wonderful."

"What was? Are you okay?"

A rush of worry clouded her senses. "It was . . . I don't know. Like a beautiful dream. Like my father—only it wasn't my father, it was like . . ." She lay on her back, looking deep into soft brown eyes. Melchi leaned in closer. A thousand eager questions buzzed in her brain. She lifted her right hand, but he jumped away.

"It's all right. I wasn't going to hurt you." She spoke the words softly as turmoil swirled in the air around her. Self-doubt. Unrelenting fear.

"What happened to you? Why are you here?" Melchi glanced around the garage.

Hailey turned. The sight of the police car brought back a flood of memories. The policemen. She could still feel the terror, but somehow it seemed remote, unimportant.

"There were two men. They tried to put me in the police car. I think they were going to kill me." Hailey pushed herself up on her elbows and sat up.

Melchi crouched before her, balancing on his toes, a misshapen gargoyle with the eyes of an angel. If only she could help him. Touch him. He was so beautiful.

"You saved my life. Thank you. I was afraid. I was so worried you—" Hailey choked on the words.

"Hailey, this is important. What happened to the men?"

"You didn't chase them away?"

Melchi shook his head. "When I got here, you were alone. Lying on the ground. Did the police chase after them?"

"The police? They *were* the police. At least, they were wearing uniforms."

Melchi jumped to his feet. "Come. We must go from here. The Mulo still hunts. They may lead it back to us."

Hailey nodded and tried to catch up to him, but he hovered just out of reach. She limped painfully after him as he melted into the shadows before her, leaving her in a wake of whispered encouragement. Her ankle screamed in protest at every step.

"I can't make it. I've got to rest."

"Right here." Melchi stepped into the shadow of a recessed doorway and motioned for her to follow. "You are in pain. If I can feel it, it can too."

"I can't help it. I think I reinjured it."

"Sit down and try to stay calm. As long as you remain calm, it will have a more difficult time finding us."

Hailey sank down onto the landing and propped up her foot. "You tell me a man is trying to kill us, and you want me to stay calm?"

Melchi shrugged and crouched beside her. "The police officers. Could you feel their emotions? Did they feel like the Mu— like the man at your apartment?"

"I don't know. Maybe one of them. It was like he was, I don't know, on drugs. The other one too, maybe. They were both incredibly strong."

"How long had they been gone when I found you?"

Hailey considered for a second. "I don't know. It was really weird. Like I fell asleep and had the most wonderful dream. It was almost like I was . . ." She turned and studied Melchi's face. "How did you know where to find me?"

Melchi looked down at the steps. When he raised his head, his drooping eyes gave him the look of a child caught with his hand in the cookie jar. "I was looking for you, after I escaped from the Mulo." He looked back at the ground. "And then I felt this . . . intense . . . I don't know. The happy realms of light where joy forever dwells." He murmured the words, as though caught up in a dream of his own. "I ran down the hill to find out, well . . . and then I saw you lying there and thought . . . I don't know." Melchi hung his head.

"It's okay. I believe you, but you aren't telling me something. What is it you aren't telling me?"

"I didn't know it was you. I thought . . ." Melchi looked back at the ground. "I just wanted to know what was making her so happy. It felt like this." Melchi dug inside his outer coat and handed her a dog-eared clipping. Something cut from a magazine.

She held it out under the dim light of a nearby street lamp. It was a picture of a little girl playing with her parents. Hailey examined the child's expression, remembering her feelings during the dream. A forgotten memory? No, her father had always been too busy. Wishful thinking more like. A fantastic daydream concocted by her subconscious as a way to cope with the situation.

But where had the policemen gone?

"Do you believe in God?" The words were out before Hailey even knew she was thinking them.

"Of course."

"Do you think He ever communicates, you know, interacts directly with our world?"

Melchi nodded. "He is all-powerful. He can do whatever He wants."

"I used to think I believed that, but now I wonder if somewhere along the way I stopped taking it seriously. I mean, if I really believed it, wouldn't I expect, you know, more stuff to happen?"

"You cannot expect what you have not seen. And you cannot see what you do not expect." Melchi took the clipping from Hailey and slipped it tenderly back into his pocket. "My master used to say that."

"Your master?"

"He took care of me when I was young. Trained me in the—" Melchi bit his lip and looked down at the steps.

"Trained you in what?"

"Well, for one thing he taught me the ways of the Mulo. The Mulo took my parents when I was a baby—and took Ortus, my master, when I was but a boy."

"The Mulo. Sabazios?"

"He goes by many names and faces. He is a master of disguise."

"When I was with him, it was like I was hypnotized. I couldn't think straight."

Melchi sat down on the steps and stretched out his legs. "We are children of the Standing. There are many dimensions humans cannot comprehend, but one of the dimensions is inhabited. We cannot see it or touch it, but our souls resonate with its music. Normal humans, only a little, but the Standing much more. They say the Mulo freely walks the roads of this dimension and only the Standing can sense its passing." Melchi's voice rose and fell in a strange hypnotic rhythm. "We resonate with it through the music. Like two tuning forks vibrating at the same frequency."

Hailey studied his face. "This is what you really believe?"

"It is the truth." The weight of Melchi's words settled onto Hailey's heart. He believed what he was saying. What a tremendous burden.

"But what does Sabazios want from me?"

"The Mulo hunts the Standing. No one knows why. Perhaps it fears us because we have the power to expose him. Or perhaps he knows the prophecy, that one of the Standing, the long-awaited child, shall eventually destroy him."

According to the lady at the bookstore, Melchi believed *he* was that child. "And the policemen? They were Mulo too?"

"I do not know what they are."

Pain mingled with worry and fear. "You're hurt." Hailey reached out to touch Melchi's leg, but he drew it back.

"It is nothing." Melchi's brow furrowed, and his eyes took on a haunted expression.

"It's okay. I won't hurt you." She slowly reached out her hand.

"Shhh! We should go now. I know a place of refuge. You will be safe there." Melchi stood, sweeping the dark street with his gaze.

Hailey stood, and her ankle started throbbing almost immediately. It was swollen to the size of a grapefruit. She took an experimental step, but the pain was too much. She sucked in her breath and took Melchi by the arm to steady herself. "You'll have to help me."

Melchi's frame went rigid, and a stab of emotion pierced Hailey—fear tinged with longing.

"I cannot. It is . . . forbidden." He pulled away from her, leaving her to lean against the wall. "It is good for a man not to touch a woman. The Mulo would find us, and I would not be able to protect you."

*Of all the stupid* . . . Hailey couldn't believe she'd heard him right. "Just let me lean on you. My ankle feels like it's broken. I can't walk." She whispered the words through clenched teeth.

"I am sorry. It is not—"

"Forget it!" Hailey turned toward the door. "Go on. Leave!"

"I will not leave you. Perhaps if you rested—"

"I said leave! Leave me alone." Tears welled up in her eyes. What was it with him? He acted as if she had some kind of—

Strong arms swept her up, lifting her behind her knees and back. "Put me down! Leave me alone. I'm . . ."

"Shhh! It is too late for that now. We must hurry."

Hailey's mind raced. She started to struggle but thought better of it. He was already running down the street, carrying her rigidly out in front of him like a man in a clean suit carries a dirty garbage can. He was incredibly strong. Just like Officer Parker.

"Do not be afraid. You will be safe soon."

Hailey trembled as tension radiated through his body. She was too heavy. She leaned into him and wrapped an arm around his neck. He gasped, and her heart pounded in her chest. The buildings bobbed and swirled around her. If only he could hold her. Crush her in his arms . . .

Her hand slipped down around his shoulders to the hard twisted mass. It wasn't real, the feelings in her head. None of it was real. She tried to jerk away from him, but he was holding her too tight. She had to think, get a grip. They were his feelings, not hers.

Melchi's footsteps beat faster and faster against the pavement. The night raced by in a blur. His breath came like great blasts from a steam engine, blocking out the sounds of the sleeping city.

"Shut your eyes," he ordered between breaths. "And keep them closed—no matter what you hear."

"Why? What are you doing?"

"Your thoughts . . . they must not reveal . . . our hiding place."

Hailey remembered the night it all started. *If I don't know where I am, maybe it won't either.* She squeezed her eyes shut and hung on tighter. The sound of pounding feet, the rolling motion, the wind in her face. She leaned closer into Melchi, burying her face in his chest. He would protect her. He would keep her safe.

His footsteps slowed and she heard voices, distant and wild.

"Keep your eyes shut," Melchi commanded.

"Wh–wh–who's she? She's not another one? Another one?" A man's voice, strange and quivering, sounded not five feet away. Hailey started to turn her head, but Melchi shifted his arm behind her head to hold her face to his coat.

"She is none of your concern. You never saw her." Melchi's voice rang out, strong and commanding. "I have come to warn you. The dark one hunts tonight. Wake the others and have them keep watch."

Hailey felt him turning. He was starting to run. She opened her eyes and let her head bounce up from his shoulder to see behind him. There, standing in a small clearing in a wooded park was a crooked man with a white beard and tattered dark clothes.

Hailey shut her eyes and leaned back into Melchi's chest. Who were the others? He was breathing harder now, but his voice had been perfectly controlled when he talked to the strange man. Why were they taking orders from Melchi?

The rhythm of his breathing and the sound of his steps lulled her. The emotions swirling in her head were gone. She was safe and alone, hurtling into the heart of the night. Afloat on a raft in a swift but silent sea.

"Can you climb?"

Hailey sighed and opened her eyes. Happy memories of falling asleep at night in her parents' station wagon filled her mind.

How many times had she pretended to be asleep so they would carry her inside and put her to bed? "I suppose so. How many steps?"

Melchi set her gently on her right foot. She followed his gaze up into a dark tree.

"Up there? Are you kidding? No way."

"I can lift you up to the first branch. All you have to do is climb onto that second branch, and I can do the rest."

"Why? You don't seriously think I'm going to spend the night in a tree."

"The Mulo is strong, but his balance is poor. You will be much safer above ground."

Something stirred in Hailey's memory. "This is your nest, isn't it?"

Melchi gasped. "You saw that in my mind?"

"No, the lady at the bookstore told us. She—"

"Us?" Melchi cast a fearful look around the dark woods.

"Me and my friend—Oh no! Boggs is going to be worried sick. I'm supposed to be spending the night at her house. You've got to take me to her. What was I thinking?"

"It would not be safe. I am marime. I will not be able to protect you. Give me a message and I will carry it."

"And leave me out here alone? No way!"

"You are ready?" Melchi bent over as if to lift her up to the branch.

Hailey considered. "First tell me who that man was. The one you were talking to."

"His name is Antwon. He will keep watch for the Mulo tonight."

"Is he a . . . homeless man?"

"He is Antwon, not the place he sleeps at night."

"I didn't mean . . ." Hailey looked away, thankful for the darkness that hid her burning face. "Okay, I think I'm ready to try climbing."

Melchi held her around her waist and hoisted her up to grab the lowest branch. Then, lifting her by her good foot, he pushed her onto the limb. The tree shook and a branch swished and suddenly he was at her side.

"I can carry you if you want."

"I can make it. I'm working with three good limbs out of four."

The branches of the tree blocked most of the moonlight, but Hailey thought she could see a smile. She followed him up through the tree, brushing occasionally against his feet just to let him know that she was keeping up. She took a deep breath and sighed. She felt free, primal. Alive.

The problems back at the lab seemed laughable now. A man, or whatever, was trying to kill her, but still life was good. The memory of her dream hovered just beyond her reach, but that was okay. It made her happy just knowing it existed.

Melchi stopped climbing and dropped onto the limb she was standing on. "I must carry you now."

"That's all right, I can make it."

"No, you will have no balance. Your ankle is too weak."

Melchi swung her into his arms and stood, balancing precariously on the limb. Then, moving away from the tree, he stepped out over a yawning void.

Hailey gasped and tightened her grip around his neck. "Put me *down!*"

"It is safe. The rope is very tight."

Her mind reeled for two eternal seconds, and then he was across. She was trembling when he set her down on a strange platform woven from little bits of rope and string.

240 OHN B. OLSON

"Of all the idiotic . . . I can't believe you *did* that! You could have gotten us killed!" Hailey scrambled across the net to the solidity of an enormous tree trunk.

Melchi shrunk away. "I am sorry. The rope is very strong—"

"Strong? One slip or a gust of wind and we'd both be dead!"

"Shhh." Melchi held up a commanding hand. "I am sorry to frighten you, but you must remain calm."

Hailey bit her lip and tested the platform. The net had been woven between two enormous branches. It seemed strong enough, but the ground was so far below.

"The morning comes soon. You should sleep now. I have two blankets and plastic to shelter you from the dew. You will be warm tonight."

Hailey fixed her eyes on the solid tree trunk while Melchi arranged the blankets and plastic. Finally he stood and stepped out onto the tightrope.

"I have walked this rope hundreds of times on nights darker than this. We were perfectly safe." He started walking across to the other tree.

"Where are you going?"

Melchi spun around on one foot to face her. "I will hide near the cedar." He turned and disappeared into the tree.

"Um, Melchi?"

"Yes." His voice sounded faintly from far below her.

"Good-night."

"Good-night, Hailey."

# ‿ 18 ‿

Athena hugged her knees to her chest, holding the thin shell of insulating newspaper around her legs. She squirmed and shivered against the dull gray of the fog-soaked morning. Her hair blew across her face, and she leaned into the cold metallic side of a newspaper stand in a futile attempt to retreat further from the biting wind.

Dark images dashed against her mind. The dim outline of Smythe's face, waiting as still as a statue in the warmth of Benedict's apartment. The woman in the car outside Randi's apartment. Leather over silk and fishnets. Whoever she was, she wasn't the police.

She shuddered and closed her hand around the jewelry through the fabric of her dress. Surely there was a way she could keep one of them. Have a fake produced? Sell one and flee the city? It could work. They couldn't cover the BART stations and all of the buses. Yeah, and then live the rest of her life in hiding. Jumping at every shadow. It just wasn't worth it.

Keys rattled in a lock. Two voices, a man's and a woman's, blew past her hiding place. Good. The jewelry store was opening early.

Athena fought the urge to get up and rush after them. She looked bad enough. No point adding desperation to the impression she would make. *God, if You're there, please help me. Let it be the woman I talked to before.*

God. She had been talking to Him a lot lately. Did she really believe He could hear her? That He even existed?

Drugs. Some sort of new techno-thingy. Genetic engineering. Spirit guides. Aliens. She went down the list of possible explanations for what was happening to her. It was freaky, but no more freaky than a God who listened to green-haired chicks. Green-haired chicks who were freezing to death.

She stood and bounced up and down to thaw her lower extremities. Then, reaching inside her dress, she unpinned the jewelry and slipped the chain of the emerald pendant over her neck. She tried to pat down her hair, but it refused to cooperate. Maybe . . .

She spit in her hands and tried to make her hair stand up. Only on the right side. That should do it. Her hair would match her torn dress perfectly.

She was filthy, but it couldn't be helped. Maybe she could even carry it off. She was famous for starting new looks. Pulling herself to her full height, she marched up to the door and yanked on the handle. It was locked.

"Great. So much for my entrance." Athena pounded on the door and waited for someone to open it, strumming with her fingertips on the glass surface.

Yes! The woman from Thursday was walking to the door with a big wad of keys. She struggled briefly with the lock.

"Good morning!" Athena called out in a loud voice as the door swung open. She smiled to set the tone. The woman would be looking to her for cues on how to respond.

"Good morning." The woman's face clouded as she looked Athena up and down. "Are you okay?"

Athena looked at her arms with a frown. "You're the third person to ask this morning. I don't think the battered waif look is catching on." She brushed by the woman and over to the engagement ring case.

The woman moved behind the counter, eyeing Athena curiously. "I've been told I need to get my ring-finger sized."

Athena leaned forward and held out a filthy left hand.

The woman went to a back counter and brought back a chain full of silver rings, all the while studying Athena with arched eyebrows. She took Athena's hand in her own. Her hands felt warm. Too warm.

"Newspaper ink—the dark pictures work best." Athena smiled. "But don't try it in a light-colored dress or you'll ruin it."

The woman opened her mouth and stared at Athena in silence. "Well, it looks like it's going to be a size six." She wrote the size on a card and slid it across the counter. "Is there anything else I can do for you?"

"Actually there is. Could you look at this chain and make sure the clasp is good?" Athena slipped the pendant from around her neck and handed it across the counter.

The woman examined the emerald and its setting. "It's beautiful. I noticed it when you came in."

"Thank you. You can see why I wouldn't want to lose it."

The lady nodded and examined the clasp and touched a probe to the prongs of the mounting. "It seems to be fine. The older pieces used a lot heavier clasps than they do now." She held the necklace up to the light and then handed it back to Athena.

Athena did a fast calculation. She had to ask for more than a bum would ask for but not so much it would look like she was trying to pawn the chain. "This is embarrassing, but if I leave the chain here with you, could I borrow a twenty? I left my wallet at home and would have to go all the way back to the Sunset to get it."

The shopkeeper studied her several seconds and then turned and took a purse out from under the back counter.

She ruffled through its contents and came back with a wad of bills. "I may be totally out of line, and just tell me if I am, but I feel like you might be in some kind of trouble. If there's anything I can do for you—something to eat, a place to stay, somebody to talk to—just say the word. All I've got is twelve dollars." She handed the bills to Athena. "And it's a gift, not a loan. Keep your necklace."

Athena blinked back the sudden tears that brimmed in her eyes. "I'm fine, but thanks for the offer." Without looking up, she turned to leave but paused as the woman hurried to the end of the counter and began digging in the pockets of a heavy jacket.

"Would you at least take my coat?" She held out a beige jacket with a gold quilted lining. "It's freezing outside. Your hands are like ice."

Athena shook her head. "I'm fine. Thank you, though." She turned her face quickly away and hurried out the door, leaning into the force of the wind.

Twelve dollars. Just like that. To a complete stranger. Athena swiped an arm across her eyes and ran across the sidewalk. Down the street, through an alley, across a public parking garage.

She ran as long as she could until finally she collapsed, gasping and panting, behind a graffiti-covered dumpster in the shadow of an open loading dock.

The woman would have given up her brand-new coat. That was a good thing. So why did it make her so afraid?

———————

HAILEY STRETCHED OUT UNDER the heavy blankets. The raucous cry of Steller's Jays filled the air and the sun, high overhead now, was just starting to burn through the afternoon haze. She looked up through the flashing branches and sighed.

That was the best night's sleep she'd ever had, even though most of it had been during the daytime.

She rolled onto her hands and knees and fell to a closer examination of Melchi's nest. Plastic garbage bags were neatly arranged in a section a little apart and at a slightly higher level from the rest. A metal pendant etched with curious glyphs hung from a small branch, and a small bundle of sharpened sticks hung next to it from another. A large, smooth pole lay at her feet across the two limbs that supported the greater part of the nest.

Curious, she reached inside one of the garbage bags and brought out a plastic-wrapped bundle. Pealing away the wrappings, she pulled out a dog-eared edition of *The Odyssey*—Fitzgerald's translation. She opened the book and gasped. The margins around the text were filled with notes.

In the same handwriting as was in Sabazios's book.

She scanned the handwritten notes. They revealed the same passion, the same appreciation for literature as the notes in *Paradise Lost*. How had Melchi gotten hold of Sabazios's book? Or . . .

Had Sabazios taken *Paradise Lost* from Melchi?

She shook her head. Neither explanation seemed probable.

She flipped to the end and started reading through the notes, engrossed in what they revealed about the author. Whoever he was, he was passionate in his identification with Telemakhos, the disinherited son of Odysseus. Maybe it was—

"Do you like Homer?"

Hailey snapped the book shut. She whirled around to find Melchi crouching on one of the larger limbs, watching her with those intense brown eyes.

"I am sorry to startle you. I felt you reading and thought it would be safe to come up. I brought chicken." He held out a white, grease-stained cardboard box.

"Where did you get this?" Hailey's words rang with accusation.

"The chicken? The Booklady gave it to me. She is very happy and wishes me to bring you to see her soon. She wants to—"

"I mean *this*." She held up the book.

"A very good lady named Miss Lila gave it to me as a present. Her son wished her to move to Chicago to be close to him. I helped her pack."

"So *you* wrote the notes?"

Melchi nodded. "It is a terrible habit. Ortus did not approve of marking up books, but paper falls out and makes it so hard to read, and—"

"So it was your *Paradise Lost*?"

"It is yours. I gave it to you as a present." Melchi's eyes were wide and pleading. "Why are you angry? I thought you would like it. The Booklady said you asked for it at the bookstore."

Hailey sighed. "Melchi, you should have put a card in it. I almost got killed because I thought it was from Sabazios. I *never* would have gone out with him if I had known it was from you." Hailey bit her lip. Way to spill her guts.

"So the flowers at your door. They were from Sabazios?"

Hailey nodded.

"I thought they were from your boyfriend."

"My boyfriend?" Hailey studied his face. Was he jealous? "Melchi, I don't have a boyfriend. I went out with Sabazios because I thought he wrote the notes in the book, and I thought what he wrote was . . . sweet." There. She'd said it. Against her better judgment, she had issued the invitation. She watched Melchi from beneath lowered eyelids.

"The man with the big black car wasn't your boyfriend?"

*The man with the big black car? The limo driver?* Hailey almost laughed. Was that why he ran off? She opened her mouth to explain but decided against it. She had issued the invitation. The ball was in his court now.

"If you will allow me, I will go to your friend and tell her you are safe, but we should eat first. We have four large pieces." Melchi opened the box and held it out to Hailey with a flourish.

She took a thigh and waited as he took a small drumstick and said a strange prayer. He ate with an enthusiasm and an eagerness that touched her. She nibbled at the cold chicken, suddenly awash with sadness. And shame.

"Melchi," she spoke his name gently, "how long has it been since you've eaten?"

"I had a big meal yester—no, day before yesterday." He took a big bite. "The Booklady is very good to me."

Hailey looked down at her piece of chicken, letting her hair fall in front of her face to hide her tears. A homeless man was sharing his food with her. He had given up his bed on a cold night and the only home he knew. She wiped the sleeve of her dress across her eyes.

No. Not a homeless man.

Melchi.

BOGGS JUMPED IN HER car and pulled out into traffic. Hailey hadn't come home last night. She'd been trying to call her all morning, but nobody answered the phone. The city slid past her in a blur. She was a VW Bug substrate in the active site of an enzyme. She could see a network of water molecules aligning and realigning themselves on the surface of the site. The order of the network was a property of the protein. The disorder, a property of the system. She mentally added energy to the molecules, letting them vibrate and flow. A multidimensional contour map of flickering blue and red.

Sleeping. That's what she was doing. Hailey was probably still asleep. She had gotten in late and didn't want to wake her up. That's what *she* would have done. And Hailey had turned off her phone so annoying people like her wouldn't wake her up. Poor thing. She'd been through so much. She needed every second of sleep she could get.

Boggs shook her head. She had to get away from the static molecular description. There was no hope for it. It had to be continuous. One with the water.

But what kind of a last-minute dinner meeting could Hailey have gone to? She'd been so vague in her note. It had obviously been written in a hurry. The half-eaten sandwich, the glass of milk—they all pointed to . . .

Humidity. It was the only answer. A large sheet of clear plastic to cover the barren ground—something permeable to oxygen and carbon dioxide but impermeable to water vapor.

She was a half block away from Hailey's house when she noticed the flashing lights. Police cars, yellow tape, a white ambulance-like van.

Boggs's stomach sank. *God, no! Please don't let it be Hailey!* She parked across the street and got out of the car.

Hailey's house was a war zone. Staccato bursts of voices and static erupted from the open squad cars while police officers stood conferring in small, uneasy groups in front of the house. A man with rolled-up shirtsleeves and a blue tie stepped through Hailey's door and hurried past a cluster of officers. Boggs ran across the street, ducked under the yellow tape, and bolted toward him, but a uniformed police officer barred her way.

"I'm sorry. This area is off-limits. You'll have to step back behind the line."

"I'm a friend of Hailey's. Hailey Maniates. She lives here." Boggs tried to walk around the officer, but he gripped her arm and directed her back toward the tape.

"Just give us a chance to do our jobs." The officer guided her under the tape with a hand on her back and a firm grip on her right arm.

Boggs twisted around to look him in the face. "Is she okay?"

"Sorry, but I can't answer that."

"Just a minute, Stevens." The man in the tie was moving toward Boggs. "You're a friend of Tiffany Gainnes or Hailey Maniates?"

"I'm a friend of Hailey's. She was supposed to be staying with me last night. Is she okay?"

"Maybe." The man furrowed his brow and ran his fingers through his hair with a sigh. "I'm Detective John Smiley, and I assure you I'm doing everything I can to find out."

"Last night I had dinner with friends. I was only gone two hours, but when I got back, she was gone. A note said she had a dinner meeting and might be back late, but she left half a PB&J and a glass of milk on the end table, and—"

"And your name is?"

"Boggs. Susan Boggs. She's been having these strange attacks, and I was just coming to make sure she was okay."

"When I met Ms. Maniates, she was sitting down, but I'd guess that she's fairly tall. How tall would you say Hailey is?" Smiley's expression was inscrutable.

"I don't know. Tall. About six or six-one."

"And Tiffany Gainnes was her roommate? How tall would you say she was?"

"I don't think I ever met Tiffany, but I got the impression she wasn't that tall—taller than me but shorter than Hailey."

Smiley nodded. "And do you have any idea where Hailey might have gone last night?"

"So Hailey's okay. She isn't—"

"Right now we don't have enough information to make that call."

"Then what's all this?" Boggs pointed to the police cars and yellow tape. "If you aren't sure—" The realization hit her like a Mac truck. Tiffany. He had asked her how tall Tiffany was. He wasn't sure about Hailey, but he was probably sure about Tiffany.

"Do you have any idea where Hailey would go if she was in trouble? Any friends she would stay with?"

"Surely you don't think Hailey had anything to do with—"

"We don't think Hailey has done anything wrong, but we think that she may be in grave danger." Smiley's eyes locked onto Boggs. "Four people are already confirmed dead, and that number is expected to climb much higher. We have good reason to believe Hailey is next on the list. Any information that could help us locate her might help save her life."

"I don't know." Boggs struggled to think where she might be. "She's more my friend's friend than mine."

"And your friend's name is . . ."

"Melissa Thomas. She's Hailey's roommate, but she's in Colorado for the week. Her grandmother—"

"I'll need the phone number where she's staying. And her address." Smiley dug in his shirt pocket and handed Boggs a card. "And a list of any other friends Hailey has in the area or any place you can think of she might go if she's in trouble. Call me at the second number. If I don't answer, leave a message."

"Okay. List of friends and places in the area." Boggs felt like a soldier in the middle of a combat zone. "Is there anything else I can do to help?"

SHADE 251

"Just call me with the list. Or the second you hear from Hailey. And if you do see her, don't let her out of your sight."

Detective Smiley turned with a nod and hurried over to a dark-green Buick. Boggs watched him make a wide U-turn and speed away.

Wherever he was racing off to, it wasn't to catch a hallucination.

# ∽ 19 ∾

The fog was rolling in again. Boggs groaned when she saw it on the horizon. Fog was the price one paid in San Francisco for clear sunny days. She zipped her jacket and tugged at the drawstrings of her hood to bring it tighter around her ears.

She had left four messages on Detective Smiley's answering machine, giving him every name and phone number she could think of: Melissa's, Nicole's, Beth's, even Mark Ackerman's—the suspiciously ubiquitous med student. Melchi, the homeless math scholar. Sabazios, the guy at the bar. Dr. Werner, the overbearing advisor. Bin, the Chinese postdoc. The weird guy that hung out in the stairwell of the student center.

A reflection in her glasses made her whirl around. A gray Honda was moving slowly up the street. The man driving the car searched the opposite side of the street. *Just looking for a parking place. Calm down, Boggsy. If Smiley doesn't call you soon, you're going to be a basket case.* She looked at her watch. 4 p.m. She might have time to go back to the bookstore after one more search of the biochem labs. And after she was finished with that, she could try Melissa's number one more time.

Boggs started to cross the street when she saw a man, on the sidewalk of a side street, waving his arms. She ignored him and crossed the intersection, but something about him made her stop and look back up the street. He signaled her over to him and then disappeared down another street. He was very tall with long curly hair and a thick bear—

She gasped. Could it be Hailey's homeless man?

Boggs turned and hurried toward the university. Her footsteps sounded sharp and urgent against the neighboring buildings. She crossed the next intersection with her head down, listening for cars.

"I have a message from Hailey." The distant whisper brought her to a sudden stop.

She turned in the direction of the voice, but the street was deserted. "Where are you?" she called out in a hoarse whisper.

"Do not look up. You are being followed." The voice came from above Boggs's head. "Go to the door on your right and pretend to knock on it."

Boggs considered running, but what if Hailey needed her help? She walked to the doorway and pretended to knock. Silence bore down on her with the weight of an invisible gun pointed at the base of her neck.

"Keep looking at the door. And listen. Hailey is safe but has need of her walking boot. Two policemen tried to kill her last night, and police guard her apartment now. I cannot get to her boot."

"Who are you? How do I know I can trust you?" Boggs spoke to the closed door in front of her.

"My name is Melchi. Hailey said to tell you that I'm the kind of person who talks life, not science in the halls. Does this mean anything to you?"

Boggs replayed her conversation with Hailey. She was saying Melchi was a friend. Could he have constructed the message himself? Might Hailey have mentioned the conversation in another context? No. It wasn't the kind of thing that would come up in idle conversation. She had no choice but to trust Hailey's judgment.

"Are you still there?"

"I am here, but I must go now. Hailey said you might be able to get her another boot. Do you think you could lose your shadows and throw a boot over the Golden Gate Park fence at the bottom of Twelfth Avenue? "

"But where *is* she? Can you take me to her?"

"I must go now. Your shadows are here."

Boggs spun around. A man in faded blue jeans and a blue flannel shirt was crossing the street, moving vaguely in her direction. She considered calling to him. Telling him to search the roof of the building. But no, she had to trust Hailey. Hailey was the only one with enough information to make sense of this crazy situation.

At least, Boggs hoped she did.

She walked back to Parnassus and hurried up the hill toward the hospital, glancing back occasionally to see if she was being followed. If she was, then they were pretty good. Either that or invisible. She made it all the way to the hospital without seeing anyone even remotely suspicious.

Boggs went first to the break rooms, hoping to find an intern or med student she knew well enough to ask a favor. Nobody. She was just about to go to the pharmacy and buy a new boot when she noticed the man in the blue flannel shirt, reading a magazine in a waiting area.

She punched the up button outside the elevator and tapped her foot. Then, looking at her watch, she pushed open the heavy door to the stairs and ran down two flights.

The homeless man was right. She *was* being followed. But why? It didn't make sense. Could he have been a part of it? Was he setting her up?

She ran across the hospital to the pharmacy and paid for a new boot. Then, hiding the bulky package under her coat, she took the stairs to the basement and ran through the dark corridors interconnecting most of the buildings on the relatively small UCSF campus.

Exiting at the back of the nursing center, three buildings away from the hospital, she slunk along narrow streets to Twelfth Avenue and ran all the way down the hill to Golden Gate Park. She climbed over the fence, pushing her way through the dense undergrowth. Then, at the edge of a tangle of bushes, she threw the boot out into a clearing and crouched down in the undergrowth to wait.

What was happening with Hailey? Paranoid schizophrenia, the police, homeless people? She watched the boot through a gap in the leaves, trying to puzzle all the pieces together.

A limb shook behind her. She wheeled, searching the sparse vegetation. Nothing. The bushes were silent and still. She turned back to the clearing with a gasp.

The boot was gone.

———

ATHENA HURRIED DOWN THE sidewalk, an important person with important places to go. She thrust both hands deep into the pockets of her new overcoat. Not bad for three dollars at the thrift store. The lining had a rip in it, and there was a large bleach stain below the left pocket, but it was a nice shade of black, and it was just long enough to drag on the ground with a majestic sweep. *Tight. Wicked tight.* She would have bought it even if she hadn't been on the run.

She turned randomly at an intersection and picked up her pace. She could always dye the pocket. Benedict had plenty of black dye back at his apartment—if only she dared go back for it. She looked up at the sky. The haze was turning into a dense fog. It would be another cold night. She needed to find a place to stay, and even more than that, she needed something to eat. Something . . .

An unsettling feeling tugged at her memory. What day was it? Saturday, Sunday, Monday? Six o'clock on a Monday night. Garibaldi's night! She and Benedict had been meeting at Garibaldi's for months.

A hollow pang stabbed through her stomach. If Benedict wanted to find her, Garibaldi's would be the first place he'd look. She forced her aching feet into a slow jog. She had a few matters to discuss with the self-centered little traitor.

She was out of breath and exhausted by the time she arrived at the small restaurant. He didn't seem to be there yet so she crossed the street and settled down to wait in the doorway of a closed clothing shop. Pulling her knees up under her new coat, she shivered in the waning light, more from hunger than from the cold.

At last she was rewarded by the sight of a tall guy in black leather and fishnet. Benedict turned at the door and searched up and down the congested street. He was looking for her, all right. Well, this was going to be his unlucky day.

He was going to find her.

She waited a few minutes to give him time to order and then a few more to give them time to bring his food. Then, darting across the street, she crept to the restaurant entrance and peeked inside.

There he was. At the table by the window.

A high-school student in a waitress apron met her at the door. "How many? Just one?"

"No, I'll wait here. I'm expecting a friend."

"Okay." The girl turned to leave as another waitress carried a steaming plate to Benedict's table.

"Never mind. I'll settle for an enemy instead." Athena stalked over to Benedict's table. "Hello, Benedict. Looking for another friend to sell out?"

"Athena!" Benedict jumped to his feet, tipping over his chair. "Where have you been? I've been looking all over for you."

"You and a hundred other hounds, but I'm not ready to donate blood to the March of Dimwits just yet." Athena sat down across the table from Benedict and pulled his plate over to her place.

"You don't understand. It's not like that. They want to help you. They've been giving me money, food, a new place to stay. And they're going to turn me. For real."

"Turn your brain to mush," Athena said between mouthfuls as she shoveled the hot lasagna into her mouth.

"Hey! That's my—"

Athena slammed her palm down on the table. "I've been out on the street, moshing with the polar bears for two nights! I've been beat up, stalked, drugged. My friends are being watched. They're watching the police stations and BART stations. And why is this happening, you might ask? How do they know where I live? How did they find out about all my friends? Because some sadistic drug lord promised my dice-brained *ex*-boyfriend he'd give him a hickey to sell me out."

"It's not like that, Athena. I promise. They want to help you. They'll give you money. Parties. Anything. This is for real. Smythe's really been turned. I've seen him. He's got powers."

"Well, I've seen him too! He was in your apartment, waiting to slit my throat."

"He wasn't going to hurt you. They just want to make sure you're safe. They're worried about you. . . ."

Athena ate Benedict's meal as fast as she could, ignoring his lame blathering. He would probably be killed when he outlived his usefulness, but there was no point trying to convince him. Only a fool argued with fools.

She pushed herself away from the table. "I want you to give your fancy friends a message from me. Tell them I don't know what they're doing and I don't care, but if anything happens to me, a detailed letter will be sent to twenty different police stations scattered throughout the Bay Area." She stood and started to walk away, but Benedict lunged for her and grabbed her arm.

"I'm sorry, but if they found out I saw you and didn't bring you back . . ."

Athena let him lead her to the door. "This is even better. I can deliver the message myself. Take me to your leaders, dice-brain. I want to give them a piece of my mind."

"You'll come with me? You're serious?"

"Sure, I'm serious, but I'm not going to jail with you. You'd better pay for your meal."

Benedict tried to pull her back toward the table, but she yanked her arm away and leaned back against the counter. He reached toward her again, but she warned him off with a look.

"You better hurry. I'm still hungry, and I expect to be well fed before I chew out your new friends."

Benedict hurried back to his table with several backward glances at Athena. She waited for the waitress to come out with the bill and then darted through the door.

————

"Do not be alarmed." Melchi climbed up through the large cedar, rattling branches as he went. "It is me, Melchizadek. May I approach the nest?"

"Of course." A musical laugh sounded, bright and sunny, through the branches. "I was beginning to think I'd scared you away. I know I must have looked a mess this morning."

"No," Melchi declared solemnly. "You did not. You—" His throat tightened. He paused to brush the needles from his beard and hair before stepping out onto the tightrope. "I did not wish to . . . startle you. I am coming now."

He pushed through a curtain of drooping limbs and stopped. Hailey was leaning back against the tree with a blanket over her legs. His Homer lay opened across her lap. She looked so comfortable, so natural.

"Good. You got my boot. Thank you."

"Not your boot. A new one." Melchi walked the rest of the way across the rope and set the boot at her feet. "The police were guarding your house. Your friend bought this at a store."

Hailey's face clouded. "Why were the police guarding my house?"

"I do not know. Perhaps they continue to search for you?" Melchi looked through the webbing to the canopy of leaves below. He shouldn't have said anything. She would worry now, and worry was an open invitation to the Mulo. "Do you have enough money to fly on an airplane?"

"What? You want me to leave the city?"

"It is not safe here. You must go away, as far from the Mulo as possible. Do you have family you could stay with? Someone who lives far away from the city?"

Hailey shook her head. Sorrow hung on the air like a fine mist. It seeped through his skin, piercing him to the innermost recesses of his heart. "I am sorry. I did not know." He crouched at Hailey's feet, looking on helplessly as tears came to her eyes. Why did he always make things worse? He was worse than the Mulo.

"So how long would I have to stay away?" Hailey's voice sounded bitter. "A year? Ten years? Living in fear? Jumping at every shadow?"

"I must fight the Mulo soon. Perhaps I will defeat him. Then you may return."

"How long is soon? And what am I supposed to do about grad school? What'll I tell my professor? I have to take a leave of absence because a monster is trying to kill me? He'll send me right back to the shrinks."

"You are a graduate student?" Melchi tried to take in the implications. That would be over sixteen years of education. She was too young. Too beautiful . . .

"You don't have to act so surprised. It's not like I've got the plague."

"No. I think it is . . . wondrous. What is your special area?"

"Biochemistry, I guess. Enzymology."

"Proteins and DNA and phospholipids and things like that? Do you know how RNA polymerase knows when to make some proteins and not others? No. Wait. PCR—how do they know what markers to use? Or the brain. What keeps chemicals from crossing the blood-brain barrier?" Melchi started to stand and then sat back down. There were so many questions he wanted to ask. The library books were pitifully incomplete.

Hailey looked at him with an expression he couldn't interpret. "The lady at the bookstore told me you never went to school."

Melchi hung his head. "I must seem very ignorant."

"No! Not at all. Just the opposite. Your writing is beautiful. It blows me away. Milton? Homer? I was supposed to read them in college but never made it through. I read the CliffsNotes instead."

"Cliff's notes?"

"Never mind. It's not important. What's important is that you've been able to teach yourself. Me—education was something that was done to me. Sometimes against my will."

Against her will? Melchi shook his head. What was she saying? It didn't make sense.

Hailey smiled at him. "For what it's worth, Melchi, I think you're one of the most interesting men I've ever met."

"Me? No." Melchi shook his head. "I don't know anything. I am . . ." A haze obscured his vision. He leaned forward, reached out with his hand . . .

*No! Holy One, help me.* Ripping himself away from her eyes, Melchi turned to face the tightrope. His right calf burned. His whole leg was throbbing. It was the poison. That had to be it. It was surging through his system, clouding his brain, infecting him to the soul. The prophecy was coming true: He was becoming the enemy.

"It is not safe here." His voice grated in his ears as he choked out the words. "You must go. As far from San Francisco as possible."

"No." Hailey's tone was rock solid. "I'm not running away. Not anymore."

Melchi eased his weight off his hurt leg and let it hang over the limb. If he had to, he would jump. He could not let himself hurt her. "Hailey?" His voice was a whisper.

"What?" A trace of irritation still clung to her voice.

"May I ask you a question?"

"Another question, you mean?"

Melchi nodded. "Is it possible for a bite to transform a person into something that person is not?"

"You mean, like a disease? Rabies is transmitted by the bites of infected animals."

"Not a disease. Something that changes the person—morally and physically."

"Creutzfeldt-Jakob disease is caused by prions, proteins that change the tertiary structure of other proteins in the brain—Mad Cow Disease. It's possible something like that could be transmitted by animal bites. If it looks enough like a naturally occurring protein in the brain, it wouldn't even raise an immune response."

Melchi risked a quick glance. "How long does it take for the transformation to occur?"

"What do you mean, 'transformation'? It's a disease, really."

"How long does it take for the disease to occur?"

"I think it's supposed to take a pretty long time. Sometimes several years. Why do you ask? Have you been hearing rumors about a disease called Sudden Onset Dementia?"

"What?"

"Sudden Onset Dementia. Boggs checked it out for me. They think it's caused by a drug addiction, not prions."

Melchi shook his head. "Is it possible for some types of people to be transformed but not other types of people?"

"Sure, I guess. There are lots of diseases that affect only a limited population."

Melchi nodded. What if the Standing were the only people who could be turned? Could that be the reason they were hunted?

The rip of tearing Velcro sounded behind him. Hailey was putting on her walking boot. "What are you thinking?"

"I'm going to go to the police. I know one of the detectives."

"But you cannot! They tried to hurt you."

"Only two of them, and I don't even know if they were the real police."

"But you . . . I . . . Once I destroy the Mulo, it will not be able to bother you anymore. You cannot go to the police. It is not safe."

"Destroy? As in murder? Melchi, this is a matter for the police. You can't go after Sabazios yourself. No matter how bad he may be, if you hurt him, they'll put you in jail. You'll be a criminal."

"But it is not human. It is not even—" He clamped his mouth shut. He had already said far too much.

"Okay. You've been evading my questions all morning. If you don't tell me everything you know about Sabazios right now, I'm leaving. I'm going to the police with or without you."

"And if I tell you, this means you will not go to the police?"

"Maybe. But I'm not running. Maybe we could work with the police to catch him. It shouldn't be that hard."

"You don't understand. The police cannot stand—"

"That's why I need you to tell me everything you know."

Melchi looked down at the webbed deck of his nest. She was almost certainly one of the Standing. Maybe if he made her his apprentice, inducted her into the Order . . . Ortus never said apprentices had to be male, not directly. And if he really was the long-awaited, didn't that give him the right to choose any apprentice he wanted?

"By telling you more, I make you my apprentice. You must agree never to reveal anything I say to anyone else."

"An apprentice. An apprentice in what?"

"Do you agree?"

Hailey shrugged. "Okay. I swear. I'll never—"

"No!" Melchi raised a hand. "Do not swear! It is forbidden. Just say you agree or you disagree."

"Okay, I agree. You don't have to get so excited."

"There is much I must teach you. It will take many days." Melchi paused, waiting for Hailey to make herself comfortable against the trunk of the tree. "The Order is very old. Perhaps over six thousand years. There is its history, its code, its tenets, the prophecies—"

"Prophecies . . . as in fortune-telling? You believe in fortune-telling too?"

"No! Never fortune-telling. That is a tool of the enemy, a web of lies designed to tangle and ensnare. The message of the true prophet comes from the Holy One. It must always be true."

"But you really believe in these prophecies, right? You believe they're about you?"

Melchi studied Hailey's expression. "You saw this in my thoughts?"

"No. The lady at the bookstore mentioned it—something about you being the long-awaited child of Standing?"

"That is the belief of my old master, but there are many prophecies and many Standing. There is the great shield, who must rise to crush the Mulo. And the strong guardian of the first dimensional gateway. Many scholars believe the two are linked, but there are others who disagree. There is also the adopted son of the first dimension, and the dawning light who stands firm against the darkness. These could be linked as well. Or they may not be linked at all. It is all very confusing. We should probably start at the beginning."

"But first, how does Sabazios fit into all this? Is he a member of your Order too?"

"No!" Melchi fought to control his voice. "He is the Mulo, the Eternal Enemy. The hunter and destroyer of my people. The Order was formed long ago to protect mankind from his reign of terror. Sabazios is but a name he takes to disguise himself in the world of men."

"But I thought you said this order was thousands of years . . . I mean, this doesn't make sense. You act like Sabazios isn't even human."

Melchi searched her eyes. Was she not paying attention? Or perhaps she didn't believe him. This was a mistake. He should not have said anything.

"Melchi?" The soft sweetness of her voice thrilled through him. Her beautiful eyes. So plaintive. So innocent.

He looked down at his hands. He should not speak. Ortus would not approve. But Ortus did not know her situation.

"The Mulo is not human, not anymore. He is unman, the eternally dying but undead. It has been thousands of years since he last walked the earth as a living, breathing man. In those days—" he looked up and met her eyes—"his name was Cain."

# ୨୦ 20 ୧୭

*Ultra Blue. 30% off.*

Athena grabbed the box off the shelf. She could already see herself with a spiky, shockin' white do. She'd look wicked good in a black lace gown. She put the black tint back on the shelf, then hesitated, her finger on top of the box—a master chess player checking her next move.

She was supposed to be hiding, not trying to stand out. There would be lots of Goths at the party, and most of them would have their hair dyed black. Especially the vampire-pretenders. If she really wanted to fit in, she'd go with the black.

Athena took her finger off the dye and carried the color remover and some black eyeliner to the register. The best place to hide when people know you're hiding is right out in the open—with shockin' white spikes.

The woman at the register was a big-boned, raw-looking woman with bright red lipstick and pink chipped nails. She took the color remover from Athena and laughed. "I knew when you walked in here you was coming to get hair dye. Is that all?"

Athena handed her a ten and forced a smile. "You know, I just remembered a costume party I'm supposed to attend. Just a second. I need to get a few more things."

She wandered through the beauty supply store, picking up expensive items at random until she had an armful. Then, dumping the items on the counter, she reached behind her neck and tugged at the tag of her dress. "Do you have a WC—um, a bathroom I could use?"

The woman nodded and took a key ring out of the register. "I'm not supposed to let customers use it, so don't take long." The woman led her through a cluttered stockroom to a dingy restroom.

"And do you have some scissors? The tag on this dress is killing me."

The woman left the stockroom with an exaggerated sigh and came back with a pair of scissors.

Athena locked the door behind her, and then, wetting down her hair in the small sink, she lopped off handful after handful of her beautiful green hair, taking care not to cut it too evenly.

Then, accompanied by a banging door and a torrent of oaths and threats, Athena bleached her hair with the mild gel.

*Blam! Blam! Blam!* The door sounded like it was going to rattle to pieces.

She took her time and teased her hair into uneven spikes. Then, checking herself from all angles in the mirror, she opened the door and sauntered out past the red-faced woman.

"That was the *worst* display of manners I've ever witnessed!" Athena said in a horrified voice.

The woman glared at her.

"I believe I've changed my mind about buying anything here. Do be a dear and put those few items back for me."

She was halfway out the door before the woman found her voice.

HAILEY WATCHED MELCHI OUT of the corner of her eye. He was sitting rigid in the taxicab, holding onto the door handle white-knuckled. His eyes darted back and forth, following each passing vehicle with the eagerness of a puppy riding in a car for the first time.

She studied his profile, trying to imagine what he would look like shaved and with a haircut. Probably pretty good. He had beautiful eyes. She noticed again the bend to his back that pushed him forward at the shoulders. The afternoon had been warm, but he never once took his coat off. Was his deformity the real reason he hid himself from the eyes of men? Was Golden Gate Park his Notre Dame de Paris?

Or was he just crazy? Hailey considered the strange stories he had told her in the park. It was all fantasy. It had to be. But he'd been so earnest, so convincing. He really expected her to believe that God had marked Cain to keep created beings from being able to kill him. It was ridiculous. And the part about Cain going back to the garden of Eden and the mark protecting him from the angel that guarded its gates. And eating from the Tree of Life. Wasn't it supposed to be the Tree of Good and Evil? And then there was the whole affair with Lilith the she-demon . . .

Okay, he admitted that that part was just a theory, but didn't that mean he believed the rest to be fact?

It was as if he were trapped in the Dark Ages. She watched him as he scanned the city streets. Vampires and she-demons aside, he seemed to be extremely intelligent, probably a borderline genius. He'd have no trouble at all passing a high-school-equivalency exam. Perhaps with her help he could even get into a good university. She could at least help him get a job. All he really needed was a loan and a little help finding new clothes and a place to live.

If he could just get over his obsession with this Mulo business.

Sabazios was just a man. There was a rational explanation for everything that had been happening. Hypnotism. Drugs in the wine. A virus. She had to make Melchi see that.

"Melchi, what if we caught Sabazios and turned him over to the police? I know you don't trust the local department, but we could contact other agencies. They can't all be bad. And we could have reporters there as a safeguard."

Melchi turned a startled look at her. "It is too strong. I would not stand a chance."

"But we're smarter than him, and there are two of us. What if we tricked him into a cage? Certainly you don't think he could escape through steel bars?"

Melchi's face brightened. "You have a steel cage?"

"No, but I know a place that will work just about as well."

"That we could use? Where?"

"At UCSF you have to go through an open balcony to get to the stairway from any floor of the science building. A heavy metal door separates each balcony from the building, and another heavy metal door separates it from the stairway. And each balcony is barred from floor to ceiling by heavy steel bars. They used to have a problem with med students jumping off to commit suicide." Hailey paused to see if Melchi was following.

"Okay . . ."

"I could get Sabazios to follow me out onto the balcony, and you could chain and reinforce the door behind me. Then while his attention is on the door, I could run through the other doors and chain them closed."

Melchi shook his head. "Too dangerous. We must not risk letting it get that close to you."

"I've been close to him before and nothing happened."

"It was toying with you. Next time it will not be so patient."

Hailey swallowed back an angry retort. He might have a point. The metal doors hadn't stopped Sabazios before, and she had no idea what they could do to reinforce them. Assuming, of course, it had been Sabazios who chased her. Somehow she couldn't picture Sabazios hanging out in research centers chasing grad students like the Boogeyman.

"What about the roof? The science building is fourteen stories high. All we have to do is get him to go out onto the roof and chain the doors. There's no other way down."

"That could work." Melchi turned in his seat to face Hailey. "Is there another building near the science building?"

"Yeah, but it's too far away. He couldn't jump, if that's what you're thinking. There'd be no way he could escape."

"But is the other building the same height? How far away is it?"

"I guess so." Hailey tried to visualize a football field overlaying the walkway separating the two buildings. "It's about the same height and about thirty yards away."

"Perfect! If I could get it to chase me onto the roof, then you could chain the door behind us. If we stretched a rope between the two buildings, I could run across before it ever got close to me."

"And then we could call the reporters and police. And no more Mulo to worry about. Right?"

Melchi frowned. "There are just two problems. Where are we going to get a chain with a lock?"

Hailey searched his face to see if he was joking. Hadn't the guy ever heard of a hardware store? "We can buy all the supplies we need. I have plenty of money."

He looked dubious. "But here is something you have not considered. How do we find the Mulo and get it to chase me to your science building?"

"That's the easy part." Hailey grinned. "I'll just call him up and ask him to meet me there. I've got his phone number."

"The Mulo has a telephone?"

"Of course he does. This *is* the twenty-first century, you know."

Melchi's eyes drifted to the window.

"So do you still think it's important to find this green-haired girl?"

Melchi nodded. "She is one of us. A child of the Standing. Even if there is a small chance she is at this Pit place, we must look. If the Mulo catches her . . ." He shrugged and looked back out the window. Hailey studied his reflected expression. There was more to this green-haired girl than he was saying.

"Have you ever ridden in a car before?"

"Yes. Many times." Melchi looked down at his knees which were pulled up almost to his chest. "But not so much after I learned hitchhiking was illegal."

"You don't travel—I mean, how long have you lived in San Francisco?"

"A little more than two months. I came here when I read about the murders in Golden Gate Park."

"I see. Where were you before?"

"New Orleans."

"New Orleans? So how did you get here?"

"A man named William drove me in his truck. I didn't hitch-hike. He was very nice. He paid for my food and everything."

Hailey felt a twinge of uneasiness. Was it something in his expression, or was she starting to feel things again? "That was nice of him."

"He was a very nice man." Melchi looked down at his knees and started picking at the ragged edge of a tear in his jeans.

"Melchi, I'm your friend, right? Do you trust me?"

He nodded.

"Then why is it I get the feeling you aren't telling me something?"

Melchi was silent for several seconds before he answered. "I met him one night in the city. Three bad men tried to hurt him, and I . . . stopped them."

"That sounds like a good thing. Certainly nothing to be ashamed of."

Melchi picked at the tear.

The image of a violent fight broke out in her mind. "You hurt one of them, didn't you?"

Melchi nodded slowly.

"Did . . . somebody die?"

"I don't think so, but I heard broken ribs. And one man's eye . . . got cut." Melchi's voice faded so much that Hailey could barely make out the last two words.

"You had a knife?"

Melchi shook his head. "One of *their* knives. I kicked it from his hand, and it . . . it . . ." Melchi bowed his head.

"So it was self-defense. No! More than self-defense. You saved a man's life." Hailey reached for Melchi's hand, but he jerked it away and scooted even closer to the door.

She pulled her hand back. "I'm sorry. You seemed so sad, I just wanted to help." She slumped back in her seat. Why did he do that? Was she so undesirable he couldn't even stand to touch her? She turned away from him and stared out her window. Why did she even care? It wasn't like she was interested in him. She was in grad school, and he . . . he hadn't even graduated first grade. It was ridiculous. He didn't have a job, an address, a phone . . .

The taxi pulled to the curb. Melchi just sat there bowing his head, a look of intense concentration blanking his features. Finally he looked up. "I think it's okay. I guess you can come with me."

"Come with you? Of course I'm coming with you." She paid the driver while Melchi fidgeted in his seat.

They got out and studied the row of run-down shops lining the street. "I still don't understand why we had to ride in a taxi. We could have lived three weeks on what you had to pay."

"If Sabazios is really looking for us, we want to be out on the streets as little as possible."

Melchi fixed her with a sharp look.

"We're fine here. This is the last place he'd expect to find us." She scanned the street. The area was pretty seedy, and it seemed to get worse further down the hill. The Pit was supposed to be somewhere on the street. If the name was any indication, it was probably at the very bottom of the hill.

She started walking and Melchi followed at her side. A man with a leather jacket and silver spikes piercing his ears gave Melchi a wide berth. Hailey moved a little closer to him. This wasn't exactly the kind of place she'd want to visit on her own. She looked up at Melchi and smiled. It was nice to be able to look up to a man. His eyes darted from person to person. She could almost feel his mind working. It was like he was using radar.

They walked down and back up on the other side of the long street, but Hailey saw no sign of the meeting place all the chat room "vampires" were talking about. They were going to have to ask someone.

A man and a woman walked arm in arm toward them. The man wore a black frock coat, and his shirt looked like it was made out of black fishnet stockings. The woman wore a black cape over what looked to be an old-fashioned corset. As they passed, Hailey noticed both of them were wearing dark eye makeup and lipstick.

"Excuse me!" Hailey turned and followed after them. "Excuse me. Do you know where The Pit is?"

The man turned with a cold stare. He looked Hailey up and down like a greedy child licking a lollipop. She still wore the blue dress she'd put on for her date with Sabazios, but it was torn and badly wrinkled. He probably thought she was a drug addict. Or worse.

Then Hailey saw them. The man's canines were long and sharp—almost twice as long as his other teeth.

"Are you with him?" The man jerked his head at Melchi, who had stepped forward to take his place beside her.

Hailey nodded, afraid to trust her voice.

"Then follow us."

The couple turned and started walking, talking to each other in low soft voices. Hailey stepped closer to Melchi and reached for his hand, but he jerked away at her touch. He stared at his palm like she'd spilled burning acid on it and then wiped it on his coat. She could almost feel the sadness in his eyes.

"Sorry. I didn't mean to . . . but I need to tell you something." She tried to move closer, but a wave of tension pushed her back. "Did you see his teeth?"

Melchi nodded and then spoke in a low voice. "But he is harmless. I have searched both him and the girl. They do not have the aura."

"But his teeth. Do you think they're real?"

Melchi shrugged. "I only know he is not the Standing, and he is not one of the Mulo-creatures."

The couple entered a bar named Alioti's, and Hailey and Melchi followed them inside. The interior was dark, lit almost exclusively with tall tapering candles set in grotesque metal candelabras. An antique bar lined the back wall, and empty round tables filled the room.

A muscular man in a red silk shirt took money from the black-clad couple and, unlocking the heavy door behind him, ushered them into a stairwell that echoed with the sound of hissing guitars. Then, closing the door behind them, he turned to Hailey and Melchi.

Hailey handed him a twenty, and the man started to lead them to a table.

"Excuse me, but we're with the couple you just showed downstairs."

The man examined Hailey through half-closed eyes and then turned an appraising look on Melchi, who stepped closer, staring down at him with a frown. The man took a couple of steps backward, then shrugged and opened the door.

The narrow stairway buzzed to the pulsing music. Hailey followed Melchi through a battering wall of discordant sounds. A rhythmic, angry voice punched through the waves like a jackhammer, pounding into Hailey's chest with a force that made it hard to breathe.

She stepped out into a dark room and looked up at Melchi to get his reaction. His mouth hung open in a silent question. He scanned the room with alert, worried eyes. Surely this was all new to him.

The walls and floor were black, punctuated by the angry reds and whites of spray-painted graffiti. Rough-hewn beams crisscrossed a high ceiling that was hung with heavy chains and cast-iron chandeliers. On the wall to their left, behind a long hacked-up bar, hung dark Renaissance prints in elaborate gilded frames.

People stood drinking from plastic cups in small clusters or sat at small candlelit tables. Fishnet, heavy silver jewelry, black corsets, hoopskirts, veils, tights. No two people were dressed alike, but taken as a whole, there was a terrifying unity around a sinister theme.

A woman in a low-cut antique white gown drifted though the sea of black hair and fabric. Her hair was blond, almost white, and her skin was so pale it blended with the satiny fabric of her gown. A trickle of red ran from twin pinpricks on her neck.

Hailey turned toward the stairs, feeling out of breath and faint. Melchi stepped to her side, stooping low so he could look up into her down-turned face. His penetrating eyes held her like an anchor in a stormy sea.

"Are you all right? Do you want to call off our search?" He had to shout to be heard over the music.

Hailey took a deep breath and then another. "Are any of these people . . . bad?"

Melchi shrugged. "I don't know."

"But this is supposed to be a vampire hangout. Aren't Mulos and vampires pretty much the same thing?"

Melchi straightened and looked around the room as if seeing it for the first time. "Come!"

Hailey's skin prickled with heightened awareness as she followed him through the crowd. She had to twist and turn through the thronging mob to keep up with him while he searched frantically to his right and left.

Ahead of them a group of almost twenty people gyrated and swayed to the music. Their movements were fluid and impossibly slow against the pounding of the racing beat. Close but not quite touching, they let their hands flow over their partner's contours. Men with women, women with women? With some of them it was difficult to tell.

A curvy woman in filmy black gauze grabbed Melchi's hand and tried to pull him toward the dance floor. He shook his head and stood his ground, but Hailey noticed he didn't jerk his hand away. Hailey moved forward, placing herself between Melchi and the woman.

"The man said no!"

The woman let go and melted into the crowd. Hailey turned to face Melchi. He was still scanning the dancers.

"Come on. Let's go!" Hailey pushed her way through the crowd and turned to see Melchi following. He didn't seem to be worried about the scantily clad women that brushed by him as he followed her toward the stairs. Some of them seemed to be brushing up against him on purpose.

She stalked up the stairs and pushed her way through the door and out onto the street. Melchi appeared at her side, but she kept her eyes focused on the sidewalk.

"What is wrong, Hailey? Are you hurt?"

"I'm fine." Her voice rang tight as a guitar string. "I suppose you enjoyed your little party back there."

"I could not find any sign of the Mulo-creatures or the girl with green hair. Why do you suppose all those people were pretending to be what they are not?"

"That's a good question. Why indeed?" Hailey stopped suddenly and turned to face Melchi. "Why does anybody pretend to be something he isn't? Maybe he likes the attention!"

"Hailey, you are angry. Did I say something wrong?" Melchi's eyes were liquid and black. Filled with sadness and pain. So much pain.

Hailey exhaled and waited for the storm to pass. "I'm sorry, Melchi. It's just that . . . you act like I have a disease or something, like you find me so repulsive you can't stand to touch me."

"It is good for a man not to touch—"

"But you didn't jerk away from the woman in the bar. You brushed by lots of women and didn't seem to mind at all."

"Did I?" Melchi looked down so that his bushy hair hid his eyes from Hailey's view. "It was wrong. I was not thinking."

"But you always seem to be thinking around me."

Melchi looked up with haunted eyes. "Hailey, I *have* to think around you. Holy One, help me, but I have thought about little else since first we met. And not because I find you repulsive.

Nothing could be farther from the truth." He looked back down at the ground. "If I dropped my guard around those other women, it was because there could be no possible danger to me—not while you are around."

Hailey bit her lip, fighting the urge to lift his head and look into his eyes. "Melchi, are you saying you find me attractive?"

Melchi nodded slowly. "But I would never hurt you. I would die a thousand deaths before I would ever let anyone hurt you."

"I know you would, Melchi," Hailey whispered through a tight throat. "I know you would." She felt like a crumpled leaf in an emotional hurricane. Too much was happening all at once. She needed time to think. If only they could put the stuff with Sabazios behind them.

"Come on, Melchi. Let's trap Sabazios and be done with him. I'll call tonight while the building is still empty.

Melchi reached inside his coat and removed a large knife. "You should keep this. Use it to protect yourself from the Mulo or anyone else who threatens you—even me."

Hailey reached out her hand and hesitated. What was he doing with such a big knife? Careful not to touch him, she took the knife from his hand and held it up to the light. An ornate crucifix stood out in bold relief against the gleaming, ornately carved blade. She studied the weapon—and her blood ran cold.

The base of the hilt was discolored by a dark stain.

## 21

Boggs paced the floor of her apartment, wracking her brain for something else to tell Detective Smiley. Something, anything to give her another excuse to call him. She had already talked to his answering machine a dozen times. Maybe she could just ask for an update. She frowned. It was getting late. Still, she could at least leave a message and ask him to call her in the morning.

A buzzer rang and Boggs lunged for the phone, knocking a half-finished glass of milk off the coffee table. The buzz sounded again. It was the intercom, not the phone.

"Nice move, Boggsy." She ran to the door and hit the talk button. "Hailey? Is it you?"

A male's voice came through the static. "Hi, this is Detective John Smiley. Is this Susan Boggs?"

"Did you find Hailey? Is she okay?"

"Miss Boggs? May I come in? I'd like to ask you a few more questions."

"Sure, please! Come on up." Boggs buzzed him in and ran out to meet him on the landing. She fidgeted as heavy footsteps plodded up the stairs. She had to calm down or he'd think *she* was crazy.

Detective Smiley turned at the landing below her and looked up with a weary smile. His haggard features showed the strain of every step he took.

"Are you okay?" Boggs noticed for the first time how his left arm hung at his side. She remembered Hailey asking the other officer about it. What was his name? Officer Murray?

"I'm fine. Just a little tired. It's been a long day."

Boggs showed Smiley into her apartment, and he sank into her couch with a sigh while she ran to the kitchen to get a wad of paper towels for the spilled milk.

Boggs wiped up the spill and perched on a dry corner of the table. "I take it you haven't found her yet?"

"We're not giving up. I've got every available officer on the force out looking for her."

"You said you had a question?"

Smiley nodded and ran his fingers through his hair. "But first could I trouble you for a glass of water? I've been on the run all day. This is the first chance I've had to sit down."

"Sure." Boggs jumped up from the table. "Would you like something to eat too? I could make a sandwich."

Smiley rose to his feet. "I wouldn't want to trouble you."

"No trouble at all. All I've got is turkey, if that's okay."

"That sounds wonderful—if it's not any trouble. I haven't eaten a bite all day."

Boggs went into the kitchen and opened the door to the fridge. Great, she'd eaten the last of the turkey for lunch.

"I'm sorry." She searched the shelves for something else she could offer. "The turkey's all gone. Would peanut butter and jelly be okay?"

"Peanut butter and jelly sounds great." Smiley walked into the kitchen and watched as Boggs fixed the sandwich. "I used to start my day with PB&Js, but I had to cut that out when I made detective. Too much time behind a desk."

She handed him a plate with the sandwich, noticing the awkwardness of his stance as he reached out to take it.

"Thanks a ton." He smiled and his blue eyes brightened. Boggs found herself wondering how old he was.

"What's wrong with your arm?" She tried to make the question sound spontaneous.

"Nerve damage from an accident I had when I was in uniform."

Boggs directed him to sit at the kitchen table, waiting for him to continue with the story. The other officer said he'd saved the life of a boy. If he were the bragging type, this was his big chance.

She started to pour a glass of milk. "I'm sorry. Is milk okay? I really should have asked."

"Milk is perfect. Thanks."

Boggs handed him the glass and sat across the table from him. He had almost finished his sandwich. Apparently he wasn't one to save and tell.

"I listened to your messages, and they were very helpful. I wanted to ask you more about this big man that contacted you about the walking boot."

"There's not much to say. I think he's a friend—certainly not a murderer. Hailey trusts him, and I trust her judgment."

"No, I don't think he's the killer either. He doesn't match the profile. But I do think he might have information that could help us. Even beyond the fact that he knows where Hailey is."

"So do you have a description? You know who the killer is?"

"Not exactly. There was a series of murders in Chicago last year. All the victims were models. Remember hearing about the Model Murderer?"

Boggs shook her head.

"Well, the CPD was able to link the murders to an underground cult known on the street as the Standing. Two witnesses described the killer as tall with an athletic build, short black hair, and a prominent scar on his chin."

"Hailey's friend Melchi is tall, but he definitely doesn't have an athletic build or short black hair. Did they say anything about a hunchback?"

"Pardon me?"

"A lump on the back—a curvature of the spine. It's pretty prominent. I doubt they'd miss something like that."

"No. Nothing about his back. Like I said, your friend isn't a suspect, but he might have valuable information."

"What makes you think this model murderer is in San Francisco?"

Smiley frowned and popped the last corner of his sandwich into his mouth. "I'm sorry to have to tell you this, but Hailey's roommate, Tiffany Gainnes, was found murdered this morning along with two police officers." Smiley looked Boggs in the eye. "You don't seem very surprised."

"I pretty much figured as much from our conversation this morning—when you asked me how tall Tiffany was."

Smiley nodded. "The body showed the . . . it was in the same condition as the bodies of the models. And lab reports confirm that it was covered with the same PCP analogue the Standing uses on its victims. Vinyl gloves were also found at the scene."

"PCP analogue?"

"A form of angel dust that can be absorbed through the skin. The Standing uses it to recruit new members. They spray it on their victims to induce euphoria and hallucination, then they use the good cop/bad cop routine to gain their trust and draw them deeper into the cult."

"Hallucinations? Hailey was experiencing hallucinations."

"Exactly. I should have picked up on it earlier, but the doctors assured me it was paranoid schizophrenia. They had CAT scans of her brain to prove it. And then I was on vacation when Murray was called out . . ." Smiley sounded bitter, almost angry. He looked miserable.

"You can't blame yourself for this. You couldn't have known."

"Actually, I should have known. I've been investigating a branch of the Standing here in San Francisco. It's different. Much less religious than its parent organization in Chicago. It seems to be run more like a business—almost like the Mafia. There are other differences too, as well as indications that the two groups are feuding, but they both use ABPA."

"ABPA?"

"Airborne PCP analogue."

"So you think the model murderer is after Hailey?"

Smiley nodded somberly and dug in his breast pocket. He pulled out a small stack of photos and handed them to Boggs. "Notice anything about these women?"

Boggs thumbed through the photos. "They're all models, right? The ones who were killed?"

"Right. The Feds think this guy just goes for models, but the truth of the matter is this blonde right there, the second from the top, hadn't been a model since she was fourteen. I'm thinking, *What if this guy isn't after models? What if he just likes tall beautiful women?*"

Boggs had trouble swallowing. "Then Hailey would definitely qualify."

Smiley nodded.

"The homeless man said something about two police officers trying to kill Hailey. How do they fit into all this?"

"That's the weird thing. Last night I got a call from UCSF Campus Security saying Hailey was down at their office complaining that two men were in her apartment fighting. Apparently, a homeless guy broke down her door and started a fight with the man she was with—a man she called Sabazios.

"Sabazios! I knew it. The homeless man's name is Melchi."

"I figured as much. Anyway I sent two officers to check it out, and they find the house ransacked but empty except for Gainnes's body upstairs. Apparently she'd been dead for some time. I was worried about Hailey, so I asked them to drive over to UCSF and bring her in to the station."

"And they never showed up."

"Oh, they showed up all right, and the campus security officer on duty released her into their custody. That's all we know—except their bodies were found back at Hailey's apartment."

Boggs went cold. "Bodies?"

"With their skulls caved in."

"And you think whoever did it has Hailey?"

"That's what I was thinking before I heard your message about the boot. Now I have to think this Melchi must have her—or at least knows where she is."

"He said she was safe. I'm praying he's right, but do you think we can believe him?"

"I don't know. Do you know where they'd hide? Any ideas at all?"

"Well, there's the bookstore I told you about. And the clerk said Melchi lived in some sort of nest in Golden Gate Park. And the science building—there are tons of hiding places in the science building."

"I've got six men searching the park right now, and I already checked the bookstore. Could you make me a list of places to search in the science building?"

Boggs shook her head. "I could show you."

"No, I wouldn't want to put you in any danger."

"Danger? I work there, remember. If you don't take me, I'm going to walk right over and look around by myself."

"Well, since you put it that way, I would enjoy the company." Smiley stood up and took his dishes to the sink. "And thanks a million for the sandwich. I was about ready to drop."

"No problem." Boggs followed Smiley to the door. "One more thing. You mentioned earlier about finding vinyl gloves at the site. Why is that important?"

"The model murderer wears vinyl gloves to handle his victims. He has to protect himself from contact with the ABPA."

———·—·———

PERFECT! MELCHI ADMIRED THE heavy steel door leading out onto the roof of the science building. A rugged steel frame, welded seams, steel rings for the chains. And the hinges were twice as heavy as the hinges downstairs. It might actually work. Assuming, of course, Hailey could really talk to the Mulo on the phone.

He checked the bicycle cables Hailey bought at the hardware store and arranged them on the top step. He still couldn't get over it. A Mulo with a phone number. Ortus would have laughed and laughed. But why not? It lived in buildings with computers and electricity. Why wouldn't it have a telephone? He pulled the spray bottle from his inner jacket and checked its seal. Then the wooden stakes from his outer pocket, the coil of nylon twine from his outer coat—

"What do you think?" Hailey's voice rang out from the bottom of the stairs.

Melchi spun around and shoved the twine and stakes back into his pockets. The force of her presence was usually so strong. How had he missed her?

"Think it will hold?" Her eyes glowed in the light of the flickering fluorescent bulb. She seemed relaxed, almost happy. Maybe they should just run while they still had the chance.

"Melchi? Are you okay? You don't think it could actually get through?"

"No, the door is good." Melchi slipped the spray bottle back into his pocket and handed her the coil of bike cables. "Everything is very good." He stood aside while Hailey threw back the bolt and pushed open the door. She stood framed against the light of the moon, a softly curving silhouette traced with crescents of silver light.

Melchi's heart pounded in his chest, filling his ears with the beat of distant drums. *Holy One, no! Not now. Please help me.* Melchi tore his eyes away from Hailey and reached down to touch his calf. It was still hot, throbbing as if it had a heartbeat of its own.

"Are you okay?" Hailey stepped back into the stairwell. She was so close. He could smell the sweet perfume of her hair. "Is it your leg? Let me look at it."

"No!" Melchi dodged to the side and slipped past her out onto the roof. "I am fine." His throat felt like it was filled with gravel. "Please. I need you to leave. To find a weight. Something I can throw across to the other building. About ten or fifteen pounds. Heavy enough to carry the rope all the way across."

"But we forgot to buy a rope." Hailey stepped toward him, forcing him to back away. "I could run back to the hardware—"

"No! My rope is . . . more than sufficient."

Her eyes widened, reflecting the moonlight glowing in her face.

Melchi forced his eyes to the roof. Her presence pulled at him with an almost irresistible force. It was too much. If it grew any stronger, he might not be able to control it. "Please, Hailey. I need the weights now."

"But shouldn't we get rope first?"

"Please!" Melchi bowed his head and squeezed his eyes shut until red lights danced in his brain.

After what seemed an eternity, he heard her footsteps retreat across the roof and clomp down the stairs.

————•+•————

TWO MORE OUT. THAT'S *three hundred and ten in and seventeen out.*

Athena stood huddled in the shadows across the street from the hotel. Two more couples walked from the hotel. People were finally beginning to leave. Twenty-one had left and three hundred and ten had entered. Another couple arrived.

Three hundred and twelve. Perfect. As many were coming as going.

She watched as another couple left the party. The guy held the door open while his date stood in the doorway laughing. He was laughing too. She could hear them as they walked arm in arm down the street and disappeared into the shadows.

Athena sighed and stepped away from the buildings, wishing she had a mirror to check her makeup. All she had to do was drop off the jewels at the front desk and get out without attracting attention. Fewer than half the guests were wearing costumes. Most of them were dressed in Goth or mundane party clothes. She hadn't wanted to look like she was wearing a disguise, so she had only used a little black around her eyes. She wished she had used less. Her short, spiked hair and the heavy, angular shading at her cheek bones changed her look enough to fool her own mother.

Benedict was the main danger, but he wouldn't be in the lobby. If she knew him, he'd be standing around a beer keg somewhere with his make-believe friends.

A solitary Goth guy walked down the street toward the hotel. This was her chance. She slipped out of her new coat and hid it under a newspaper rack. Then, with a sigh, she tore a slit in her dress along the seam and ripped a ring of fabric from the bottom edge of the dress. The thin fabric refused to tear evenly, and the tear rode up much higher than she wanted as it circled behind her, leaving a six-inch gap between its starting and finishing points. Oh well. At least nobody would be looking at her face. Ripping the fabric down the seam, she stashed it with her coat and ran to catch up with the guy.

Latching onto his arm, she leaned in close to him, ignoring his initial cry of surprise. Athena swung forward around his arm to give him a better look.

"Mind if I join you?"

"Wha—?" The youth's eyes went wide as he looked into her face.

"I saw you from across the street and thought, *This guy I have to meet.*"

Athena smiled and led him through the doors.

Good. She'd found a young one. He wouldn't give her any trouble at all. She leaned on the youth's arm, noticing the growing swagger in his step. She swung her feet around each other in smooth arcs, stepping and twisting just past center to add a little extra sway. Now all she had to do was steer him to the front desk and—

"The party's over here." He turned and headed toward the archway at the other end of the lobby. She nodded and blinked her eyes. Her head felt like a swarm of bees had decided to nest in her brain. A group of black-clad guests loomed ahead of her, swaying to the music spilling out of the ballroom.

"First I need to drop off—" Athena looked up and froze. Benedict stood less than ten feet away. His eyes were focused on the doors, but . . .

She leaned her head on her new friend's chest and whispered, "Put your arm around me. I'm cold."

The kid complied with frightening alacrity and led her toward the archway. She looked up at him, careful to keep her face averted as they passed within a yard of where Benedict stood.

"Not that it matters, but what's your name?" the kid asked as they stepped into the ballroom. His voice was a full octave deeper than it had been when she grabbed his arm.

"Not that it matters, but none of your business." Athena twisted free of his grasp and pushed her way through the crowd toward the hors d'oeuvre tables lining the wall. She had to get back to the desk, but she was so light-headed she could barely think. She needed food. One little bite and she'd go.

She glanced behind her to make sure she wasn't being followed and almost ran into a tall man in a black suit who was hurrying through the crowd.

"Excuse me." He looked straight at her and rushed on past. It was the man in the white turtleneck—one of Sabazios's little helpers.

The music throbbed in her head, distorting the faces around her. Another suit was running to the entrance as well. All the more reason to bide her time.

She loaded a plate with a huge mound of food and started eating in earnest. A couple of women glanced her way and broke out in tittering laughter. Fine, let them laugh. She wasn't hiding anything. Turtleneck had looked her in the eye and walked on by. They could laugh all day for all she cared. She was starving.

Setting her plate down on the table, she filled a plastic cup with blood-red punch. The sweet liquid burned as it went down, warming her from the inside out. She added another ladle full. Another. The best way to hide was to fit right in. She laughed out loud and stuffed a huge California roll in her mouth. Hiding in plain view. Hiding in style.

Grabbing another cup of punch, she drifted over to the dance floor. The thrashing music drove through her, making the room tilt and spin to its beat. She was happy and warm and free—in the perfect place wearing the perfect disguise. Nobody would recognize her. She was invincible.

The music lifted her, buoyed her up, carried her in its arms. The room swirled around her as she swayed back and forth to the beat. He'd looked right at her and walked on by. Maybe she didn't need to give the jewels back after all. If they were that stupid, she could just sell the ruby and buy a big house for her and all her friends. And she'd throw big parties. Every night. And wear her long satin dress with the emerald necklace. And her new coat.

With all the money she'd have, she could buy all the dye she wanted.

## ↷ 22 ↶

*What is Melchi's problem?*

Hailey paced across the lab and unscrewed the cap of one of the compressed nitrogen canisters. She hefted the heavy metal cap in her hand. It weighed two or three, maybe even four pounds. She'd need four or five of them, or did it have to be a single object? She set the top down and scanned the room. Of course he hadn't bothered to explain. He'd been so eager to get rid of her, he was practically jumping up and down. It was like he had a Hailey allergy. He was afraid to touch her, talk to her, even be in the same room with her. Why couldn't she just accept it? He was a raving, out-to-lunch, pass-the-drool-rag lunatic.

She hobbled back across the room and pulled her keys from the top drawer of her desk. No. What was the point? He couldn't use a weight until he had a rope. That little ball of string he'd tried to hide in his pocket wasn't going to hold his weight. And the pieces of wood—was she crazy or were they sharpened stakes, like in the old Dracula movies? What kind of a cuckoo's nest had she flown over? The guy lived in a tree, for crying out loud. He was in love with Eve and ran around like some kind of interdimensional Dr. Who with a sonic screw loose.

And a plastic squirt bottle.

Why did that bother her so much? Had the lady in the bookstore mentioned something about a squirt bottle? Or had it been Detective Smiley? And why was Melchi so afraid to touch her? He didn't seem to mind touching anybody else. Sure, he'd said all that stuff about other women not being a danger. So was that what she was? A danger to him? It didn't make sense.

Something just wasn't right.

She sat down at her desk and switched on her computer monitor. Googling for Melchizadek brought back all kinds of craziness, but nothing specific to Melchi. She tried *Melchi* and *Melchy* and *Melky.* Still nothing. Finally she logged into the UCSF Library system and tried a MELVYL search. Nothing for *Melchizadek* or *Melchi.* She typed *Melky* into the search form and started clicking through the results. The third link hit her like a punch to the stomach.

A photo of a younger, better-groomed Melchi.

She scanned the document, gripping the desk to keep from jumping out of her chair. The man, known only to the doctors as "Melky," had been in a mental institution in Chicago for over three months. He'd been committed for a severe case of paranoid schizophrenia and had escaped in a struggle that ended up destroying the entire wing of a mental hospital.

Hailey stared at the screen. Suddenly everything fit. Melchi genuinely believed the monsters were real; that's why he seemed so innocent. As far as he knew, he *was* innocent. He was a hero battling against what he believed to be the forces of darkness! And somehow he had managed to draw her into his delusions too. No, that wasn't right. Maybe she didn't see the same monsters he saw, but she definitely saw something. Something she couldn't control even though she knew better than to believe. They were *both* crazy. The monsters were all in their heads. She was no better off than him.

Or was she? At least she'd never done anything violent. A lump formed in her stomach. What did the article mean by *a struggle that ended up destroying the entire wing of the hospital?* Had anyone been injured? Had anyone been . . .

Her eyes wandered back to the picture. No. She couldn't imagine Melchi fighting security guards. He was too kind, too gentle. It just didn't fit. And how had he become what he was now? The knife and sharpened stakes. What kind of a man would even *think* of using such weapons, let alone carry them around in his pockets? Was that what he was so afraid of? Was he afraid he might use the weapons . . . on her?

A noise sounded behind her. She slapped the off switch of her monitor, knocking it onto the floor, and dropped out of sight.

———————

"THANKS." BOGGS STOOD BACK while Smiley opened the door of his car and pushed a pile of folders to the side. She climbed inside and glanced over at the stack. The top folder was labeled *Melchizadek.* The corner of an official-looking paper protruded from the top. She slid it further out of the folder while Smiley walked around the car. The report was about the death of two police officers.

It was dated that day.

She read it out of the corner of her eye while Smiley slid behind the wheel. Two officers had been found dead at Hailey's apartment, but the report said the officer named Bill Jennings had been killed at least six hours after the officer named Thaddeus Parker. He was thought to be—

Smiley straightened the pile and set them in the backseat. "Sorry about the mess." He gathered up a handful of coffee cups and candy wrappers and tossed them onto the floor behind him.

"My housekeeping skills are a little rusty. I haven't had company in a long time."

Boggs nodded. Should she confess to snooping? He didn't seem to have noticed.

Smiley pulled the car away from the curve in a sharp U-turn. He seemed at ease behind the wheel, but she noticed he was going almost twice the posted speed.

"So why do you suppose the officers took Hailey back to her apartment? Weren't they supposed to take her straight to the police station?"

Smiley shrugged. "The whole thing doesn't make any sense. After listening to your messages, I thought maybe they might have gone back for Hailey's walking boot, but there's still a lot that doesn't fit. For example, why has Hailey gone into hiding? And if she isn't hiding, how did the homeless man know to give you that coded message? It was pretty clever."

"And why weren't the officers killed at the same time?"

Smiley looked across the seat at Boggs with a startled expression, then grinned. "You *are* good. Got any theories on that one? I have to admit, I'm baffled."

"It sounds like you've been checking up on me."

"Sorry, nothing personal. It's my job. But rest assured, nobody I talked to had anything but glowing praise for you. The words *brilliant* and *genius* came up quite a lot." Smiley stopped the car in front of the science building and climbed out.

"Great." Boggs got out before Smiley could come around for her. "I take it the coroner ruled out simultaneous injuries with different times of death?"

Smiley nodded and followed Boggs up the stairs. "And I take it you have a key?"

Boggs checked her watch. "They shouldn't be locked yet."

Smiley pulled a door open and held it for Boggs. "Well, where do we start?"

*We.* Boggs shrugged and led Smiley to the elevators. "I guess we should check Hailey's lab first and then the autoclave rooms, animal rooms, cold rooms, the seventh-floor ladies' room, the intern lounge . . ." She led him to the elevators, and they rode up to the ninth floor. "So was the coroner marking the times of injuries or the times of death?"

"Both. They were simultaneous."

The elevator doors opened out onto the ninth floor, and Boggs led Smiley to Hailey's lab. The door was locked, but the lights were still on.

A crash sounded inside the room. Boggs caught the sound of a startled gasp.

Hailey!

Smiley pulled out a gun and burst through the door. A scream sounded, and Hailey jumped back into a lab bench.

"Hailey, are you okay? Are you alone?" Smiley pivoted to the right and left, sighting down the barrel of his handgun.

Hailey leaned back against a lab bench with her hand to her heart. She was pale and visibly shaking. Finally she nodded. "You scared me to death!"

"We've been looking all over for you!" Boggs pushed past Smiley and gave her friend a hug. "Where have you been? We've been worried sick."

Boggs drew back and noticed the worried expression on Hailey's face. She was watching Smiley as he checked the rest of the room.

"Didn't you get my message? I tried to send word I was okay." Hailey tottered across the aisle and leaned against her desk.

"Melchi delivered your message, but we were still concerned.

We know what's been happening to you. You're in serious danger."

Hailey glanced at Smiley again. She seemed nervous. Was she afraid Melchi was listening? Hiding somewhere nearby? Then Boggs noticed the broken computer monitor on the floor. Something was definitely wrong.

"Hailey, are you hungry? Want to go get a bite to eat?"

"What?" Hailey frowned.

"You want to get something to eat?"

Smiley shot a look at Boggs. She motioned with her eyes and glanced down at the monitor on the floor.

"Actually, I know a great Greek restaurant if you're interested." Smiley motioned with his gun and moved silently toward the door.

"Would somebody tell me what's going on?" Hailey looked from Smiley to Boggs and back again. "What are you doing? Why are you here?"

Smiley poked his head out into the hallway, searching to the left and right.

"Are you okay?" Boggs whispered. "Where's Melchi?"

"I already said I was okay, but you still haven't answered my questions. What's going on?"

"We've got to go. Now!" Smiley stormed back into the room. "Hailey, I'm sorry, but we can talk on the way."

"On the way?" Hailey exclaimed. "I'm not going anywhere until someone tells me what's going on."

Smiley glanced at Boggs and stepped closer to the desk. "Hailey, I'm sorry to have to tell you this, but Tiffany has been murdered."

Hailey gasped and brought her hands to her mouth.

"It happened last night, probably several hours before you had campus security call the department. We think her killer was after you."

Hailey slumped down into the desk chair, her eyes wide and staring. Boggs bit her lip. After everything Hailey had been through, what was Smiley trying to do? Make her snap for real?

She shot Smiley a dirty look and crouched beside Hailey to take her hand. Why was he being so rough on her?

Smiley ran his fingers through his hair. "I'm sorry. I didn't mean to be so direct. I just need you to take this seriously. I want to take you into protective custody. You may be able to help us catch this guy, but your safety is our first priority. I can get you into a safe house, either here in town or down in L.A., but it's important we move now."

Hailey shook her head. "Sorry, but I can't. We already tried that, remember? The two officers you sent tried to kill me."

"What? Kill you? That's impossible." Smiley started pacing the floor beside Hailey's desk.

"Hailey," Boggs spoke in her gentlest voice, "the two officers that picked you up were found dead at your apartment."

Hailey sat in her chair, staring straight ahead. Boggs squeezed her hand but got no response.

"They grabbed me and put tape over my mouth and tried to wrestle me into their car," Hailey finally said in a dull, lifeless voice.

Smiley stopped pacing and crouched in front of Hailey. "Hailey, this is important. Did they show you their badges, their IDs? Were they wearing uniforms?"

Hailey nodded. "But the officer named Parker, his uniform didn't seem to fit. The pants were too long."

"Hailey, those weren't police officers. They were impostors. The officers I sent were killed at your apartment."

"But one of them showed his picture ID. His uniform fit."

Smiley leaned forward. "Hailey. I want you to think. Was there anything about him—dilated eyes, clumsiness, slurred speech—anything at all that might indicate that he was under the influence of drugs?

Hailey nodded. "All those things. He was totally out of it. His partner said he was taking cold medicine."

"It fits." Smiley stood up suddenly and walked to the corner of the lab. Boggs could hear him speaking softly on his cell phone.

"Hailey, the killers, the people after you—they're part of some kind of a cult that uses hallucinogenic drugs to manipulate their victims." Boggs moved to kneel in front of Hailey. "That's what's been happening to you. You don't have paranoid schizophrenia. They've been spraying a PCP analogue on you. It's absorbed through the skin."

Smiley walked back to the desk. "Hailey, I need to get you out of here. I just called for backup. They'll be here any minute. You'll be completely safe."

Hailey shook her head. "I can't. I need to stay here. I've got some . . . things I need to do." Hailey closed her eyes and bowed her head.

"Hailey, are you waiting for Melchi? Is that why you want to stay?" Boggs gave Hailey's hands another squeeze. "It isn't safe. He might be part of the cult."

"Actually, the homeless man isn't a suspect, but he could have some information that could help us," Smiley interjected. "Susan told me he's been hunting people he thinks are vampires. He might be hunting the killers. Do you know where he is?"

Hailey sat with her head lowered and her eyes closed.

"Hailey? Do you know where we might be able to find Melchi? We just want to talk to him. That's all."

Hailey didn't move.

Smiley went back to pacing the floor, clearly perturbed. "Hailey, this is your life we're talking about. It isn't a video game. You don't get another quarter. You only—"

He stopped in his tracks and emitted a low whistle, staring at the lab bench near Hailey's desk. Then, using a Chem-Wipe from a nearby box, he picked up a long knife by its hilt. "Hailey, I need to know: Where did you get this?" His voice was hard as steel.

Hailey turned in her seat and stared up at him with a sagging jaw and vacant eyes.

"This isn't just about you. People's lives are at stake. At least eight people are already dead, including two police officers. Two good men with wives and children that loved them. If I have to arrest you for obstructing justice, I will. But I need to know where you got this knife."

Tears filled Hailey's eyes and streamed down her face. "Melchi gave it to me, for protection." She stood and stumbled toward Smiley. "But he hasn't done anything wrong. It's Sabazios. Melchi would never hurt anybody. He's . . ."

"It's okay, Hailey. I'm not saying he's done anything." Smiley set the knife back down on the bench. "It's not my job to determine if he's guilty or innocent. I just have to bring him in. So we can talk to him. Find out what he knows. I know you know where he is. Please tell me and it will make things easier for all of us."

Hailey was silent for several seconds. Finally she looked up. "He's . . . on the roof."

"Where? Here?"

She nodded and slumped back in her chair. "We were setting a trap for Sabazios. He's waiting for me to bring him these weights."

"What kind of a trap?"

Smiley's cell phone rang and he snapped it to his ear. "Okay, good. Keep two units on the street, and the rest of you move to the roof of the building to the right of the hospital entrance." He put his hand over the receiver and looked toward Boggs. "How many entrances to the roof?"

"Just one, at the top of the front stairs near the elevators."

"Is he armed?" Smiley shot the question at Hailey.

"No, of course not. He's just a homeless man who—"

He lifted the phone back to his ear. "Suspect is on the roof of this building. There's only one entrance, at the top of the stairs near the elevator. He's a male Caucasian, about six foot eight with long black hair and a full beard. Proceed with extreme caution. Suspect may be armed and dangerous. I repeat. Suspect may be armed and dangerous."

"But he's not!" Hailey reached for Smiley's phone.

The detective snapped the phone shut and drew a gun from a holster inside his jacket. "Okay, ladies. Let's get you someplace safe."

———

HAILEY SAT AT HER desk, staring at the wall in front of her. Melchi had escaped from a mental hospital, and now Tiffany was dead. And if Smiley was right, there might even be a serial killer after her. Did that mean she was back to not being crazy? Or did he just think there was a serial killer because she *was* crazy? Her stomach felt like lead. Why didn't she just go ahead and throw up? Get it out of her system and be done with it.

Somehow everything felt more real, more terrifying now that it was a serial killer instead of a Gypsy vampire. At least with a vampire after her, she could pretend it wasn't really happening. It had been a fantasy, an elaborate dream, with supernatural monsters and a supernatural hero who could save her from them all. But the article on the Internet had shattered that dream. There were no monsters. No knights in shining armor to come to her rescue.

Smiley said something, and Boggs dragged Hailey onto her feet. She let herself be guided through the door and out into the hallway.

"Please, I want to talk to Melchi. Just let me—"

"Shhh!" Smiley raised a finger to his lips. "No talking. Be as quiet as possible. Where are the stairs?" His voice was barely audible.

Boggs led the way down the hall to the stairs while Hailey's thoughts rattled and bumped in her head. Had she done the right thing telling Smiley where Melchi was? This way at least they'd be able to get him help. Besides, what choice did she have? Smiley and Boggs would never let her out of their sight.

Smiley held up his hand and slipped though the door into the stairwell. Searching up and down, he signaled them forward, leading them gun first down the stairs.

Melchi would be okay. He hadn't knowingly done anything wrong. They couldn't hold him responsible for his disease. He was a good man. He had nothing to fear from the police. Unless . . .

No. She pushed the thought from her mind. If he genuinely thought he was doing the right thing, how could anyone hold him morally responsible? Was it still a sin if he genuinely believed he was serving God?

She followed Smiley down the stairs, pausing at each landing while he searched the flight below. A mechanical whir made her jump. Smiley jammed his hand into his pocket and brought out a cell phone. "Smiley." He cupped his hand around his mouth to muffle the sound. "Are you sure? Well, check it again and send the other two units into the other building. Hurry!"

He grabbed Hailey by the arm and started pulling her down the steps. Her ankle twinged. He was going too fast—

The door behind Hailey exploded open, and a huge arm grabbed her around the waist. Smiley spun around with his gun as she was lifted off her feet and pulled through the open doorway. The door slammed in front of her. Melchi slid a metal pipe through the door handles milliseconds before they buckled outward with a loud crash.

"Hailey!" Boggs's frantic shouts sounded though the doors.

Hailey spun to face her homeless man. "Melchi, how did—"

"Shhh." He swept her into his arms and ran with her down a hallway. They were on the sixth floor, running toward the nursing building.

"Melchi, it's okay. It's just the police. They're trying to help us."

Melchi shook his head as he jogged down the nursing center's stairs. "They're . . . like the Mulo. They work for him."

"No. I was wrong. The policemen that attacked me were imposters. Put me down. We've got to go back or they'll think you're a murderer."

Melchi shook his head. "The one in the stairs. He's one of them. Don't let his pretty face fool you."

"His pretty face? Melchi, put me down! Right now!"

Melchi pounded down a set of dimly lit stairs, jarring Hailey's vision with the force of each step.

"I'm going to be sick." Hailey squirmed, throwing her weight backward, trying to twist out of his grasp. Melchi's hold on her tightened, pinning her arms painfully in an iron grip.

"Stop, you're hurting me."

"I'm trying to save your life."

They burst through a door at the foot of the stairs and emerged into orange-tinted night. Melchi paused, searching up and down the dark street, then took off running down the hill.

Racing past the blur of rushing buildings, joggling down a deserted street, the full moon danced, streaking the sky at the impact of Melchi's feet.

"Please, Melchi. Put me down!"

He tensed but didn't respond. His eyes were sweeping the road ahead of him. He ran down the hill, faster and faster, until they plunged into a sea of dark fog. Filmy shadows swirled past them, the outlines of lashing trees.

Hailey shut her eyes as a branch slashed her face. "Melchi, stop! Listen to me." Why wouldn't he listen? This wasn't like him at all. Surely he wouldn't hurt her. "Melchi, put me down!"

"Quiet! It will hear you!" he hissed between breaths.

"*What* will hear me? We're in the middle of the park."

"The Mulo. Don't you feel it?"

"No!" Hailey lunged with her feet and tried to squirm out of his grip, but he was too strong. Inhumanly strong. He shifted her in his grip and started running even faster. Her skin tingled as she remembered the police officers. She could feel their hatred burning at the base of her skull, burrowing up through her brain.

"It's getting closer," Melchi hissed. "Surely you must feel it now. We have to hide."

Anger, lust, deep unquenchable hunger—her mind was suddenly awash with swirling emotions. What had he done to her? She'd felt fine a few seconds ago. Slowly, carefully, she reached out and brushed a fingertip across her arm. Sure enough. Her skin was moist to the touch.

"No!" She twisted and turned and threw her weight from one side to the other. "Why are you doing this to me?" Dark shapes flashed against her mind. Uncontrollable rage. It was engulfing her. Suffocating her in its grip.

*Shhh . . . be quiet.* A remote voice rose above her panic. *Calm down. This isn't real. You've got to calm down and think.* Hailey bit her lip and focused on the pain. *Think. Think of something. Anything.* What did she have? Was there anything she could use as a weapon?

She took a deep breath and brushed her fingers once more across her arm. Then, reaching up with her moist hand, she touched it to Melchi's face.

He gasped and pulled away. She felt a tremor ripple through the muscles of his arms. Good. It was working.

"It's too fast." His voice was hoarse and strained. "We have to hide."

"Okay. Put me down and I'll help you find a hiding place."

"Wait." He leaped high in the air and landed with a jolt. "I think I can make it. One more minute . . ."

Hailey stopped struggling and felt his grip on her gradually begin to loosen. His breath was coming in ragged blasts now. The emotions were starting to fade. He was getting tired. She could feel his arms drooping lower and lower. Just a few more moments and he'd be—

"Hold on!" He swung her head first over his shoulder. Then there was another jolt and he was scrabbling up a tree.

Hailey reached out with flailing arms and grabbed at his coat. He was climbing fast, but if she could just twist around. . . . She kicked her legs up and over his shoulder, but the backs of her knees caught on a branch.

"Careful." The arm was instantly around her. "Sorry, but there was no time." He lifted her off his shoulder and helped her onto a branch. "You must climb higher. The Mulo will be here soon. I will try to lure him away."

"Go on. I'll be fine." Hailey clung to the tree trunk as another wave of hunger crashed down on her.

"You must get higher. *Quickly!*"

A malicious presence tingled at the back of her neck. She could feel something down there. Something powerful, angry, hungry.

She felt her way through the darkness, climbing higher and higher. She was just reaching for the next limb when an arm swept her off the branch and lifted her into the air. The tree swayed dangerously around her. Bright moonlight flashed. Then she was deposited on a network of woven cords.

"Be quiet." Melchi's beard tickled her face as he whispered in her ear. "I'll lure him away and be right back." The ropes shook and he was gone.

Gripping the net with both hands, Hailey sat up and looked around. She was in his nest. All she had to do was climb back across the tightrope and she would be free.

Hands outstretched, she made her way slowly to the edge of the web. Then, stretching her arm out into the void, she felt for her lifeline.

The tightrope was gone.

# ∞ 23 ∞

A raging blast cut through Athena, holding her transfixed and numb, swaying back and forth to the rhythm of screaming guitars. Bodies crashed against her, dashing her against the slashing light. She was hot. Weak and trembling. She took a few shaky steps toward the edge of the dance floor and was thrown onto her hands and knees by the violence of her stomach's convulsive hurl. People stood back, watching her, horrified. Staring.

Their mouths moved, but only music came out. They weren't supposed to be looking at her. They weren't supposed to notice.

She pushed herself onto her feet and stumbled toward an exit sign. Angry red letters above a lush paneled door. The floor pounded and rattled beneath her feet. Pushing bodies. Grasping hands. She fought her way through the milling crowd.

Her skin tingled with a chill sweat. Her stomach tightened, convulsing her whole body in an agony of breathless suspense. Before the crowd could close back around her, she ran for the door, throwing her weight against its stubborn bulk. The door swung open and a man's voice bounced off her senses. Tuxedos carrying trays. She grabbed a bottle off a rolling cart and took a sip to wash away the foul taste in her mouth.

Shouting voices. Turtleneck and two of his stooges were walking up a well-lit hallway. She ran forward, bounced off an intersection, and kept running. Another turn and she crashed through a swinging door. Another hallway, wide and carpeted. The interplay of mirrors on rich wood paneling. Hundreds of Athenas with brilliant white hair. She pushed her way through the reflections. Her hair still looked good. It was shocko-dazzling. She hit another wall and turned again, pushing her way into shadow. A dark alcove. She searched the walls for a restroom sign. Dress or pants, it didn't matter. Anything would do.

Men's voices bore down on her from behind. She crawled to the back of the alcove and tried to squeeze behind a potted tree as the voices came closer.

"Don't you feel it? It's fuzzy, but I think she's this way."

"Think she's been drinking?" A door opened and shut again.

"Probably. We'd better call Ibanescu, just to make sure. Sabazios wants this one bad." Another door opened and there was a banging noise. They were right around the corner.

"Think he wants to take her through the portal?"

"Nah, she's only a number three. I think he's gonna start breeding them."

"It's about time."

Athena shrank behind the plant as the footsteps passed her by. What had the big man said? They were tracking her by her thoughts? She shut her eyes and tried to blank her mind, but the image of the potted plant kept reforming in her brain.

Great. She staggered to her feet and started running in the opposite direction. Stupid brain never could follow orders. She lifted the bottle in her hand and took a long swig of the foul-tasting liquid. That should teach it.

She stumbled down another hallway and ducked through an

open doorway. A dirty metal staircase led down into darkness. She took another gulp and descended into the shrouding darkness.

Feeling her way along a rough wall, she turned down a narrow alcove. A pile of boxes. Metal equipment, musty with the smell of damp earth. One more swig and she was wading through a sea of cardboard, crunching and stomping and tipping against the wall.

A fuzzy red spot danced before her eyes. Larger and larger it grew until it filled her vision, swallowing the darkness and blotting out her mind.

———————

"HAILEY." A GENTLE VOICE cut through the nightmares swirling in Hailey's brain. "Hailey, wake up. We must leave now."

A hand touched her shoulder and she jerked awake, grabbing at the platform beneath her. She blinked her eyes against the darkness and tried to focus on the shadow hovering at her feet, but the nightmares . . . they were still inside her head. Shadowy trees gliding past her like ghosts. Gnarled branches reaching out for her with grasping hands.

"We must hurry. The Mulo will soon discover my trick. We do not have much time."

Hailey nodded and leaned on her elbow to see around the crouching figure. A thin line stretched out from the platform behind him.

"Hailey, back at the university. I am very sorry I . . ." His voice was a ragged whisper. "I could not think of another way. He was a Mulo-creature, and his compatriots were all around. I did not mean to hurt you, but you didn't seem to understand. They would have killed you."

Hailey studied the faint outlines of his face. He seemed so genuine now. So gentle. Had the episode passed? "Melchi, could you help me get down now? I need to get home."

"Of course." He leaned down over her and lifted her in his arms.

*Oh great. Here it comes.* She shut her eyes and tensed as the world started bobbing up and down beneath her. Even with her eyes closed, she felt light-headed and dizzy, but the sensation soon passed as the branches closed around her and she was set gently on a solid branch.

"You would prefer to climb down yourself?"

Hailey nodded and threaded her way through the dark branches. When she got to the lowest limb, Melchi jumped down and lowered her gently to the ground.

"We must move quickly now. The Mulo approaches from the south. I fear I must carry you."

"But . . ." The protest died on her lips. Even if he let her walk, she wouldn't be able to get away from him—not with her ankle. Maybe he was better now. Maybe he'd take her home.

He lifted her in his arms and set off through the woods at a slow jog.

"Melchi." She paused to consider her words. The last thing she wanted was to trigger another episode. "When you left me, I noticed the tightrope was gone."

"I unhooked it to protect you from the Mulo. A roll of fishing line is tied to the end of the rope. It was easy to pull back up."

"So where are you taking me now?"

"Away."

She waited for him to say more, but all she could hear was the steady hiss of his breath. Suddenly, his arms tensed. He started running faster. A leafy branch slashed against her feet.

Anger boiled up inside her. "Melchi, where are you taking me?"

"Quiet! It has discovered our trail."

"There is no *it*!" She threw her head back and tried to twist out of his arms. "Don't you get it? The monsters are all in our heads." A shiver of fear tingled like a cold mist across her skin. She shuddered and pressed her hands to her eyes. "Melchi, no! Please—"

"Shhh!" He shook her and veered suddenly to the right. "You must not respond to it. Blank your mind."

Hailey shut her eyes and tried to concentrate above the storm raging in her head. Of course he sounded convincing; this was all real to him. She had to keep her head. Think . . .

Shadowy trees pounded past her. Phantoms of swirling mist. She had to do something or the nightmare would never end.

The gloom suddenly lifted. They were running through a small clearing. The light of the full moon filtered down on them through the fog, giving the plants and trees an eerie glow. He was slowing now. Finally he stopped and looked down at her with flashing eyes. Her heart pounded in her chest, and her throat constricted. She stopped struggling and relaxed into his arms.

His grip on her loosened. "I am so sorry." He breathed the words straight into her soul, filling her with a deep yearning sadness.

She leaned toward him, encircling his neck with her arms. Something was wrong. A voice in her head, distant and faint, sounded a nagging alarm. His neck. She ran her hands across his neck and shoulders and found only hard, smooth muscle. Gone were the disfiguring knots. She lifted her upturned face toward his, but he jerked back, suddenly alert, searching the darkness with half-closed eyes. He set her on her feet and stepped behind her, his ragged breathing tearing the air. He sounded exhausted.

"It is too late. The Mulo moves too fast."

At his agonized words, Hailey searched through the trees in the direction they had just come but could see nothing. "What makes you think there's something here? Can you see it?"

"I feel it. It knows we are here."

A cool mist drifted past her, sending a shiver up her spine. An uneasy feeling, vile anger that licked at the back of her mind. The hunger. She could feel it returning. Was it possible he was right? Could there really be something out there?

Hailey turned and searched the darkness. She limped toward Melchi, but he retreated before her, disappearing into the swirling mist and then reappearing like a phantom. Her ankle twinged and the pain reverberated through her mind, growing into a bitter rage. Gritting her teeth against the pain, she broke into a shuffling run. "Melchi! My ankle. Help me! You said you would take me home."

Melchi stopped, holding out his hands to warn her back. "It is too late. I must fight him. It is the only way."

Hailey took another step toward him.

"Please, don't touch me. I must stay pure."

"But you've been carrying me all night."

"Saving your life was the greater good. Now the greater good lies with purity. Only that can—"

Melchi stepped suddenly around Hailey and stood facing the far side of the clearing.

"You must go. Now! Hide. If we get separated, you must meet me at the bookstore. Wait until noon. It will be safer then."

"Get out of here? I don't even know where we—"

Just ahead of them, only twenty yards away, a hazy apparition rose up through the darkness. Shifting shadows. Swirling mists. The force of its presence slammed Hailey in the chest, knocking her backward.

"Am I interrupting something, Melchizadek? Does the girl know the evil you purpose in your heart?" The shadow approached them, radiating darkness like a sputtering candle flickers light.

Hailey backed away, recoiling at the voice.

Sabazios. But why . . . ?

"Run, Hailey! Get away."

She watched in wide-eyed fascination as Melchi slowly advanced toward the immaculately dressed man. Why was he here? To rescue her?

"You disgust me, Melchizadek. Pretending to be so good when your heart is black with evil. Does she know about the dreams? Does she know about the others?" Sabazios stopped in the middle of the clearing. Hailey could just make out his features through the shadows that clung to him like a cloak.

"Don't listen to him, Hailey. Run!" Melchi glanced back at Hailey, and in the same instant Sabazios charged.

"Melchi!"

Sabazios swept across the field, a dark thunderbolt in a sea of roiling clouds. He struck Melchi with resounding force, and the two of them flew several feet before hitting the ground and rolling over and over and over.

"No!" The word erupted from deep within, tearing though her paralysis. "No!" She ran toward the struggling pair, tearing with her hands at the red mist churning in the air around her. She tripped and went down hard. An angry whorl pressed down on her. Hands, arms, gleaming teeth. She beat at the earth with clenched fists. The grass was alive, slashing at her face with razor-edged blades.

"No!" She fought her way to her knees, rising through the phantom images of combat pressing her from all sides. Melchi. He was back on his feet. Circling Sabazios. Reaching into his jacket.

A surge of rage washed through Hailey, doubling her over with its intensity. She fought her way to her knees, burst through the surface of a black and oily sea. Panting, she fought against cramping muscles and tried to stand.

The rush of feet and the thud of closing bodies. Spinning, tumbling, back on his feet again, Melchi held a white cylinder between himself and a slowly circling Sabazios. Pumping, Melchi sprayed a fine mist from the tiny bottle.

Sabazios threw his head back with a bellowing laugh and threw himself feet first through the air, hitting Melchi full in the face with a loud snap. Both bodies tumbled to the ground.

Melchi lay on the ground motionless, while Sabazios, still laughing, rolled to his knees. He crouched down low over Melchi's neck in a motion that was at once smooth and unnatural.

Animal revulsion welled up in her. Her stomach surged as she backed away. A blast of black exultation knocked her back. Bushes tore at her face. Branches slashed against her arms, her body. The trunk of a tree spun her around. Numb to everything but the terror behind her, she ran blindly through the dark and swirling fog.

She emerged into the open space of light-speckled city. Out of breath, stomach and sides knotted in an agony of cramping muscle, she limped toward the cover of the narrow, concealing streets.

"Help me," she whimpered, bouncing off one door and pounding furiously on another. Jabbing at doorbells, hammering on walls, she ran from house to house, leaving a trail of lit windows and closed doors.

The outline of an enormous church rose up in front of her. She staggered toward it, eyes focused on the crowning cross, concentrating on its outline, a shield to ward off thoughts of the fight. Sabazios had attacked first. It couldn't have all been in Melchi's head. But Melchi had sprayed him with the spray bottle. It didn't make sense. Was it all in *her* head? The question filled her with nauseating fear.

She stumbled up the steps of the church and reached for the handle of a massive wooden door.

"God, please help me . . ."

The door opened at her pull, and she stepped into a large sanctuary, illuminated only by the glow of a backlit cross. Limping down the aisle, she collapsed at its base.

"God, please help me. Please make Melchi okay. Please . . ." She lowered her head into her hands. "Holy one, protect us!"

But even as she prayed, she knew.

It was too late. The enemy had won.

# IV

This must not be! We have sworn together that it must not. Thus we are ministers together of God's own wish: that the world and men for whom His Son died, will not be given over to monsters, whose very existence would defame Him. He has allowed us to redeem one soul already, and we go out as the old knights of the Cross to redeem more. Like them we shall travel towards the sunrise; and like them, if we fall, we fall in good cause.

Bram Stoker, *Dracula*

## ↩ 24 ↪

Melchi stood transfixed as a woman in a rose-colored gown slinked down a path to the door of a sparkling white house. She turned at the door and looked back at him. Hailey's radiant face. She called to him with a voice of laughter and sunshine. Another dazzling smile and she stepped inside, motioning for him to follow.

Melchi moved toward the house as if in a daze. Delicate flowers dissolved under his feet, filling the air with a heady perfume. He stepped through the door into a small room. The air was deliciously warm. He started to take off his coat but froze at the sight of a rose dress lying in a heap on the floor.

"Melchi, come in. I'm waiting for you," Hailey's voice sang to him from behind a closed door.

He stepped toward the door. "Hailey? Is that you?"

"Of course it's me. Come in."

His hand was pulled toward the door handle. Something was wrong. He struggled, tried to pull away, but his hand moved to the knob, gripped it, started to turn it.

No! Sweat beaded on his face as he fought to pull himself away. He couldn't do this. Wouldn't.

The image of a dark face appeared through the door. Too late. A click reverberated through the knob. The door was opening.

*"No!"* Melchi burst through the surface of the shimmering dream. The Mulo was staring down at him with gleaming eyes. Seductive images danced at the periphery of his vision. His eyes were losing focus . . .

Melchi pretended to relax under the soothing spell, shutting his eyes and smiling as though contented. Then swinging his fist with every ounce of his strength, he hit the Mulo square in the jaw.

A flash of hot anger rent the night. Melchi rolled back onto his feet and crouched, ready, searching the mist for his assailant.

Black, dancing shadows surrounded him. It was Hailey; she was walking through the mist.

"Carry me, Melchi. Crush me in your arms."

She stepped aside, breaking into two, four, eight rippling images. Her voice hung on the night air, dancing with the mist.

Billowing fabric hissed out an alarm. Melchi swung around, aiming a high kick at the shadow behind him. The blow connected, wrenching his knee at the impact. Red hot lights burned into Melchi's brain.

He had hurt it. Surely he had hurt it.

*"Shkaaa!"* the Mulo roared and attacked.

Melchi fell back under the blows. Dodging, blocking, feeling the fury of its strength. A kick to the ribs. A blow to the face. He ducked under a high spinning kick and countered with a sweeping kick in the other direction. Nothing. He spun, searching the shadows. Then he saw it. Lying on its back on the ground. It wasn't moving.

Melchi pulled a wooden stake from his pocket and crept toward the figure, on the alert for a trick. The Mulo was silent. Still.

Melchi raised the stake over the heart of his mortal enemy. Something wasn't right. He hadn't hit it that hard. He pushed the body with his free hand. Nothing. Crouching even lower, he reached out and felt for the carotid. Impossible. How could it be dead? He had hit its arm.

Melchi checked the forearm. The ulna was broken, but the radius was still intact. Surely it wasn't enough to—

An unseen hand thrust Melchi backward. Shadows flickered inside his head. An invisible raptor clawed at his brain with razor-sharp talons. Shredding his mind. Filling him with evil. It tore its way up through his soul, clawing, tearing, scratching . . .

Was it fighting to get in or out?

Melchi staggered back and threw up his arms to protect his face. Slashing, cutting, tearing. He turned and ran, screaming into the night. Gray mist streamed past him, carrying with it the bodies of dark trees and grasping branches. The presence followed him, dodging in and out among the trees, straining to higher and higher speeds.

The presence was with him.

The presence was inside him.

Black wings beat against his senses. Pent-up rage. A foaming sea of malice broke through the feeble dikes of his training. He was hungry. He had always been hungry.

The crash of the surf sounded, clean and fresh against the storm of his mind. The sea bluffs. He ran for the sound. Straining to hold onto the last shreds of self-control, he fought down the beast raging inside him.

Hailey's voice called out to him. A doorway stood at the center of his mind. He reached out a cruel, taloned claw and turn the doorknob.

At that moment he reached the highest point of the bluff. Without even slowing his pace, he flung himself off the cliff into the crashing, foaming bay.

The inky water closed about him with a shock, paralyzing him in its icy grip. He plunged deep beneath the surface into black, mind-numbing cold. A swell sucked him down and sent him rolling. Then, with bursting lungs, he was thrust to the surface and pounded against a craggy rock. He clung to the algae-covered outcropping as the surf tugged and pulled at his body.

Another wave washed over him, sweeping him off the rock and sending him tumbling. Coughing and spewing, he was drawn slowly out to sea, but a low wall of jagged rocks caught him in their teeth.

He pulled himself up onto the rocks and managed to draw his numb body into a loose ball. He lay coughing, gagging, listening to the crashing of the surf, waiting for the next wave to sweep him off the rocks and end his suffering. Why had he even tried to fight it? Either way he was damned.

But surely the sea would have been more merciful than the cold semi-life that haunted him now.

———————

HAILEY WOKE WITH A start. A soft fluttering sound was coming from the back of the church. Slowly, careful not to make the slightest sound, she inched away from the backlit cross. She needed a place to hide. How long had she been asleep?

The floor behind her creaked. Soft footsteps. They were getting closer. She tensed, preparing to spring up and run.

"Miss? Excuse me, Miss?" a man's voice called out from the aisle. He sounded harmless enough.

Hailey sat up and blinked at the man watching her from the other side of the podium.

"I'm sorry, Miss, but you shouldn't be here. There's a shelter on Mission Street with comfortable beds. And if you need groceries, we direct inquiries to the food pantry on Pennsylvania Avenue, which we help to support."

"I'm sorry." Hailey closed her eyes and tried to think. A thousand images crowded into her mind. Melchi in the vampire bar. All those women touching him. Smiley in the stairwell. The park. Melchi laying on the ground with Sabazios kneeling over him.

"Pastor, can I start cleaning out the flowers?" A slight, white-haired lady bustled into the back of the church. "Oh my. Are you all right, dear?"

"She was sleeping here when I came in. Harold forgot to lock the doors again."

Hailey buried her face in her hands. Sabazios. What was he doing in the park? He'd attacked Melchi first. Before he'd even had a chance to use the spray bottle. It didn't make sense.

"Oh dear." The elderly lady began to rummage in her ample purse. "Do you . . . do you need something to eat? I could get you—"

Hailey shook her head and climbed unsteadily to her feet. Her ankle was as heavy as a watermelon.

"Lydia, I already told her about the food pantry. You know you shouldn't give them money."

Averting her eyes, Hailey limped to the back of the church and pushed her way through the cross-adorned doors. The morning was gray and lifeless. A chill breeze blasted her in the face. She took a step down the stairs and cried out as her leg buckled beneath her, sending her tumbling down the steps. She lay on the cold cement, gritting her teeth against the pain. Over and over the sickening snap of Sabazios's kick to Melchi's face sounded in her head. She'd just run away and left him there. At the mercy of Sabazios or the Mulo or whatever he was. Had she done the right thing? Whether he was good or bad or schizophrenic or a combination of all three, she shouldn't have abandoned him. He could have been seriously injured. Or worse.

"Oh!" A high-pitched squeal sounded behind her. Running footsteps. "Oh dear. Are you all right?" A warm hand rested on her forehead. Another one squeezed her hand.

"It's okay." Hailey looked up into the face of the older woman. "I'm fine. It's just a sprained ankle."

"You're hands are cold as ice. I'll call a doctor."

"No!" Hailey sat up and tried to climb onto her feet. "I don't need a doctor. I just need to get to a bookstore."

"A bookstore?" The tiny woman took her hand and gave it a little tug while Hailey found her balance and stood up on one foot. "Are you hungry? I can't drive, but my apartment is right next door. I've got some nice vegetable soup I can heat up in a jiffy."

"I'm fine, thank you, but I'm really in a hurry. I have to get someplace right away. My friend may be hurt."

"Oh dear. I don't have much money." The woman's voice trembled to match her fluttering hands. "Five dollars, but Pastor Jim—"

"Could I use your phone?"

The woman's face brightened. "There's one in the church. Pastor Jim's in the office, but we could use the one in the kitchen. I'm sure he wouldn't mind."

Hailey limped back into the church, doubly hampered by her ankle and the old woman's eager assistance. Passing through the auditorium, they walked down a wide hallway into a large, eighties-era kitchen.

"Thank you." Hailey picked up the receiver and started to dial Boggs's number. But if Boggs thought Melchi was dangerous before, what would she think now? After what happened in the stairwell, she'd be certain he was the serial killer. Smiley had probably alerted the whole city.

She put the phone back on its cradle and turned to the old woman hovering at her side. "I'm sorry to be so much trouble, but do you have a phone book?"

"We have three." The woman grinned and pulled a stack of heavy volumes out of a drawer. "Is there anything I can do to help? People say I'm a real good listener."

"Thanks, but I'm afraid there isn't much anybody can do. Besides the phone, I mean. I really appreciate your letting me use it."

"You're very welcome." She sidled up to Hailey and put a swollen, blue-veined hand on her arm. "I'm going upstairs now, and I'm going to pray for you." Her face crinkled into a smile. "You just watch and see if things don't get a whole lot better real soon." Her head bobbed up and down as she shuffled toward the door. "You'll see."

"Thanks, I appreciate it," Hailey called after her. "Could you pray for my friend too? He's . . . in need of lots of prayer."

The tiny woman nodded and slipped through the door.

Hailey flipped to the yellow pages and looked up bookstores. There it was. Elsewhere Science Fiction and Fantasy. She punched in the number and waited. Either nobody was there or they just weren't answering. The image of Melchi laying crumbled and bleeding on the ground flashed through her head. She needed a doctor. A doctor who made park calls.

She flipped back to the white pages. Mark . . . what was his last name? *Ackerman? Akkerman?* She thumbed through the pages. There it was. The only *Mark Ackerman* in the book.

She punched in the number and waited.

"Hello?"

"Hello, Mark? This is Hailey."

"Hailey? Oh my gosh! Are you okay? People have been looking all over for you. Your friend called three times just this morning."

"Mark, I need you to listen to me. I'm in trouble. Somebody is trying to kill me, but I can't trust the police and I can't . . . I don't even know if I can trust myself. Could you do me a big favor?"

"Sure, anything." The eagerness in his voice made her hesitate. She didn't know any more about him than she knew about Melchi.

"I have to meet a friend in Golden Gate Park, and he might require medical attention. Do you think you could look at him?"

"Sure, I'd be happy to. Can you give me an idea what's wrong with him? I'll need to know what to bring."

"I don't know. Bring the most complete first aid kit you can get your hands on without telling anyone you have it. It could be anything. Concussion, cuts, broken bones, bite wounds . . ."

"Bite wounds?"

"Mark, please. This is serious. You have to promise you won't tell a soul. Nobody can know."

"Okay . . . if you say so. Where are you?"

"First promise me you won't tell anyone. Not even the police."

"Okay, I promise, but—"

"I'm at a big church on Cabrillo Street. Could you pick me up right now? We might not have much time."

"Sure, I'm not that far away. But my first aid kit is pretty minimal. It sounds like you need—"

"Just bring what you have. If you need something else, we can always run back and get it later."

"Okay, but if it's a bite wound—"

"Mark, please, just hurry. Someone could be dying."

"Okay, hold tight. I'll be right there."

"Mark!" Hailey blurted into the phone before he could hang up. "Thanks. I really appreciate this."

"No problem. What are friends for?"

———•———

"WHAT ABOUT THE GOLDEN Gate Bridge?" Boggs paced back and forth within the tight confines of Smiley's cubicle. "Have they thought about that? He could walk her out across the bridge."

Smiley got up from his desk and shook his head. "Too public. He'll be trying to—" His cell phone rang and he snapped it to his ear. "Smiley. Whatcha got?"

Boggs looked on while Smiley barked orders into the phone. It had been twelve hours since Hailey's abduction. They could be in another state by now. She could already be . . . no, Boggs couldn't go there. Not now. They were still in the city. They had to be. Smiley was right. The guy was too smart to run for it. He'd lie low a few days. Wait until the search efforts had died down.

"So what were you saying?" Smiley hung up the phone and fixed her with penetrating blue eyes. "The Golden Gate Bridge?"

"No, you're right. It's too public." Boggs leaned back against the desk. "What about that rival cult? The one here in the city? Do you know where they meet? He might have taken her there."

"Not likely. The Hand wants him dead almost as much as we want him alive."

"What about the cult in Chicago? Maybe someone there might be able to help us."

Smiley shook his head. "I've already got a man on it. No joy so far, but who knows—" His phone rang again. "Smiley." His face tightened and he let out a loud oath.

"What's happening?" Boggs stepped toward him, but he was already hurrying out of the cubicle. "John, wait!" Boggs ran after him, following him through the crowded office and down the stairs. "What's wrong? Did they find her?"

"Not yet." He turned at the bottom of the stairs and waited for her to catch up. "That was the lab. They've got a match on those prints."

"What prints?" Boggs followed him through the door and outside into the parking lot. "Would you just slow down?"

"The lab matched the fingerprints they lifted from Melchi's knife." Smiley stopped at his car and opened the door for her. "It's been confirmed. They belong to the model murderer."

# ✧ 25 ✧

Red light bored into Melchi's brain. He opened his eyes and squinted into the dazzling sun. He should be dead. Why was he still alive?

A dull haze shrouded his vision, cloaking his world in ghostly twilight. He rolled onto his stomach, fighting to work life back into his cold, aching muscles.

"Hailey!" His voice grated in his ears. He pushed up onto his hands and knees and groaned onto his feet. His clothes were heavy with dripping seawater; they hung on him like sandbag ballasts, dragging him back down to the earth.

"Hailey!" He picked his way on numb feet through the rocks and gulleys at the base of the cliff. The surf roared in his ears, swirling around the rocks, reaching out to him with great tendrils of foam and spray. Slowly he picked his way up the rocky cliff. His hands and fingers were a sickly shade of red-splotched blue. Aching and stiff and frozen to their core.

The coldness was upon him.

Ortus had warned him about the coldness. He had always said to guard against it, but all his precautions had been in vain. Deep inside, he'd always known it would win in the end.

He followed a path up an eroded gulley. The squeals of gulls broke against the tangled mass of images slithering through his mind. Rock walls floated and shifted before his eyes.

"Hailey!" His throat was raw with the taste of blood. He squinted his eyes against a hard, penetrating light. Its warm golden rays streaked and smeared, refusing to stick to his cold world of grays and blacks.

Finally, pulling himself over the ridge, Melchi collapsed under a gnarled cedar. His breathing came in pants, shallow and rasping. *The Mulo. What had it done to him?* He could feel the beast churning inside him, fighting, scratching, tearing . . .

He had to find Hailey fast, before the beast clawed its way out.

Struggling to his feet, Melchi tottered through the trees. Running, falling, picking himself up off the ground, he ran deeper and deeper into the maze of bewildering trees.

Quiet footsteps. Stealthy breathing. Suddenly the woods were buzzing with dozens of invading presences.

Melchi turned, doubling back on his steps. They were after him! Swarming to him like a pack of wolves. He crouched low to the ground. Crawled from one tree to the next. Through a long winding creek bed, along a tangle of tall plants. He ran desperately through the wooded park, but the evil was everywhere. Putrid, suffocating, weighing him down like the waters of the dark foaming sea. The cold inside him spread throughout his body, taking hold beneath his wet, clinging clothes. Deeper than the ocean, blacker than the pits of death, he could feel it feeding the beast inside. He put his head down and ran faster, but he knew he couldn't escape it.

He was the beast. The evil was inside him.

A shout rang out in the distance. A surge of exultation crashing through the trees, blasting through Melchi's senses, bringing him to his knees. They had found her. His fate had been sealed. Even if he managed to fight his way to her side, he'd never be able to wrest her away. They were far too powerful, and he was far too weak. And even if by some miracle he was successful, what then? Who would protect Hailey from the beast inside *him*? How would they elude the monsters? For that he needed a better plan.

For that he needed Hailey's drugs.

———————

HAILEY CROUCHED BEHIND A trash bin and watched as a red Mustang pulled in front of the church. She searched up and down the street as Mark got out of the car and looked around. He seemed to be alone.

"Mark! Over here!" She stood and hurried across the road.

Mark turned and jogged over to meet her. "Am I ever glad to see you. I've been worried sick! After what happened to Tiffany . . ."

"Thanks for coming." She gave him a quick hug and hobbled over to his car. "We need to get to the park. Somewhere around Forty-fourth Avenue."

"What's going on? The police, your friend . . . and what's all this about a homeless man?"

"He's . . ." Hailey's throat tightened. Tears were starting to form in her eyes. "Mark, please. There might not be much time." She climbed into the car and fumbled with her seat belt.

"Time for what?" He closed the door behind her and ran around to the other side. "Can't you tell me anything?" He shot her a pleading look as he slid behind the wheel. "I want to help you."

She swiped a sleeve across her eyes. How could she explain?

"It's okay, you don't have to say anything. But anytime you want to talk, I want you to know I'm here." He pulled away from the curb and sped down the street.

Hailey nodded and closed her eyes. "It isn't that." She bit her lip and tears welled in her eyes again. "I just don't know. Everything's gotten so crazy. Nothing makes any sense. All I know is I have to help this . . . homeless guy I met. He's got paranoid schizophrenia, which may have made him do some terrible things, but he's hurt, and I just know I have to help him."

"What kind of terrible things?" Mark asked in a gentle voice. "Did he have anything to do with—"

"I don't know. But it's not his fault. You don't know what it's like—to feel things that aren't there, not to be able to tell whether a person is a homicidal monster or just an ordinary guy. Of course he's going to fight back. To him they're really monsters. It was self-defense."

"What was self-defense? What did he do?" Mark took a right and circled around Stanyan Park.

"I don't know. Maybe it was just my imagination, but I think there was a fight, and I think Melchi might have been hurt."

"And Melchi—that's the homeless man, right?—he's the one that needs first aid?"

Hailey nodded and looked through her window as the trees of Golden Gate Park rushed past her in a shadow-streaked blur. The park was so big. How was she going to find him? They could search for days.

"So if the homeless man can't be held responsible for his actions, why not just call the police?"

"Because Melchi thinks the police—" A strange sensation tingled at the back of her mind. What was it? Had she recognized the trees? "Stop the car!"

"*What?*"

"Stop the car!"

"Here?" Mark pulled the car over to the side of the road. "I thought you said Forty-fourth."

Hailey climbed out of the car and stepped down into an over-grown ditch.

"Hold up. Wait a second." Mark ran up behind her and set a large toolbox-sized case on the ground to help her climb over a wire fence. "This is where the guy is?"

Hailey shrugged and pushed her way deeper into the woods. She could feel something—the high-pitched shrieks of invisible bats fluttering all around her. She swatted at the air around her ears. It was getting louder, more insistent. She clomped through the underbrush, weaving in and out between the trees. Mark was right behind her, just off to her left. She could feel his eyes on her, boring holes into the back of her head. She picked up her pace, pushing herself through the stabbing pain in her ankle.

"Are you sure—"

"Shhh!" Hailey held up a hand and pointed off to their left. Something was out there. A flicker of darkness moving against the trees. Could it have been Melchi? She angled toward the spot and quickened her pace even more.

Mark was out of breath now. She could hear him stumbling and crashing like an elephant-sized puppy.

"Quiet!" She turned to survey the area ahead of them. The trees opened into a clearing. Something about the drooping branches of the trees . . . A surge of adrenaline buzzed in her brain. She started running. Faster. A splotch of black and gray showed through the long grass.

"Melchi!" She ran toward the sprawling figure. He wasn't moving. Why didn't he move? She slowed to a stumbling walk, pressed a hand to her mouth. "Melchi?" She crept over to the body and gasped.

It was Sabazios.

She just stood there, staring in wide-eyed horror as Mark knelt beside the body.

"Is he . . . ?"

Mark touched Sabazios's neck and shook his head. The trees tilted and swayed around her. Hot burning eyes prickled at her skin. Mark's mouth was moving. He was looking down at her, shaking her, filling her head with a thousand biting ants.

Hailey screamed and twisted out of Mark's grasp. Then she was running. Back across the clearing, in and out through the trees. They had to get to the car. He was there. All around her. She could feel him clawing his way into her mind.

A bush caught her foot and she went crashing to the ground. Rolling, scrambling onto her feet, she ran through a maze of tearing, scratching limbs.

"Hailey!" The word echoed all around her. "Hailey!" Footsteps behind her. Thudding, crashing, shaking the ground beneath her feet. They were getting closer. Closer. She couldn't get away.

"Hailey, stop!"

She shrieked as Mark appeared next to her and a hand tugged on her shoulder.

"Slow down! What's wrong?"

Hailey wrenched free of his grasp and angled toward the road. She could hear the sound of traffic. The flash of reflected sunlight. "Come on! Faster! Get to the car!"

She plunged through a clump of saplings and hit the low wire fence at high speed. Her head and shoulders were thrown to the ground as her legs and feet went recoiling into the air, flipping her onto her back.

Her head rang like a cracked bell. She felt a little nauseous, but the buzzing, swirling sensations were gone.

"You okay?" Mark's face was a fuzzy dark shadow against the sky.

Hailey blinked her eyes. What had made the buzzing stop? Had Mark done something? "We've got to get out of here." She crawled onto her feet and limped over to the car.

"Why? Was that the homeless guy? What's going on?" Mark helped her into the car and ran around to the other side.

"I don't know. Just drive."

"Where?" He started the car and pulled slowly forward.

"There's a bookstore on Irving Street. I need to get there. Fast."

Mark nodded and made a wide U-turn.

Suddenly a man in tattered clothes appeared right in front of the car. Mark slammed on the brakes, but the car skidded forward, hitting the man with a sickening thud.

Silence rang in her ears as Hailey sat shaking in her seat. Then there was a hand. Reaching, clawing at the hood of the car, the man pulled himself slowly to his feet and faced them. Blood dripped from the corner of his mouth, and a jagged gash ran down the side of his face. He leered at them and climbed with lurching, spasmodic movements onto the hood.

Feral eyes locked onto Hailey. A twisted smile distorted his features. Then, rearing his head back, he smashed it into the windshield.

———

"SHHH." MELCHI LED THOMAS along the narrow walkway and dropped to his hands and knees. "Stay right here. Don't move." He crawled along the foundation of the townhouse and peered around the corner. Good. There were still just two of them. Two men sitting in an unmarked car just across the street from Hailey's house. He reached out toward the men with his mind. Still nothing. Either they were normal Gadzé, or they were extremely good at cloaking their presence.

He crawled back and climbed to his feet. Thomas had wandered over to a walled-off area and was poking through the trash cans.

"Okay, Thomas. I need you to pay close attention." Melchi took the ragged man by the shoulders and guided him away from the noisome distractions. "There are two men sitting in a burgundy car across the street from a house with yellow plastic tape. Okay? Two men sitting in a dark red car. Understand?"

Thomas's wide face split into a broad smile. "I'm goin' help Melvi save lives of beautiful girls. And I'm not goin' say Melvi's name neither."

"Good." Melchi patted him on the shoulder. "In a few minutes I want you to walk over to the men in the car, and I want you to knock on their window. Keep knocking until they open the window, okay? Then ask them if you can do some work for them. You must not ask for money, just ask if you can do some work. Okay? If you ask them long enough, they will give you money. Then you can go get a cheeseburger."

Thomas's eyes went wide at the mention of cheeseburgers. He grinned and made the cooing sound that meant he was excited.

"Okay. So what are you going to do?"

"I'm goin' get a cheeseburger."

"Right. But what do you have to do first?"

"Talk to the car and don't tell them Melvi's name."

"Good. Keep asking them if you can do work for them, and they'll give you money. Okay?"

Thomas nodded. "Money for a cheeseburger."

"Right." Melchi stepped forward and gave his friend a hug.

"Mmmm . . . Mmmm . . ." Thomas bounced up and down at the knees and pounded Melchi's back, but Melchi just held on tighter. Lots of people gave Thomas money, but hardly anyone gave him what he needed the most.

A couple minutes later, after Thomas finally started to calm back down, Melchi pried himself away. "Are you ready? Go to the red car and ask the men if you can do some work for them."

Thomas took off like a guided missile. Melchi watched as he shuffled out to the sidewalk and crossed the street. He was practically running. That wouldn't give him much time.

Melchi charged down the walkway to the back of the townhouse and vaulted fence after fence until he reached Hailey's backyard. Then, creeping along the side of the house, he peeked out at the car across the street. Thomas was already at the car. Melchi dashed across the porch and slipped through the broken front door.

Where would they be? There were so many places in houses to put things. Melchi thought back to the month he and Ortus had slept inside a house. He had kept his weapons and clothes upstairs in his bedroom. He crept up the stairs and stopped at the top of the landing. A door opened into a large bedroom. On the floor, just inside the doorway, a taped outline of a human body lay across a dark red stain. Melchi hesitated. Maybe this wasn't such a good idea. It was almost noon, time to meet Hailey at the bookstore. He looked back down the stairs.

No. He needed the drugs. He and Hailey would be on the run for a long time. How could he live with himself if, by finding her, he was the means of causing her death?

He leaped over the stain and turned in a slow circle to survey the bedroom. Two beds, two chests of drawers, a closet full of clothes. How could anyone possess so many things? There were enough clothes to keep every homeless person in the city warm. And so beautiful . . . He stepped toward the closet and reached out a hand to touch one of the hanging gowns. No, he shouldn't be there. Turning away from the closet, he strode over to the desks and searched them inside and out. A small plastic bottle. It was probably amber-colored with a white prescription label. He searched under the beds, the bedside tables, the bookshelf. Finally, he turned to the tall chest of drawers. *Holy One forgive me. Protect me from what I'm about to see.* Squinting his eyes to blur his vision, he opened the top drawer and patted his hand across its contents. The next drawer, the next, the next . . .

His hand closed around something hard and cylindrical. It rattled at the touch. Pulling it out of the drawer, he opened his eyes and held it up to the light. Geodon! According to Hailey it did the same thing as a Haldol-Lorazepam-benztropine cocktail.

He ran down the stairs and opened the kitchen window. The sun was already high in the sky. No time to check on Thomas. He had to get to the bookstore.

————

HAILEY SCREAMED AS THE windshield exploded in a shower of glass. A bloody hand groped through the jagged hole, feeling its way toward her.

"Mark! The car. Go!"

Brakes squealed as a black car skidded to a stop in front of them and started backing up. Mark fumbled with the keys and his car engine roared to life. He threw it into reverse. *Crunch!* They hit a white van.

Now the van was pushing them forward.

*Smash!* The black car hit them hard, knocking the injured man off their hood. Seething madness. Dark and desperate hunger. Mark gunned the engine with a squeal of shrieking tires. Black smoke rose up around them. The smell of burnt rubber.

A hooded figure appeared at Hailey's door. She screamed and swatted at the lock. "Go! *Go!*" She shoved Mark through his door as a hailstorm of glass hit her in the back. Four more hooded figures were getting out of the van.

"Run!" Hailey shook Mark off as he tried to drag her across the street. "Go! Get help!"

He took off running for the woods. She started to run in the opposite direction but a body hit her from behind, driving her into the pebbled asphalt.

"Hel—"

A gloved hand pressed against her mouth. She struggled, kicking and clawing at her attacker, but he was inhumanly strong. He picked her up and shook her like a chew toy. The hand clamped tighter across her mouth and nose. She was falling into a thick noxious cloud. Swirling darkness. Her whole being shuddered. She was beginning to fly apart. *Oh God! Oh God! Please help me.* The black spirals were tightening. She couldn't breathe.

Pain exploded beneath her. The dawn of sudden light. Crusts of blackened rock. Crystals of amber sand. She was lying face down on the road.

"Hailey? Are you okay? Get her head down. Easy. Raise her feet." The voice was faint and distant. It sounded like Boggs.

Hailey tried to sit up, but gentle hands held her down. "It's okay, Hailey. Take it easy. You hit your head."

"My head? Boggs?" Hailey shook off the restraining hands and looked around. Boggs was crouched in front of her with Detective Smiley peering over her shoulder. "There were men in hoods. And a bleeding man. They tried to—"

"It's okay. We saw them as we drove up." Boggs reached out and brushed a hand across her hair. "They dropped you and ran when they saw the blue light."

"Do you think you can stand?" Smiley said. "We need to get you out of here."

Hailey nodded and Smiley helped her to her feet. She looked back at the dented car. "Where's Mark?"

"Mark Ackerman? He was with you?" Boggs turned a questioning look on the detective.

Smiley shrugged. "Tall with red hair, right? Either he was gone when we got here or he was wearing a black hood." He helped Hailey into the front seat of his car while Boggs climbed in the back.

Hailey glanced at the clock on the dash. 12:03 p.m.

Smiley got in and started up the car.

"Wait a minute! Where are we going? I have to be somewhere at twelve."

"Where?" Smiley pulled out into traffic.

She studied Smiley's face. Could she trust him? His manner seemed too relaxed, too . . . something. "Nowhere in particular. Right here is fine. Just stop the car and let me out."

"Hailey!" Boggs cried out from the backseat.

"I'm sorry, Hailey, but I can't do that. It's too dangerous." Smiley kept on driving.

"What do you mean, you can't do that?" Hailey lashed out at him. "I'm a free person. I haven't done anything wrong. You have no right—"

"Hold on a second. If you want out, I'll let you out. But not until you have all the facts. Just hear me out, and I'll drop you off wherever you want to go—assuming of course that's what you still want. Deal?"

Hailey nodded.

"Okay." Smiley turned at a light.

"So where are you taking me?" Hailey tried to keep the tremor out of her voice.

"To the police station. It's the safest place to talk."

"Please, just let me out here." Hailey reached for the door.

"Whoa! We don't have to go to the station. It's okay. We can talk here." Smiley pulled the car to the side of the road and turned in his seat to watch her. "You don't go until we've talked. We have a deal, right?"

Hailey just sat there and waited.

"Okay, first of all I totally get what you're going through. I know these past few days have been really hard."

"Okay . . ." Hailey reached for the door, but a hand closed around her arm.

"Let me just give you a scenario and see if it rings any bells. You start hallucinating and it scares you, right? Somebody attacks you and a hero in shining armor comes miraculously to your rescue. He tells you about an evil enemy with terrifying powers but says he can protect you. He's the only one you can trust. Everyone else is out to get you. You're worried and confused and scared to death you're going crazy. It's only natural you turn to him. He's the one with the answers. The only one who understands." There was a long pause. "Well? Am I right?"

Hailey stared right through him. She said she'd listen. She didn't say she'd agree.

"Okay. Little by little he starts to draw you into his cult, bit by bit feeding you new information. He gives you his knife, a scroll of the history of his order, maybe a medallion with cultic runes on it. Tell me if I'm way off base."

Hailey's stomach sank as she pictured the medallion hanging on Melchi's nest. Melchi hadn't given her a scroll, but he had told her the weird story about Cain. "How do you know all this?"

"It's happened before. Many, many times. There's a cult called the Standing. I'm just describing the way it operates—the way it recruits new members. I know this is hard for you to hear, but if it makes you feel any better, the man you're protecting probably believes it himself."

Boggs's head appeared between the seats. "Hailey, remember how the doctors thought you were paranoid schizophrenic? Well you're not. Your hallucinations were caused by an airborne PCP analogue used by the cult. But Melchi's hallucinations aren't. He was diagnosed with paranoid schizophrenia four years ago. I've seen the paperwork myself. There was even a picture of him. He was at a mental institution for over three months before he managed to escape."

"So?" Hailey shrugged. "Maybe he was misdiagnosed. They were wrong about me."

"I know you want to believe him. I wanted to believe him too." Boggs's eyes were wide and pleading. "Not because he just *seemed* like a good man, but because he *is* a good man. He just happens to be a good man with a mental disorder. He honestly believes there are monsters out there, but the monsters are all in his head."

Smiley leaned forward. "Hailey, if you don't help us find him, he might hurt somebody. The voices in his head are telling him the other people are evil."

"You're wrong." Hailey shook her head. "I've seen them. They *are* monsters. They attacked *us*. Melchi had to fight. It was self-defense."

Boggs looked to Smiley who just nodded. "I didn't mean to imply the whole thing was in Melchi's head. His enemies are real enough. Remember I told you about a rival cult here in San Francisco? Melchi might have called it the Hand? Well, members of the Hand are at war with the Standing. They believe roughly the same things, and they use basically the same tactics. But they're better organized and way better funded. If Melchi was attacked, he was probably attacked by members of the Hand. Did they try to spray him with drugs?"

Hailey bit her lip. Melchi had sprayed Sabazios, not the other way around. But if Sabazios had a spray bottle too . . . that could explain the weirdness that first time she had met him. And the way she felt on their first date.

Could she really have been drugged?

Boggs placed a gentle hand on her shoulder. "Hailey, remember you said Melchi didn't want to touch you after he rescued you from the guy with the knife? Maybe that was because you were covered with PCP analogue. He didn't want to get it on him."

Hailey looked down at her lap and nodded. She could still see Melchi that night at The Pit. He hadn't minded all those other women touching him. Just her. Especially when she started getting that tingly feeling—like after he put her down in the park.

"Hailey, help us find him," Smiley coaxed, "before he hurts someone else. I know this is hard, but we were able to get fingerprints from the knife he gave you. They matched the prints of the model murderer."

"No." Hailey shook her head. "He's not a murderer."

"No, he isn't," Boggs said. "He's a good man. But he's a good man with a mental illness. Who knows? Maybe the disease turned those women into monsters. Maybe he was attracted to them and that scared him. Whatever it was, it could happen again if we don't find him. He needs our help."

Hailey closed her eyes, squeezing out twin streams of tears. It couldn't be true. It just couldn't. But what had he been doing on her roof? Normal people didn't sit on people's roofs. And why was he hiding behind a beard and all those coats. And his neck. Last night at the park his neck had been perfectly smooth.

"Hailey, think about it." Boggs voice broke through the storm of her emotions. "He was talking about Mulo—Gypsy vampires. Mind reading. Prophecies. This isn't a movie; this is real life. You're a scientist. Think about it."

Hailey buried her face in her hands. She felt nauseous, wretched. Why wouldn't they leave her alone? She sat for a long time, hunched over in the seat with Boggs stroking her hair and patting her back, just like her mother used to do.

"So what do you want from me?" She flung the question at the floor.

"My main concern is your safety." Smiley's voice was soft, almost gentle. "I can get you to a safe house where neither cult will be able to get to you. You need some time to rest. After that we can talk about how you can help us catch him."

Hailey nodded without looking up.

"Hailey, it's for the best." Boggs leaned over the seat. "Melchi needs help. He's in danger—from the other cult as well as from himself."

"I just need to know one thing," Smiley said. "Were you supposed to meet him at noon? Where were you going to meet him?"

Hailey nodded. "At the Elsewhere Bookstore on Irving Street." She closed her eyes.

*Just call me Judas.*

# ∽ 26 ∾

Athena opened her eyes. A loud mechanical roar was coming from somewhere behind her. The noise rattled her skull like a jackhammer, sending echoes of throbbing pain coursing through her brain. She blinked and tried to swallow. Her mouth tasted like a sewer rat had crawled inside to die. Where was she?

Struggling to a sitting position, she searched her surroundings while her numb legs came tingling back to life. Dirty concrete walls, piles of lumber, empty boxes. The outline of some sort of miniature bulldozer sat in a large corridor running perpendicular to her own. Dim light filtered through the dusty haze hanging in the air. It was coming from the left side of the passage, the same direction as the noise.

She stretched out her legs and heard the sound of scraping glass. A half-empty champagne bottle, right by her leg. Then it all came rushing back, like a half-remembered nightmare. She was at the hotel. The party. She'd been drinking. Had someone drugged her? Images flashed through her mind. They had chased her through the hallways. It all felt surreal.

She climbed to her feet, but her legs erupted in a paroxysm of tingling pinpricks. Leaning against the wall, she searched the rest of the passage. It dead-ended at an equipment-covered wall.

A real-life jackhammer leaned against a stack of pickaxes and shovels.

The roar of the machinery suddenly died down. Athena swung around. Men's voices. They sounded like they were still a good distance away, but they were getting closer.

She dropped to the floor and pulled a large piece of cardboard over the top of her. A blob of light shimmied and danced along the wall of the corridor as the voices grew louder. It sounded like three or four men, construction workers if their vocabulary was any indication. They were talking about a guy named Simmons getting in a fight with his boss. She flattened herself against the floor as four burly men walked past her alcove. Apparently they didn't have that ESP thing going because they walked right by without the slightest pause. She listened as they clomped up what sounded like a flight of metal stairs and slammed a door behind them.

Now was her chance. She squirmed out from under the box and climbed slowly to her feet. The area was dark as a tomb. Trailing a hand along the wall to maintain her balance, she tiptoed to the bulldozer and turned right to follow the workers. The stairs were only fifteen feet away. She crept up the steps until she came to a cold smooth door. Feeling for the knob, she turned it first to the left and then to the right.

It was locked.

* * *

HAILEY SLOUCHED IN THE front seat of the car. The skin around her eyes felt tight and crusty. She knew she looked terrible, but she didn't care. Smiley sat, fidgeting in the seat next to her. Waiting.

She was sick of all the cloak-and-dagger stuff. Sick of running. Why couldn't she pack her own bag? It wasn't like she would have been there alone. Boggs didn't have a clue about clothes. Not hers anyway. She looked terrible in Crayola.

She looked down at her shredded hose. She looked awful. Her legs were scraped and bruised. Her dress was torn and dirty. Why had Melchi picked her? Because she was tall? Was that all people saw when they looked at her?

Another tear rolled down her cheek. And why hadn't she run when she had the chance? Why had she been so attracted to Melchi? She wiped her face with the back of her arm. Maybe that was it. There was no attraction at all, so he wasn't intimidating. He was a dirty, deformed homeless man. He'd never been to middle school so he'd never learned to make fun of huge, clumsy geekettes. He was completely safe—except that he was the most dangerous of them all.

The passenger door opened, and Boggs handed her a small, blue suitcase. The case her mom had bought for her seventh-grade summer camp.

"Sorry it took so long. I couldn't find the tennis shoes you had on when I brought you home from the hospital. Your house is kind of a mess."

Hailey bowed her head. Tiffany. She still couldn't believe it was really happening.

"Hailey, I'm sorry. I . . ." Boggs reached through the door and gave her a hug. "I know this is hard, but you'll get through it. I'll be praying for you. And Melchi."

"Thanks." Hailey swallowed. "I mean it. Thanks for everything. I–I don't know what I would have done without you."

Boggs smiled and closed the door. "John will take good care of you. Just listen to what he says."

Smiley started the car and pulled out of the parking lot. Boggs was still standing by her car waving as they pulled out into traffic and disappeared from view. Hailey slumped back in the seat and closed her eyes. She felt like she was leaving the country. Like she'd lost everybody who had ever loved her.

The car took a sudden turn. Hailey opened her eyes and looked over at Smiley. His face was taut, and he kept glancing up at the rearview mirror. He swerved around a pair of slow cars and squealed around another corner. His body radiated tension like a bonfire. Were they being followed? Hailey swallowed back the question. All of a sudden it wasn't a game anymore. Speeding up, slowing down, dodging in and out of traffic. Hailey slumped low in her seat, afraid to distract him from the life-and-death business of making sure they weren't being followed.

"Okay, I'm going to have to ask you to close your eyes," he finally announced. "It's for your own protection, as well as for the protection of others."

Hailey nodded and shut her eyes. If she didn't know where the safe house was, nobody could force her to tell. If she didn't know where she was, *it* wouldn't either.

Dozens of turns later Smiley slowed to a stop and told her she could open her eyes long enough to get out of the car. They were in some kind of partially underground parking garage. Dirt clods and chunks of brown rock covered the cement deck. It felt more like a construction site than a safe house.

Smiley took the suitcase from her and ushered her through a set of dusty doors. "Okay, you'd better close your eyes again." He put an arm around her and guided her through what must have been a long hallway. The farther they walked, the more the smell of dust and exhaust fumes gave way to the smell of potpourri and new carpet. Elegant voices. The subdued tones of chamber music. Wherever they were, she got the impression it was pretty nice.

Smiley stopped and Hailey heard the chime of an elevator. He guided her forward, and she could smell the rich scent of polished wood. *Very* nice. A thrill of excitement tingled through her. A million thoughts at once buzzed in her brain.

When the elevator finally opened, Smiley led her down a long hallway and stopped again. She heard the sound of a key in the lock of a door. Smiley ushered her forward, and the door shut behind them. "Okay, you can look now."

Hailey opened her eyes and waited for her vision to adjust to the soft light. The room was beautiful. A massive, antique canopy bed dominated one end of the room while a nice Victorian sofa group set off the other.

"Nice, huh?" Smiley set her suitcase on an antique writing desk and swept his hand to indicate the room with a flourish.

Hailey grew suddenly tense. She was in a hotel room with a man she hardly knew, and nobody knew where she was. She backed subtly toward the wall. What had she gotten herself into?

"I'll have room service bring up a menu, but for now you should get some rest. I'll swing by in the morning and we can talk." Smiley opened the door and stepped outside. She heard the reassuring snap of the lock.

Hailey sighed and sank down onto the sofa. What was her problem? She was getting so paranoid. She had to relax, trust God. Everything was going to be fine. It would all be over soon. They would find Melchi, and he'd finally get the help he needed.

Paranoid schizophrenia. She knew exactly how it felt, not being able to trust your senses. Not even being able to trust yourself. Just thinking she had it had been bad enough. But to live that way for four years? Constant vigilance. Never getting enough sleep. Living in perpetual fear of the monsters just around the corner. Poor guy. To believe he was all alone, that only he could protect the world from all those monsters. So much stress and responsibility. No wonder he'd been so desperate to find someone else like him. It was too big a burden for any man to bear alone.

She reached out and pulled a magazine from the marble-top table by the sofa. There was also a GameBoy and a couple of books: *Mrs. Dalloway* and *To the Lighthouse.* Both by Virginia Woolf.

Hailey got up and looked around the room. A door opened into a large bathroom with an enormous whirlpool tub. Another door opened into a closet. She went to the window and threw open the curtains. Ornately carved bars only partially obstructed her view of the city. Why all the cloak-and-dagger stuff getting here if there was an outside window in the room? She limped around the bed and checked the phone. It was dead.

*Virginia Woolf.*

Then it hit her. Smiley hadn't stopped at the hotel desk. He already had the key to the hotel room. And that reassuring sound of the lock sliding into place . . .

She ran to the door and yanked on the knob. It was locked all right.

From the outside.

---

MELCHI VAULTED OVER AN old wooden fence and ran across a toy-littered yard. He hit the next fence at an all-out run, twisting and turning in the air to avoid a hedge of thorny roses. Another fence, hard-packed dirt, and a yapping terrier.

He flew over an ivy-covered wall and darted across a deserted street. The sun was already past its zenith. He didn't have time for stealth. The longer Hailey spent in one spot, the easier it would be for the Mulo-creatures to find her. Assuming they hadn't found her already.

He sprinted up the sidewalk and turned onto the Booklady's street. The store was only two blocks away. He reached out with his mind, filtering though the turmoil of the city, searching the roiling caldron of activity for the slightest trace of her presence.

Maybe she was asleep. Or reading. Or deliberately blanking her mind. Melchi slowed to a walk and crept toward the bookstore, all senses on the alert. Something wasn't right. Patches of ominous silence stood against the maelstrom of the city, large black holes against a radiant sea of stars.

He scanned the busy street. Everything looked normal enough. The sidewalks bustled with life. Shopping bags, sunglasses, coats and jackets draped over shoulders. Contentment and warmth. The suppressed joy of a sunny afternoon.

Then he noticed them. The man in the expensive business suit, stopping, turning around, walking back down the street. And the woman at the corner grocery. Sunburned and wearing a black strapless gown. How long had she been considering those tomatoes?

*Holy One, shield me . . .*

Melchi crouched down and spun around. A small army of black-clad figures was emerging from a dented white van. High-pitched screams, squealing tires, people running into the street. The men staggered toward him, lurching and stumbling like grotesque marionettes controlled by a drunken puppet master. Pale skin, impossibly black hair. The one on the right looked like the missing boy—the one from the papers whose roof he had investigated. An inhuman snarl issued from deep inside him. Long, gleaming canines . . .

Melchi darted out into the street, but a black car squealed to a stop just in front of him. Black eyes, the metallic glint of a gun—

He turned back to the sidewalk and charged through the center of the lurching mob. Spinning, kicking, striking out with precision force, he felt the nauseating snap of breaking bones beneath his fists, the thud of falling bodies, but still they kept coming at him. Faces slack, arms dangling, they dragged themselves toward him, throwing themselves against his whirling fists.

*Holy One, forgive me. Holy One, please . . .*

Melchi ducked under a charging creature and ran for a break in the crowd, but a thunderous roar blasted through his senses, sending him tumbling into the street. White-hot power licked at the back of his mind, burning through his brain, tingling across his skin. He could feel it bearing down in him, coming at him from all directions.

He picked himself off the ground and tottered across the street. It was behind him, rumbling through him. Wave upon wave of twisted pleasure. Exultant, triumphant, glorying in his helplessness and pain.

A dark shape streaked across his tear-blurred vision. Another creature, right in front of him. He leaped into the air, pulling his feet up for the strike, but then he saw the face. Black lips, large luminous eyes . . . it was a woman.

He tried to twist around, tried to keep from hitting her, but his momentum sent him careening into her like a cannonball. He reached around her head, spun himself behind her to take the impact of the fall, but she landed with a hollow thump, the sharp exhalation of air from her lungs.

"I'm sorry. Forgive me, I—"

Then she was on him, biting and clawing like a crazed mountain lion.

An angry voice cried out, and a loud explosion hit him in the left shoulder. The woman looked up and stared at him. Hollow painted eyes, black-smeared lips. Her face distorted and melted away into a hazy pool of light. Melchi reached for the light, but his left side wouldn't move. His shoulder. He turned his head, tried to focus his eyes on the shiny silver cylinder protruding from his arm. A fringe of red cotton. What did it mean? Red was the color of blood.

Two blurry faces appeared right above him. "In the truck. Now! And keep your claws out of him. The boss wants this one for himself."

———·———

HAILEY PACED BACK AND forth across the floor of her room. A silver tray with her dinner sat untouched on the writing desk. The men who delivered it wouldn't even speak to her. One brought the food in while the other guarded the door. Facing in, not out. He was the jailer and she the prisoner.

How could she have been so stupid? Melchi had been right. Smiley was one of the cult members, just like Sabazios. That was the only possible explanation. And she'd told Smiley exactly where to find Melchi. For all she knew he could already be dead. Thanks to her and her big mouth. And to Boggs. Had she been in on it too? Was that why she'd been so nice to her? Who else was in on it? Dr. Goldberg? Mark Ackerman? The police officer who came out to check her apartment?

She grabbed the suitcase Boggs had packed for her and dumped its contents out on the bed. Jeans, sweatshirts, underwear—not exactly the ones she would have chosen, but still they were close enough. She dug through the pile and discovered her Bible and a small book. Melchi's *Paradise Lost*. A wide sticky note was stuck to its cover.

> *Thought you might want something to read. I'm*
> *praying for you and Melchi. Remember, all things*
> *work together for the good . . .*
> Love, Boggs

Tears burned in Hailey's eyes as she hugged the book to her chest. Boggs didn't know. A cult member wouldn't have written that note. She couldn't have known.

Which meant there was still hope. Boggs wasn't the type to sit quietly by and do nothing while her friend stayed locked up in a safe house. She'd start asking questions eventually. Smiley had to know she'd start asking questions. What would he tell her when—

"No." Her legs buckled and she sank to the floor. "No. God, please protect her. Please help her to be all right."

A whining roar sounded inside her head. First Melchi and now . . . What had she done? The floor seemed to tilt beneath her, twisting her stomach into a knot. "God, please help him. Please keep him away from the bookstore. Please."

Cold sweat tingled across her skin. Her stomach tightened. She climbed to her feet and tottered across the room. She had to get to the bathroom before she—

A shudder rumbled up Hailey's spine. She could feel it. Hunger. Anger. She was about to have another episode.

She pressed Melchi's book to her chest. Her whole body was trembling with a putrid, alien rage. She had to hold on. Had to control herself. She hugged the book tighter, fighting the urge to rip it to shreds.

Keys rattled behind the door. She hid Melchi's book under a magazine as the lock slid back with a resounding snap. Hailey shrank back against the wall, watched in horror as the door swung open in the stopped-frame motion of a terrifying nightmare.

A stranger stood in the doorway. Dark-skinned and lopsided, as if the right side of his face had melted. His black eyes drank in the room like ravenous black holes.

"Hello, Hailey. How good to see you again."

The voice. Had she heard it before? Her ears told her she hadn't, but something about it tugged at her memory with terrifying familiarity.

"I trust the accommodations are satisfactory. Ah, but you haven't touched your food. We must eat to keep up our strength. We have a bright future ahead of us, you and me. You are a child of great destiny."

"Who are you? What do you want from me?"

"From you? Absolutely nothing. Just the opportunity to offer you a priceless gift." The man stepped closer. "The gift of immortality."

"I'm warning you. Stay away from me."

"Ah, you don't believe me? Why look at me. I'm thousands of years old, and I don't look a day over twenty-five."

"Trying to convince me you're Cain? You might have fooled Melchi, but I'm not buying it."

"Cain? What an amusing idea. Wherever did you dream up such a thing?" The man approached Hailey, holding her rigid with the intensity of his gaze.

"I don't care who you are, just keep away from me." Hailey tore her eyes away from his. She swayed on her feet, staring hard at the undulating floor.

"Hailey, I'm hurt. Don't you recognize your old friend? At one point I daresay you even loved me." Strong hands seized her face and forced her to look up into his eyes. Large and black, they reached through her being and tore at her soul.

"Ah, I see you finally recognize me. It's your old friend, Sabazios."

## ∞ 27 ∞

Lurching shadows, flailing arms, a face with black-smeared lips. Melchi tried to run, but his arms and legs were dragged down by a dozen grasping hands. Angry voices echoed in his brain. He was falling.

Ice-cold water closed around him, shocking him back to his senses. He opened his eyes and looked up through a shimmering veil of liquid light. An explosion of bubbles erupted from his mouth and nose. They were drowning him, holding him under the water with a powerful, vice-like grip.

Melchi arched his back, tried to twist out of their hands, but there were too many of them. *Holy One, help me!* He had to control himself. Stop struggling. Quench the need for oxygen burning in his lungs.

Suddenly he was jerked upward. His face broke the surface of the water with a sputtering gasp. He coughed and spewed and inhaled as much air as he could. Deep breaths. In and out. Any second they would plunge him back into the water. In and out. Any second they would . . . what? What were they waiting for?

He looked around the ring of staring faces. Handsome men in expensive suits, beautiful women resplendent in glittering gowns and sparkling jewels. The air was heavy with their suffocating presence. They were so young. How could they have become so twisted in such a short period of time? Hatred, perversion, putrefying decay—it all burned into his brain like sulfur and brimstone, filling his head with poisonous fumes and choking desires.

"What do you want from me?" Melchi struggled to free himself, but they only clung to him tighter. Chains rattled across the shiny brass tub. Metal cuffs bit into his wrists and ankles. They weren't taking any chances. He wouldn't be able to break free. But what did they want? He had killed the Mulo. If they wanted to punish him, why didn't they just get it over with?

He stared defiantly at the ring of glassy-eyed figures. Their faces were expressionless, flat, and lifeless—as if all the joy had been sucked out of the world. Behind them a huge marble statue towered over their heads. The likeness of a grotesque hand covered with cultic runes and symbols. A large snake coiled across the back of the fourth and fifth fingers. Sinister, hypnotic, it filled Melchi with dark despair, a sense of impending doom.

A door creaked open and a band of white light swept across the ceiling. Slow, heavy footsteps. The candles dimmed as the room filled with a torrent of raw swirling power. Suffocating, infectious, the familiar presence pounded against Melchi's senses, filling him with guilt, self-loathing, and shame.

"Hello, Melchizadek." The voice was deep and unfamiliar, but the rush of power underlying each word was undeniable.

Somehow, some way the Mulo had come back.

Melchi looked on in horrified fascination as a man stepped into the light. Short, dark-skinned, powerfully built . . . it couldn't be a disguise. But the eyes. The man's presence bombarded him with terrifying familiarity.

"So nice of you to join me." The man smiled a lopsided smile. His right eye and the right corner of his mouth drooped like hot wax held over a flame.

"I will never join you." Melchi forced every ounce of defiance he could muster into his voice. "You might as well kill me now because I'll never become like one of them."

"Kill you?" The man threw back his head and laughed. "After all those years working to keep you alive? Providing a teacher to train you? Leaving a trail of bread crumbs to make sure you followed me from city to city? Why would I want to kill you now?"

Melchi lunged forward, but the chains brought him up short. A twinge of pain stabbed up from his left calf. The creature's bite. Had the Mulo been waiting for the bite to turn him?

A foul touch slithered through his mind. The Mulo's eyes were boring into his. Then it growled and turned to the man at his right. "I thought I told you not to injure him!"

"But, Boss, we didn't—"

"His left leg. See to it now! I will not take a maimed piece of meat!"

Maimed? The man motioned to two huge men who hoisted Melchi's leg out of the water. Cutting open his pant leg with a large pair of sheers, they inspected the bite wound on the back of his calf.

"Who's responsible for this?" The Mulo's fury filled the room. "I gave explicit instructions!"

"This didn't happen today. It's old. See?" The man nodded, and the two others raised Melchi's leg higher in the air. "It's all infected."

"Get the doctor up here to clean it up. I want the host ready in an hour!" The Mulo stepped forward and turned another lop-sided smile on Melchi. "I do apologize for the accommodations, but I promise you, tonight you'll experience luxury you never even dreamed possible."

"It will take more than a bite to turn me." Melchi stared defiance into the Mulo's drooping face. "I will never serve you. Even if you drain me of my last drop of blood."

"What a delightfully barbaric idea." The Mulo reached across his body with his left hand and slowly drew a jewel-encrusted handle out of his right pocket. He snapped his wrist, and a long gleaming blade flipped out of its sheath. It was a straight-edged razor.

The same kind Melchi had seen in the missing boy's room.

———

HAILEY GRABBED AN ANTIQUE Tiffany lamp and yanked its power cord from the wall. She smashed the heavy lamp into the floor, over and over, until the base cracked open and she was able to disconnect the wires and pull the cord free. Then, carrying the metal base to the television set, she swung it like a hammer, pounding a large hole in the back of its plastic case. Good, the circuitry was still intact. She picked up the power cord and ripped it down the middle, splitting it into two cables. All she needed was an insulator and she could—

A key grated in the lock of the door. The snap of the deadbolt being drawn back. Hailey turned the back of the television to the wall and stuffed the power cord behind the dresser as the door swung open with a smack.

Four robed men stepped into the room. Hailey's stomach turned as the force of their presence tingled across her senses. She shrank back, pressing herself against the wall. The lamp! The pieces were scattered all over the floor. They would know what she was doing. She could feel them slithering across her mind.

They already knew.

The dark figures glided across the room, sweeping past the broken lamp. Gloved hands locked around her arms, dragged her kicking and screaming out into the hallway. She was weak, cowardly; her every thought was of herself. She would never escape them. They were too powerful, irresistible, eternal. And she was just a slab of meat.

A foul presence pushed into her mind, burning her thoughts into a pile of swirling ashes. *He* was there. The bridegroom waiting to meet his bride.

*No!* The scream caught in her throat as her muscles shuddered and went limp. She was dragged into a candlelit chamber. A ring of hooded figures stood around the base of a massive stone hand. The figures stepped back, opening the circle to reveal an ancient marble table. Dark stains. Candlelight glinting on liquid black.

*God, please protect me. God, please protect me. God, please . . .*

The figures lifted her off her feet and placed her face up on the table. An icy chill soaked into her skin. She could feel it spreading through her body, numbing her to the division of body and soul. A low humming noise filled the room. The murmur of voices. Groaning, chanting, the echo of sibilant whispers.

One of the robed figures stepped forward and held up a silver bowl. Pressing the bowl to his lips, he tipped it back and passed it around the ring. He drew back his hood to reveal a heavy face. Sagging folds of flesh around piercing black eyes. He looked into her eyes, bearing down on her with the weight of his gaze.

Hailey tried to look away. She fought through the chilling numbness, tried to lift her arms and legs, but something held her fast. Coarse fibers cut into her wrists and ankles. The pain was a distant spark. A flickering campfire on a hill far away. The chanting started again. It was getting louder, boring like hot coals into her mind.

She stood upon a rocky summit, lifted high above the twinkling grids below. All the cities of the world. A diamond-studded carpet, cool and soft beneath her feet.

A dagger flashed in her hand. A thin sliver of moonbeam, encrusted with translucent jewels. The baby at her feet attacked her with a soul-piercing wail. Her hand trembled. The dagger was too heavy. The blade slipped closer to the crying child. It didn't matter. The child wasn't real. Nothing was real. It didn't matter. Nothing mattered.

The dagger grew heavier and heavier. It was too much. Why didn't the baby stop crying? It wasn't real. Surely it didn't count if it wasn't real.

Hailey slammed her head back against the stone table. The chanting stopped, and the world dissolved into a starburst of dull red light.

One of the figures threw back his hood. It was the dark-skinned stranger, the one calling himself Sabazios. He leaned over her, siphoning away her soul with thirsty black eyes.

Hailey collapsed under the weight of his presence. She was too tired. She couldn't hold out much longer. The hunger gnawed at the shell of her empty being. Only hunger. There was nothing else left.

"It's not working. She's infected. She has to be," a voice cried out from the foot of the table.

Hailey's mind suddenly cleared.

"Don't you think I'd know if she was contaminated?" The room rumbled as the dark-skinned man spoke. "She's one of the Standing. Of course she's strong, but I'll break her. Five more minutes and she's mine."

The chanting started again, and a blast of raw malice ripped into her mind like a forest fire. The crying child. The dagger. Sparkling, twinkling lights. She was too tired. He was going to win eventually. Why prolong the suffering?

The dagger throbbed in her hands once more, shaking with the violence of the silent sobs that wracked her body. Its glistening point dropped lower and lower. She was too weak. She couldn't hold out.

*God . . .*

Suddenly an explosion of light washed through Hailey's body. Agonized screams filled her ears. Shouting voices. Hailey opened her eyes to pandemonium. Tangled figures picking themselves off the floor. A clot of men trying to get out the door.

"I told you she was contaminated!" the slack-faced man screamed. "I told you, but you wouldn't listen!"

"But why couldn't we see it before? Did it happen just now?"

"It doesn't matter!" The room pulsed with rage as the dark-skinned man strode up to Hailey and pulled a dagger from under the folds of his robes. "We still have the other. We can kill this one now." He raised the dagger high above Hailey's chest. "Or we can use her to test the gateway. There aren't many Standing left. It seems a shame to waste her."

"Kill her now!" the slack-faced man shouted. "What are you waiting for? Be done with it!"

"Why the rush, Ute?" the dark-skinned man sneered. "Are you afraid?"

The man looked back and forth at the others in the room. "We know the gateway works. Kill her now!"

"Do we?" The dark-skinned man smiled. "Are you willing to be the first to ride a Standing into a hostile dimension? You're willing to risk a perfectly good mount on a thousand-year-old prophecy?" He turned his back on Hailey and stalked toward the door. "Throw her into the gateway and report back to me. If she survives, we'll launch our assault at midnight."

*HAILEY!* HER SILENT SCREAMS still reverberated in Melchi's head. She was somewhere nearby. He kicked out with his legs and pulled with his arms, tipping the Mulo-creatures this way and that. Wrenching his arm free, he swung at one of the men, but the chain snapped taut inches from the man's face.

The guards pounced on his arm and drove him back to the floor. He twisted and lunged and screamed, but it was no use. He couldn't get to her. Even if he could escape the creatures, he still wouldn't be able to get out of his chains.

Reaching out with his mind, Melchi tried to project thoughts of comfort and love and joy, but she was too far gone. Overwhelming suffering and despair filled his mind. Was it coming from him or her? At this point he couldn't tell. He had given her his word that he would protect her, and he had failed. Everything he'd told her about the Mulo, everything he'd lived his whole life believing, it was all a lie. His training, the legends, the prophecies.

How could he destroy a being that couldn't die? It was hopeless. He had killed one of the Mulo's bodies, and it had just picked up another one, like a rich man changing into a new set of clothes. And now it was going to change into him. It had cut his hair, shaved off his beard, and put medicine on his leg. Any minute now it would walk into its closet and put him on like a freshly laundered suit. How could he have been so stupid?

"Okay. Lift his head up!" The man the Mulo had talked to earlier was standing over the group, looking down at Melchi with an expensive-looking camera clasped in his hands.

The creatures pushed Melchi into a sitting position. He tried to shake them off, but his arms were too tired. He swung his head back and forth as the man reached down with a brush and tried to run it through his freshly cut hair.

"That's okay. It don't have to be neat for the picture." The man stood back and aimed the camera at Melchi's face. "Everybody get back!"

Bright lights flashed in Melchi's eyes, filling them with floating spots. Melchi grimaced and tried to distort his features, but the man didn't seem to care. He just kept bombarding him with flashes of light.

"What are the pictures for?" Melchi finally asked. "If you are trying to blind me, a burning hot poker would be much more efficient."

The man lowered the camera and walked back to a hidden corner of the room. When he returned, he was carrying a sheath of typewritten papers and a tiny plastic box.

"Give me his right hand!" The man knelt beside Melchi and opened the plastic box.

The Mulo-creatures pulled on his arm, stretching it out toward the man. Melchi tried to fight them, but they were too strong. He gritted his teeth as the man moved the box closer and closer to his trembling hand.

"First his thumb." The man's voice was thick with cruelty.

Melchi balled his hand into a fist, but his fingers were slowly pried open. He winced as the man pressed a cool moist surface to the tip of his thumb. Then his thumb was pressed against one of the papers, leaving a large black spot. That was it? They were taking his fingerprints?

"What are you doing? Just tell me and maybe I'll cooperate!"

The creatures ignored him and pressed finger after finger to the page. When they were finally done, the man took the papers, now covered with black spots, and hurried from the room.

"What do you want from me?" Melchi lashed out as a fiery rage flared up in his mind. "If you wish to kill me, kill me, but—"

The door flew open and the Mulo stepped into the room. Anger rippled through the air, tingling across Melchi's skin like a swarm of biting fire ants. He threw back his head and screamed, reveling in his power and strength.

"Enough!" The Mulo's shout slammed into Melchi's chest like a blast of icy wind.

Melchi fell silent and stared up at the Mulo's face. "Let the girl go. Do what you must with me, but let her go."

"Such heroism. How very noble." The Mulo's words shook with barely suppressed laughter. "Especially since I can already do whatever I want with you."

"So why take photographs and fingerprints? Do you seek a ransom?"

"A ransom." The room rang with cruel laughter. "Perhaps it is a ransom, of sorts. A very large ransom, actually. But unfortunately I'll have to pay it myself—plus a sizable chunk to your government as an inheritance tax."

"Inheritance tax?" Melchi's head buzzed as the truth finally dawned on him. He was to take Sabazios's place.

*By becoming the enemy, he shall shield the world from the enemy's dark stain . . .*

The door swung open, and the man who had taken Melchi's picture hurried back into the room. "The papers are backdated and ready for the lawyers. I've inserted the fingerprints and photos."

The Mulo turned on him with a scowl. "And you're sure you didn't detect any signs of infection?"

"The doctor cleaned the wound and gave him antibiotics—"

"The enemy!" The Mulo snapped. "Are you sure he's not infected by the *enemy?*" A flick of his wrist and the guards backed away.

Melchi scrambled backward as the Mulo stepped closer. If he could just get him to come within his reach. One more step, one more . . .

The Mulo's eyes locked on him, sending a torrent of burning pain rushing through Melchi's body. Darks wings beat against his mind. The slash of tearing talons. Melchi lifted his arms, tried to tear his eyes away, but the dark orbs engulfed him, sucking him into their depths.

*No!* Melchi felt the scream tearing through his body. He was of the Standing. He must stand firm. To quit struggling was the only unforgivable sin.

Finally, after what seemed an eternity of darkness, the sensation began to subside, leaving Melchi trembling and gasping for breath.

The Mulo turned and faced the man in the doorway. "He's weaker than I hoped, but he hasn't been infected. Finalize the papers. I want to take him within the hour."

The man nodded and backed out of the room.

"You won't be able to turn me." Melchi lifted his eyes to the Mulo's and forced himself to return his unblinking gaze. "I'll fight you all the way—even if it kills me. But if you let the girl go, you have my word, I'll give up without a fight."

The Mulo's eyes flashed. The faintest flicker of doubt edged the anger filling the room.

"But there must be proof," Melchi continued. "I must see Hailey with my own eyes. She must walk out of here unharmed and unmolested."

The Mulo's eyes narrowed.

Melchi pictured the girl on the roof and was overcome by a surge of burning desire. To be able to see Hailey just one more time . . .

"Yes." The Mulo's face twisted into a hideous smile. "Your desire to see the girl, it seems, is stronger than your wish to set her free."

Melchi took a deep breath and returned the Mulo's gaze. "Before you release the girl, you must also give me one more time with her. One full hour, just the two of us in private. And then you must let her go. If these conditions are met, I will not fight you."

The Mulo laughed, sending surges of perverse pleasure coursing through the room.

Melchi gritted his teeth and focused his thoughts on Hailey's beautiful smile, the soft curve of her lips, the sting of Ortus's betrayal. The Mulo couldn't be killed. What was the point of trying? All his life he'd been a fool.

Once—just one time before he died—he wanted to taste what he had been missing.

# ✂ 28 ✂

Hailey let her body go limp as the men dragged her down the hallway. Her shoulders ached, and their hands dug into the muscles of her arms, but she forced herself to relax. They were already breathing hard. Just a little bit longer, and they would tire themselves out while she conserved her strength.

"This is crazy." The youngest in the group hadn't quit complaining since the new Sabazios had walked out of the room. "A mount this strong? We should be breeding it. The infection isn't passed down from generation to generation. It's the environment, not genetics."

"Shut up!" One of the elders hissed. "The boss hears you and we'll be rattling around in gadje for an age."

"That's what I'm saying. If he'd just breed them, there'd be enough Standing to go around . . ."

The men turned a corner and stopped in front of a black metal door. One of the elders pulled out a set of keys and fitted one into the lock. The handle turned, and the door opened with an echoing groan. The smell of alkaline dust and cold damp earth. Dirty metal stairs descending down into complete darkness.

Two of the men grabbed her legs and hoisted them over their shoulders. For a terrifying second she thought they were going to throw her into the pit, but then they stepped forward and carried her down the stairs.

The stairwell plunged into darkness as the door swung shut behind her. Was that the gateway they were talking about? What was waiting for her at the bottom of the stairs? She sucked in her breath and listened, every sense at the alert. All she could hear was the echo of their grinding footsteps and the huffing of their breathing. Now was the time to make her move. While it was dark and they were still on the stairs.

But what was at the bottom? If she fell, would she ever be able to get back up? The door might have locked behind them.

A flashlight snapped on, flooding the narrow passage with bobbing light. Construction equipment, a tunnel dug into solid rock . . .

An uneasy feeling tingled at the back of her neck. The men stopped and looked around. They seemed to be confused.

"I told you to shut up!" someone growled. "Don't expect me to go down too. I said all along—" The door at the top of the stairs had opened, filling the tunnel with light. A dark silhouette stood in the doorway. Black slacks and a white turtleneck. "Sabazios changed his mind," the man called down the stairs. "Forget the gateway. He wants you to carry her up to the breeding room and lock her inside."

"See?" The younger man crowed and swung the group around to face the stairs. "I told you it'd be breeding. Soon we'll be standing up to our knees in Standing!"

---

MELCHI STARED INTO THE mirror in open-mouthed wonder. His face. How long had it been since he'd seen his face? He tried a smile and turned his head from side to side. What if she didn't like it? He ran his fingers through his hair. It was so short and the clothes. . . . He looked just like the man with the big black car.

He backed away from the mirror and admired the fit of the crisp white shirt and silk trousers. A voice inside his head screamed out a warning, but he shrugged it aside. The clothes he wore couldn't make him unclean, even if they *were* owned by the Mulo.

He looked down at the pile of jackets and clothes puddling on the floor. At least they hadn't taken his backpack. His things were wet, but—

A knock sounded at the door, and three men in black suits stepped into the room. Melchi smiled once more at the mirror and turned to meet them.

"I told the Mulo I do not require guarding. He knows I would never do anything that might harm the girl."

"He also knows you don't know where her room is. We have come to escort you."

Melchi nodded and followed the men out of the room. He was going to see Hailey. He played the thought over and over in his mind. Her voice, her smile, the way she looked in the rose-colored dress . . . there, that was enough. The Mulo would be able to read those feelings for miles. He looked down and focused his attention on the sheen of his new black shoes. They were so light and supple. It was like walking barefoot. The bright buckle of his leather belt, the swish of his fine new trousers, one more impression of Hailey . . .

The men stopped outside a reinforced steel door and inserted a key into the lock.

Melchi swallowed hard. His heart was throbbing in his ears. He would be alone with her—in her bedroom.

He couldn't go through with it. The whole idea was insane.

The door swung open, and the men thrust Melchi inside the room. He stood there gawking as she lifted her head from the bed.

Her eyes were red and puffy, filled with so much pathos and pain. He took a step toward her, tried to say something, but the words caught in his throat. It was his fault she was here. Every tear she shed had been his fault.

He stood by helplessly as she crawled across the bed and backed her way across the room. She was terrified. Her fear battered his senses like a drum.

"It is okay." He choked out the words in a hoarse whisper. "I will not hurt you. You must believe me." He took another step, and she jumped back like she'd been shot. She tumbled into the dresser, knocking her elbow into the television with a loud smack.

"I am sorry." Hot tears burned in his eyes, distorting his vision. "Please, forgive me. I never meant for you to get hurt."

---

HAILEY BRACED HERSELF AGAINST the dresser as a flood of wild emotions swept through her. Sorrow, yearning, intense pain . . .

She was so sorry. She had never meant to hurt him. She had never meant to hurt anyone. But she was so beautiful. So painfully, agonizingly beautiful . . .

She swept her hand across the dresser as the man took another step toward her. His eyes . . . so beautiful. Beautiful and achingly familiar . . . they opened up around her, drinking her in like the parched desert sand soaks up rain.

"No!" She tore her eyes from his face. He was one of them. She had to keep her head. She slid her fingers across the dresser, felt the flimsy halves of the split power cord.

"Hailey, what is wrong?" The voice stabbed into her heart, flushing a flock of fluttering emotions. He was in her head again. Looking down on her tear-stained face. The soft curve of her jaw. Her lips . . .

She lifted her eyes, and the man's features filled her world. Warmth suffused her, tingling across her skin like the caress of a thousand flower petals. The feelings . . . they couldn't be real. He was one of the monsters. He couldn't possibly be in love.

Pulling out the power cord, she jabbed the stripped wires into his chest. A loud pop sounded as the television's capacitors discharged into his jerking body with the smell of burnt flesh.

The man collapsed onto the floor, and her head instantly cleared. She was finally alone, all by herself inside her own head. But her heart still throbbed at the memory of those familiar, achingly beautiful eyes.

———

"GOD, NO! PLEASE, MAKE him be okay."

A soft hand touched his cheek. The tickle of hair sliding across his face. He opened his eyes and blinked. Hailey's face was inches from his own. Tears streamed down her cheeks, dripping onto his neck.

She gasped and her eyes went wide. "Are you okay? I'm so sorry. I thought you were—"

"What happened?" Melchi tried to sit up, but she laid a restraining hand across his chest. An electric chill spread out from her touch, tingling its way throughout his entire body. His thoughts spun off in a hopeless tangle. He should do something, but what? His mind was a complete blank.

"I'm sorry, but you looked so different. And all those feelings inside my head. I thought you were one of them."

Melchi nodded. His heart felt like it was going to explode. She was so close.

"Are you okay? What's wrong?" She was frowning now. A hand stroked his forehead, brushed across his hair.

*Holy One, no!*

Melchi rolled across the floor and leaped to his feet. He stood there, rigid and tense, gulping down air like a drowning man. "How long have I been here? How long was I out?"

"What?" Hailey turned a worried look toward the door. "Just a few seconds. Not long at all."

He reached in his pocket and pulled out a handful of white tablets. "Quick. You must take these. Hide them in your pockets." He held the pills out to her, wincing as she took them from his hand.

"What pockets? What's happening?"

"The Mulo's men will come for you soon. They'll take you outside and pretend to let you go. You have to swallow these pills and run as fast as you can. Keep running until the drugs take effect. I'm not sure how, but I think they may sever our connection to the other dimension. If that's true, then the Mulo-creatures won't be able to sense you. You won't be able to sense them either, so be careful. It's your only hope of escape."

"But what about you? You're coming too, right?"

"I cannot." Melchi looked down at the carpet. "I am sorry. It is my fault you are here. My arrogance, my selfish desires. I was a fool. I should have sent you out of the city the first time I saw you."

"Melchi, slow down. What did you do?" Hailey sounded upset now. "Why are they suddenly willing to let me go?"

"The Mulo will only pretend to let you go. Its creatures will try to follow you. You must take the medicine. They will not expect that. It is your last best hope."

"And what about you? What are you going to do?"

Melchi stared at a shard of broken lampshade.

"Melchi! I'm not doing anything until you talk to me. What are you going to do?"

"I must remain here."

The room was silent for a long minute. Hailey took a hesitant step toward Melchi, looked up into his eyes. "You can give up if you want to, but I'm not leaving you here."

"I am not giving up. This is the only way—"

"The only way? What happened to the prophecy—the one where you defeat Sabazios and we all live happily ever after? Or was it all just a story you made up to lure me into your cult?"

Melchi opened his mouth, but what could he say? The prophecy didn't make sense. How could he defeat a being that could not be killed? Finally he shook his head. "The Standing is not a cult; it is a birthright. And I did not create the prophecy. One day the long-awaited will come, but it will not be me. I tried to kill the Mulo and failed. Perhaps we misinterpreted the prophecy. Ortus always said the Mulo inhabited a different dimension, but I refused to understand. Maybe it can only interact with our world through humans like you and me. I might be able to injure its human host, but I will never be able to touch the Mulo itself. There is nothing I can do."

"So that's what you were doing with the spray bottle? Trying to break the connection between the Mulo and its host?"

"I—" Melchi looked back down at the floor as his face flooded with heat. "I was a fool. I thought if I sprayed it with holy water . . ."

"As in vampires? You thought it was a vampire?"

Melchi shrugged. "There are many stories . . . The Mulo hunted the Standing in Romania and Bulgaria for many years. I thought perhaps the legends were true."

"So why wouldn't you touch me? All this time I thought you were spraying me with something you didn't want to get on your skin."

"It is good for a man not to touch a woman."

Hailey glared back at him. "That's not what the passage means, and you know it."

"It is not a passage. It is a commandment. A commandment I have broken too many times." He turned away and faced the back wall. "Do you still not understand? I am marime—*unclean*. The Holy One intended me for great things, but I have squandered my inheritance on selfishness and wicked desires. I'm a corroded tool, a shattered sword. I cannot stand against the Mulo. The Holy One will cast me out of His hand."

Footsteps behind him. A soft touch upon his shoulder.

Melchi stiffened. "You would not torture me if you knew what I am. You would take the medicine and run. As far from me as possible. A beast lives inside me. A beast as evil as the Mulo."

"I don't believe that." Hailey's gentle voice sounded close to his ear. "I know you were in a mental hospital, but that doesn't make you evil."

"I do not have paranoid schizophrenia." Tears started to blur Melchi's vision. "It would be better if I did, but that excuse is not left to me. The doctors thought I had the disease only because they could not feel the Mulo's presence."

"Is that what happened in Chicago? You were attacked by the Mulo?"

Melchi wiped a hand across his eyes. "It attacked me at the hospital. I tried to protect them, but I could not stand. I was . . . too full of sin."

"Shhh . . . it's okay. You can't blame yourself. It was the Mulo. You didn't do anything wrong."

"I almost got them killed. The doctors were so kind to me. They gave me food and a warm place to live. I wanted so much to please them. I never set out to lie, but they kept asking the same questions. Over and over and over . . ."

"It's okay. You did the best you could."

"No!" Melchi rounded on the girl. "It is not okay. Lying is a filthy, despicable sin! Do you not understand? I am fallen, corrupt, wicked through and through."

Hailey bit her lip and looked over at the door. "I don't know how to ask this . . . but Melchi, have you ever even read the Bible?"

"Of course not. I am not a priest. Ortus taught me the commandments, but he was no priest either."

"Whatever he taught you, he was wrong." Her voice was low but firm. "You don't need to be a priest to read the Bible. And you certainly don't have to do anything to be worthy of God's love."

"But you don't know what I am. The evil desires . . . even now I can feel them."

"Really?" Hailey's eyes flashed. "So now you're saying you're better than God? Grow up and get over yourself." She turned and walked over to the television.

"What?" Melchi stared after her. What had just happened? "I never said—"

"No?" Hailey pierced him with an icy stare. "You said you were willing to sacrifice yourself to give me a chance to escape."

Melchi nodded. "But I never said I was better than—"

"So what if you found out I told the Mulo's people where you were? Would that make a difference? I went out on a date with your mortal enemy, did you know that? I even tried to electrocute you. Does that mean you won't help me escape?"

"But you did not mean to—"

"It doesn't matter. What if I lied to you? What if I told you I hate you and never want to see you again? Would you still be willing to sacrifice yourself?"

Melchi looked down at the floor. What would it take for him to turn away from her? He couldn't imagine such a thing. Not even if she were a murderer or a prostitute.

"Melchi, I know there haven't been many people in your life to show you love, but you can't judge God by people. If you can still . . . care for me after all I've done, just think how much more God must care for you. He was willing to die for you, to pay the penalty for all your shortcomings. If you could just get over yourself and tell Him thank you, you could forget all that unclean nonsense. He died to pay the penalty for the uncleanness, but you keep throwing it back in His face, telling Him it wasn't good enough."

"No." Melchi shook his head. "I would never . . ." His eyes brimmed over with tears. She was talking about Jesus. He'd heard the story of Easter but never thought—

No. He looked down at the floor and shook his head. It was too easy. "If God already paid the penalty, then what do I have to do? I must do something."

"Because God didn't do enough?" Hailey stepped toward him. "You honestly think He needs your help?"

"No, but—"

"Just tell Him thank you. Once He declares you to be clean, it doesn't matter what the Mulo says. God will never see you as anything but perfect. Do you believe that?"

He wiped a sleeve across his eyes. He wanted to. But could it really be that simple?

"Melchi, I'm not just repeating a bunch of legends. This is something I've actually experienced. Do you trust me?"

He studied Hailey's face. Finally he nodded. He trusted Hailey, and she trusted God.

It was enough.

———

HAILEY DRAGGED THE TELEVISION set closer to the door and stretched out the wires. Still too short. She needed more wire. The alarm clock cord? The lamp?

A loud crash sounded behind her. "Shhh!" She ran back across the room. Melchi was using one of the posts of the canopy bed as a battering ram to smash through the drywall. "Quiet. It's too loud. The guards will hear you."

"But I think we can get through to the other side. If the next room is not locked, we should be able to—"

A sharp *snap* sounded behind her. Hailey spun around as the door burst open and three burly men pushed into the room. The largest man lurched toward her, baring a mouthful of filed yellow teeth. A maniacal gleam lit his eyes as he reached toward her with red-stained hands.

A blur of spinning motion pushed in front of Hailey. A sickening *crack* rang out. Melchi spun past the falling man and struck out with the bedpost. *Smack! Smack!* He spun the post around and threw it at the door, wedging it open before it could close.

Hailey watched in horrified fascination at the other two men toppled backward and landed on the floor with a sickening double *thunk*. She stood anchored to the spot, staring at the bodies of the three men. Her heart pounded in her ears, freezing time and space.

Melchi stepped toward her. Tears glistened in his eyes. "I am sorry, but they would have hurt you. I could not let them hurt you. I had no choice." His voice broke, and he looked down at the ground. His shoulders shook as a low moan escaped his lips.

"It's okay. You did the right thing." She stepped forward and wrapped an arm around his back.

He gasped and his whole body went rigid.

"It's okay." She pulled him into a gentle embrace. "And it's okay if you want to hold me. I feel it too. I know you would never hurt me."

His shoulders were shuddering now. Tears ran onto her forehead. She shouldn't have done that. Now wasn't the time. He had lost his parents even earlier than she'd lost hers. He'd probably never been hugged.

She pulled gently away. "Melchi, we've got to go now. Quick, before anyone else comes."

He nodded and wiped a sleeve across his eyes. Then, taking a deep breath, he walked over to the door and stooped to retrieve his bedpost.

"Are any more out there?" she whispered and peeked out into the empty hallway. "Can you feel anything?"

"The hotel is full of them. There are too many to be certain."

Hailey nodded and crept out into the hall. The faint glow of an exit sign showed above a door to their right. She jogged down the hall and pushed through the door into an uncarpeted stairwell. Melchi followed her down the stairs, shooting her concerned looks every time she stumbled or paused to catch her breath.

"Your ankle still hurts," he whispered behind her. "Does being forgiven mean I could carry you down the stairs and still fight the Mulo?"

"I'm fine. But yes, it does." She leaned against the railing and hopped down onto the landing.

Sixth floor. Five more flights to go. They were going to make it! And the way Melchi handled that bedpost, even if someone tried to stop them, they still might be able to get through.

They had just reached the fourth floor when they heard the shouting. Voices. At the top of the stairs. The pounding footsteps of what sounded like dozens of men.

"Keep moving!" Hailey plunged down the stairs. Her ankle jolted and throbbed, but it didn't matter. The men were getting closer. She and Melchi had to move faster before someone raised the alarm.

She pushed out onto the first-floor hallway with Melchi right behind her. Racing past a bank of elevators, she struck out toward the sunlight. There. Up ahead of them. Glass doors.

It was the lobby.

An explosion sounded, the echoing report of a gun. Hailey dove for the floor and rolled against the wall. Five figures stood framed against the light, barring their way out. Another gunshot. The figures were walking toward them.

Two hands clamped around Hailey's waist and turned her in the air. Melchi. He pulled her to his chest and bounded back through the hallway. Multiple gunshots rang out as the elevators bounced and jolted by. The bedpost jabbed painfully into her side. Running footsteps behind them.

"Stop! They'll kill us," Hailey cried, but Melchi kept running. The end of the bedpost smacked into a doorway, spinning them around. Another hallway, carpeted and lined with gilded mirrors.

Melchi plunged down the hallway and took another left. Scarred walls. Scuffed, dirty floors. She'd been there before. The black metal door.

"Quick, turn here!" she hissed. "Over there. The big black door!"

Melchi ran to the door and yanked on the knob. "Locked."

"I think it's an exit. An underground passage." She squirmed out of his arms. "Try it again!"

Melchi smashed the bedpost into the door frame, bending it away from the door. Hailey tried the knob. This time the door swung open with a grating creak. She stepped onto the stairs and pulled the door shut behind them.

The stairwell was almost pitch black. Somewhere in the depths below, a soft scraping noise echoed in the darkness.

"It's okay." Hailey reached out and traced Melchi's arm to his hand. "There's a tunnel down here. I think it leads to a—"

A muffled shout sounded behind them. Running footsteps.

Hand in hand they pounded down the stairs and pushed forward into the blackness. Hailey closed her eyes and tried to remember the layout of the area. There had been a tunnel just beyond a small Caterpillar. She felt her way along a concrete wall until it opened out into a narrow, jagged-edged passage.

"Hurry!" Melchi dragged her into the tunnel, pulling her behind him at a quick jog.

A rock turned under her foot, tipping her into a rocky wall. Another rock clipped her shoulder, but still she clung to Melchi's hand. The tunnel was getting lighter now. She could just make out Melchi silhouetted against a dim light, probing the tunnel with his bedpost, a dark knight jousting with an invisible foe.

Melchi stopped suddenly, and she almost ran into him.

"What's wrong?" She stepped around him and froze. The tunnel had widened into an elliptical chamber. At the far end of the chamber, behind and to the right of a large pile of rocks, a strange, shimmering light bisected the room at a sixty-degree angle. She angled around the rocks and stood before the wall of light, turning her head to the side.

A field and trees! The translucent light showed the trunks of hundreds of light-dappled trees—growing *sideways,* across the wall of the chamber. And they were moving. Dead leaves fell horizontally through the air.

"What is it?"

Melchi didn't move. His eyes were wide and unblinking. He looked as if he was seeing a ghost.

"Melchi?" She reached out for his hand, but it was cold as stone. "What is it? What's going on?"

"I think this might be the gateway." His hushed voice held the unmistakable tremor of terror. "We have to get out of here."

# 29

Melchi stared through the sheet of light to the rocky wall beyond. The tunnel was a dead end. What was he supposed to do? Protect Hailey or protect the gateway? And what did protecting the gateway mean?

"Come!" He turned and led the way back down the dark passageway. "Check the walls for a branching tunnel. It will not take long for them to figure out—"

A deafening roar shook the tunnel. A drizzle of dust and fine sand.

Trembling hands clamped around his arm. A soft whisper sounded in his ear. "What do we do now?"

Melchi raised a finger to his lips. "Go back and wait by the gateway. Just don't touch it!" He pushed her back toward the end of the tunnel and turned.

The scrape of footsteps ahead. Beams of flickering light. A dark shadow sizzled and sputtered against the wavering lights. A rumbling growl, low and guttural, sent chills tingling across his skin.

Melchi gripped the bedpost tighter. There could be no escape.

He had led Hailey to her death.

"Melchizadek." The shadow rose up before him, filling the tunnel with dark malice. Behind it a mob of eight or nine men held a struggling girl with spiky white hair.

"I thought we had a deal, boy. I give you an hour with the girl, and you give yourself to me. I honored my part of the bargain."

"The deal was for you to let her go!" Melchi stepped forward, the bedpost at the ready.

"Very well then." The Mulo waved a hand and two large Mulo-creatures stepped forward. "These men will escort both her and this girl out of the hotel and take them anywhere they want to go."

Melchi stared at the girl. There was something about her face. . . . Had he seen her before?

"Melchi, no!" Hailey called out from behind him. "Don't trust him. He's lying. You know he's lying."

"But your dear Melchi gave me his word." The Mulo's face twisted into a mocking smile. "He no longer has a choice."

Melchi took another step forward. "You must get through me to reach Hailey."

"Ah . . ." The Mulo motioned the other creatures forward. "So you are willfully and knowingly breaking our agreement? I had hoped you would prove to be more honorable, but I suppose I should have expected it. What's the honor of a murderer worth, eh, Hailey?"

"I am not a murderer."

"Oh?" The Mulo raised an eyebrow. "Tell that to the men in Hailey's room."

A pang stabbed through Melchi's chest. They were dead? He hadn't meant to hit them that hard.

"Melchi, don't listen to him. You had no choice. It was self-defense."

"Self-defense?" A thunderous laugh echoed through the tunnel. "They weren't even armed. They had orders to escort Hailey out of the hotel. Unlike some people, I am a man of my word. Once I make a deal, I keep my end of it."

"But I—" Melchi blinked his eyes. His brain was filled with fog. He had to think. "If I hadn't—"

"Don't listen to him!" He felt Hailey's hand on his arm. "Don't you see what he's trying to do?"

"I simply state the truth." The Mulo stepped forward. "The important question is: What is Melchizadek trying to do? Right, Melchizadek? Did you tell her why you wanted an hour alone with her?"

"I wanted to save her life."

"Come now. That's not what was in your heart then. I could see the lust filling your thoughts. Even such an innocent thing as her hand on your arm. It's all you can think about. Admit it. Your heart is desperately wicked. Lust fills your mind even now."

Melchi hung his head. The Mulo was right. Hailey's life was in danger, and all he could think about was the warmth of her touch. He pulled his arm away and tried to focus on his training, but his mind kept drifting back to her face. She would be better off without him. If the Mulo was still willing to let her go . . .

"Melchi, remember what you told me," Hailey's voice rang out. "You're going to destroy him. It's your destiny."

"Is that what he told you? That *he* was destined to destroy *me?*" Mocking laughter echoed through the tunnel. "Well, Melchizadek, we both know that's impossible, don't we?"

"I never said 'destroy.'" Melchi stepped in front of Hailey. "The long-awaited child will rid the world of the enemy's threat. This is the prophecy. It must happen."

"But how will the child of prophecy do this? Did you tell her that?"

A surge of anger flared up inside Melchi. He took another step toward the Mulo, gripping the pole tighter in his hands.

"'The long-awaited child of prophecy will become the enemy to rid the world of the enemy's threat.'" The Mulo's mocking words filled Melchi's head. "Isn't that the *full* prophecy, Melchizadek? Did you tell her that?"

"You cannot destroy an enemy by becoming that enemy," Melchi said. "That part of the prophecy refers to the crucifixion of the Christ. It has to."

"Does it?" The Mulo sneered. "A prophecy written in A.D. 866? How convenient for the prophet."

Melchi raised his pole higher. The Mulo was lying about the date. Ortus would have mentioned it . . .

The Mulo sighed dramatically. "It's disheartening, isn't it, Melchizadek? After all this time, finally to learn we both want the same thing. I want to see the prophecy fulfilled just as much as you do. I must get through to the first dimension, but only a child of the Standing can take me across the gateway. You want to rid your world of my threat, but I'm too powerful to be destroyed. There's only one solution. Don't you see it?"

Melchi shook his head. The Mulo was lying. It was after something else. If only his mind were clear enough to see it.

"All you have to do is give yourself to me, to become the enemy, as it were. And I'll be able to leave your world and enter another. By joining with me, you will rid your world forever of my threat."

"No. That cannot be true." Melchi's head felt like it was full of biting fleas. "I will never join you!" He leaped forward, but the Mulo fell back in a blur of motion.

"Wait!"

The command froze Melchi in midstrike. The Mulo, the ancient one himself, stood before Melchi, smiling at him down the barrel of an enormous handgun.

"What's the matter, boy? Didn't anyone ever tell you this is the twenty-first century? You can put your stick down now—unless Ortus taught you how to deflect bullets."

Melchi lowered his staff. The *Mulo* was hiding behind a gun?

"Drop the stick, Melchizadek, and listen to me. After all the pains I've taken to raise you, it would be a shame to kill you now. Or perhaps I'll just kill the girl instead?" He swung the gun to point at Hailey.

The staff slid through Melchi's fingertips and clattered to the ground. "Hurt Hailey and I shall surely kill you."

The Mulo laughed. "You just don't get it, do you, boy? You already killed me, and it didn't do a bit of good."

"I don't care how much you try to twist things. I am the long-awaited child of prophecy. I *will* find a way to destroy you."

The Mulo laughed again, a deep resonant peal that filled the tunnel with reverberating echoes. "Do you have any idea how many children of prophecy I've taken? In fact, I do believe I was a child of the prophecy when I impregnated your mother."

"You lie!" Melchi stepped forward and up came Sabazios's gun.

"Yes, Melchizadek. That makes me your father, doesn't it? Like father, like son. We were destined to be joined. You can't fight your destiny."

Melchi stepped toward the Mulo. He was only two yards away from the gun. If he was fast . . .

"Ah, is this what you want?" The Mulo tossed the gun to Melchi. "Go ahead. Shoot. I'm tired of this host. It doesn't have nearly the control of a full-blooded Standing. Once it expires, I think I'll try one with a few more curves. A tall one with beautiful eyes and long brown hair."

"Shoot him, Melchi!" Hailey shouted behind him. "He can't inhabit me. He's already tried."

Melchi pointed the gun at the man-creature in front of him.

"I must confess, it would be difficult." Sabazios opened his arms wide. "But I'd manage in the end. Fortunately, however, I have other options." He turned and two men pushed the girl with spiky hair forward. Her hands were bound with heavy rope. The way she stood swaying on her feet, she looked like she was about to pass out.

"Melchizadek, meet Athena. As you can see, she's one of the Standing as well. So what's it going to be? I suppose you could shoot the girl first and then shoot me. Or you could give yourself to me, and I'll let both girls go free. It's your choice. You're the one with the gun."

He held out his arms and waited as Melchi sighted down the gun. At his chest. One squeeze and he could send a tiny metal stake through his empty black heart.

"Of course, if you're going to shoot me, you'll have to switch off the safety first. That lever there on the side. Go ahead. Don't keep us waiting. Athena and Hailey are growing weary."

Melchi's grip tightened around the gun. It all came back to the prophecy. He was the first guardian. The only way to beat the Mulo was to join with him. The only way to save his world was to help the Mulo get to another. He didn't have a choice. It wasn't the best solution; it was the only solution.

"Melchi." Hailey's whisper sounded right behind him. "How much are you loved?"

He raised himself to his full height and looked the Mulo in the eye. It might be the only solution, but it was wrong. He was a child of the Standing. He would stand firm.

"I will not let you hurt these women." Melchi tossed the gun to the ground. "And I will not give myself over to you. I have already given myself to another."

"I'm sorry to hear that." The Mulo reached in his jacket and pulled out another gun. "That gun wasn't loaded anyway, but this one—"

Melchi rolled the bedpost onto his toe and snapped it into his hand.

The Mulo just laughed. "That's what I liked about Ortus. He always trained my mounts so well. Strong, quick, excellent physical conditioning. Why do you suppose he had you spend so much time with the staff? It certainly wasn't for fighting. Not in this age of automatic weapons."

"I may be defeated, but the Holy One's purpose cannot fail." Melchi stepped forward, raising the bedpost to ready position. "I am the first guardian of—"

The tunnel exploded with three echoing blasts. Melchi leaped as his bedpost jerked this way and that in his hands.

Silence. A swirl of eerie blue smoke hung in the air. The smell of burned powder.

Melchi was still standing. He looked wide-eyed at the bullet holes in his staff. How did—

"Impossible!" The Mulo aimed the gun at Melchi's face. "Where did you learn—"

"You are right." Melchi angled the staff toward the gun and took another step forward. "It is impossible. I cannot possibly do what I just did."

A wave of molten rage hit Melchi in the chest, knocking him backward. The staff jumped in his hand as another explosion rang in his ears.

Leaning into the battering storm, he raised his bedpost as a half dozen snarling Mulo-creatures charged him. The flicker of black shadows against flashing white teeth. Glinting knives, swinging clubs.

He spun around, sweeping his staff before him, but the tunnel was too narrow. The bedpost grazed a wall and was ripped from his hands as a heavy shoulder slammed into his gut and drove him to the ground.

Clawing fingers, champing teeth. Melchi rolled with his assailant, snapping his body around to slam him into the ground. He ducked beneath the slash of a knife, struck out with a fist, pushed a body into the wall and dove. A twisting roll and he was back on his feet, spinning and kicking and raining down blow after blow after bone-cracking blow.

"Enough!" The command cut through the swirling rage.

Heaving and panting for breath, Melchi turned to the right and left, waiting for the next attack, waiting for one of the bodies to move. Then he saw the Mulo, standing in front of the gateway, pressing a gun to the side of the white-haired girl's head.

Melchi looked up and down the tunnel, searching the bodies littering the floor. "Where is Hailey? What have you done with her?" He reached out with his mind. Malice, anger, a fiery wall of blazing power rose above a weak and tremulous presence. No, that was the girl, not Hailey. Where was Hailey?

Sabazios's face twisted into a smile. "What's wrong, boy? Did you really think she would stay with you? After learning what you really are?"

"Where is Hailey?" Melchi charged down on the Mulo and leaped across the chamber.

"Back!"

An explosion of rage slammed into Melchi, driving him back into the side of the tunnel. The force pounded against him, pinning him to the wall, crushing the air from his lungs. He tried to fight back, tried to pry a hand from the wall, but he couldn't move.

Blood pounded in his ears. Red lights swam before his eyes. He couldn't breathe. Couldn't hold out much longer.

"What's the matter, Melchizadek? You aren't going to hit me with your little stick? I thought you were the all-powerful child of prophecy."

Melchi gasped for breath. "Where—is—Hailey?"

"Running from you, I would imagine. She fled through the gateway. Search for her yourself. She's gone from this world. The only way to see her again is to come with me. We'll conquer the first dimension together. A certain tree grows there. One bite of its fruit will give you immortality, unlimited power. Think of it. You can live forever with Hailey as your queen. The sovereign rulers of an entire universe."

"Don't listen to him!" The white-haired girl lunged forward only to be jerked back again. "He's afraid—" She cried out as the Mulo jabbed the gun back against the side of her head. Blood oozed out from beneath the barrel. Her eyes fluttered. Her arms and legs jerked and twitched in agony.

"Let her go!" Melchi reached out with his mind, past the girl's violent suffering, past the tunnel, through the hotel, out into the streets of the blind and uncomprehending city. Hailey wasn't out there. The Mulo had sent her through the gateway, irresistible bait for an unavoidable trap.

The Mulo's eyes locked onto Melchi's, pushing deeper and deeper into his mind. "At last you begin to see reason. The gateway is unavoidable. It is our destiny."

"If you are so powerful, then why hide like a coward behind a gun?" Melchi glanced down at the floor. One of the Mulo-creatures had dropped its knife. If he could just pry himself off the wall . . . "Do you know what I think? I think you wonder why I was able to stop the bullets. Why you could not inhabit Hailey. I think you wonder and are afraid. Someone is fighting for us. Someone has engineered this situation from the beginning of time."

"*I* am the engineer! I planned this moment for centuries." The Mulo shook the girl, lifted her kicking and shrieking off her feet. "Give yourself to me or the girl dies!"

A soft scrape sounded behind the Mulo. The whisper-soft dribble of cascading pebbles. A dim shadow rose up from behind the pile of rocks.

"Okay!" Melchi shouted. "Stop hurting her. But I want your word. As soon as I take you through the portal, you must release me. I must be free to go to Hailey on my own." He called up the memory of Hailey in the rose-colored dress and held it to his heart as the shadow crept toward the Mulo. The memory of Hailey on the rooftop. The time he'd first met her in the park . . .

The shadow crept closer. Hailey's silhouette, bathed in the soft light of the shimmering gateway. She lifted a large rock above her head. Took another step closer . . .

The Mulo swung around with a growl and swatted the rock from Hailey's hands.

Melchi cried out as the blasting force subsided. Peeling away from the wall, he crumpled to the ground. The knife! He lunged for it as a gunshot rang out.

"No!"

Sabazios grabbed Hailey by the neck. He lifted her kicking and shrieking from the ground and swung her toward the gateway. He drew her back, prepared to throw—

Melchi snatched up the knife and sent it spinning through the air. It embedded itself to the hilt in the Mulo's arm. Hailey's flailing body fell to the ground with a thud.

Cold laughter battered against Melchi's senses. He was hurled against the wall, pressed back into the rocks until they dug into his bones.

The Mulo slowly turned and pulled the bloody knife from its arm. "Too late, boy. That was your last mistake." It flipped the knife in its hand, drew it back over its head.

The white-haired girl spun around and, lowering her shoulder, rammed into the Mulo. It stumbled backward toward the gateway, reached out a flickering hand . . .

Blinding light flashed through the tunnel—and they were gone.

The force crushing Melchi to the wall receded, dumping him onto the ground.

"Hailey!" Melchi scrambled across the chamber to where she stood, staring into the gateway.

There, standing sideways against the shimmering trees, the Mulo lifted the struggling girl into the air and shook her. Melchi looked on helplessly as the Mulo grabbed her by the face and forced her head backward. Slowly it drew her exposed neck toward its gaping mouth.

"Melchi, no!" Hailey threw her arms around him as he stepped toward the gateway.

Suddenly the trees bent double as a bright light streaked through the air and exploded into the clearing behind the Mulo. A massive creature rose from the impact crater. Flashing golden wings, halos of radiating light, it drew an enormous sword from a flaming sheath and swept it across the field.

The gateway flashed as a fluttering shadow erupted from its shimmering surface and burst screeching and screaming into the tunnel. The beat of black wings tore through Melchi's senses. The slash of ripping talons. Pain mingled with rage ripping through his brain. Tearing, cutting, gouging deeper and deeper into his soul.

Melchi fell over backward. Rolled over and over across the floor, clawing at his face, covering his head with his arms. *Holy One, help me. Jesus, please . . .*

And then it was gone. He lay on the floor panting as the dark presence slowly receded into the dim shadows of the underground tunnel.

"Melchi?" A soft hand touched his cheek. Gentle fingers combed through his hair. "Are you okay? Is it gone?"

Melchi opened his eyes and looked up into Hailey's down-turned face. "The girl . . . is she . . . ?"

Hailey's eyes went wide. She sprang up and looked into the gateway.

Melchi climbed to his feet and moved to stand beside her. The field lay empty. Both bodies were gone. Only the crater and a few leaning trees gave any indication of the violence they had just witnessed.

He turned to Hailey and reached out to her, trying in vain to touch her with his mind. "You . . . took the medicine? So the Mulo would not see you?"

She nodded and looked back down the tunnel. "Do you think he, the Mulo . . . do you think it's dead?"

Melchi shook his head. "We stopped it this time, but it will be back. It cannot be destroyed. We can only hope to stand."

Hailey leaned toward him and stopped suddenly short. She looked up at him with wide tear-bedazzled eyes. As sweet and innocent as a frightened child.

Catching his breath, he reached out trembling fingers and took her by the hand.

# ⌒ 30 ⌒

Melchi sat doubled over in the front seat of Boggs's VW Bug, watching as the world flowed past him, steady and silent as the passage of time. Scrubby trees, stately buildings, torn billboards . . . they all disappeared into his past, never to be seen again. Everyone who had ever cared for him, every friend he'd ever made, he had left them all behind.

And now he was leaving Hailey.

An image leaped into his mind: his profile as seen from the backseat. A torrent of cascading emotion, the stab of exquisite pain. He dug his fingernails into his thigh and forced his eyes back to the car in front of them. He had no right to intrude. Hailey's thoughts were her own.

"Well," Boggs called out from the driver's seat, "Officer Murray phoned right before we left. He said they found Smiley barricaded in his apartment, raving like a lunatic. The department is trying to dismiss it as an accidental drug overdose, but the UCSF team is calling it another case of Sudden Onset Dementia. The police have already rounded up a dozen members of the hotel cult and anyone want to guess how many of them also have SOD?" She paused, letting the question hang in the heavy silence. "Five of them. Five out of twelve. What do you make of that?"

A wave of bitterness and pain radiated from the backseat. Melchi ducked and turned to look behind him. Hailey was hunched over her knees, staring off into space. Fresh tears glistened in red puffy eyes.

"I am sorry," he said in a soft voice. "I can only imagine how hard it must be for you to leave the university. Your classes and friends . . . I give you my word. I will do everything in my power to hunt the Mulo down. Boggs will let you know as soon as it is safe to return."

Cold, hard silence.

Melchi's throat tightened as Hailey's features dissolved into a curtain of sparkling haze. The force of her suffering was overwhelming. The Mulo would be able to feel it for miles.

"Everything's going to be fine," Boggs called back to her. "Students take leave of absence all the time. Dr. Werner will understand. Once Officer Murray tells him what happened, he'll give you all the time you need."

"And how long will that be?" Hailey's voice was ragged and torn. "Till I'm dead? The Mulo can't be destroyed. How long am I supposed to wait?"

"Eventually it must journey to another city," Melchi said. "To force entry into the gateway, it must find another . . ."

"Another what?" Hailey demanded. "Another person like me? I'm supposed to run away and wait for it to destroy someone else's life?"

"You have no choice. If you stay here, it will find you. I will not be able to protect you for long."

"And what about you? You're staying. What's to keep it from finding you?"

"I have no classrooms or houses to tie me to one place. No possessions to prevent me from changing hiding places. And now perhaps, with thanks to you, I will be the hunter instead of the hunted."

"A hunter with a quarry that can't be killed?"

Melchi shrugged. The Mulo had hidden behind a gun. He had taken a hostage. Surely that must mean something.

He turned and forced his attention back to the front window. The road rose above the ground in a broad sweeping curve. Massive roadways twisted and curved around them. Ribbons of concrete and steel.

So soon. Melchi sucked in his breath as he read the large green signs that indicated they were already at the airport. Soon he would be alone.

"What if I stayed with Boggs?" Hailey's voice sounded at his ear. "I'm on a leave of absence. I don't have to go to class."

Melchi shook his head. "It is too dangerous. You must remember what happened to your last roommate."

He winced as a new wave of pain rang through his thoughts. "I am sorry. I did not mean . . ." He swiveled in his seat, but she had already turned to face away from him. "Hailey."

The car swerved suddenly and slowed to a stop. "Okay. Here we are." Boggs got out of the car and folded her seat forward to let Hailey out.

Melchi watched helplessly as Boggs opened the hood and pulled Hailey's suitcase from the car. Then, throwing the door open, he twisted his body around to squirm through the narrow doorway. He took a step toward Hailey and stopped. The way she looked at him. Uncertain eyes. A bewildered, crinkled brow. It was like she was still afraid of him. Had he hurt her so much?

"So . . ." She stood before him, rocking the suitcase back and forth on its wheels. "I don't know what to say." More rocking. "Thank you for pretty much repeatedly saving my life . . . over and over again . . ."

Melchi nodded. "I . . . it was my great pleasure."

"Promise me you'll be careful, okay?" Shimmering eyes caught him up, holding him in an agony of breathless suspense.

"I—" He stepped forward, motioning incoherently with leaden arms. "I will try."

"Oh! I almost forgot." She reached down, unzipped the outer pocket of her bag, and pulled out a large burgundy book. "It's not new, but I've underlined a lot of important passages and even written some notes. Not as many as yours, but I want you to have it. Something to remember me by."

He sucked in his breath and took the book. The cover was soft and supple with a beautiful leather grain. Letters of shining gold were engraved on the front. It was a Holy Bible—*her* Holy Bible. His throat constricted as tears filled his eyes. He looked up at Hailey and opened his mouth, but he could only stare. There weren't enough words.

"It's okay. You don't have to be a priest to read it."

He nodded and tried to swallow. It was too nice. He would get it dirty. It would be ruined. Hundreds of conflicting emotions churned in his head. Agony and elation. Happiness and an intense desperate longing more powerful than hunger or thirst or physical pain.

She stepped toward him, closer, until she was only inches away. "I don't have to go. I could stay and help you fight."

Everything in Melchi leaped at the thought. To be with her every day, to provide for her, to fight to keep her safe . . . but he could not be so selfish. To let her sleep exposed to the elements when she could have family and friends and warm dry houses with books and all the water she needed.

"I am sorry." He could barely choke out the words. "To sleep in the rain without food or money or shelter or warmth . . . it is too dangerous."

She nodded and turned suddenly away. Then, taking up her rolling suitcase, she walked through a set of automatic glass doors and disappeared from sight.

———————

HAILEY INSERTED A CREDIT card at the check-in kiosk and tapped her way through the screens. What was her problem? After everything she'd been through, she should be looking forward to a vacation. She loved staying with the Robinsons. Little Lisa with her fat dimpled cheeks and big brown eyes. Davie with that mischievous smirk. They were as close to family as she could ever ask for.

She showed her ID to the woman at the desk and set her suitcase on the scale. Fresh tears pooled in her eyes as the woman tagged it and flopped it onto the conveyor belt. She was just being stupid now. A nutso, caramel-covered, headcase with whipped cream and a cherry on top. She had to accept it: Life as she knew it had ceased to exist. Everything was different, and there was no going back.

She walked past the check-in counters and drifted through the faceless crowd. Lonely voices echoed over the PA system. Recorded messages, artificial tones. She followed the arrows to her gate and zigzagged back and forth through the taped-off lanes to stand in a slow-moving line.

*They also serve who only stand and wait.* Where had she read that? Was it a note in Melchi's book? She thought back to her time reading under the spreading branches above his nest. He had slept on the ground that night. No blankets, no place to lay his head. He had chosen discomfort so she could be comfortable. He was sacrificing everything to protect her and who knew how many others like her. Children of the Standing.

Like the girl with spiky white hair. The thought filled her with an aching void. So young and petite and fragile . . . They could have become friends. She could have been the little sister Hailey never had. But she had sacrificed her life to save them. Strangers she didn't even know.

Now Melchi was going to do the same.

Hailey spun on her heel. "Excuse me. Sorry. I need to get through." She pushed through the crowd and ducked under the barrier. Running back across the terminal, she searched the walls for a phone. Why hadn't she taken the time to get her cell phone fixed? She should have bought a new one right away. And while she was at it, she should have bought Melchi some supplies. A sleeping bag, a rain tarp, some new clothes. She could have made such a difference in his life. How could she have been so thoughtless?

She ran on and on but couldn't find a phone anywhere. Finally, frustrated and out of breath, she slumped against a vacant information counter and closed her eyes. Suddenly she was back in Melchi's arms, weaving in and out through the dark trees of the moonlit park. A blanket of warmth settled over her—safety and contentment, shelter from the ravages of the storm. He had been shaggy and disheveled and filthy, but it hadn't mattered. She'd loved him even then. Before she'd even seen his face.

"Excuse me, sir?" She rushed after a man with a Bluetooth headset jutting forward from his ear. "Could I use your phone? It's an emergency."

The heavyset man eyed her warily. Took in the cuts on her face. The scrapes and bruises covering her arms.

Without a word he reached in his coat pocket and handed her a phone.

"Thank you. Thank you so much." She punched in Boggs's number and pressed the phone to her ear. *Come on. Pick up. Answer the phone.*

A click sounded and an electronic voice sent her to Boggs's voicemail.

"Hi, Boggs. This is Hailey. Whatever you do, don't let Melchi out of your sight. Okay? Tell him I'm staying and I need to talk to him. I'll be right there. Just don't let him go. Please." She hung up the phone and handed it back to the man.

"Is everything all right?" His eyes strayed back to her arms. "If there's anything I can do—"

"Thanks, but I'm fine." Hailey turned and started walking. Then she was running. Down the escalator and across the terminal to the AirTrain station. Her luggage could wait. If airport security didn't catch it, the Robinsons would have to mail it back. But she had to get back to the city, had to get to Boggs before she let Melchi go.

Because once he went into hiding, she'd have as much chance of finding him as the Mulo would have of finding her.

———

A GUST OF WIND sent daggers of ice stabbing through Hailey's wet clothes. Blast after blast of pelting rain, soaking into her skin, running into her eyes. She wiped a sodden sleeve across her face and looked up into the dark, angry sky. Melchi was out there somewhere. Huddled and shivering against the cold. No shelter, no heat. Even his coats were gone. All he had was the thin suit Sabazios had given him. Ridiculously expensive but worthless against the elements.

She sloshed though a puddle and leaned into the biting wind. Where would Boggs have taken him? She had checked Boggs's apartment, the science building, the bookstore, the park. Surely they wouldn't go back to Tiffany's apartment. Even with Smiley gone, there could be other corrupted police. And then there was the Mulo. If he had found another body, he could be searching for them right now.

Or did he even need a body to search? There was so much she didn't know. She had to find Melchi. She had been a fool to leave him, even for a moment.

Limping across a partially flooded intersection, she turned into the wind and made her way up the streaming sidewalk. The bookstore was closed when she checked it earlier. Maybe the owner was back. Maybe she'd seen Melchi and could tell her where to find him. It was worth a try.

Hailey squinted into the rain, shielding her eyes with her hand. Was that a light in the bookstore window? She stumbled forward, faster and faster until she was running. She plodded up to the entrance and reached for the door with senseless hands.

Loud voices sounded through the rain. A burst of sudden laughter.

Pushing the door open, she stumbled inside and stood wet and dripping on the mat.

Silence. A jolt of alarm rang through her head.

"Hailey?" Boggs's voice called from the other side of the shelves. "What are you doing here. I thought you were—"

Then she saw him. Wide-eyed and gorgeous with his short hair and fitted white shirt. Melchi charged between the bookshelves and caught her up in a powerful hug. Warmth flooded her senses, soaking through the numbness of her skin, thawing her from the inside out.

"I thought you were— Why did you not go to Wisconsin?" He set her down and stood back to look at her. "Are you hurt? The Mulo, it didn't—"

"No. I'm fine. I just couldn't leave you. Not to fight alone. I want to help."

"But—"

"Don't leave her at the door, boy." The bookstore owner's gravelly voice. "Bring her in. Offer her a chair."

"I am sorry. I . . ." Melchi swept his eyes around the room and turned to usher her into the store. As soon as he stepped out from between the shelves, Boggs darted past him and locked Hailey in a laughing embrace.

"You're soaking wet. Here." Boggs took off her jacket and draped it around Hailey's shoulders. "Come inside and get warm. There's a space heater."

Hailey squished her way into the bookstore and looked around. The bookstore owner leaned over the counter, looking for all the world like a leathery Cheshire cat. Two strangers sat against the far bookshelf on stools.

No, not strangers. The guy in the leather jacket was the officer who had come out to check her house. But who was the guy in the expensive-looking suit? She shot a questioning look at Melchi.

"So what are you doing here?" Boggs grabbed Hailey's arm and led her over to the stool in front of a small space heater. "Was your flight cancelled?"

"I'm not going." Hailey fixed first Boggs and then Melchi with a firm stare. "I've thought it over, and I've decided to stay and help Melchi stand against the Mulo."

"But—" Melchi stepped toward her. "You are not—"

"Please." Hailey held up a hand. "Just let me finish. I know it'll be tough. Sleeping outside, not having food or clothes or money."

The bookstore owner broke out in a cackling laugh.

Hailey looked around. Boggs, the officer, even the stranger was laughing.

"This is *my* decision." She raised her voice and turned to face Melchi. "Not yours. I know it's dangerous, but how can I fly to Wisconsin knowing you're suffering out in the rain and cold? I appreciate all you've done, but this is too big. You can't take the whole thing on by yourself. I can help. I've got enough money to buy sleeping bags, canteens, a tent—"

More laughter. Boggs was braying like a hiccupping donkey.

Heat rose to Hailey's cheeks. She took a deep breath and let it out slowly. "Would someone please tell me what's so funny?" She looked back at Melchi. "This isn't a joke."

"Please," the bookstore owner said between gasps, "tell her what's so funny, Melchi."

Melchi's eyes went wide and his face turned scarlet. "I . . ." He looked helplessly around the room.

"Melchi, what's wrong? What did you do?"

The stranger in the suit laughed and slid off his stool. "Maybe I can help clear things up. I'm John Vorreiter." He reached out and shook her hand. "I take it you're Melchizedek's girlfriend?"

Hailey shot Melchi a look, and his face turned an even darker shade of red. He looked like he wanted to crawl under a chair.

"I'm his friend. At least I thought I was."

"I see." The man smiled. "The friend this gentleman said was too beautiful and well-educated and good even to consider someone like him."

"What?" Hailey stared at the man, too shocked to say more.

"But given the fact you canceled your trip and walked here in the pouring rain and are willing to become a penniless homeless person, I'm inclined to disagree with him."

"I see." She risked a shy glance at Melchi. "I guess that was kind of funny."

"Oh, that wasn't the funny part."

Hailey turned back to the man.

"The funny part was when you said you had enough money to buy sleeping bags."

Boggs and the old lady burst once again into laughter.

Hailey's cheeks were really burning now. She was even redder than Melchi. "That's not what I meant! I said I could buy supplies. Melchi—"

Everyone was laughing again.

"I'm sorry." The man in the suit took off his glasses and wiped his eyes. "I promised to explain and I will. I just wanted to establish to your *friend* here that you cared for him before you heard the news."

"What news? What are you talking about?"

"I work for the law firm of Rubart, Cushman, and Doucette. Before his death Sabazios Vladu registered with us a legal and binding last will and testament which effectively makes young Melchizadek here a billionaire. In addition to stocks and bonds and properties all over the world, he also owns the hotel everyone seems to be so interested in."

*"What?"* Hailey waited for the man to crack a smile. "No. When he thought he was going to inhabit . . ." She looked around the room. "Sabazios wrote you into his will?"

Melchi looked down at the floor. "I am a child of the Standing. Of course I cannot accept it. They want me to take his name."

"Only legally," the lawyer said. "You're free to go by whatever name you choose."

"But I cannot live in a house. I cannot—"

"Melchi, wait!" Hailey stepped over to him and took him gently by the hand. "Don't you get it? It's the prophecy. You've become the enemy. You're Sabazios Vladu. Now that you own the hotel, you have the means to protect the gateway. You have the resources to do so much good. And the Mulo has nothing. As long as you're still standing, you've already got him beat."

"But I cannot be a billionaire." Melchi shook his head. "I know nothing about caring for money. I am just a simple homeless. You must take it."

Hailey looked down at the strong hand engulfing both of her own. This couldn't be happening. The whole thing was crazy. "Sorry Melchi, but I won't have time. I'm going to be too busy helping you fight the Mulo."

"Helping me?" Melchi's eyes went wide. He leaned in closer and whispered in her ear. "Maybe then, it would not seem like so much if . . . if we could share the burden?"

Hailey's breath caught in her chest. Was he asking her to . . . ? She looked into his eyes—and nodded.

Maybe crazy wasn't so bad after all.

# Acknowledgments

I was a brand-new writer back in the spring of 1998 when I showed up at the Mount Hermon Christian Writers Conference, clutching the early draft of *Shade* in my sweaty little hands. Would the editors like it? Would they hate it? Did I have what it took to be a writer? That very first night I sat down with one of the editors to whom I had submitted my manuscript for review, and he asked the dreaded question: "Did you send me a manuscript?" I nodded my head, and he studied my name tag with a frown. Apparently he didn't remember my name. That was a good sign, right?

"Wait a second. . . . You're *that* John Olson? I wouldn't touch that book with a sixty-foot pole. . . . It was terrifying!"

That was my first introduction to Steve Laube, the man who would go on to become my editor, agent, advisor, and friend.

Of course, I didn't know all this at the time. I just knew there was a circle on Steve's napkin called the market and that apparently my manuscript was a sixty-foot-pole length outside that circle. By the time the third day of the conference had rolled around, I was a bacterium infecting the toe jelly of a flea on the belly of a pregnant dachshund. I snuck into the fiction editors' panel discussion and sat in the back of the room to let the real writers get their dose of *face time* with the editors.

One of the editors on the panel, a spunky redhead with enough charisma to make an empty football stadium feel claustrophobic, started talking about a manuscript she'd received. The more she raved about it, the further down in my seat I sank. If only she would give the author's name, maybe I could get some pointers from him. Funny thing was, the story sounded a lot like mine.

But I knew she couldn't be talking about me. First, she said the author understood women, which ruled me out right away. And second, I hadn't sent her my manuscript.

When she quoted from my proposal, I about jumped out of my chair. Karen Ball liked my book? I couldn't believe it. *Shade* had been discovered!

During the last ten years Steve and Karen have both been great friends and tireless champions for this project, but it's only been recently that the circle on Steve's napkin has gotten big enough for us to take the project public. During those years I've had a never-ending supply of encouragement, help, and support from Scumlings (Lori Arthur, Candy Campbell, Jan Collins, Karen D'Amato, Tasra Dawson, Donna Fujimoto, Judith Guerino, Ellen Graebe, Nancy Hird, Margaret Horwitz, Randy Ingermanson, Kelly Kim, Kim Lavoie, Sibley Law, Carl Olsen, Amy Olson, Patty Mitchell, Michael Platt, Jennifer Rempel, Lynne Thompson, Allison Wagner, Katie Vorreiter, and John Zelaski); Winklings (Katie Cushman, Jenn Doucette, Jim Rubart, and Katie Vorreiter); the Third Element (Dragon Coensgen, Julian Farnam, and Michael Platt); subject matter experts (Jennifer Vallier, Mel Hodde, Robinette, Haeyoung Sohn, Lyndsey Cadoo, Athena, JaneA, Sally Olson, Maki Katsumoto); and most of all from my family (my selfless mom, my database-brained dad, my brilliant brother Bill, my catalytic sister Kathy, my always entertaining son Peter, my master-editing daughter Ari, and of course my loving, encouraging, first-to-read, last-to-discourage wife Amy).

But the project never would have made it past page 10 if it weren't for the encouragement of my friend and brother Peter Sleeper and his wife Sherah. Not only did Peter spend many hours brainstorming with me, but he also cared enough to charge me fifty bucks every week I didn't write a chapter. With friends like that, who needs the IRS?

—John B. Olson